This Is Next Year

This Is Next Year

PHILIP GOLDBERG

AVAILABLE
PRESS

Ballantine Books · New York

An Available Press Book
Published by Ballantine Books

Copyright © 1991 by Philip Goldberg

All rights reserved under International and Pan-American Copyright Conventions. Published in the United States by Ballantine Books, a division of Random House, Inc., New York, and simultaneously in Canada by Random House of Canada Limited, Toronto.

Library of Congress Catalog Card Number: 91-91923
ISBN: 0-345-36647-6

Cover design by Ruth Ross
Cover photograph courtesy of The Bettman Archive

Text design by Holly Johnson

Manufactured in the United States of America

First Edition: April 1992
10 9 8 7 6 5 4 3 2 1

To Archie, my father and friend

This Is Next Year

Part One

Part One

Chapter One

Rooney's Lot was a comma in a run-on sentence of brownstones, brick row houses, and small apartment buildings. Long ago, when its soil was fertile, the small plot might have yielded tomatoes and beans for the early settlers of Brooklyn. By 1955 it had become host to isolated sprays of goldenrod and ragweed, a single desperate oak, a forest of rocks and rubble, a rusted bicycle frame, tin cans and bottles whose labels had been peeled and faded by the elements, the shell of a Philco console radio, a wooden chair with three legs, a blue sofa whose puffy innards spilled through the slashed upholstery like the guts of a slain beast, a bureau without drawers. To the neighborhood children, it was as if each discard had been placed in Rooney's Lot for a purpose, like the seesaws and monkey bars in a public playground. The sofa might be a doctor's examining table, the radio the control panel of a rocket ship, the cans and jars hand grenades to be tossed on imaginary Japs and krauts.

That day, perhaps because of the damp heat, it was quiet in Rooney's Lot; the only items in use were the two that had been put there for the express purpose of recreation. A girl sat in an automobile tire that dangled like an amulet from a rope tied to the brawny arm of the oak. Her companion, a red-haired boy, gave her a vigorous shove from behind, and she soared upward toward the rooftops. Back and forth she swung, her lithe body stretched in a streamlined horizontal to gather speed, her head tilted back so she could watch the mosaic of leaves blur against the blue-gray sky, a dizzying sight. At the nadir of her arc, her black ponytail swept the ground like a silken broom.

I was involved with another piece of apparatus: a box spring bolted to the rear wall of an apartment building, strategically distant from the nearest windows. It had been hung there, in vertical orientation, like the featured painting in a gallery, precisely sixty feet and six inches from a pitcher's mound, an asymmetrical dome that had been assiduously molded out of the stubborn dirt. The architect of this setup was my father, Frank Stone. He had designed it some years earlier, primarily for the use of my older brother, Hubbell. Having determined that his firstborn son would grow up to pitch for the Brooklyn Dodgers, Frank Stone had named his child after Carl Hubbell, the great left-handed pitcher of the thirties, who, although he toiled for the archrival Giants, had earned my father's enduring respect. When the infant Hubbell turned out to be a lefty with a penchant for throwing rattles out of his crib in a trajectory that appeared to match his namesake's screwball, my father's dream took on the aura of prophecy.

Frank Stone gave his son spherical toys to match his size and guided his left arm into proper throwing motion before Hubbell was old enough to say baseball. He recorded the distance and accuracy of Hubbell's throws the way some parents chart their children's height. With our father at his side—coaching, teaching, cajoling, inspiring—Hubbell followed his destiny cheerfully through Little League and Pony League and high school, and now, in the summer after his graduation, he was pitching for an American Legion team while my father pulled every string he could to ensure that Dodger scouts did not miss out on the remarkable prospect right under their noses.

What was destined to be enshrined as the Hubbell Stone Memorial Box Spring had been erected so that my brother could work out when no one was available to catch for him. On it my father had painted, in red, a rectangle whose width was that of home plate and whose length measured the precise distance from Joe DiMaggio's knees to his armpits. At the time the box spring was installed, Jolting Joe had been the archetypal opposing batter; the rectangle was his strike zone.

I was hurling baseballs at the target that day because I liked to try my hand at pitching now and again. I did this clandestinely, since my father believed rather strongly in early specialization. At birth I had been designated a shortstop and given the name Roger after the Hall of Famer Rogers Hornsby. The s had been dropped at the insistence of my mother, who did not want her son going through life being mistaken for a plural. I had been given a preschool education similar to Hubbell's, only I was tossed objects of various kinds, often when least expected, to sharpen my reflexes for fielding. The training had worked well enough to make me a neighborhood star and captain of my Little League team, as well as land me a coveted spot on Happy Felton's Knothole Gang, which preceded Dodger home games on Channel 9.

I toed the rubber and rotated a baseball in my palm, placing the tips of my first two fingers on the stitching just so, angling my thumb for proper rotation. Arms raised overhead, I twisted my torso, kicked my left leg high and hurtled forward, snapping my wrist as I released the ball, and followed through. DiMaggio leaned away as the ball sped toward his hip, only to curve sharply and clip the inside corner of the rectangle. It was my twenty-seventh consecutive strikeout.

It was time to call it a day. I had, that morning, played eighteen innings at my customary position on a hard, dusty diamond in Lincoln Terrace Park, where rocks were embedded like land mines in the grass. My knees, the target of bad-hop grounders, needed to be patched; my stomach needed to be fortified. I gathered the scuffed and tattered baseballs scattered around the box spring, counted them, and shoved all but one into my duffel bag. The remaining ball I enclosed in my mitt—a Pee Wee Reese model by Rawlings—and secured it in place by wrapping two thick rubber bands around the leather. This ritual, along with periodic application of neat's-foot oil, maintained the glove's pocket and its supple texture.

The maze of alleys and cellars that I wound through to reach home was refreshingly cool after my hours in the sun. From trash cans the putrid incense of yesterday's meals rose and hung in the humid air like fog. Well-adapted cats had knocked over the metal lids to scrounge for scraps of fish and lick clean the drops of milk that had spilled from cartons. Fans whirred from apartment windows, their buzz mingling with the clang of pots and pans, the shrill exhortations of mothers, the music and static from radios.

A ditty called "The Yellow Rose of Texas," which that summer was whistled as often in the Brownsville section of Brooklyn as in Brownsville, Texas, segued into an ad for Palisades Amusement Park: "So skip the bother and skip the fuss, take a public service bus. Public service sure is great, it takes you right up to the gate." I had been to the park on the cliffs of New Jersey once; it had a roller coaster and the world's largest saltwater pool, complete with a machine that created artificial waves, but I preferred Coney Island, a ten-cent subway ride away and home to an assemblage of dazzling lights, heroic rides, succulent hot dogs, and an ocean with genuine salt water and waves.

A door opened and Jesse Hicks, the superintendent for a group of apartment buildings, including my own, walked backward into the alley. He was pulling a dolly with bags of garbage on it. Each building was equipped with a dumbwaiter, on which the tenants transported their trash to the bottom floor. There, Jesse would collect it and haul it into the alley to a row of cans. Once a week he carted the cans down a small flight of steps and up another for collection on the sidewalk. The janitor was a tall man with a body of steel and a face that was older than its years, worn out from his efforts to preserve his natural dignity in a world that treated men of his color like the trash on his dolly.

"Hi, Jesse," I said.

Jesse smiled. He was a handsome man with warm black eyes and strong features, but his teeth were as yellow and black as they were white, and his eyes were stained red by whiskey and the smoke from the fires he stoked all winter in coal-burning furnaces. Jesse paused in his labor, lifted the old gray fedora he always wore, and wiped his forehead with the sleeve of his plaid shirt. "Hey, there, partner. You keeping your eye on the ball like I told you?"

I told him I was, right up to the moment the ball hit my glove. "That's good," said Jesse. "Mom and Pop all right?" I assured him they were fine. "That's good. You tell 'em Jesse said hello."

"You promised you'd tell me more about Cool Papa Bell," I reminded him, referring to the legendary outfielder from the Negro Leagues, whom Jesse claimed to have met. He had once told me that Cool Papa Bell was so fast he could hit the light switch and get into bed before the room got dark.

"Jesse always keeps his word," he said. "But I can't right now, my friend, 'cause I got work to do."

I heard the scratchy sound of a big band record and, more prominently, the clamor of drums. "Is that Otis?" I asked. Otis was Jesse's teenage son; they lived together in the two gritty basement rooms that came with the super's job.

"Yeah, he's playing them drums," Jesse sighed. There was irritation, not pride, in his voice, and a dollop of pain. He yanked the dolly into motion and resumed his backward walk. "You drop by sometime soon, hear? Jesse'll tell you about Cool Papa Bell."

I skipped down the five steps that led to the cellar and opened the door. It was cold and black and it smelled of trash and the mounds of coal that would heat the building in winter. When my eyes adjusted, I could see Otis, shirtless, the sweat on his skin glistening like polished ebony in the light that entered the cellar with me. He flailed at a snare, a bass, and a tinny cymbal to the tune of Count Basie's "C-Jam Blues." His limbs were in constant, electric motion, but his face was as serene as a stone saint, and the corners of his mouth curled slightly in an expression that even an eleven-year-old like me could recognize, without knowing the word, as ecstasy. I watched, enthralled, until the song ended and Otis stopped playing.

"Hi, Otis," I said.

His eyes were open now and he looked directly at the lighted doorway in which I stood, but he did not appear to see me. The phonograph needle scratched repeatedly on the label of the 78 rpm record. Otis started drumming again, as if the repetitive scratches constituted a tune. He closed his eyes once more; his body writhed like a snake's. And as he worked his drumsticks up to cruising speed, his mouth opened and his head dropped backward, as if his neck could not support the weight of his bliss.

Softly, I closed the door. I climbed back up the steps and walked down the alley, wondering if Otis was ill or if I had done something to offend him. I thought of Otis as my pal. Just recently, another boy my age had been beaten and robbed when he wandered too far past the schoolyard that marked the border between ours and the black neighborhood, which was referred to as *over there*. Otis had told me, "Any of them bad nigger boys bother you, little man, you tell 'em you's a friend of Otis Hicks. No one bother you then." Gratefully, I had filed the advice in my mind, hoping I would never have to use it, but I never received a satisfactory explanation for why I was forbidden to say the word nigger while Otis used it with impunity.

In a second-story window a woman with arms like legs of

lamb leaned heavily on the sill and fanned her face with a magazine that featured a photo of Rita Hayworth, whose flaming red hair spilled languidly onto bare, ivory shoulders. Rita had just divorced her fourth husband, singer Dick Haymes, who had succeeded Orson Welles and Aly Khan in her bed. The woman in the window, who no doubt sniffed at Hollywood morality while privately envying Rita's connubial versatility, eyed me with suspicion, as if at any moment I might unzip my duffel bag and send a baseball crashing through her windowpane. In the window adjacent to hers a young boy in a bright green shirt launched gobs of spit between the iron bars of a fire escape, no doubt picturing himself a fearless bombardier on a strafing mission over Berlin or Tokyo.

"Barry!" growled the woman. "How many times I gotta tell ya to quit that stupid spitting?"

"I ain't gonna spit on no one," the boy protested.

"Don't talk back to your mother."

As I turned a corner, a drop of liquid splashed onto my shoulder. It wasn't spit—it was water, dripping from the freshly scrubbed garments that hung from the clotheslines that crisscrossed the alley like shoelaces. I was on intimate turf now, in the narrow corridor that separated my building, 510 Howard Avenue, from its identical twin, 514 (why there was no 512 was a mystery I had never been able to solve). The underwear dripping excess water belonged to Sammy and Sylvia Finkelstein. I knew this because of the circumference of the boxer shorts—a tad shy of the Roman Colosseum—and the prodigious grandeur of the brassieres, whose cups could double for basketball nets. The lacy slip and white panties, fetchingly petite by comparison, belonged to the Finkelsteins' daughter, Ruth, a sophomore at a state teachers college who was home for the summer. A corner of Ruth's bedroom was visible from mine—*only* a corner, alas, just enough for me to see her bare arm and, on rare occasions, a shoulder and a bra strap, when, at night, she draped her undies oh-so-delicately over a chair.

My mouth began to salivate, a Pavlovian response to the smell of tomato paste simmering in olive oil with freshly pressed garlic. The scent emanated from the kitchen of Angie Corso. Angie was the wife of Mike the Barber and the mother of two sons: Ignazio, who was Hubbell's age, and Louie, my friend. Angie's Sunday suppers—mounds of macaroni, plump meatballs, and spicy sausages, topped with her incomparable sauce and fresh Parmesan cheese which each diner scraped onto his plate with a grater—could sate the population of Naples. As I proceeded down the alley, the sweet, pungent smell was joined by another, far less appetizing odor: the liver and onions of Hilda Klinger. Hilda wielded her frying pan not with the artistry of Angie Corso, but with the insolence of a private doing K.P. She served her family not with Angie's proud and passionate flair, but with the panache of an orderly at an asylum dispensing sedatives to inmates.

It occurred to me as I inhaled the competing fumes that the personalities of the men who daily consumed Angie's and Hilda's cooking had been forged in their respective kitchens: the Corsos, lusty, sensuous, affable; the Klingers, sullen and belligerent. This theory explained to my satisfaction the long-standing feud between the two families.

As I neared the back door of my building, I realized that I was hearing the opening passage of Beethoven's Moonlight Sonata for the fifth or sixth time. The pianist, Louie Corso, had been unable to get the thirteenth note right, falling a shade flat or sharp each time. When his next attempt also failed, Barney Klinger's voice roared from his third-story window and bounced from wall to wall like a handball: "Hey, Liberace! Get the goddamn thing right, willya, or I'll take an axe to your goddamn peeaner."

"Mind your own business!" Angie retorted from her kitchen.

A hush fell over the twin buildings. Radios were lowered, cooking ceased, arguments suspended in mid-sentence. Only the hum of window fans could be heard as Louie began his next, and possibly final, attempt at Moonlight Sonata. He trod the keys as if they were eggs, adagio con prudence. When he reached the troublesome note, he hesitated for a split second and then— bravissimo!—he got it right. Louie was rewarded with applause and whistles from a dozen invisible supporters as he plunged with renewed gusto into the sonata. Barney's window slammed shut.

I entered the cool stairwell inside my building.

Our second-floor apartment, four bedrooms and only one bathroom, was spacious and airy, with high ceilings and patterned woodwork adorning the walls and door frames. It was, however, ancient. Chunks of plaster fell from the ceilings in regular flurries, the floorboards creaked under the linoleum, the plumbing and appliances were arthritic. Washers and sprockets and hinges and bolts expired faster than the landlord would replace them. The owner was looking to sell, we had heard, in hopes of using his profits to buy some units in the fast-growing borough of Queens. Our furniture, too, was old; only the floral slipcover on the sofa and a brass floor lamp, purchased with Green Stamps, had been with us fewer than five years.

It was the kind of dwelling that families by the thousands were deserting for suburban tract homes and garden apartments with spiffy appliances and Formica cabinets and Danish modern bedroom sets. My mother wanted to upgrade too, but she had no interest in the new developments in Queens or Long Island which other housewives viewed as Eden. Her dream was to live in Greenwich Village, near the theatres and concert halls of the great city and the coffeehouses where interesting, cultured people gathered around scintillating conversation. Her move to the Village was on hold until we could afford it. To my father, a Brooklyn loyalist, a new apartment in, say, nearby East Flatbush, would do just fine. We could not afford that either.

I myself did not care to move at all. I liked my cozy room with its view of the alley and a patch of sky and Ruth Finkelstein's window. And I loved the neighborhood; to me, it had everything a family could want: friends, shops and candystores within walking distance, convenient subway and bus stops, and streets, parks, and vacant lots to play in. It pained me to hear the news, announced approximately once a month, that yet another family was moving.

My brother Hubbell was at the kitchen table eating a meat loaf sandwich and reading *The Catcher in the Rye.* Hubbell was a shade under six feet tall and had, according to my father, the perfect build for a pitcher, lean and loose-limbed, with a strong upper body. He was handsome in a fine-featured, dark-eyelashed, Tyrone Power sort of way, the kind of cute young man that so-called nice girls wanted to bring home to meet their mothers.

Hubbell did not think he was good-looking at all. He hated the space between his two front teeth (my mother said it gave him character), he thought his eyes were not a dark enough shade of brown and that his hair was too fine and hard to manage. To remedy that last shortcoming he had recently acquired a new look: a flat top, about an inch and a half tall, with the sides left long and combed straight back. This style served two purposes, Hubbell informed me: he did not have to deal with pompadours that would not stay put no matter how much hair tonic he applied, and his ears would not stick out like Dumbo the elephant.

So engrossed was Hubbell in the tragedy of Holden Caulfield that he was oblivious to the ketchup that gushed from between the slices of bread like blood from a severed artery, spilling onto his fingers and the table. When he was not playing ball or doing something associated with improving his pitching skills, my brother was usually reading. Sometimes he would do both simultaneously, reading a book while squeezing hand springs to strengthen his grip, for example, or reading a magazine during a game when his side was at bat. The reading addiction was something I had also acquired; like Hubbell's, my eyes were drawn to the printed word as irresistibly as to bare legs or exposed cleavage, and I could not fall asleep at night, no matter how tired I was, without a fix of at least a page.

My mother was responsible for this affliction. She had not resisted her husband's determination to see his sons play ball in the major leagues, but she resolved that their intellects would not atrophy in the service of sport. She introduced each of us to the public library at the same time my father initiated us in the arcane mysteries of Ebbets Field. As a result, her three sons (Hubbell, my younger brother Hank, and I) could read at second-grade level before they entered school. Frank Stone tried to turn this skill to his advantage by indoctrinating us with such masterworks as *The Sporting News,* novels like *The Kid from Tompkinsville,* and scorecards. My mother countered with good books, doling out literature in sequential doses according to our ages.

This early reading gave the Stone children an edge in school, of course, but it was not without its drawbacks. When Hubbell was in kindergarten, for example, my mother was called in by his teacher, who thought the poor five-year-old was so shy that, instead of mixing with his classmates, he spent his recesses pretending to read. My mother had to prove to the teacher that her son was not pretending. Hubbell went on to be as good a student as he was an athlete, and when his illustrious years at P.S. 144 drew to a close, he was selected for the Special Progress class. Going S.P. meant he would complete junior high in two years instead of three. My mother was delighted, for it meant that Hubbell's classmates would also be exceptional and his curriculum advanced. My father disapproved. He felt that when Hubbell got to high school, he would be at a disadvantage having to compete at sports with boys a year older than he.

The stalemate was settled in the progressive, Dr. Spock-like manner to which my mother tried always to adhere: they let Hubbell decide for himself, just as they let him decide whether or not to have a bar mitzvah. On that occasion, Hubbell had followed an exemplary rational procedure: he looked around at his acquaintances and observed that Jewish kids who had to study Hebrew after a full day in public school were abjectly miserable over the state of affairs, while Gentile kids came home at three o'clock, changed clothes, and played ball till the sun went down. It was no contest. Hubbell, in the eyes of certain relatives and friends, would never be a man. In the case of the S.P. decision, Hubbell deduced that one less year of school in a person's lifetime was a reasonable reward for having brains, and he would work extra hard at baseball to make up for losing a year of on-field experience. He skipped the year and ultimately graduated from high school, that previous June, at age seventeen.

Skipping a year did not prevent Hubbell from becoming the number-one pitcher for Thomas Jefferson High or receiving honorable mention on the all-city team. It might have had other consequences, however. Perhaps because he was a year younger than his classmates, Hubbell had been particularly eager to be accepted. This, coupled with the fact that he found schoolwork inherently boring, made him especially vulnerable to Regular Guys' Disease. Regular Guys were not brains. Regular Guys did not show off in class by raising their hands and answering questions; they made their marks with wisecracks about the teacher, brainy boys, and female classmates. Regular Guys did not study beyond what was absolutely necessary to get by, and if that was not good enough, they cheated, cleverly and fearlessly. Regular Guys did not stand out by scoring good grades; they stood out by scoring points on the playing field and chicks on Saturday night. Like most men in our neighborhood, Hubbell aspired to Regular Guy status, so he became an academic underachiever. Nothing his teachers did could make him live up to his scholastic potential. Because he was smart, and because he liked to read, Hubbell had been able to sail through high school with a B average without trying.

That would not get him into a top-notch college, which pained my mother, although not as much as it would most moms who possessed a bright male child. Hubbell was happy and well-liked, he had a good and generous soul, and he had his path laid out for him. He would be a career jock, but he would stand out in that world as a literate, articulate, socially conscious exception to the rule, the sort of player the sporting scribes would flock to for witty, insightful quotes, and who would, upon retirement, do something with his mature years. As for my father, a prototypical Regular Guy, Hubbell's attitude toward school made him ecstatic. Time spent on math was a waste, he felt, unless it could help his son calculate the trajectory of a curveball or analyze a box score; history was useless unless it included the history of Jews in baseball, a short course indeed; English was okay if it helped you comprehend the subtleties of a scouting report. Without his wife's knowledge, Frank Stone coerced his firstborn son to not mail in his college applications. Doing so, he believed, would jinx his chances of signing with the Dodgers.

"In about a year, you'll be ready for this book," said Hubbell as I placed the ingredients for my lunch on the table. "It'll change your whole life."

"What's it about?" I asked. "A catcher, like Roy Campanella or something?"

"That's right," said Hubbell. "It's about this catcher for the Chicago Cubs. See, he's so sick of losing games, he starts drinking. He drinks large bottles of Canadian Rye and—"

"You're full of it. What's it about, really?"

Hubbell pondered a moment, then he looked off to the side, as if directing his gaze at a television camera. "Ladies and gentlemen," he intoned, "the young man wants to know what this book is about. Well, some say it's about a sick, neurotic boy. I say it's about a sensitive soul that's tormented by a world full of phonies."

For a delicate-looking guy of average build, Hubbell's voice was surprisingly deep and resonant. Because my mother had lost the hearing in one ear when she gave birth to me (it was not my fault, she reminded me often), Hubbell had learned to speak loud and clear to compensate for the handicap. Like his precocious reading ability, his husky voice brought him to the attention of ignorant school authorities. When he was in the sixth grade, Mrs. Schaefer, the wicked witch of P.S. 144, called in my mother for a conference with the principal, Dr. Gross. This pair of self-righteous pedagogues tried to convince Mom that her son had a serious problem with his throat or vocal cords. They wanted him to see a specialist. My mother replied, politely, "Bushwah."

Schaefer and Gross accused her of being a typically self-indulgent mother who ignored the welfare of her children in favor of playing mah-jongg and gossiping at the beauty parlor. My mother told them she did not play mah-jongg or gossip under hair dryers, and what's more they were pompous farts who did not know their asses from their elbows. Dr. Gross called her a foul-mouthed fool. Mom clipped him one just below his mustache.

"Sounds boring," I told Hubbell. "You have any baseball books?"

Hubbell laughed and went back to his sandwich and *The Catcher in the Rye.*

I spread thick layers of peanut butter, grape jelly, and marsh-mallows between two slices of spongy Silvercup white bread, then poured a large glass of cherry Kool-Aid to help the sticky concoction slide down my throat.

My mother entered the kitchen. She was carrying a broom, which, as soon as she saw us, she held before her mouth like a microphone. She sang in unison with Frank Sinatra, who, from the radio on top of the refrigerator, was crooning the nation's number-one hit: "Fairy tales can come true, it can happen to you, if you're young at heart . . ."

"Listen to the words, boys," said my mother. "Stay young. Don't let them get to you."

Exactly who *them* was I could not say, but I sensed that the advice was worth remembering because she repeated the theme frequently. My mother had always done her best to live up to the spirit of the anthem. She was forty but she looked and acted much younger. As a girl growing up in the neighborhood, Skinny Jeannie had been known as a tomboy, a prankster, a daredevil, the kid most likely to play hooky from school or place a thumbtack on a teacher's chair or razz a pompous politician on the stump. According to legend, she would hang by the backs of her knees from the fire escape and tap dance on the ledge of the roof.

Her older brothers would earn pocket money by taking Jeannie around the neighborhood and issuing the challenge, "My kid sister can lick your kid brother." There were men in the neighborhood who still remembered the black eyes they received when, as boys, they had gone too far in teasing little Sidney, Jeannie's twin brother, an effete pianist who, it was theorized, had lost his share of testosterone to his sister in utero. "Your mother left the womb twenty minutes before me," Uncle Sid would tell us, "and she's been a step ahead of me ever since."

Five feet two and a wiry 108 pounds, my mother could throw a ball almost as well as a man, better than many in fact, and not with the namby-pamby, wrong-foot-forward style of a girl. She leaned into her tosses and whipped the ball sidearm. She could chin herself on a bar ten times and jump rope with effortless dexterity, even performing the difficult Double Dutch. Despite these skills and her one-of-the-guys demeanor, she was treated as a lady by the men in the neighborhood, a singular sign of respect. She was considered pretty in an unglamorous, even *anti*-glamorous way. Aside from a thin coat of lipstick, her only concession to vanity was the auburn tint she used to camouflage the premature gray that would otherwise have spread like ivy over her head. She considered time spent in a beauty parlor nearly as much of a waste as visiting a house of worship. She dressed plainly but well, partly because she disliked shopping and partly out of habit. As the only daughter in a poor family where hand-me-downs were the principal sources of clothing, she learned to make the most of very few garments.

"And if you should survive to a hundred and five, think of all you'll derive out of . . . goddamn it!"

She spied a cockroach scampering across the floor and swiped at it with the broom. "She swings and misses!" cried Hubbell.

She swung again. "Strike two!"

The insect disappeared behind the sink.

"Is the once-great Jeannie Stone over the hill, fans?" asked Hubbell. "Has she lost her reflexes?"

"Must be a new breed," said Mom. "I swear, they get faster all the time. I can't wait to move to the city."

"I hate to tell you this, Mom," said Hubbell, "but they have roaches in Greenwich Village too."

"A much better class."

Hubbell asked her for some Kool-Aid. My mother poured a glass of milk and placed it before him. He stared at her inquisitively. "Your father says you should drink more milk," she explained. "Something about pitchers needing calcium."

"What the hell is he, a doctor?" Hubbell snapped. "Jesus Christ! It's not enough he thinks he's Casey Stengel. Now he's Albert Schweitzer too?"

My mother was not accustomed to this sort of belligerence. Frank and Jeannie Stone were, by temperament and ideology, advocates of permissive parenting. They gave their offspring very little to resent or rebel against. When it came to our baseball training, my father was demanding, but the regimens he concocted had always been introduced not by authoritarian fiat but with a sense of shared excitement, even joy, and he never had to assume the role of disciplinarian—one which would not have come naturally to him—because Hubbell and I complied with the program not out of obligation or fear, but for the sheer fun of it, and our agreeable attitude was reinforced by friends who repeatedly told us how lucky we were to have a dad who played catch with us anytime we wanted and knew so much about sports, not to mention his repertoire of jokes and his carefree attitude toward schoolwork.

However, that summer, tension had entered the master plan for Frank Stone's firstborn. Unlike other standout seniors, Hubbell had not been approached by the Dodgers. My father said not to worry. He figured that the scouts must have caught Hubbell on an off day, and besides, he contended, by skipping a year of school Hubbell had deprived himself of a full year's worth of development. He revised the plan. New workouts were designed, the pace of training stepped up. Hubbell was enrolled in a league that played its games at the Parade Grounds—a destination that required two subways and a bus to get to—because scouts were known to stop by in search of untapped talent.

During this time my father's coaching style acquired some rougher edges; he demanded more, pushed harder, barked louder. At the same time, the spirit of adolescence had stiffened the spine of my brother. Hubbell spent less time at the box spring. Less often did he round up volunteers to swing a bat so he could work on some new wrinkle in his delivery. The dumbbells he lifted to keep his arm strong clanged and thumped less consistently from his room. Whereas the old Hubbell always had a ball in his hand, squeezing it and snapping his wrist to keep his grip and delivery strong, he was just as likely now to be carrying a newspaper or a portable radio. And no longer did he follow without hesitation the injunctions of his mentor; if something didn't make sense, he asked tough questions and sometimes even argued. I sensed that a late-inning rhubarb was about to erupt.

"Drink the milk," said Mom. "You'll thank him when you're pitching in Ebbets Field."

"No, thanks," said Hubbell. He pushed the milk aside.

"What's with you lately?" Mom asked.

"Nothing's *with* me. I don't like milk, that's all. If I feel like drinking Kool-Aid, or Coke, or *beer* for chrissake, then I should be able to, that's all. Drop it, okay." And he reopened *The Catcher in the Rye*.

Mom dropped it, as requested. This was her husband's terrain. Besides, she could hardly interfere with the reading of a novel she herself had given her son.

"You can use some calcium yourself, Mr. Shortstop," she said, and poured me a glass of milk.

"Are there any Oreos to dunk into this junk?" I asked.

"There are always Oreos in this house. There may not be meat and there may not be vegetables, but there's always Oreos. Your brother sees to that."

She returned to her sweeping. The radio played "Cherry Pink and Apple Blossom White." Soon, Hubbell stood up to leave, dutifully placing his empty plate in the sink and dropping his napkin in the trash bag, but pointedly leaving the glass of milk on the table. With my mother's back turned, he bolted down a swig of Kool-Aid straight from the pitcher. He winked at me, said goodbye, and headed for the front door. He was always heading for a door in those days.

"Wipe the Kool-Aid off your mouth," my mother called. "If you're gonna be a sneak, better not be sloppy about it."

Hubbell smiled, wiped his mouth with his arm, and left shaking his head. Mom shook hers too, but for different reasons. Suddenly, she was startled by a drumroll of padded footsteps and the darting shadow of a creature considerably larger than a cockroach. A terrified hamster dashed across the linoleum. Mom hopped out of the way, then backed against the stove to avoid an orange and white cat in feverish pursuit of its prey. The hamster deftly avoided the cat's claws and sprinted toward the living room.

"Hank!" yelled Mom.

Hank, the brother who saw to it that we never ran out of Oreos, pounded into the kitchen in pursuit of the animals. "Bwana, get back here!" he called.

The cat had been named after a native in a jungle movie. My brother had been named after Hank Greenberg, a great first baseman and the only Jew in the Hall of Fame. Shortly before her third child was born, my mother had announced that she would not tolerate naming him Tyrus, after Ty Cobb, just because her husband wanted an outfielder to go with the pitcher and shortstop he had already sired. In fact, she insisted, the new child would not be named after *any* baseball player. It would be named after a dead relative, as was the custom in Jewish families.

Not that my mother gave a hoot about tradition. She violated, proudly and ostentatiously, every custom and ritual that had ever been prescribed. We set foot in synagogues only when forced to attend someone's wedding or bar mitzvah; we lit candles only when the electricity went out; at Passover we gathered together and gaily consumed forbidden food, which we always had in abundance because the neighbors brought to our apartment whatever they had to get rid of for the holiday. So vivid was the memory of food shortages that they would rather contribute to the violation of holy writ than throw out anything edible.

It was not for religious reasons, then, that my mother had put her foot down on the issue of naming her third child. One reason was she was tired of offending her relatives on minor issues such as the naming of children; she preferred to save her defiance for bigger concerns, when she could truly get a kick out of it. When the initials of the dearly departed were bypassed in favor of Carl Hubbell and Rogers Hornsby, elders on both sides of the family had been hurt. In the case of his firstborn, my father tried to ameliorate the damage by claiming that his grandmother, Naomi, had a middle name that began with *h*. When I came along, he discovered a long-forgotten great-uncle named Rubin. So unconvincing were his explanations that my mother's aunt took to sending Hubbell and me birthday cards each year addressed to names of her own choosing. So skilled was this woman at rewriting history that whenever we saw her, she would fondly recall my older brother's bar mitzvah, even though there had been no such event.

My mother refused to name her child Tyrus for another reason as well: she could no longer endorse my father's unique brand of superstition, which she considered as primitive as setting a place at a Passover meal for the spirit of Elijah. She told her husband, "Frank, the spirit of Ty Cobb is not going to descend on your child just because of his name."

For my mother the issue was closed when her cousin Henry, with whom she had been close, was killed in the Allied invasion of Normandy. If male, she decided, her child would be named Henry; if female, Harriet. Frank Stone could not deny his wife's wishes at a time of grief. But when he held his newborn son in his arms, lo! he beheld a miracle, and he rejoiced in the irony of it all. Eleven-pound, six-ounce Henry was destined to be a big, slow-footed power hitter, just like Hank Greenberg.

My father's prediction turned out only partly true. Hank grew to love sports as much as the other Stone males, but his body turned out to be suited only for activities that did not require moving. Normal height for a ten-year-old, he weighed 142 pounds at his last weigh-in. My mother had to dress him in the hand-me-down pants of grown men with thirty-four-inch waists, cut off and hemmed at the knee. As poorly coordinated as he was smart (he was in line to be a contestant on *The Whiz Kids* radio program), Hank was the kid who got left out if an odd number of players assembled for a ball game. If the other guys were feeling particularly charitable, he would be allotted as a kind of handicap to the team that had the advantage, and assigned to a position in which he would do the least harm.

Apparently oblivious to the guffaws and taunts that accompanied his athletic endeavors, Hank never sulked, never complained, never elected to avoid embarrassment by sitting on the sideline. When he got into a game, he played with passion; when left out, he volunteered to coach, and performed that task with equal verve. Win or lose, he left the field with the same goofy grin, his eyes narrowing into Oriental slits that made him look like a jolly, imperturbable Buddha. Hank was, by nature, a sanguine fellow who was simply of the opinion that sports were supposed to be fun.

He even seemed amused by his nickname. My father had tagged his third son Round Man when he perceived the obvious: my brother had no angles on his body. He was all curves and hemispheres and arcs. Even his fingers were more like ovals than cylinders. His face was a perfect circle, unbroken even at the top, because his hair was cropped about a sixteenth of an inch from his scalp and it seemed never to grow in, although you would not have noticed this feature as he chased Bwana the cat through the kitchen. Round Man was wearing a pith helmet.

"Bwana, get back here!" he yelled as the animals scampered into the living room.

"Go get 'em, Round Man!" I said.

My mother and I arrived in the living room to find Hank bent over, his spherical rump pointing skyward, obscuring the rest of him. Bwana was tucked under his arm, trying to wriggle free, as Hank groped with his free hand under the sofa where the hamster was hiding.

"I told you to keep those animals in your room," said my mother.

"You think it's easy?" Round Man replied. "They don't like being all cooped up." Softly, he addressed the hamster. "Come here, Bruno. Come on . . . ."

"Bruno?" said my mother.

"He named him after Bruno Sammartino, the wrestler," I

explained. "He has another one named Gorgeous George."

"They're a tag team?"

"Quiet," said Hank. "He's already scared."

"Poor thing," said my mother. "Just make sure that rodent doesn't crap on—"

"Don't call him a rodent," Round Man hissed, as if he were protecting an adopted child from the knowledge of its sordid heritage.

He was wearing short pants, which had climbed up the curve of his behind, exposing a crescent-shaped slice of plump white flesh. I could not resist. I reached into my pocket for my stinger. This weapon was engineered by bending one arm of a bobby pin and looping it around until the tip reached halfway up the other arm, which remained straight. The loop was secured by placing the tip on the inside of the straight arm so the device ended up shaped like the *and* symbol in penmanship. When the curved arm was pressed against a solid surface, the tip sprang loose with a sharp kick.

I stung my brother perfectly on his exposed tush just as he had finally gotten hold of Bruno and dragged him into the open. Hank yelped, jerking his arm instinctively to protect his rear. This gave Bwana the opening he needed. The cat had started meowing and scratching as soon as it saw the hamster, and now it lashed out with its claw. It missed Bruno but caught the back of Round Man's hand. Hank lost his grip. Both animals wrenched themselves loose again and started careening around the living room like billiard balls. Round Man called me a mean shit.

"That cat is vicious," said my mother, kneeling to make sure Hank was all right. "I knew he'd be trouble the minute I laid eyes on him."

"He's not vicious," Hank contended. "He just has to learn the difference between hamsters and mice."

"And *you* have to learn the difference between a home and a zoo," said my mother.

The problem was my brother loved animals even more than he loved baseball, and there was little opportunity to indulge his passion in the wild. The neighborhood fauna consisted mainly of temperamental cats and ornery mutts, some dusty sparrows, robins with rust-colored breasts, pastel parakeets in cages, and a

variety of thriving insects. If you wanted to inspect more pictur-
esque species, you went to the zoo at Prospect Park. Or to Round
Man's bedroom. His menagerie currently consisted of hamsters
and gerbils, a trio of turtles, a tank full of guppies, goldfish, and
angelfish, a praying mantis named Sebastian, a cocker spaniel
named after Davy Crockett, Bwana the cat, and a parrot named
Gleason. As per the agreement he worked out with my mother,
Hank had full responsibility for the care and feeding of his pets,
and he housed every one in his room.

Soon, my brother had captured both beasts and tranquility
was restored. I resumed my lunch; my mother resumed sweeping.
"Listen," she said, "when you go out, I'd like you to pick up a
few things. I need some milk and some—"

The phone rang. My mother answered. She listened a moment to the voice on the other end, then said gravely, "Hold on,
Cecille." Frowning, she placed the phone on the table and poured
a cup of coffee from the percolator. She lit a Camel and sat down
at the kitchen table, angling the chrome and vinyl chair so she
could cross her legs in comfort. She was settling in for one of her
marathon conversations.

"Did Herbie leave her again?" I asked.

Her hand darted to the receiver in hopes of covering it
before the sound waves of my voice got there. "I wish he would,"
said Mom. "He won't let her be president of the PTA."

She reached into her blouse and pulled out her hearing aid.
It was a metal box, about the size of a pack of cigarettes, which
hooked onto her bra. She inserted the earplug in her bad ear,
placed the hearing aid itself on the receiving end of the phone and
spoke into the other end. No matter how many times she told me
that her hearing loss was not my fault, I still felt guilty when I saw
that gadget.

"Cecille, we'll have to find someone else fast or the fascists
will take over and—"

Cecille interrupted with a woeful plaint that I could hear
across the table. "Calm down, honey," said my mother. "It's all
right. Go on, tell Jeannie all the gory details."

According to my father, Mom was a sucker for sob stories,
misfits, and self-pitying neurotics who flocked to her like lepers
to Lourdes. Listening to Cecille's domestic lament, she turned

toward the wall, as if to shield her child from the odious details. I seized the opportunity. Palming the rest of my sandwich so I could finish it on the run, I slipped discreetly away. I had more important missions than to run errands for my mother. The Dodgers were about to play the Braves at Milwaukee, and if Brooklyn won, they would clinch the National League pennant. They needed me. I heard my mother call my name as the front door slammed behind me.

Chapter Two

On a weekday afternoon four days before the start of the school year, the sidewalks of Brooklyn belonged to women and children. Fecund mothers in pastel dresses striped by the shadows of fire escapes rocked baby carriages while keeping a steady eye on their toddlers to make sure they played a safe distance from the curb. Eager wives carted home bags of groceries to feed the proud breadwinners who would, in a few hours, emerge from the subway, their necks sticky with sweat, their fingers and shirts stained by newsprint, their hearts filled with the postwar dream of a prosperous security. Old women born in the ghettos of Eastern Europe or the villages of Sicily huddled on the stoops. Some were gliding cheerfully into their twilight; others watched the young with sour disdain, as if the America of chrome-lined automobiles, transistor radios, and Bermuda shorts was the Rome of Nero.

One such sour drop was Mrs. Kass, who lived across the hall from my family. A bovine septuagenarian, Mrs. Kass sat on an aluminum folding chair at the top of our stoop each day, all day, until her husband, a buyer and seller of junk who was half his wife's size and cursed with the name Jack Kass, returned home to haul her upstairs. Her face, which had the color and texture of a turnip, looked as if it had been frozen during an attack of heartburn. She sat still as stone in her vigil, so still that my father had named her the Sphinx. That summer, however, the nickname had became a tad obsolete: Mrs. Kass had acquired moving parts. Her hands had started to shake, just her hands, above her lap, in randomly timed episodes, as if her wrists were receiving jolts of electric shock. According to my mother, Mrs. Kass had Parkinson's disease and we ought not make fun of her. I found that explanation unsatisfactory. I was certain that, in her dementia, Mrs. Kass believed she was a minstrel playing a banjo that only she could hear.

I was a good-natured boy, it was generally agreed—friendly and well-mannered. But I admit to a mean streak in the case of the Sphinx and others like her. Before she'd become ossified, the virago would erupt in brain-jarring shrieks each time a kid slammed a door or bounced a ball within fifty feet of her. Once, she had poured ice water on a bunch of us because we were playing handball against a brick wall two stories beneath her window. Now that she could barely *drink* water, much less throw it, and her lips rarely uttered anything more complex than a long, sustained *oy,* it was with sadistic pleasure that I would forget to hold the ponderous iron door when I exited the building.

Emerging into daylight from the long, cool corridor, I flung open the door and vaulted the four steps to the street. The impact of the landing sent shock waves through my black U.S. Keds and up my legs to my belly. The door crashed shut with a thunderous clang inches from the Sphinx. I looked back. She hadn't budged. But I noted with pleasure a slight narrowing of the eyes and a further downturn in the deep crevices that ran from her nostrils to her jaw. I also noticed, above her head, a bit of graffiti that someone had scrawled in chalk overnight: EAT IT.

I sauntered, guiltless, up Howard Avenue. A pair of retired men argued heatedly over which Communists—the Russians or Chinese—were the bigger threat to the peace and security of the free world. Aside from them, the only men visible were the shopkeepers. Among the wrinkled, defeathered chickens hanging from their feet in his window, Sharfin the butcher, his white apron streaked with blood, regaled his customers with the virtues of kosher meat. Sharfin fed a slab of beef into the top of a grinder and watched it ooze out the other end in spaghettilike strings, ready to be molded into hamburger. Sam the fruit-store man, a tall Ukrainian with fiercely dark eyes and a thick black mustache, weighed a cantaloupe and added its price to the list of figures he jotted down with a thick black pencil on a brown paper bag. Between entries, Sam would reflexively lick the lead tip of his pencil, an action I attempted to emulate in school only to end up with a rank taste in my mouth and black spittle on my notebook.

In the shop next to Sam, a nearsighted old laundry proprietor named Gen H. Lee hunted among rows of packaged shirts for a number that matched the one on the ticket of a woman who barked directions: "Up . . . higher . . . to the right . . . not *light,* right!" My father would have us believe that Gen H. Lee was General Harry Lee, the only surviving Civil War officer of Oriental descent.

On a wooden chair outside his grocery, next to a rack of mops and brooms that belonged to the hardware store next door, sat Happy Horowitz. A pink-faced man with a sacklike jowl and a tweed cap that he wore year-round to conceal a bald, wart-riddled scalp, Happy was taking a break while his wife Henny sorted out a dozen eggs for a customer. In a dark corner Henny held up each egg to a lamp. By illuminating the egg's interior, she could detect an embryo, and if she did, the egg would be discarded as unfit for consumption.

"Roger the Dodger," said Happy when he saw me. "You ever read this book?" He held up a copy of *From Here to Eternity.*

I shook my head. "Never read it, eh?" he said. "You like James *Joyce,* not James Jones, right?"

I squinted at him inquisitively. "It's a joke," said Happy. "You ever see the movie, with Burt Lancaster? About the war?"

I said I had, and in my mind flashed the love scene on the beach with Lancaster and Deborah Kerr, the waves lapping their naked thighs.

"I was in the war, you know," said Happy. "I was a sentry at the naval base in Norfolk, Virginia, and you know what? The whole time I was on duty, not one Nazi ship landed on the shores of the U.S. of A. Not one. You could look it up."

His face lit up like the brake lights on his Studebaker; his laugh climbed from the deepest crevasses of his lungs and burst forth in a series of whiny sounds that resembled an asthmatic attack.

"What's so funny?" asked Henny. She had finished waiting on her customer.

"You wouldn't understand," said Happy.

"Which means I've heard it a hundred times," Henny translated. "Have a piece of halvah, sweetheart." She handed me a chunk of the sesame-based confection. It was sweet and chewy and laced with chocolate.

"Give me a sentence with halvah in it," said Henny. I juggled the word in my mind: *hal*-va, hal-i-*va, hol*-i-va. But I could think of nothing beyond the obvious, and the obvious was not what Henny's game was about.

"I give up," I said.

"That's a holluva nice car over there," said Henny.

"That's not fair," I protested.

I could still hear Happy laughing when I reached the intersection of Howard Avenue and Sterling Place. The only corner in the neighborhood to merit capitalization, the Corner was the hub of street life, especially in summer when that block of Sterling became Play Street and the asphalt strip burst forth in a whirligig of games. Kids jumped rope, flipped baseball cards, aimed pennies and rubber heels at chalk-drawn lines, rolled marbles, shot basketballs into apple crates with the bottoms removed, glided on skates and scooters, sputtered by on bikes with playing cards attached to the spokes to make them sound like motorcycles, competed in potsy, skelly, hopscotch, jump-rope, kick-the-can, hide-and-seek, ringolevio, dodge ball, Johnny-on-the-pony, and, on days when the Police Athletic League brought its equipment around, shuffleboard and volleyball. But mostly they filled the air with spaldeens, the ubiquitous pink rubber balls with the Spalding logo that were used for stickball, punchball, boxball, off-the-wall, stoopball, Chinese handball, hit-the-penny, throwing sewers— which entailed throwing, not a sewer, but a ball, from one manhole cover past the next without your opponent catching it on the fly—and a host of other games, nameless, improvised, ingenious.

There was a mysterious organicity to street games; they replaced each other in rhythmic sequences like buds, blossoms, and leaves. Somehow, as if the dates were engraved on calendars, everyone knew when, say, marble season ended and scooter season arrived. The games stopped only for rain and sleep. Even in winter, missiles flew past Sterling Place windows. Only those were made of pigskin or snow.

Neighborhood drivers avoided Play Street whenever possible. Those who dared enter risked collisions with flying bodies and other lethal objects and endured the angry stares and impatient injunctions of kids who felt that the street belonged to them. They also had to confront Ippish. Ippish was a self-appointed traffic cop with a twenty-five-cent tin badge pinned to his shirt, who protected the sanctity of Play Street by standing in the intersection and prohibiting cars from entering. Ippish was mentally retarded. According to my mother, the unfortunate young man had a twenty-two-year-old's body (the trunk of a bear, topped with a rodent face) and a six-year-old's brain. I imagined a lump of gray matter floating like a matzo ball in the soup of a gallon-sized skull.

Each summer day, Ippish worked up oceans of sweat waving at the cars that sped up and down the gentle slope of Howard Avenue, shooting nasty looks at drivers who had interrupted the games by entering from the other end of Play Street, thrusting out his hand in staunch rebuke to any who might entertain thoughts of turning into the street off Howard. That the one-way street was clearly marked against such an intrusion was a matter of no consequence to Ippish.

That day Ippish was protecting a stickball game. Of the several varieties of this universal urban sport, the one favored in my neighborhood was played with two or three on a team: a pitcher, a catcher, an optional outfielder. It was a primal, no-frills battle between pitcher and batter. No bases, no running, no pitching on a bounce the way sissies in certain neighborhoods played the game. The customary equipment was: a stick that had once been attached to a mop or a broom (hand-me-downs from mothers or hot merchandise pilfered from hardware stores); a glove for the catcher, typically one too battered to be used for baseball or softball; a spaldeen, ideally one that was neither overly lively nor so dead that it would ricochet off a swinging bat like a shot put. Home plate was a manhole cover. The rules were simple: a ground ball that got past the pitcher was a single, as was an uncaught pop fly that did not pass the next sewer; if a fly ball soared past the first sewer, it was a double, a sewer and a half and it was a triple, two sewers or more and it was a home run. Since the street was narrow and the sidewalks were foul territory, batters had to hit straightaway to score runs. And good stickball pitchers were tough to hit. They knew how to dig their fingertips and knuckles into the spongy pink of a spaldeen and make the ball dance. Control, however, was difficult to master, so games generally featured a plethora of walks and an equal amount of strikeouts, since batters were so eager to hit something they would swing wildly at anything close to the plate.

The players that day were the Big Guys, young men sixteen to nineteen, who let me hang out with them on occasion for three reasons: I played ball well enough to fill in if they had an odd number of players; I was a dependable source of arcane information such as Duke Snider's batting average in 1953; and because I was Hubbell Stone's kid brother.

That these young men let me take drags on their smokes, that my presence did not inhibit their critiques of the female anatomy or curtail their use of dirty words, was a mixed blessing. My association with them made me feel older and wiser than I actually was and instilled in me a poise that would serve me well in later life. But my social climbing made me, on occasion, insufferably snobbish around kids my own age, and it informed me of matters I might have been better off waiting to discover in a more natural way. Already, for example, I was anxious over what seemed to be an interminable delay in the sprouting of pubic hair.

At bat was Harry the Horse, an acne-riddled behemoth who played guard on the high school football team. Harry was about as aggressive as a notary public, but his size lent him a certain intimidation value both on the gridiron and the streets. The pitcher, Marty Klinger, went into his windup, all jerky elbows and knees and clench-jawed intensity. The eldest son of the ill-tempered Barney and Hilda (the purveyor of liver and onions), Marty was about to take a second crack at getting through his senior year in high school. He did not want to do this, preferring instead to follow in his father's footsteps and work the docks as a longshoreman. Hilda insisted that her son finish school and make something of himself. "He's making something of himself all right," my brother Hubbell once remarked. "He's making of himself a first-class asshole."

I turned away from the stickball action when something caught my eye. Next to Mike's Barber Shop was a poster of Miss Rheingold. The face on it changed from month to month, but it was always a pretty young face with a radiant smile and teeth that should have been advertising toothpaste, not beer. The message was always the same: "My beer is Rheingold, the dry beer." This was another mystery I had been unable to solve: how can beer be dry, and if it could, why would that be a selling point? This month's Miss Rheingold was a pert brunette whom I'd admired since her coronation. Now she had a long black mustache and a pointy beard like Fu Manchu. Above her head were scrawled these words: "Miss Rheingold eats it raw." An orally fixated vandal was on the loose.

I heard the familiar sound of a stick whacking a spaldeen, and a familiar voice call, "Base hit!"

"Waddayou, nuts!" roared Klinger. "It was foul by a mile."

"Fair ball," said the umpire, resolutely folding his arms.

"Who the fuck made you official umpire anyways?" said Klinger. "You're not only a dwarf, you're a moron."

It took guts to stand up to Marty Klinger, especially if you stood five feet tall and had to call balls and strikes while standing on a milk box so you could see over the squatting catcher. But Mr. Big was a man of courage. A Brooklyn College junior, he had stopped growing at an age when most adolescents begin their surge to full stature. Because his size precluded meaningful participation in sports, Mr. Big specialized in umpiring, a job he dispatched with gusto and Solomonic integrity.

"Hey, kid!" I heard Klinger's call and, hoping I was not the kid in question, walked toward the entrance to Jake's Luncheonette without looking in his direction. But his next command was unequivocal. "Hey, you! Stone!"

I turned and pointed inquisitively at my chest to verify that it was indeed I who was being paged.

"You see any other Stones around here? Was that foul or what?"

I had no idea; I had been distracted by Miss Rheingold. But I could not resist sticking one to Klinger. "Fair ball," I said.

The other players laughed. "What is he, an expert?" said Klinger. "He's just a fucking kid!"

"Shut up and pitch," said Mr. Big, "before you have a conniption."

Such moments made my daily egg cream that much sweeter.

Jake's Luncheonette was the place where Play Street players refreshed themselves and grown men ate when their wives were not home or they didn't feel like going home themselves. It was one of two places where the Dodger faithful would congregate to watch ball games, the other being Mickey's Saloon a block away.

In the glow of his nineteen-inch Admiral television and a neon Coke sign that read THE PAUSE THAT REFRESHES, Jake Ratner assembled sandwiches, sizzled burgers and bacon and eggs on a greasy grill, whipped up impeccable sodas from a row of syrup dispensers and seltzer spigots, spun thick malteds in silver containers on the whirring blades of a mixer, and brewed what was said to be the strongest cup of coffee in Brooklyn. All this he did single-handedly while carrying on a steady stream of conversation, sometimes several at once.

I made it a point to arrive at Jake's well in advance of game time in order to secure my customary stool and partake of an egg cream. This had become a ritual of mine earlier that summer, when I discovered a positive correlation between drinking an egg cream and Dodger success on the diamond. The breeze from a swivel fan brushed my face as I approached the marble counter. A big hand yanked the brim of my cap down to my eyebrows and around to the side. "Waddaya say, kid?" said Jake.

Jake was a likable, gentle man, avuncular and funny, but this cap-yanking routine of his was infuriating. I had several interchangeable T-shirts with Dodgers spelled out on the chest in graceful script, but I had only one official Dodger cap, blue with a fancy white B on the front. I had purchased it for a dollar that spring and had trained the beak to curl just right by rolling it up and shoving it into a drinking glass for three days. Worn for the first time on opening day, the cap, even more than my pregame egg cream, was largely responsible for the Dodgers' achievements that season. One day I intended to tell Jake that it is not wise to mess with a lucky cap.

Of the three men sitting at the counter, two were close friends of my father. I had known them all my life. Burt Sugarman was a husky man with blond hair clipped as close and straight as a putting green; he worked nights collecting tolls on the Cross Bay Boulevard Bridge. Sal (Sappy) Sapienza had recently retired from the transit police with a small pension and a leg made gimpy by a bullet. The bridge of Sappy's nose was a series of peaks and valleys; it had been broken four times. The third man looked vaguely familiar. Older than the others, he was pale, with stooped shoulders, white hair, and bags under his eyes that were big enough to store marbles. He wore an old-fashioned brown suit and a striped tie with a white shirt whose collar was yellow at the edge. I pegged him as the kind of man who would wear a suit and tie even when he didn't have to.

"Irv, you know who this is?" Jake asked him, jerking his thumb in my direction.

Irv looked me over for several seconds. "Frankie Stone's kid," he ventured. "Hubbell, right?"

"Not Hubbell, you idiot," said Burt. "Hubbell just gradu-ated high school, for chrissake. He'll be pitching for the Dodgers in a year or two."

Irv was delighted with the news. "Yeah? No kidding. An-other Jewish ballplayer, like what's his name, the rookie from Lafayette High School, the lefty . . ."

"Sandy Koufax," said Sal.

"Yeah, Koufax," said Irv. "A Jewish boy. He's got some future, that kid."

"Waddayou, kidding me?" said Jake. "He's a stiff."

"If he's a stiff," said Irv, "why did they give him so much money?"

"To get Jews into the ballpark," said Sal.

Irv did not buy that theory. "What are you talking? Did you see his fastball?"

"Hey, you can throw fucking cannonballs," said Burt, "but if you can't hit the side of a barn, what the hell good is it? I guarantee, two years from now he's selling shoes. Now, Hubbell, *there's* a pitcher. Smart. Knows the game. Frankie taught him good."

Irv subjected my face to further scrutiny. "So, if you're not Hubbell, you must be . . . let's see . . . Roger. Roger and out!"

I had earlier concluded that mankind was divided into two categories: idiots who, upon hearing my name, said things like Roger and out, and those who did not. Just by looking at this Irv guy, I could tell that, if he ever laughed, spit would leak from the corners of his mouth. And I was right; he laughed, and spit leaked out, along with a sibilant sound that could have passed as the hissing of a hysterical snake.

"Jeez, you were this big when I lived around here," Irv continued. "How old are you?"

"Almost twelve," I said.

"Almost twelve," he echoed. He stared at me, reflecting on the deeper meaning of the information he'd just received, making a series of clicking sounds with his tongue and teeth. Then, having arrived at a profound conclusion, he sighed deeply, shook his head, and exhaled into my face. His breath stunk of stomach acid and remorse. "Time flies," he said.

"Jeez, Irv, you're a regular Einstein," said Sal.

Irv ignored the remark. "So, how's your old man? Still driving a cab?"

I nodded, wondering whether it was mockery I detected in the way he asked the question, or pity. It was certainly not respect.

"Now there's a guy who made something of himself," said Irv. He was not referring to my father. He nodded at the TV screen, where the logo read: TALKING SPORTS WITH SONNY SCOTT. A low-grade growl rattled along Jake's counter as the logo dissolved into the face of the show's host. It was an oily face, snide and arrogant, the lips twisted to one side in a permanent sneer; a vain, angular face, topped off by an expensive but too-obvious toupee. Sonny Scott had grown up as Solly Skapinsky in the neighborhood. He and my father had played ball together. Solly was a spark plug, a good-field, no-hit, do-anything-to-win outfielder; Cyclone Frankie Stone was a rock-solid third baseman, a strapping slugger whose swing reminded people of Mel Ott. Solly and Frankie advanced in unison to the middle rungs of semipro ball, but their friendship disintegrated along the way when they fell in love with the same girl.

As long as the girl was ambivalent, rejecting neither suitor, encouraging both, the two young men worked out an uneasy but peaceful coexistence, balancing the demands of teamwork and the imperatives of the mating instinct. But when Skinny Jeannie got engaged to my father, Solly stopped talking to his old friend and sulked, until one day, during an intersquad practice game, when the two players were assigned to different teams, he got his revenge.

It was a wild play, the details of which had changed over the years with the telling, and it ended with my father covering home plate and Solly racing down the baseline determined to score. He arrived just after the ball. My father applied the tag. Solly barreled full-speed into him like Bronco Nagurski trying to cross a goal line. The collision was brutal; both men crashed to the earth in a tangled heap, and the full weight of Solly's body landed on my father's leg. When the dust settled, my father was bleeding from spike wounds, his shoulder was out of joint, and his ankle was bent at a grotesque angle. Never again would he throw without pain. Never again would he stride into a pitched ball with quite the same potency. They tried him at first base, but even that was too demanding, and the sweet swing of Cyclone Frankie Stone was consigned to softball games in the neighborhood schoolyard, where the left field wall became known as Frankie's Fence, so often did he pelt it with doubles.

It took Frank Stone another two years to get the girl of his dreams to marry him, but he finally succeeded. His other dream, to play with the Dodgers in Ebbets Field, died in the dust at home plate that day, only to be resurrected, vicariously, when he became a father. Hubbell would be first to redeem the dream; I would be second. Together, we would be the only brothers other than Paul and Lloyd Waner to make the Hall of Fame. My father even held out hope that the Round Man would, at puberty, undergo some hormonal miracle that would enable him to assert his hereditary grace and agility and join his siblings in Ebbets Field and Cooperstown.

Solly Skapinsky played one year in the low minor leagues before it became evident to management that his drive and his moxie would never compensate for his shortage of skill. Embittered, he moved out of the neighborhood, changed his name to Sonny Scott, and got a job in radio. When television came of age, he moved to the local NBC station. Now he was known throughout New York as the acerbic, opinionated host of *Talking Sports,* a provocative and controversial figure whom sports fans either loved or hated. In our neighborhood he was more than hated, he was despised, not just for his intentional maiming of Cyclone Frankie Stone, but for lying pretentiously and turning his back on his roots. Sonny Scott's official biography had him growing up in Connecticut and attending Yale University before being offered a minor league contract. A congenital heart condition, he claimed, forced him to retire prematurely and offer his athletic erudition to the listening public. Solly Skapinsky had committed the ultimate offense: he stopped being a Regular Guy. He became a snob, a phony, and he had escalated those crimes to unspeakably heretical heights by publicly proclaiming his allegiance to, first, the Republican Party, and second, the New York Yankees.

"Mister So-Called Sonny Scott is not our favorite poisonality," said Jake.

Skapinsky's voice had a peculiar quality that made accented syllables sound like the yaps of a terrier. "Well, what can I say? I picked the Dodgers to finish fourth and they ran away from the rest of the league. They've been lucky all season."

"Lucky, my ass!" said Burt, and a chorus registered agreement.

"But let me tell you this," Scott continued. "All the luck in the world won't help them if they play the Yankees in the World Series. The Dodgers will do their old foldo routine. They're over the hill. Their manager's a moron. And they got about as much guts as the Italian army."

Sal let loose a curse in Italian, adding emphatic hand gestures. Jake changed the channel.

"Jeez, I'd like to get my hands on that scumbag," said Sappy.

"I saw him once," Irv reported. "On Fifth Avenue, outside this fancy-schmancy building with a doorman and everything. He got into a Cadillac the size of a tank."

Perhaps out of deference to me and the Stone family honor, the men pointedly did not permit Irv to pursue the subject. Jake turned his attention to the grill; Burt decided to phone his wife; Sappy unfolded a copy of the *Daily News.* "Let's see what's in the paper," he said.

The *News* was the paper of choice in the neighborhood, the Regular Guy's paper. Anyone who read the *New York Times* was assumed to be putting on airs or gearing up for social climbing. *Times* readers worked in offices. They were pencil pushers and eggheads. The working stiffs in my neighborhood were, for the most part, New Deal Democrats and union loyalists who did not approve of the pugnacious, Red-baiting, reactionary bluster that filled the editorial page of the *News,* but they read the tabloid anyway for its snappy, street-smart headlines, its photos of luscious babes (complete with measurements), and its made-for-the-subway format. Mainly, they preferred the *News* for its sports section. It was in the back of the paper, and it was, on most occasions, the first, and frequently last, place to which the reader turned. *News* writers, principally Dick Young, wrote about ball games the way Brooklyn fans watched them: knowing, opinionated, witty, aggressive, brutally honest.

On that day, September 8, 1955, Konrad Adenauer, the Chancellor of West Germany, was on his way to Moscow to meet with Nikita Khrushchev about normalizing relations. The *News* feared that the Russkies would bulldoze Adenauer into reunifying his country, a move they felt would inevitably turn Germany into "just another prisoner nation of the Red Slave Empire." Yeah, well, at Jake's, reunification meant reuniting the Dodgers with the National League pennant, which Willie Mays and the New York Giants had pilfered the previous year, and the only slave empire that mattered belonged to the New York Yankees, who had won the World Series six of the previous eight years. Turn the page.

The Commerce Department reported record highs in personal income, employment, and construction spending—a *triple boom.* Terrific news, thought the men of Jake's, but to them a triple boom meant consecutive home runs off the bats of Duke Snider, Roy Campanella, and Gil Hodges. Turn the page.

Emmett Till, a fourteen-year-old Mississippi black, had been killed by two men because he allegedly saluted a white woman with a wolf whistle. "The South stinks," said a letter to the editor, and the men at Jake's agreed with all their hearts. This was a tragedy, an abomination. The bigoted trash should be lynched. But, say, speaking of Negroes, where the hell would the Dodgers be without Jackie Robinson, still a firebrand at thirty-six, and Campanella, roaring back from career-threatening injuries with an MVP season, and big Don Newcombe, a shoe-in for twenty wins? Turn the page.

Flip quickly past the ads for Philip Morris and Chesterfields and Dodges and Packards and Amana ranges and Frigidaires. Pause briefly for the 37–24–36 Italian starlet in the tight sweater. Accelerate past the invitations to see *Marty* and *Love is a Many-Splendored Thing* at our local movie houses. Fly by the pictures of society brides and obituaries of people we never heard of. And stop at the only pages that matter, where the headline reads: FLOCK CAN CLINCH TODAY.

That day, the day it was announced that *Peter Pan* would soon return to Broadway, the Dodgers—the Flock, the Brooks, the Bums—could, with a victory over the Braves, move a step closer to the Never-Never Land of a World Championship. This was a mythical realm that we, the tenacious and adoring fans, refused to accept as make-believe. Autumn after autumn we had clawed at Never-Never Land with our fingernails, sniffing its fragrant air, only to be yanked back to earth before our feet could touch ground, as if destiny were a ship to Hell piloted by Captain Hook. And spring after spring we gathered ourselves up and, with a faith stronger than Peter's and Wendy's and all the Lost Boys', we soared once again on the fairy dust of hope; 1955 was no exception.

Chapter Three

My father looked like a movie star: Jeff Chandler, whose dark, high-cheekboned looks enabled him to play both Western heroes and Indians such as Cochise. The resemblance was so striking that on several occasions my father had been mistaken for Chandler and had even signed the actor's name for insistent autograph hounds. He was six feet two and weighed 208 pounds. That made him exactly a foot taller and one hundred pounds heavier than my mother, a nice compatible symmetry for a couple, I believed.

He was a handsome man with a strong, wide-nostrilled nose, brown eyes with a slight Siberian slant, and dark hair combed straight back in rolling waves. His smile was generous and infectious. But the physical features that fascinated me most were the odd patches of color on his skin. His complexion was olive-toned, but the sides of his shins, where for some reason no hair grew, were milky white; the fingers on his right hand were yellowed by nicotine; his left arm up to the middle of his bicep was several shades darker than the right because he drove his cab, in all but the most inclement weather, with his arm resting on the open window.

Frank Stone had become a cab driver when he was forced to give up his dream of playing third base for the Dodgers. He had a wife and a future big leaguer to support, and with the Great Depression still raging and jobs so scarce that his own father could not get him into the plumber's union, he borrowed money and paid someone off to get a hack license. He had tried sales because everyone said he was articulate and had an affable, winning personality, but his boiling point was too low for such work; he couldn't stand people saying no to him, and he could tolerate even less indecision, ambivalence, and changes of mind. When you drove a cab, the customers came to you, and they needed you as much as you needed them.

On occasion my father would take me with him to work. Early in the morning, sometimes in the chill stillness before the street lamps were turned off, we would ride the subway into Manhattan, walk a few long blocks to the banks of the Hudson River, and enter the garage, where the other cabbies would surround me with their whiskery faces and coffee-scented smiles. I would ride up front with my father, first mate to his captain, proud that he always knew where to go and the best way to get there. It seemed to me he had a gift for handling passengers; big shots and riffraff, the friendly and mean, the loquacious and inanimate, the kvetches and the kind, those who treated him like an expert who knew his job and those who treated him like a coolie—he knew how to deal with all of them, even the ones he wanted to toss out on their ears. He would introduce me to each and every rider, and to the nice ones he would relate how I got my name and how I would follow my older brother's footsteps into baseball immortality.

It seemed to me a terrific way to earn a living, navigating a big yellow vehicle through the great stone canyons of the city, meeting a new person every few minutes—here a tycoon, there a peon, here a dowager, there a maid—entering their lives, however fleetingly, transporting them with dispatch to their chosen destinations. It was life on the move. It was a noble vocation. It sure beat running some shop in the neighborhood with the same tiresome customers buying the same humdrum goods day in and day out, or having some despot of a boss breathing down your neck, or sitting hunched over some desk in a stuffy room choked by a necktie. All this I understood from listening to the grievances of men with other occupations.

For most of my life my father seemed to agree with my assessment. Every night, it seemed, he would come home, tired but cheerful, with another tale of life in the city—of a big-tipping drunk, of a traveling salesman with a repertoire of jokes, of a particularly sage choice of routes, of a shop with the best doughnuts he'd ever eaten, of a jerk who tried to stiff him out of a fare, of a foreigner who couldn't pronounce Lexington Avenue, of a gambler who made bets on how fast he could get to his destination, of a jilted woman who broke down and cried, of a couple he

transported to the hospital a minute before he'd have had to
deliver a baby in the backseat.

But he had changed over time. Hacking had become a living,
not much more. At times he even seemed to be ashamed of his
profession. And, that year, he started openly complaining: the
traffic, the cops, the politicians, the hack bureau, other cabbies,
tourists, truck drivers, bus drivers, passengers. They were all out
to make his life miserable. Plus, he needed to make more than the
eighty to ninety dollars a week he was pulling in, and he was
being held back in that aspiration because the new dispatcher, one
Sy Kramer, had it in for Cyclone Frankie Stone. Kramer would
not give him the most productive shifts despite my father's senior-
ity, because my father refused to dish out the kickback Kramer
demanded. There were even times when my father would show
up at the garage and find out there were no cabs to drive—unless,
that is . . . But my father would not give Sy Kramer a dime. Sy
Kramer was not only a Yankee fan, he was the brother-in-law of
Solly So-Called Sonny Scott Skapinsky.

What my father wanted was his own taxi medallion. This was
a shield-shaped piece of tin that was affixed to the hood of a cab
and signified private ownership. A medallion cost about seventeen cents to manufacture, but it was a holy grail to cabbies with
an entrepreneurial bent. A beat-up old Checker cab worth seventy-five bucks might as well have been a solid gold Cadillac if
it had a medallion on it, for no new medallions had been issued
in New York since 1937, the year Hubbell was born, and a cabbie
who owned one could earn twice as much, even after expenses,
as he could driving for a fleet—and still more if he hired the cab
out to another driver when he wasn't using it. My father knew
that for twelve thousand bucks, maybe even ten, he could pick up
a medallion on the black market. Only he was a long way from
having that ten grand.

My mother believed that her husband was fooling himself if
he thought a medallion would be a panacea. She wanted him to
drop the cab business entirely and try something new, something
that would let him use his brains. Her man had a good mind,
Jeannie Stone insisted. She knew him in high school, when he was
so wrapped up in sports he never cracked a book, but was sharp
enough in class to fool his teachers into believing he'd studied.

Later, during their courtship, she realized that her Frank was, by nature, a man of considerable wit, curiosity, and intelligence, but with the lazy mind and skimpy ambition of the Regular Guy. Over the years, she claimed, Frank Stone had let his once-lively brain atrophy without any challenge beyond vicariously managing the Dodgers and orchestrating the baseball destiny of his sons. She did not know what Frank Stone might do other than drive a cab, but she wanted him to find work that required of him something more challenging than figuring out the fastest route from Wall Street to Central Park West.

In temperament if not appearance, my father resembled his own. Grandpa Abe was half a foot shorter than his eldest son, although he weighed nearly as much. A loud, boisterous Regular Guy, he liked Camel cigarettes, card games, dirty jokes, and, rumor had it, busty young girls like his wife, Grandma Rosie, had been when he married her fresh off the boat from her village in the southwest corner of Russia. He himself was born in America, and he too looked like a movie star. Two of them, in fact: if Sydney Greenstreet and Peter Lorre had had a son, he would have looked like Grandpa Abe. He had a moonface with a double chin, and eyes that looked as if he were about to cry, although crying was something he did only when the fumes of a raw onion, his favorite condiment, floated into his nostrils.

A hoarse-voiced man who had to clear his throat of phlegm between sentences, he was a plumber in the construction trade, a union man who installed pipes and fixtures in new buildings. To Grandpa Abe, a man of fierce loyalties, the Brooklyn Dodgers ranked just behind Franklin Delano Roosevelt and ahead of his union for claims on his heart. Grandma Rosie was a distant fourth.

It was through these two men, our elders, that Hubbell and I, and later Hank, had been passed the legacy of the Brooklyn Dodgers. As in other homes, the Dodger heritage was handed down from father to son, brother to brother, repeated like the story of Passover or the Passion of Christ, that it shall not be forgotten. It was our folklore, our living mythology, an oral history with the pathos and redemptive promise of the Old Testament.

Prehistory began in 1890, when the Brooklyn franchise joined the National League. They were called the Trolley Dodgers because Brooklynites were accustomed to dodging the conveyances that raced along the tracks that laced the growing city, which was not yet part of New York. They were also known as the Bridegrooms because six players had married during the winter of 1890. The team won the pennant that inaugural year, but fired their manager anyway.

The first epoch of the modern era took shape with the construction of hallowed Ebbets Field in 1913, the same year, significantly, that Frank Stone was born. My brothers and I knew at an early age that in the first regular season game ever played at Ebbets Field, a Dodger outfielder named Casey Stengel made a spectacular catch but the home team lost to the Phillies, 1–0. Grandpa had been present that day, or so he told us. So vivid and insistent were his tales that his heirs could recount other landmark events as if they too had been in attendance: the longest game ever played, a twenty-six inning 1–1 tie with the Boston Braves; the unassisted triple play in the 1920 World Series by a Cleveland infielder with the double-take name of Bill Wambsganss; the first night game in Brooklyn, June 15, 1938, when Johnny Vandermeer of Cincinnati pitched his second consecutive no-hitter; the third strike that catcher Mickey Owen dropped, giving the Yankees a reprieve that they turned into a victory in the 1941 World Series. Like Bible students who memorized the names of prophets and saints, we could recite by heart the oddball monikers of luminaries such as Leo the Lip Durocher, Dolph Camilli, Pistol Pete Reiser, Babe Herman, Zack Wheat, Dazzy Vance, Van Lingle Mungo.

Our elders recited the tales in tones laced with the sweetness of nostalgia. But when the discourse turned to the turgid history of the latter-day epoch, legend turned to lamentation, laughs to groans, the twinkle of fond remembrance to tearful woe.

The trouble started when the Bums got good. After winning the pennant in 1941, they hired Branch Rickey, who had built great teams in St. Louis, to run the club. During the war, the man who would earn nicknames like Mahatma, The Brain, and El Cheapo, quietly stocked the Dodger farm system with talent, and by 1946 his new team was good enough to force his former team into the first pennant playoff in history. The Dodgers lost to the Cardinals, and the spirit of "Wait till next year" was born in

Brooklyn. The phrase started out as a promise, in a headline in the *Brooklyn Eagle,* but it would, through repetition each year, evolve into a liturgy, a lament, a battle cry, a curse.

In 1947, the year Chuck Yeager broke the sound barrier, Mr. Rickey broke a more recalcitrant barrier by unleashing on a segregated nation a black marvel named Jack Roosevelt Robinson. Jackie's immense spirit had an incalculable impact on race relations, and his unique skills galvanized the Brooklyns. He and shortstop Pee Wee Reese, the spiritual leader, formed the nucleus of a team for the ages. In subsequent years Rickey added power-hitting, smooth-fielding Duke Snider; Carl Furillo, a durable line-drive hitter and rifle-armed right fielder; Billy Cox, an acrobatic third baseman with a vacuum cleaner for a glove; Gil Hodges, a muscular catcher who was converted to a first baseman and covered the bag like Nijinsky; Junior Gilliam, a rock of consistency and versatility; Don Newcombe, the iron man of the pitching staff; Preacher Roe, a crafty southpaw whose slow breaking balls drove batters mad; Carl Erskine, a gentleman Hoosier with a wicked overhand curve; and Roy Campanella, the home run-clouting catcher whose dignity and intelligence anchored the team.

This matchless squad dominated the National League for a decade. Half its starting lineup—Reese, Robinson, Campanella, Snider—would jog straight to the Hall of Fame, and the others, if not immortal, consistently made All-Star teams or were among the league leaders in one category or another. The Dodgers won over ninety games in five consecutive seasons, a feat never before accomplished, and they would have made it seven years in a row had they not blown the last game of the 1950 season. Despite that record, or perhaps because of it, they left behind a heritage of heartbreak.

In the nine seasons preceding 1955, the team had finished as low as third only once, in 1948, a bizarre year in which manager Leo Durocher quit in midseason to pilot the hated Giants. Otherwise, the postwar legacy consisted of four second-place finishes, three of which were decided by gut-wrenching defeats in the last game of the season, twice in the last *inning* of the season—and four pennants, each of which was followed by a World Series defeat at the hands of their aristocratic uptown rivals, the Yankees. No fans could ask for more excitement. No fans could endure more frustration or crave redemption more fervently. The Bums had never won a World Championship. Not for us the ultimate glory. For us, the bitter taste of almost. For us, the screech at the wretched street sign, STOP, WRONG WAY.

A writer once said that Yankee fans did not root for their team; they applauded it. Dodger fans didn't root either; we worshiped, we adored, we rejoiced, we beat our breasts and rended our garments and wept. Yankee fans—whom I always envisioned in three-piece suits toting the *Wall Street Journal* to the Stadium—knew who they were; they were winners. The Yankee symbol was a top hat. The Dodgers' symbol was a bum in a flea-bitten derby.

Dodger fans—in khakis and denims, schlepping the *Racing Form* and sandwiches in brown paper bags on the bus to Ebbets Field—had a monstrous identity crisis. Were we winners? Damn right we were, pal. Did it feel like we were? Hell, no. Well, then, were we losers? No way. Did it feel like we were? Yes, goddamn it! Every miserable winter, as we replayed in our minds the games we should have won, second-guessing managers and players and umpires and God, as we lifted our voices and wailed, "If only he'd have pinch hit," "If only he'd have caught that ball," "If only he'd have bunted," "If only . . . ," we felt exactly like losers.

According to Grandpa Abe, it was a lot easier to be a fan in the twenties and thirties, those pennantless decades when the Bums earned their nickname. That hapless bunch of wackos was expected to lose. They were, said Grandpa, like gals you took dancing, had a good time with, but whose sex was off limits and you knew it, no buts about it. The postwar Dodgers were flirts, coquettes who let you neck with them and feel them up and maybe even reach into their bloomers. But they would not let you go all the way. "Wait till next year" was the equivalent of "Not tonight—I'm not ready yet." It sent you home aching, but willing, in fact eager, to go back and try again.

If true love is about obsession; if it means thinking constantly of the love object, talking about it, sacrificing to be with it; if it means identifying so completely with the beloved as to feel you are part of it, embracing its needs and desires so totally as to make them your own, rejoicing as if for yourself when its goals are fulfilled, and suffering as miserably when they are dashed; if love is measured by loyalty and tenacious devotion and immense expectation, or by the ferocity with which you defend the loved one from defilers and slanderers, or by the pain you feel when the beloved lets you down, then the Stone men, like all true fans, were lovers.

We loved the Dodgers, not with the gooey idolatry that fools bestow on movie stars, nor the fulsome worship of religious fanatics, but with the forbearance and faith that comes from intimacy. We knew our players not just as athletes in flannel uniforms or names in box scores or pictures on baseball cards, but as persons. I knew that Jackie Robinson's wife was named Rachel and that he had graduated from UCLA, where he'd played football and basketball and ran track. I knew the church in which the Hodges family worshiped. I knew that Carl Erskine and his wife, Betty, hailed from Anderson, Indiana, and that Oisk had won his first World Series game on October 5, 1952, the Erskines' fifth wedding anniversary, in the fifth game, after giving up five runs in the fifth inning. I knew that Pee Wee Reese lived on Ninety-seventh Street in Fort Hamilton, that his real name was Harold, and that he had obtained his nickname not because of his height but because he'd been a marble champion in Kentucky and marbles were called pee wees. I knew who roomed with whom on the road and where they kept apartments in Brooklyn. I knew that Furillo was moody and short-tempered and kept to himself, that he and Johnny Podres, a party guy and ladies' man, lived at the Hotel Bossert in Brooklyn Heights. I knew that some of his teammates thought Robinson was too outspoken, and that Jackie considered Campanella an Uncle Tom. I knew that Campy was half Italian and grew up in Philadelphia. I knew that Newcombe was six feet four, 235 pounds, and very temperamental. I knew that Duke and Beverly Snider had an avocado ranch in California, even though I had never eaten an avocado in my life and thought it must be a species of cattle.

Those daring young men were not just a team we rooted for, they were *us*. Even in winter they were still in our minds and hearts, like brothers and sons away at school. With snow on the ground we talked about them, read about them, reveled in their achievements, bewailed their mistakes, drew sustenance anticipating their homecoming. Apart from the need to purchase tickets,

Ebbets Field was like a neighborhood park, a place you walked to or hopped a quick bus or subway ride to, where you could sit in the sun with like-minded fellows and watch a bunch of guys play ball.

Ours was a family kind of love: critical, honest, informed. Flaws were exposed and weaknesses scrutinized; resentment and rage were vented openly. The traumas induced by the bond were as lethal as any inflicted by parents or siblings or spouses, and we learned from them bitter and enduring lessons. What happened on the playing field and in the Dodger front office at 215 Montague Street had a profound, if perversely irrational, influence on what was said and done in the homes, streets, stoops, and shops of Brooklyn.

A psychologist might have postulated that a Yankee fan, reinforced each season in the conviction that victory is inevitable, would develop a sanguine, confident attitude about life, but perhaps also a dangerous complacency. A Dodger supporter, on the other hand, might develop a superior ability to bounce back from defeat with life-giving hope. But that hope was polluted by a relentless sense of apprehension. It ain't safe out dere.

Like my father and grandfather, the Regular Guys of the neighborhood were working men with jobs, not professions, jobs they stumbled upon or lucked into when times were tough, jobs they kept at all costs because they remembered the Depression and feared that another position might not be easy to come by. These men carried inside themselves a kind of shadow that could darken the windows of their perception at any moment. It was an almost metaphysical sense of anticipatory gloom, a disquietude that made life's small triumphs and fleeting moments of serenity seem like nothing more than decoys. If life seemed peachy, if things were going just the way you wanted them to, if the future looked glorious, you could count on someone puncturing your balloon with a crooked smile, or a sigh, or a pregnant remark like, "We'll see," or, most ominously, "Don't tempt God."

To the men who lived with it, this subtle sense of dread was not some psychic tumor to be dug out and biopsied by a disciple of Freud, or a bad habit to rise above with that 1955 best-seller, *The Power of Positive Thinking.* It was life. It was the way things were. It was history. Perhaps it started back in the old country, where life had been unendurable. Perhaps, since most of its adherents were Jews, the heritage stretched back to antiquity and was handed down, generation after generation, climaxing with bold punctuation marks at the Holocaust. It was nothing to be ashamed of, this unspoken doctrine. It was something to cherish and protect, for *it* would protect *you*. From what? From letting your guard down. The Babylonians are coming. The Romans are coming. The Inquisition is coming. The cossacks are coming. The Nazis are coming.

The Yankees are coming!!!

For whatever its antecedents, this look-over-your-shoulder mentality was reinforced season after season by the national pastime. The long-suffering fans had reached the point where, if the Dodgers had a lead, someone was bound to mutter what everyone else was trying not to think: "Dem Bums'll find a way to lose."

For me, an heir to the tradition, the sense that disaster was never far away had a name and a form: The Thing.

The Thing had entered my life in the summer of 1951, when I was seven. I had gone with some friends to a matinee at Loew's Pitkin, an Art Deco palace where stars twinkled on a domed ceiling of midnight blue and plaster caryatids linked Cecil B. deMille to Sophocles. We saw half a dozen cartoons, a Flash Gordon serial with Buster Crabbe, and a feature film called *The Thing*. The title character was a seven-foot vegetable from outer space with huge, powerful hands that ended in claws. The Thing lived on blood, and his regenerative powers were such that if you chopped off one of its limbs, it would grow back again.

The monster's flying saucer had lodged in the ice when it crash landed at the North Pole. A bunch of American scientists were dumb enough to thaw it out, and The Thing proceeded to terrorize them, popping up for a bite of flesh any time some jerk opened a door or turned a corner or left his pet dog alone. At one point The Thing came face to face with a dovish technocrat who pleaded with the creature to communicate with Earthlings. The appeasing egghead got swatted aside like a fly. Thankfully, some military types figured out a way to barbecue the monster on an electric grid, and the Free World was once again safe from foreigners. The movie was set in the North Pole, not the Mojave Desert, for a reason: it was about the Cold War.

When I left the Pitkin the air was as flat and sticky as a three-cent stamp, and The Thing was making it commemorative. I shivered all the way home; in my mind I was still at the North Pole. The Thing could have reached out from any doorway or dark corner and clamped its enormous hands around my neck. When I arrived at my building, I ran up the stairs, and when I reached the second-floor landing, my key already in my trembling hand, I saw my mother. She was startled, then relieved to see that the intruder was her own son. I dashed to her side. She was preoccupied, tearing up books and pamphlets and tossing the shreds down the dumbwaiter chute, acting as if the chore were as routine as discarding the bones and scraps of a lamb chop dinner. But I could tell she was nervous.

At the time, Korea was ablaze and Joe McCarthy's bloodhounds were sniffing after pinkos, urging citizens to inform on their friends and families. My mother's brother had, in the thirties, been a card-carrying Communist whose magnetic soapbox oratory had roused many a rabble. When he died, my mother stored his leftist literature in our apartment—in closets that were already host to back issues of the *Daily Worker,* books by and about Karl Marx, and subversive fiction like *Looking Backward* and *Heavenly Discourse.* Now it was time to dump the entire stash before some informer stumbled upon it. My mother worked quickly, looking out for neighbors. Evidently, The Thing had ties to the House Un-American Activities Committee.

For weeks I would leave the apartment only when one of my parents was going out or when I heard friendly footsteps on the stairwell. When forced to go out alone, I would plunge down the hallway steps two at a time and dash full speed down the long dark corridor to daylight, never so glad to see Mrs. Kass keeping vigil on the stoop. I would walk near curbs to avoid closed doors; I took wide turns around every corner; I carried a pocket knife whose blade was about as long as one of The Thing's claws. At night I made my parents turn on the bathroom light before I entered, and I refused to go to sleep until one of them had checked under the bed and in my closet. During this period, the

Dodgers' lead over the Giants—thirteen and a half games when I saw *The Thing*—dwindled inexorably.

By the time school began, I had gotten over the phobia, or so I thought. Then, on October 3, 1951—a day remembered in Brooklyn more vividly than the December day a decade earlier when Pearl Harbor was bombed—The Thing reappeared.

A few days before, on the last day of the regular season, the Dodgers had faced Philadelphia. It was the third year in a row that the Bums had to win that last Phillies game to stay alive for the pennant, for the Giants had, miraculously, caught up. In 1949 the Dodgers had won that final game; in 1950, they had lost. Each game had gone extra innings. So did this one. In the twelfth frame the Phils loaded the bases. Don Newcombe, pitching heroically, struck out the enemy's best power hitter, Del Ennis. Then Eddie Waitkus lashed a line drive that seemed headed for right field and a Phillie victory. But Jackie Robinson dove and snared the ball in midair. As he hit the ground, Robby's elbow rammed into his rib cage and he lay in the dirt, unconscious. But he revived and stayed in the game, and two innings later he carved his initials in my heart by belting the game-winning home run.

Thanks to the dramatic victory, the Bums tied the Giants for first place. Now the bitter rivals faced off in the second pennant playoff in league history. The Giants won the first game, the Dodgers the second. The winner of the third would play for all the marbles in the Fall Classic. The world's attention was glued to the Polo Grounds, a weird oblong in upper Manhattan at the foot of Coogan's Bluff. The Giants were the home team because of a peculiar decision by the Dodger brass. Having won a coin toss, they had a choice: play Game One in the Polo Grounds and Games Two and Three (if needed) at home, or open the series at Ebbets Field and play the next two away. When they chose the latter alternative, the men at Jake's Luncheonette concluded that subversives had penetrated the Dodger organization.

October 3 was an overcast day, so dark that the lights in the Polo Grounds were turned on in the third inning. All over the city businesses shut down and bars filled up with baseball fans, thousands of whom had not been fans until that week. I watched the game in my living room on the twelve-inch DuMont console we had purchased the year before. Joining me were Hubbell, then thirteen, my father, and my grandfather. By common inheritance we were baseball bleeders, and we were about to hemorrhage.

The Bums led 4–1 going into the bottom of the ninth inning. Three generations of Stones stood up and stretched, as sanguine as our heritage would permit. Newcombe was pitching well; he had struck out the side in the eighth inning. Three more outs and the pennant would be ours. I went to the bathroom. As I peed, I felt the clammy hand of The Thing on my neck. Terrified, I zipped my fly and sped back to the living room, urine dripping down my leg. My mother was pouring coffee for the men. She asked what time they would like dinner. Take the night off, they advised her. They figured they'd be out celebrating pretty late.

Hubbell sat cross-legged on the floor. In his right hand, the *wrong* hand, was the ragged baseball glove that my father had used in his semipro days, the very mitt he wore on the fatal day of his collision with Solly Skapinsky. He had ceremoniously passed on the heirloom to his eldest son on the occasion of Hubbell's thirteenth birthday, in lieu of the typical bar mitzvah gifts. The sacred mitt was already an anachronism with its flimsy padding and severed laces and fingers that were barely longer than a mitten's. Naturally, my father did not expect Hubbell, a lefty, to use the glove in games, but he did expect him to keep it well-oiled and supple, and, the most inviolable injunction, to wear it once, only once, when he took to the mound in a Dodger uniform. If Frank Stone would not play in Ebbets Field, at least his mitt would.

With a snap of his wrist, Hubbell threw a baseball into the glove, then threw it again and again in a rhythmic pattern of thwacks that became a relentless backdrop to the tension of the game. His concentration was remarkable even then; he said nothing, just watched the screen and thwacked the ball in his glove, occasionally moving his lips as if broadcasting his very own play-by-play.

My father sat in his customary chair and lit a Pall Mall. My grandfather sat on the sofa. The Thing sat down next to him.

Alvin Dark, the Giant shortstop, led off with a chintzy ground ball that wriggled through the Dodger infield. "Like it had eyes," marveled my father.

Don Mueller was up next. The outfielder was as pesky as a bumblebee and just as pernicious; he knew how to sting a pitched ball so it landed where no one could catch it.

"Why the hell is Hodges playing so close to first base?" asked my father.

"Hubbell, tell your old man why Hodges is playing close to the bag," said Grandpa Abe, as if it were a test.

Hubbell did not turn from the screen. "He's holding the runner on, to keep him from stealing," he said.

"Who the hell cares about the runner when you got a three-run lead?" said my father. "Let him run wherever the hell he wants. You gotta protect the hole."

Mueller hit the next pitch to precisely where the first baseman would have been stationed if my father had been manager instead of Charlie Dressen. Hodges lunged for the ball and missed it by inches. It trickled into right field. Instead of an out, maybe even a double play, the Giants had two men on base and the tying run at the plate. Newcombe induced Monte Irvin to pop out. We breathed deeply. Two outs to go.

But Whitey Lockman stroked a double between Andy Pafko in left and Duke Snider in center. Dark crossed the plate, making it 4–2. Mueller hustled to third, and as he slid off balance into the bag, he broke his ankle. There was a long delay as the trainer tended to the injured player. The Thing was prolonging the agony.

"Get Newcombe the hell outta there!" my grandfather advised Charlie Dressen.

My father disagreed. "Let him finish. At a time like this, you go with your best."

"What are you, kidding me?" countered Grandpa. "Remember last year? Dick Sisler?"

Dick Sisler? Last year? I remembered. And while they carried Don Mueller off on a stretcher and Clint Hartung came in to pinch-run, I had time to relive the gruesome moment once again. It was the last game of the season, another extra-inning game with the Phillies, and the Dodgers should have won it in the bottom of the ninth when, with the score tied, Duke punched a single to center field. Cal Abrams tried to score from second but he rounded third too wide and weak-throwing Richie Ashburn, who happened to be playing very shallow because he expected a pick-off attempt, threw home and beat Abrams with room to spare. Then, in the tenth inning that should not have been necessary, Newcombe hung a curve ball and Dick Sisler slammed it to left field. Duke and Abrams both chased it . . . and ran out of room.

I had watched that game with these same forebears in the same room on the same television. It was a black-and-white set; color had not yet been introduced. But somehow, a year later, when my grandfather evoked the image, I saw Dick Sisler rounding the bases in my mind, and his cap and the stripes on his Phillie uniform were bloodred.

"Sisler, shmisler," said my father. "Don't take out Newk."

If my father said Newcombe should keep pitching, that was good enough for me. Around the neighborhood it was often said, "No one knows the game like Cyclone Frankie Stone."

Bobby Thomson walked toward the batter's box, representing the Giants' winning run. From the third base coach's box their manager, Leo Durocher, razzed Newcombe unmercifully. All day long the Lip had done this, hoping to provoke an attack that would get the temperamental hurler thrown out of the game. Charlie Dressen walked to the mound. Meeting him there were Pee Wee, Robby, and Rube Walker, who was catching in place of Campanella. Campy had been injured in Game One, and to this day there are those who believe that life in the borough of Kings would have been different had that not been the case.

"Walk him," demanded my father. "First base is open."

"What are you, nuts?" countered Grandpa Abe. "Put the winning run on base with Mays on deck? Forget about it."

"Walk him," my father repeated. "Thomson's hot."

Hubbell stepped up the tempo of the ball thwacking the sacred mitt. Dressen signaled for a relief pitcher.

"Jesus Christ, he's taking him out," said my father.

"Bring in Labine!" said Grandpa Abe.

"What, Labine?" my father said. "Labine ain't even warming up. It's Erskine or Branca. Bring in Oisk! Bring in Oisk, for God's sake! Anybody but Branca."

But Dressen did not listen. He brought in Ralph Branca, who, in 1947, had won as many games as he had years—twenty-one—but who had not won more than fourteen since and had been a mediocre 13–12 that season.

"Jesus Christ! Thomson hit a homer off that bum in the first game," said my father.

"Holy shit," said Grandpa Abe.

We yelled at Charlie Dressen, trying to change his mind. The Thing was rather amused.

Valiant Newcombe, who would carry straight into alcoholism a bum rap for choking in big games, lumbered dejectedly to the clubhouse. Giant fans prayed for the Miracle of Coogan's Bluff. But they were not passive supplicants. They roared deafening encouragement to Thomson and taunted Branca, hoping to rattle him as he made the long trek to the mound. The numbers on the pitcher's uniform seemed to grow bigger and bigger until they covered the entire TV screen: 13. THIRTEEN. THIRTEEN!

My father lit another Pall Mall. The first one was still burning in the ashtray. "Gimme a smoke," said my grandfather.

"Forget about it," his son replied. "You're not supposed to—"

"Gimme a goddamn cigarette!" It was the traditional last smoke of a condemned man.

My grandfather could not sit still any longer. Despite the chill in the air, he was wearing just a sleeveless undershirt and white boxer shorts with blue stripes, and the shorts had crept up his ass. He stood up and yanked the shorts free and paced around the coffee table puffing on a cigarette as Ralph Branca warmed up to meet his destiny. The Thing stretched his legs languorously across the vacated sofa.

On Branca's second pitch Thomson lashed a low line drive to left field. "Easy out! Easy out!" said my father. And in Ebbets Field, or any normal ballpark, it would have been. But this was the Polo Grounds, where the foul poles were practically in the infield. The only way left fielder Andy Pafko could have caught that ball was if he had a ticket for the bleachers.

The living room became a maelstrom. I remember Thomson circling the bases, waving his arm in the air and skipping like a child, and Durocher and his players jumping up and down, hugging each other, converging on home plate to embrace their savior, and the vanquished Bums frozen in ghastly disbelief, then trotting or running toward center field to escape into the solitude of their clubhouse five hundred feet from home plate—all except Jackie Robinson, who hated losing almost as much as bigotry (he watched closely in case Thomson failed to touch a base) and the stunned silence of Red Barber, and, from a neighbor's radio, Russ Hodges shouting, "The Giants won the pennant, the Giants won the pennant . . ." over and over like an incantation, and Hubbell's baseball careening off the edge of the TV console and smashing the mirror that hung above the sofa, and my father's fist pounding the plaster wall, and the wretched shrieks from other apartments, and my mother charging into the room with Round Man a step behind holding a pet turtle in each hand, and my father wailing in pain as the wall opened up and his knuckles shattered on a solid beam, and my grandfather stretched out cold on the linoleum floor in his boxer shorts, clutching his chest and gasping for air. And The Thing's unearthly laughter.

My mother had the presence of mind to pump and pound my grandfather's chest. My father dropped to his knees and yelled in Grandpa's face, "Pop! Pop! Snap out of it, goddamn it!"

The old man was still breathing, but barely, and his eyes were glazing over. "Breathe!" my mother commanded, and she leaned all her weight on his chest. Grandpa's eyes closed. My father smacked him across the face. But he hadn't realized that his hand was broken. The pain shot through him and his body jerked and trembled as if he'd stuck his finger into the socket of a lamp. He screamed so loud I could feel my eardrums snap and quiver like rubber bands.

"What's going on? What's going on?" the terrified Round Man kept asking. He clutched his turtles protectively to his bosom.

"Roger, get Dr. Goldsmith," my mother commanded. "Hubbell, call an ambulance."

Hubbell ran to the phone. I ran to the window. The first person I saw was Sylvia Finkelstein. I called her name and told her to fetch the doctor quick. Round Man retreated to the sanctuary of his room, where his menagerie was in its early stages.

"Pop! Pop! Don't go, you son of a bitch!" My father slapped Grandpa Abe with his good hand.

The old man's eyes opened. They were glazed over and unfocused. He wheezed and summoned his strength and managed to utter his final words: "They shoulda walked the sonofabitch."

Because Dr. Goldsmith responded to house calls like the Lone Ranger, Grandpa was still alive when they carted him off in an ambulance. I never saw him again. His casket was open for viewing in the funeral home, but I refused to look inside. I stood as far away from the corpse as I could, against a wall, watching the mourners with Round Man at my side, the two of us choking in our stiff blue suits and red ties. The mourners shook their heads a lot. They groaned. They sighed. They paid respects to Grandma Rosie, who wept all night, dabbing her eyes with a lace hanky that must have had the absorption capacity of Brighton Beach.

I felt Round Man and I were on display, the skinny kid and the fat kid, like cardboard cutouts of Laurel and Hardy. As soon as they saw us, the mourners would point us out to their companions and either bite their lips and shake their heads or commence to sob. Like my grandmother, we were a trigger point for tears. The casket was another trigger point. I noticed that everyone who looked into it either started bawling or blew his nose. Nothing on Earth, short of a promise that my gaze would restore Grandpa to life, would get me near that coffin. As a result, it would be another four years, when the Sphinx finally bit the dust, before I would see my first real live dead body.

We buried my grandfather in a cemetery on Long Island on a crisp sunny day, under a canopy of red and orange leaves. At the same time, the Giants and Yankees met in the second game of the World Series. No such scheduling conflict would have been permitted had the Dodgers been Series participants, of course. Then again, Grandpa Abe would never have died with the Bums about to play in a Fall Classic. The game did not diminish the attendance at the funeral by a single soul. The friends and family of Abe Stone boycotted the Series. We hadn't even read a newspaper account of the first game. If there was a God, we figured, he'd find a way to make both teams lose.

I stood amidst a sea of black gabardine, between Hubbell, who bit his lip to fend off tears, and Hank, who was studying a pair of squirrels scrounging for acorns. A rabbi with a voice like a violin delivered a textbook eulogy that described a dear, departed soul who bore no resemblance whatsoever to the deceased. That was because the rabbi had never even met my grandfather. If he had, he would not have shown up, because my grandfather liked rabbis about as much as he liked Herbert Hoover. A wan, frail man with the beak and flapping gullet of a turkey, the rabbi droned interminably about what a good, decent, hardworking man God had called to his side.

When he directed us to pray for Grandpa's soul, my mother decided she had had enough. She marched up to the rabbi's side, thanked him politely, and addressed the gathering. The rabbi was so taken aback, he shuffled obediently to the side as if time was short and my mother was the next scheduled speaker. "What do you say we talk about the real Abe Stone," my mother said. "I loved my father-in-law more than I loved my own father. I don't know how good and decent he was—that's a matter of opinion—but he was an honest man with strong feelings about justice and a sense of fair play. He hated hypocrisy and he hated phonies, and, if he could, he'd give the rabbi here the old raspberry. And if any of you cover your mirrors or sit shivah or sing kaddish or any of that crap, he'd give you the raspberry too, because most of all Abe Stone hated bullshit. Abe *loved* a lot of things, though. He loved good schnapps and bawdy jokes and strong horseradish and herring on day-old pumpernickel. He loved his union and Eugene V. Debs and honest Democrats and Milton Berle and Benny Goodman and all his kids and his grandchildren and his Brooklyn Dodgers. And don't go making the mistake, like I heard some of you saying before, that the Dodgers killed him—or whatsisname, the guy who hit the home run . . ."

"Bobby Thomson," came the whispered response from the congregation.

"Bobby Thomson did not kill Abe Stone," my mother continued. "Abe died because he had a bum ticker and he didn't take care of himself, not because of a home run and not because some God he never believed in decided to lower the boom. His heart was bad and it stopped. Period. He'd laugh in your face if you made anything more out of it, and he'd laugh even harder if you prayed for his soul. He'd tell you not to waste your breath. So let's do it Abe's way, all right? Go home and drink a toast to his memory and take a minute to think about why you'll miss the old bastard."

And she buried her face in my father's chest and wept.

I did not need much time to figure out what I would miss about Grandpa Abe. I would miss riding up the temporary elevator in a building he was working on, just the skeleton of a building, and Grandpa showing me off to his fellow workers. The week before he died, he had taken me to an office building under construction a few blocks from Times Square. With the wind whipping our faces, we ate hero sandwiches and admired the view of the skyscrapers and the long green carpet of Central Park, unimpeded by walls. I would miss sharing a bag of peanuts with him at Ebbets Field, and watching him play pinochle, and sweating beside him in the steam room at the Russian Baths, and watching him get apoplectic at the racetrack when his sure thing galloped in last. I was grateful to Grandpa Abe for experiences like those, and for his sleight-of-hand tricks, and the dollar bills he handed me surreptitiously, and for changing the family name from one with about forty-seven letters, forty-five of which were consonants, to something tight and tough like Stone.

I agreed with my mother: Bobby Thomson did not kill Grandpa. Neither did Number 13, Ralph Branca, nor Charlie Dressen, who summoned the star-crossed reliever from the bullpen. They were merely hired hands. The real killer was The Thing.

After his lethal visit on Dat Day, as October 3 came to be known, The Thing made a brief appearance at Grandpa's funeral, then returned from time to time over the years, a kind of spectral presence that sent a shiver of terror up my spine, a harbinger of doom. Whenever he appeared, something dreadful would follow: my parents would have an ear-splitting argument; some creep would spring out from behind a car like a jack-in-the-box and whip my Dodger cap off my head or pelt my neck with a pea-shooter; a teacher would catch me trading baseball cards instead of practicing my penmanship; I would twist an ankle and miss a week of playing ball; I'd have to eat Grandma Rosie's cooking;

some icky girl would get a crush on me; the Dodgers would lose. The Thing was versatile and unpredictable. If The Thing had his way, some Bobby Thomson would always be waiting in the on-deck circle of life.

Despite strenuous efforts to erase it, my mind retained a vivid picture of Thomson crossing home plate after the Shot Heard Round the World, his teammates exulting like men brought back from the dead, which is just what they had been. Time diminished none of the picture's clarity. It remained there, The Thing's indelible reminder that, no matter how terrific life might seem to be, you must never turn your back because there is no such thing as a sure thing. Not even a three-run lead in the ninth inning.

Chapter Four

Because, for lovers, hope springs eternal, that spring "Wait till next year" had metamorphosed once again, taking shape as the bold assertion that Jake had spelled out in Dodger-blue crayon and Scotch taped above the team photo on his cash register: 1955 *IS* NEXT YEAR!!!

"I'll have an egg cream, Jake," I said.

"Coming right up, kid."

Before Jake could start making my drink, my brother Hubbell arrived with his buddies, Dizzy and Benny. The inseparable trio was, to me, like the three ingredients in an egg cream: Hubbell was the milk, nourishing and wholesome; Benny was the chocolate syrup, as much for his sweet personality as his complexion; and bubbly Dizzy was the seltzer.

Benny Mason was short and thin, and he wore thick glasses and neat, carefully selected clothing. He was such a pleasant young man, such a gentleman, that he had, years before the Brown vs. Board of Education decision, effortlessly integrated the Corner. Benny's single handicap was his athletic ability; he played ball like a white girl. This trait would have marked any other neighborhood boy as a target for unspeakable torment. In Benny's case, everyone held his tongue; not only was everything else about him highly respected, but no one wanted to give the impression that he was picking on Benny because he was a Negro. Such was the ambivalence that race aroused that many of these same sensitive souls were openly predicting that the neighborhood would soon turn into a jungle if the encroachment of blacks from *over there* continued unabated.

Benny was also a rarity in that he could openly express ambition without losing status as a Regular Guy. He was so excited about starting his freshman year at City College that he was already toting his required texts around with him. Benny was determined to be Somebody. Exactly what, he wasn't sure; some days he aspired to make lifesaving scientific discoveries like Jonas Salk; other days he dreamed of becoming a captain of industry, or a distinguished professor, or a physicist who would conquer outer space—for space, Benny felt, was going to be big. Hubbell had his friend pegged to become the first Negro mayor of New York City.

Dizzy, whose real name was Sheldon Finkelstein, was the younger brother of Ruth, she of the lovely lingerie, and the older brother of my pal Artie. A loose-limbed, beady-eyed, kinky-haired, trumpet-playing beatnik-in-training, Dizzy had recently taken to hanging out in Greenwich Village coffeehouses on Friday nights. He claimed to know Lenny Bruce personally. He always wore a black beret and, that summer, a black armband in memory of Charlie Parker, who had died in March. He kept a picture of Bird and his namesake, Dizzy Gillespie, glued to his trumpet case. The case was always with him. He would take out his horn and blow a few riffs whenever the spirit moved him, or he would toot on the mouthpiece to keep his chops in shape, or he would use the case itself as a tom-tom, supplying the backbeat for whatever happened to be going on around him. One thing Dizzy did not do was keep still. When he walked, he loped elastically; when he talked, he bobbed and weaved like Sugar Ray Robinson. Hubbell said that Dizzy aspired to become the hippest white man in America.

Dizzy smoked Kools. He lit one as he marched with Benny to the back of the luncheonette and surveyed the selections on the jukebox.

Hubbell joined me at the counter. "How's it going, champ?" he said, and he pulled the brim of my lucky cap down to my eyebrows. There was something about that cap that compelled people to play with it.

When old Irv recognized Hubbell, he marveled at how much he'd grown, and initiated a discussion about the future of Frank Stone's oldest son. The other men waxed poetic about Hubbell's destiny, how he would be named Rookie of the Year, how the first time he pitched in Ebbets Field he would, as a sign of respect, wear on the wrong hand the patriarchal mitt. Everyone in the neighborhood had a stake in Hubbell's future, especially the older generation, which once had a stake in the future of Cyclone Frankie Stone.

My brother seemed uncomfortable with the conversation. Like his sometime defiance of my father's training guidelines, this too was a new phenomenon. Hubbell used to relish such attention. He would light up like a jukebox when people talked about his pitching and his future. When he returned from a triumphant game, he would relive in colorful detail his every pitch, seeming to enjoy the telling as much as the playing. Now, when people talked about his brilliant future, he no longer gloated, he no longer luxuriated in the attention. He would turn away as if embarrassed, and sometimes he would snort something cynical or change the subject.

The transformation was baffling and troubling. Hubbell had always been even-tempered, sunny, patient even with jerks like Irv. Now he brooded a lot, and at times he got so cranky and irritable I feared he would not stay young at heart but grow old and petrify like the Sphinx. My generous, considerate brother, who always had time for me, who told me stories and helped me with my homework and took me places off limits to other kids my age, was now losing patience with my merciless stream of baseball questions. The last time Round Man asked if Hubbell would get him a job as bat boy when he signed with the Dodgers, he snapped at him as if he'd been asked to sleep on the street so Hank could have a larger bedroom for his pets. I did not know what was going on in Hubbell's mind, nor dream that I was witnessing the early stages of a rebellion that would throw my family into chaos. I merely concluded that the only explanation for his erratic behavior was the same one that my mother used to account for Hank's obesity and the disconcerting giggles of teenage girls: hormones.

Jake asserted that Hubbell would surely receive a bigger signing bonus than the one given to Sandy Koufax. Irv raised one eyebrow and arranged his mouth in a crooked smirk. Jake defended his position: "It so happens, a couple of years ago, Hubbell pitched against Koufax in a sandlot game. Koufax was what, two, three years older? But Hubbell beat him good. A shutout, if I'm not mistaken."

"I gave up three runs, Jake," said Hubbell.

"Which means the other guy gave up more, right?"

"Jesus Christ, I'm not even sure it was *him,*" said Hubbell. "And even if it was, he struck out about twenty guys. Anyone who hit the ball got on base on an error, that's how bad his team was."

Ignoring Hubbell's explanation, Burt said, "He got twenty grand, Koufax. I figure Hubbell should get twenty-five, maybe thirty."

"He got fourteen," said Hubbell. "Plus six in salary—the league minimum."

"You'll get more."

"Oh, for chrissake, why don't you take book on it?" said Hubbell. He meant it facetiously, of course, but the men decided that betting on the size of my brother's signing bonus was not a bad idea at all. Sappy said he'd organize a pool.

Annoyed and exasperated, Hubbell joined his two friends, who had by then activated the jukebox. Strips of red, blue, and yellow lights ran up the sides of the machine and curved around the top, with bubbles flowing through them in perpetual motion. The sound of Fats Domino's "Ain't That a Shame" thumped across the room.

"How about that egg cream, Jake?" I said.

"Coming right up, kid."

"Waddayou put that jungle music in there for?" asked Sappy.

Jake shrugged. "The kids like it."

"My kid plays that crap in the house, he's out on his ass," said Burt. He yelled to the boys in the back, "Lower that goddamn thing! I can't hear myself think."

"How could you tell the difference?" Dizzy cracked.

"Waddayou, a wise guy?"

The three men at the counter took turns attacking the new music that had, in recent months, assaulted the air waves and battered their ears like Rocky Marciano. The principal perpetrator was "Rock Around the Clock," upon which a torrent of fury had been unleashed, not just because of its volume, or its twangy electric guitar riffs, or its booming backbeat, but because of a basic image problem: it was the theme song for the movie *Blackboard Jungle.* Thus, at the outset, was rock 'n' roll linked to juvenile delinquency.

"One, two, three o'clock, four o'clock, rock," sang Sappy, imitating an orangutan. "Didja ever hear anything so goddamn dumb? I bet that moron needed help counting to twelve."

Bill Haley and the Comets' record was the first rock 'n' roll song to achieve the status of national hit. That week it was number two on the Hit Parade, right behind Sinatra. "Ain't That a Shame" was number five—not Fats Domino's record, but the tame cover version by Pat Boone. The white bucks rendition might have been acceptable to the men at Jake's, but the teens in my neighborhood were too hip for that. Thanks to Dizzy's persistence and Benny's powers of persuasion, they had lobbied successfully to gain a voice in jukebox selections. Hence, the sounds at Jake's were as integrated as the Brooklyn Dodgers. The beat that Jackie Robinson had brought to major league basepaths now pounded the walls of the luncheonette, as it soon would the rec rooms of middle America and eventually bars and bedrooms around the world, so that in five years European adolescents who did not know the meaning of the words would sing in English, pronouncing vowels as if they had grown up on the Mississippi Delta.

"It's a sin, that music," concluded Irv.

"How's my egg cream doing, Jake?" My egg cream was doing nothing, and I knew it. Caught up in conversation, Jake was still holding the empty glass in his hand. I had to get him back on track before it was too late. My pregame ritual called for finishing the egg cream before the National Anthem ended; I had learned the hard way that finishing late was bad luck. And one simply did not gulp or guzzle an egg cream as if it were beer. One sipped an egg cream like a fine wine.

"Coming right up, kid." He reached for the chocolate syrup dispenser. At the sight of that gesture, saliva gushed into my mouth.

"I'm gonna unplug the goddamn jukebox," said Sal.

"Hold on, Sappy," Jake commanded. He addressed the teenagers: "Hey! That's the last song."

"What do you mean?" said Dizzy. "I put in a quarter. I got five more songs coming."

"I'll give you back the quarter. You know the policy: no music when the ball game's on."

"I believe the game doesn't start for another fifteen minutes," said Benny. It was just that sort of precise observation, stated with disarming diplomacy, that had given Hubbell the idea that his friend would become mayor after first distinguishing himself as a jurist. Dizzy grinned and proferred his palm for Benny to slap.

"All right, you asked for it," said Jake. "Shut it off or I'll get rid of all that . . . whatever the hell you call it, and fill the whole damn jukebox with Patti Page and Eddie Fisher and Perry—"

"But we made a deal, man," Dizzy protested.

Jake reinforced his threat by breaking into song. "I remember the night, of the Tennessee Waltz, when an old friend I happened to see . . ." He sounded like an impatient teakettle.

The boys wailed, and Dizzy pretended to vomit. "All right, okay, we give up," he cried. "Stop singing, man, I can't take it." "Ain't That a Shame" was the last song we heard.

"How about that egg cream, Jake?" A militant whine had crept into my voice.

"Coming right up, kid, specialty of the house." This time he meant it. He lowered the glass to the spigot on the chocolate syrup dispenser. Then, because Hubbell and his friends had sidled up to the counter, making the crowd big enough to constitute an audience, he asked, "Did I ever tell you guys I invented this drink?"

He had, of course, a thousand times. But Irv had never heard the tale. "Get outta here," he said. "*You* invented the egg cream?"

Jake pushed his bifocals up over the hooked portion of his nose and patted down the long strands of gray hair that were plastered across his scalp like stripes on a flag. A smile of sweet remembrance spread on his face. "Yeah, it was 1927. Hell of a year. Lindbergh flew the Atlantic. Ruth hit sixty home runs. I invented the egg cream. We changed the world, the Babe and Lindy and me."

"Yeah, sure, you're a regular Thomas Edison," said Irv.

Jake was undeterred by skepticism. "I was working in my father's joint on Delancey Street, over on the Lower East Side. One day this guy comes in and orders a chocolate soda. So I start making the soda and he changes his mind. 'Make that chocolate

milk,' he says. So I get out the milk. 'No, make it a soda.' So I go
for the seltzer, and he says, 'Nah, I think I'll have chocolate milk.'
So I says, 'Milk, soda, make up your mind, for chrissake.' But the
guy can't decide. I swear, he must've been right out of Bellevue
or something, this maniac. So I says, 'All right, you can't make up
your mind, I'll give you milk *and* soda.' So that's what I did. It
was a joke, right? But the guy drinks it and he goes nuts. It's so
good he orders another one. Now the other customers get wind
of this and they want to taste it, and they flip out too, and I spend
the whole day putzing around with this new invention, and the
next thing I know people are coming in from all over the city
asking for this drink, and before you know it every schmuck and
his brother is serving the friggin' thing like *they* invented it, and
all of a sudden it has a name! I should have patented the friggin'
drink. I'd be a rich man by now."

"How *did* it get the name?" Irv asked.

"Who the hell knows?" said Jake. "There's no eggs in the
friggin' thing, there's no cream in the friggin' thing. Never was.
I'm telling you, the whole thing's absoid."

I didn't know if Jake had invented the egg cream. No one
knew. But I thought that one day, after my playing days were
over, I might become a journalist and dig up the truth of the
matter once and for all and uncover in the bargain the origin of
the drink's enigmatic name. I had looked it up one day in every
dictionary in the big public library at Grand Army Plaza. I had
found egg-and-dart, eggbeater, eggs Benedict, egg crate, egghead, eggnog, eggplant, egg roll, eggshell, egg timer, egg white,
and egg yolk, but no egg cream. Further research was needed.

Maybe I would write a poem about the egg cream one day,
immortalizing the drink as Keats had Grecian urns. Then again,
maybe I'd find a way to bottle Jake's recipe. It would blow Coke
and Pepsi into the wasteland of American commerce. At the very
least it would corner the market on discerning drinkers with taste
and class. The ads would read: "Jake's Egg Cream—the champagne of soft drinks. When an ordinary beverage simply will not
do." My smiling visage, beneath my Brooklyn Dodger cap,
would appear above the copy, hoisting a cold one.

He may not have invented it, but Jake made the best damn
egg cream in the world. And, finally, he got around to making

mine. Hubbell introduced him with a perfect imitation of Ed
Sullivan: "And now, ladies and gentlemen, right here on our
stage, just back from a round-the-world tour of candystores, the
king of the egg cream, the incomparable Jake R-R-R-Ratner."

This was a new talent that Hubbell had unveiled that summer. He would do uncanny imitations of TV personalities like
Sullivan and Dave Garroway, and especially sportscasters like
Red Barber and Mel Allen and Vin Scully. At first these routines
were quite entertaining, but now it was getting spooky, and sometimes tiresome, living with a guy who felt compelled to introduce
everything you did and then do play-by-play on it.

Hubbell announced, "We're about to begin, fans. And Jake
opens with his unorthodox syrup-first style."

With the heel of his hand Jake squirted the chocolate syrup
into the glass, just so. "You don't want your egg creams too sweet
and you don't want 'em too tart," he explained. "The key to the
thing is the ratio of ingredients."

"And now, the milk," said Hubbell. Delicately, Jake poured
milk straight from a carton onto the waiting syrup. He held the
glass up to eye level, examined the contents through his bifocals
and adroitly added about three more drops.

"Remarkable skill and precision," said Hubbell. "And he
picks up the long spoon, demonstrating exactly why Jake Ratner
is the best spoon man in the league." With a graceful swirl of his
wrist, Jake placed the glass under the soda water spigot, inserted
a long-handled spoon and let the seltzer flow. It deflected off the
spoon and cascaded down the side of the glass onto the mixture
of syrup and milk. "Perfect touch," said Hubbell. "Not too weak,
not too strong."

When the glass was about half full, Jake let the seltzer hit the
drink directly and he stirred, wielding the spoon majestically, like
Toscanini with a baton. The mixture turned by phases brown,
then cocoa, then tan, with a white foam peak. "You want it
foamy," said Jake. Then, looking as if he smelled something foul,
he added, "But you don't want to turn it into a goddamn bubble
bath, like that joint next to the train station."

The joint in question was run by a family who had recently
relocated from the Washington Heights section of Manhattan and
had the impertinence to hang an orange and black Giant pennant

on their wall. The audience booed. "These are loyal fans at Jake's," said Hubbell. "It looks just about done, ladies and gentlemen. The glass is almost full . . . and there it is!"

Jake stopped the flow of seltzer, scooped off some foam from the side of the glass with his finger and licked it. His smile pronounced it satisfactory. He held up the finished product for all to admire, as if he had just removed a ceramic vase from a kiln.

"Let's hear it for the incomparable Jake Ratner!" said Hubbell.

Dizzy whistled loudly and applauded by thumping his trumpet case. The others joined in.

"Bee-you-tee-ful," said Burt.

"Da poifect egg cream," said Sal.

"You're all nuts," Irv concluded.

Jake permitted himself a modest bow. "Where you sitting, kiddo?"

I pointed to my customary stool at the end of the counter, the seat closest to the window that looked out onto Play Street. Jake winked. With the confidence of a master, he flung the glass. The spectators gasped. The glass slid rapidly on its own moisture along the marble counter, leaving a trail of tan liquid in its wake. It gathered momentum and then, just as it was about to plunge over the edge, it came to a full stop in front of my stool. Not a drop had spilled. Jake grinned and winked at me.

"It's all in the wrist," he said.

Chapter Five

Sunlight glistened on the gossamer foam that clung to the rim of the glass. I sipped the perky sweetness of my egg cream.

On the Corner, Ippish frantically blew his whistle at a Chevy Bel Air that started to angle as if it might turn into Play Street. The driver, who was merely making a U-turn, shouted at his accuser so violently that Ippish was transformed from brave upholder of the law to cowering child. Appearing to shrink about two feet, he shoved his thumb into his mouth and began to shuffle away. Mr. Big, the umpire, knew what to do. He caught up to Ippish and, speaking as he might to a real police officer, implored him to stick around and protect the stickball game from outlaw drivers. Ippish returned to his post, his back as straight as a stop sign, his chest puffed out to display his badge.

An errant spaldeen rolled into a sewer. Harry the Horse tried to retrieve it by sticking a wad of chewed-up Bazooka bubble gum on the tip of a stickball bat and reaching into the sewer in hopes that the ball would stick to the gum. Meanwhile, Marty Klinger tended to his grooming. He whipped out a long black comb from his back pocket and combed his dirty-blond hair so that the sides swept back and met in the rear in a duck's tail. With two fingers he carefully drew the front curls onto his forehead. He ran both sides of the comb across his jeans to remove a viscous layer of hair tonic, shoved the comb back in his pocket, then rolled the sleeves of his white T-shirt over his shoulders, exposing triceps chiseled by barbells.

Klinger was performing for the benefit of two girls sitting on a brownstone stoop across the street from Jake's. One, a slim brunette with a ponytail, wore navy-blue Bermuda shorts and a powder-blue halter top. The other, a redhead with bangs and a pert shoulder-length flip, wore a white pleated skirt. She sat with her knees up to her chin, engrossed in filing her nails and listening to her companion speak. Apparently, she did not realize that the white V of her panties was visibly aglow at the intersection of her thighs.

Klinger managed to keep an eye on the girls while pretending not to notice them at all. Hoping that they, in turn, noticed him, he preened until Harry rescued the ball from the sewer and threw it to him. Klinger snared the spaldeen one-handed, his studied nonchalance suggesting that the catch was no more difficult than plucking a floating feather from the air. Then, scowling at Harry, he rubbed the ball free of sewer sludge.

"Play ball!" said Mr. Big. "The count is two and one."

"Bullshit!" said Klinger. "You're cheating me again, you fucking midget."

The girls grimaced; they did not approve of vulgarity. In more civilized language, Klinger started to explain why the count should be two and two, not two and one, when he was interrupted by the beep of a car horn behind him.

It was a big, black Buick convertible with a sleek strip of chrome on the side and a foxtail hanging from the antenna. The driver was Ignazio Corso, son of Mike the Barber and Angie. Iggy was as handsome as Sal Mineo and as cool as James Dean, the two idols whose photos were taped to his glove compartment. Iggy glided to the curb, lit up a Lucky Strike, and said something to the girls on the stoop. I deduced that he was inviting them for a ride. Giggling, the girls huddled together to confer.

Klinger shouted at Iggy. In his agitated body language and the shrillness of his voice, there was more than a demand to move the car off the stickball court; there was history. The Klingers' hatred of the Corsos went back about eight years to the time Mike the Barber had solicited the aid of some persuasive *goombahs* from Little Italy to convince Barney Klinger not to muscle in on his bookmaking monopoly. Marty's personal resentment started before he and Iggy reached adolescence. It seemed that, whatever they did, Iggy would come out on top. If they played ball, Iggy's team would win. If they made a bet—which they did often, on anything from a kid's hopscotch game to which line at a box office ticket window would move faster—Iggy would win. Most of all it was his inability to match his rival's success with girls that drove Klinger to a frenzy. He would never admit it, of course, but

Marty had imitated Iggy's hairstyle, his walk, his manner of dress and speech, even his smile. He did everything but dye his hair jet-black like the hair of his nemesis. Girls kept falling at Iggy's feet and stepping on Klinger's.

To top it off, Harriet Klinger, Marty's sister, was currently residing in a home for unwed mothers. She would not talk about anything connected with her pregnancy. The Klingers believed that Harriet's silence had been purchased by the Corsos under threat of violence, and that her child had been conceived in the infamous backseat of Iggy's Buick. It was that very Buick that scraped the blackboard of Klinger's brain more than anything else. Mike the Barber had pulled some strings to get his son a phony, but foolproof, driver's license before he was legally old enough to drive, and he had accepted the convertible as payment from a gambler who was down on his luck. The wheels gave Iggy an advantage in the mating game that he scarcely needed. The mere sight of the Buick was enough to sauté Klinger's blood corpuscles.

In reply to Marty's demand that he move the car, Iggy issued a steady stare and blew a slow stream of smoke in his adversary's direction. He turned again to the girls, beckoning with a wink, a tilt of his head, and a smile that wrinkled a nostril and raised one side of his upper lip. It was a devilish smile that would, one year later, be practiced by teenage boys before mirrors across the nation. It was Elvis Presley's smile. Iggy had it first.

The girls stood up decisively, exchanging mischievous grins. Klinger shouted, "Get that friggin' jalopy off the court!" Iggy's middle finger rose up slowly, like the periscope of a submarine. When it reached full height, he twitched it mockingly several times, then leaned across the seat and opened the passenger door for the giggling girls.

Ippish ran up to Klinger and asked if he would like to have Iggy arrested. "Get the fuck out of here, you moron," said Marty. He aimed a kick at Ippish's behind, but he missed, lost his balance and nearly fell. His face turned red, then green, then red again, like Christmas lights.

Iggy waited for the girls to settle the matter of who would sit where. The debate ended when the ponytail shoved the redhead into the front seat, nudged her closer to the driver, and climbed in after her. Pointedly ignoring Klinger, Iggy took his time tuning his radio to WNEW, where Sinatra was likely to be heard. He draped his right arm over the seat, his hand dangling above the redhead's shoulder as if it might, at any moment, reach into her blouse. Then, with a sudden burst of speed, he took off. Burning rubber, he aimed the car right at Klinger. Marty leaped out of the way. He fired the spaldeen at the speeding Buick, but it bounced off the rear fender and caromed across Howard Avenue.

"Fuck you, you guinea bastard!" yelled Klinger. Without looking back, Iggy flashed the finger once again and whipped the Buick around the corner, tires squealing. Ippish ran after it, blowing repeatedly on his whistle.

"I'm gonna kill that wop son of a bitch," vowed Marty.

"Shut up and get the ball," said Harry the Horse.

Ippish returned, winded and frustrated by justice unserved. Marty showed his appreciation the only way a guy could with Hilda Klinger's liver and onions festering in his intestines: he delivered a series of noogies to Ippish's head.

Tilting my head back to down the thick, syrupy remains of my egg cream, a moment sublime for lovers of the beverage, I contemplated important subjects: the meaning of cool, the advantages of owning a car, the pink underside of thighs, and the bright splash of panties under a pleated skirt.

Jake's quickly grew crowded. The stickball game was suspended because no one could find the ball Marty Klinger had thrown at Iggy's car, and Marty refused to spring for a replacement. Plain Cokes, cherry Cokes, lemon Cokes, and lime rickeys were ordered and rapidly dispatched by Jake. Camels and Old Golds and Chesterfields were lit. I inhaled the smoke that drifted my way, a secret depravity that would lead to nicotine addiction at the age of sixteen. I saw no harm in this. My mother smoked two packs of Camels a day, and my father matched her consumption with king-sized Pall Malls, and all they had to show for it was an occasional coughing fit. Even Duke Snider smoked—he endorsed Lucky Strikes in the Dodger yearbook—and he had forty-one home runs so far that season.

The atmosphere was so relaxed, I wondered if I was the only one who appreciated the importance of nailing down the pennant that day. True, the Dodgers had seventeen games left to play, and all they needed was to win one of them. But my philosophy was: clinch fast and take it easy until the World Series. Protect the regulars, give them lots of rest, get the reserves in shape, arrange the pitching rotation just right. After all, who knew better than Dodger fans that anything could happen? Campy could break a knuckle on a foul tip, Duke could crack his head on a wall chasing a fly ball, a batter could smash a line drive off Newcombe's nose . . . The Thing has his ways.

There were other, more compelling reasons to get it over with pronto. If the Bums should win one of their next four games, they would break the record for the earliest pennant-clinching in league history. This would be a powerful portent. Furthermore, I had come to realize that it was bad luck for the Dodgers to clinch a pennant without me, and with school about to begin and games scheduled primarily in daylight, the odds that I would be present for the event would grow slimmer each day. Logic and history were my witnesses: I had never seen a pennant-clinching game, and the Bums had never gone on to win a Fall Classic.

"So, what do you think, kid?" said Burt Sugarman, dunking a cheese Danish into his coffee. "What's the scoop on the game?" As the offspring of Cyclone Frankie Stone and the brother of a future Rookie of the Year, my opinions were respected in the neighborhood. I told Burt that the starting pitchers were Bob Buhl for the Braves and Roger Craig for Brooklyn, and I predicted that the Brooks would jump on Buhl early and win going away.

Indeed, the Dodgers struck quickly. They scored four runs in the first inning, not with their estimable power, but with three walks, a hit batter, and two singles. They were as versatile in virtue as The Thing was in iniquity.

Roger Craig set down the Braves easily in the first two innings. It was still 4–0 in the third when my mother arrived.

Most neighborhood mothers were a threat to the reputations of their sons. They would scold them in front of their friends. They would make them stop playing to drink their milk or do their homework. They felt obliged to inform them of the condition of their bodies—"You're exhausted," "You're filthy," "Look at your knee, you're bleeding to death"—as if the poor guys' nerve endings were too dull to sense these things themselves. They issued injunctions that made young men feel like babies: "Don't play near the gutter," "Don't drink too much soda," "Don't get sweated up!" Why didn't they just post signs?

Jeannie Stone was different. She had a sense of priorities. She knew that endeavors such as playing stickball and cataloging baseball cards and sitting on a stoop discussing philosophy with your buddies were more important than eating on time, and she knew that sweat, dirt, and blood were small prices to pay for a normal boyhood. When my mother showed up on Play Street, it was either by coincidence or necessity, not because she was hatching some diabolical plot to humiliate her son. And she never outstayed her welcome. I was proud of her for that.

Mom waltzed into Jake's with a cheery smile in a sleeveless yellow dress and functional pumps.

"Yo, Jeannie," said Harry the Horse.

"Jeannie, baby," said Dizzy.

"Hi, fellas," she said, placing a bag of groceries on an empty stool. "Jake, give me a two cents plain."

As the seltzer streamed into the glass unaccompanied by syrup, my mother leaned over as if to kiss me. I jerked my head away. She faked left, went right, and pecked me on the cheek. Blood rushed to my face, turning it crimson. Earlier that year I had demanded an end to the practice of kissing in public, and Mom had dutifully acceded to my wishes. But she was not above exacting a little revenge.

"You snuck out on me," she said.

"You were on the phone. I couldn't wait all day."

"Oh, I see. Busy man, can't do errands for his mother."

"You and Cecille can talk for ten hours."

"Can't deny that," Mom admitted. "But it's no excuse."

Hubbell then went public with a discussion that had been taking place out of earshot. "Hey, Mom, these guys don't believe you can stand on your head."

"They're just jealous," said my mother.

"Come on, Jeannie, show them," urged Mr. Big.

Dear God, I thought, please don't let her do it. Get her out of here. Not that I thought she might fail if she accepted the challenge. I'd seen her stand on her head dozens of times, and although she was probably rusty and was even older than Pee Wee Reese, I figured she could still deliver the goods. Nor was I afraid of being embarrassed, as I had been once before when, slightly tipsy, she stood on her head on the bandstand at a wedding reception. She had learned from that occasion to protect against unnecessary exposure when turning upside down with a dress on.

No, I wanted her to remain right side up and get out of Jake's on the double because, for all her virtues, my mother was a jinx. If she was in a room when a Dodger game was on television, disaster would inevitably follow. The evidence was irrefutable. She had made appearances in the deciding games of both the 1952 and 1953 World Series, and, on Dat Day, while I was being ambushed in the bathroom by The Thing, she had been serving coffee to my father and grandfather in the living room and had lingered just long enough for the Giants to start their lethal rally. My theory had been confirmed repeatedly over the years, but I did not have the heart to inform on my own mother.

She borrowed a handkerchief from Benny, the only guy whose handkerchief was clean enough to lend, and laid it out flat on the floor. She tucked her skirt between her knees, anchored her head to the cloth and her hands to the tile and flipped her legs into the air. "And she's up!" said Hubbell. "A perfect vertical. Will she do her famous rotation?" She did. Guiding herself with her hands, she rotated clockwise 180 degrees before lowering her feet gracefully to the ground.

"How about that, ladies and gentlemen!" said Hubbell. "A perfect ten!"

My mother's performance earned her a hearty and respectful round of applause. By then there were Braves on first and second. I hustled her to the door to mitigate the jinx as much as possible. On the way, she said, "Here's how you can make up for running out on me. Supper's going to be late, and I can do without one of your father's tantrums. So do me a favor. Catch him on his way home and stall him."

I accepted the assignment.

By the time my mother left the luncheonette, Johnny Logan had smacked a line drive through the gap in right-center field for a triple, driving in two runs. The Dodgers escaped the inning with no further damage, but their lead had been cut in half.

In the following frame the Braves got two more men on base and Walter Alston replaced Craig with Karl Spooner. Spooner had been brought up from the minors at the end of the previous season, when the pennant was out of reach. In his first start, he shut out the Giants on three hits with fifteen strikeouts. Four days later he shut out Pittsburgh with twelve strikeouts. The spectacular debut prompted the *News* to run this wishful headline: SPOONER, ONLY SOONER. All winter the cocky prodigy from Oriskany Falls, New York, was the subject of eager speculation: was he a southpaw Bob Feller or a flash in the pan? The question was still unanswered; in spring training he developed a kink in his shoulder, and had been limited to spot appearances all season.

With his fastball darting like a bee, Spooner struck out the first two batters he faced to end the inning. I had removed the jinx just in time. By the sixth inning the Bums had a 10–2 lead and I felt the smooth calm of certain victory wash over my body.

Above the rooftops a flock of birds swirled in formation, like granules of pepper stirred into a blue-gray soup. A breeze rustled the leaves of an unappreciated maple tree that was viewed as a nuisance, an entrapper of spaldeens, rather than as nature's only brush stroke on a monochrome canvas. A trio of boys rode by on scooters fashioned out of milk cartons, two-by-fours, and roller-skate wheels, followed by children on foot who were chasing the siren song of the Good Humor Man's bell. A game of punchball was delayed when a truck parked near the sewer that served as second base. Promising the players a rapid departure, Marvin, the seltzer man, clambered aboard the truck and hoisted a box of seltzer bottles onto his shoulder for delivery to a row house. A lanky boy in dungarees took a running start and leap-frogged over a fire hydrant.

The Big Guys had left the luncheonette to start another stickball game, a fresh ball having materialized. Some were choosing sides, others were loosening up their arms. I did a double-take: Hubbell was on the chalk stripe that marked the pitcher's mound, throwing a spaldeen. The shock was overwhelming. My father had forbidden Hubbell to throw spaldeens, on the theory that doing so would endanger his pitching arm; and, to my knowledge, Hubbell had honored the injunction to the letter. This blatant violation was practically patricidal. But, evidently, Hubbell was not prepared to challenge authority directly. For when Benny called his name and pointed up the street, my brother tossed the spaldeen to Mr. Big and hurried off the court.

My father loped down the incline of Howard Avenue from the direction of the subway station. He was wearing sturdy gray work pants and an olive-green shirt with a circle of sweat on the lower back and a smaller circle under each arm. His steps were heavy with fatigue, his dark skin glistened with the glow of honest sweat. He looked older that summer. The gray hair that distinguished his temples had spread hastily upward over his scalp in a kind of chromatic reversal of what was happening on the edges of our neighborhood, where black tenants were filling the vacancies created by departing whites. A paunch had appeared where once a flat gut had girded the strong upper body that powered the sweet swing of Cyclone Frankie Stone. The belly was accentuated by a posture that slouched a bit farther with each indignity my father suffered in his cab-driving day.

Recalling my mother's entreaty, I left Jake's and jogged across the street to stall my father. I followed him into the establishment of Mike the Barber. The shop was thick with the scent of witch hazel. Mike was sweeping up clusters of blond hair, listening to my father, who beseeched him earnestly. Their backs were turned to the door; they did not see me.

"Come on, Mikey, you know I'm good for it," said my father. "I ain't going nowhere."

"Nothing poisonal, Frank. It's just, business is business. What if all my customers—"

"Who's gonna know, for chrissake? We're talking a few days here, maybe a week at most."

They were not talking about haircuts. Their transaction had to do with Mike's real business: bookmaking. My father had been gambling again. I saw The Thing in the mirror; he was sitting in a barber chair, eyeing his claws as if deciding whether to have them manicured.

In his eagerness to put together the ten thousand dollars for a taxi medallion, my father had taken to wagering on sporting events, but each sure thing had instead diminished his savings. Perhaps it was a subconscious wish to remain impoverished that compelled my father to bet on losers, for he seemed to make his most ludicrous mistakes right after a winning bet. Maybe he felt that if he had real money, my mother would insist on moving to Greenwich Village, and that would have been a flagrant violation of the Regular Guy code. After Manhattan, what would come next? Reading the *New York Times*? Voting Republican? Rooting for the Yankees? In any event, he gambled and he lost, and finally my mother had had enough; she swore that she would walk out on him if he so much as bet another nickel on a horse race. If Mike were to tell his wife or any of his customers that my father had been placing bets, the word would surely get back to my mother and she would leave us. She was a woman of her word.

Mike Corso was a short, chunky man with a flat, circular face and jet-black hair that hugged his scalp like a sheet of tar. Regardless of the weather, he wore black pants and a long-sleeved white shirt with the sleeves flounced out by a rubber band. He always had a thick stogy clenched in his teeth, and when he wasn't cutting hair, he was going over figures in the little memo pad he used to record transactions, or leafing through the pictures of naked women in the magazines he kept around the shop for customers.

The barber looked up at the taller man who implored him with his eyes. He smiled crookedly, a beam of light reflecting off his gold tooth. He transferred the cigar from one corner of his mouth to the other and sighed. "Do me a favor, willya, Frankie? Quit picking losers. I hate taking your dough."

"Don't worry about it, Mikey," said my father, gratefully slapping his friend's back. "You'll have the fifty by the end of the week."

They turned and saw me. "Look who's here," said Mike, "a chip off the old blockhead."

There had been a time, not long before, when my father would kneel down at such a moment and I would run to him and surrender to his enormous hands, and he would grab me under the arms and hoist me high in the air, up above his head, arms extended. He would toss me and catch me and flip me over and pretend he had dropped me, only to snatch me out of gravity's grasp and hug me to his chest. Then he would plant a wet kiss on my cheek, his whiskers scraping my skin. I was too old for that now, but there were times I wished it wasn't so.

He removed my cap and tousled my hair. "Take a haircut while you're here," he said. In Brooklyn, we *took* haircuts, we did not have them or get them.

I backed away, inching toward the door. "I don't need one yet."

"What do you mean, you don't need one? It's over your ears already."

"That's because the cap pushes it out."

"Cap, my ass. You look like a bum."

"I just *took* a haircut."

Evidently, my word was not good enough. "Mike, when was the last time he was in here?" my father inquired.

"Jeez, it's gotta be two months," said Mike. It was a conspiracy.

"Get out of here!" I protested. "It's nowhere near two months."

"You have to take one sooner or later," my father reasoned. "Why not get it over with? School starts soon."

"That's just it," I explained. "I'm not starting school with any new haircut. He makes me look like Howdy Doody."

On Mike's radio Vin Scully reported that the Braves were about to come up for their last at-bat. Karl Spooner had yet to give up a hit. "The Dodgers are clinching the pennant," I said. "I'm not going to miss the celebration for some stupid haircut."

That was an argument my father would have difficulty rebutting in good conscience. He shoved the cap back on my head and turned me in the direction of the door.

"Friday, Mike," he said.

But Mike did not hear. He was staring out the window, so astonished by what he saw that his mouth hung open and his cigar dangled precariously from his lower lip. Outside was a Lincoln Continental that looked like it was made of jade and could comfortably seat about fifty basketball players. The driver was Barney Klinger. He was wearing a sharkskin suit and a silk necktie, and as he talked to his son Marty, he gestured with his hand; light flared out from a pinkie ring like sparks from a welding iron.

"What the hell is going on?" Mike wondered.

"Beats the shit out of me," said my father. "All I know is, he's been walking around like he looted Cary Grant's closet, and now he's driving a goddamn ocean liner."

"Look at that rock on his finger," said Mike. "You don't get these things on a longshoreman's salary, I can guarantee you that."

"Must be moonlighting."

"Yeah? Doing what? Brain surgery?"

"Maybe he hit it big at the track," Dad conjectured, "or maybe he's dealing junk or something."

This struck me as the most preposterous theory of all. Jack Kass, the Sphinx's husband, had been dealing junk for a living all his life, and it was only in the last year that he'd been able to trade in his horse-drawn wagon for a dilapidated truck. It was well-known that the Kasses' children were helping to support them; you couldn't make ends meet selling rags and scrap iron and other junk, let alone get rich.

"Must be taking book again," said Mike. "Some guys, dey just never loin."

As my father and I approached the Corner, the stickball players, who did not include Hubbell, paid their respects. "Hey, Frankie!" said Harry the Horse.

"Waddaya say, Harry old boy?"

"Hey, Frank," said Mr. Big, "can you lend me a buck? I'm a little short this week."

"Jesus, Big, will you get another line already? That one's older than the Sphinx."

He walked up to Harry, who stood in his batting stance next to the sewer that served as home plate. "Look at you, Horse, you got your foot in the bucket. Move it up, like this." He tried to nudge Harry's rear foot closer to the plate. "More," he said. "No, no . . . here, gimme that."

He grabbed the bat and demonstrated a more efficacious stance. "Go ahead, Frank, take a swing," said Mr. Big. The other boys added their invitations. "Yeah, let's see if you're over the hill," said Harry.

"Okay, wise guys," said my father. "Come on, Klinger, gimme your best shot."

Klinger fired a fastball about three feet wide of the plate. My father swung and missed. The boys razzed him.

"Just warming up," he said. "Come on, you bum, put it over the plate."

Klinger grooved one. Cyclone Frankie Stone stepped into it, executed the sweet swing, and clobbered the ball. As he watched the spaldeen soar majestically over the maple tree, a grin spread over his face like he'd just won the World Series. The boys cheered. My father tossed Harry the bat and flipped a quarter to Mr. Big to replace the ball, which had landed on the roof of a distant brownstone.

Tall and erect, his stomach somehow flat again beneath the broad chest, he strode toward the Corner where Hubbell and his two best buddies had been watching. "These bums thought I was over the hill," he said.

"My man, my *main* man," said Dizzy. He removed his sunglasses, as if my father would not otherwise recognize him.

"Hey, Sheldon, does your mother know you converted to Negro?"

"Too much. Gimme five, daddy-o." Dizzy extended his palm. My father slapped it. Then he turned to Hubbell.

"How'd it go today, champ?" he asked, massaging his son's left shoulder. "Work out on the box spring?"

"Hundred and twenty pitches," said Hubbell. He was lying. He hadn't been near the box spring in days. "Ran some laps, did the weights."

"Good, good. How's the arm? Maybe later we'll toss a few, keep it loose."

"I don't know, Pop," said Hubbell. "Don't want to overdo it, you know."

The conference was interrupted when someone announced that the Dodger game was over. We had clinched the pennant. I suggested that we watch the celebration at Jake's, calculating that my mother would need considerably more time. But Dad led me toward home. He did not want to go to Jake's. He wanted to shower. He wanted to eat. He wanted to see his wife. Inadvertently he provided me with an opening. "Make sure you cut that hair before school starts," he said, yanking on a tuft that spilled out from under my cap.

"If you make me," I said, "I'll tell Mom you're gambling again."

He spun me around. With a thick forefinger bumpy with calluses from gripping steering wheels, he lifted my chin, forcing me to look him in the eye. "You didn't hear a thing. Understand?"

"My silence will cost you an egg cream."

He was incredulous. He was annoyed. But he was also impressed. "I've raised an extortionist," he said.

"What's that?" I asked. "Is that like an exterminator?"

"Sort of," said my father.

The circumstances demanded a second egg cream. It is not every day that your team clinches a flag earlier than anyone in the history of the world. The atmosphere at Jake's was happy but subdued, the pennant having been a foregone conclusion, but things picked up when the Big Guys arrived and Dizzy blew a fanfare on his trumpet.

"Drinks on the house!" yelled Harry the Horse.

"You want free drinks?" said Jake. "Take them to *your* house."

In the Dodgers' clubhouse the requisite beer and champagne was poured on the heads of players, coaches, and broadcasters. It was done with a sense of ritual, not release. The players were glad it was over; they were eager to rest their bones and heal their wounds and get ready for another crack at the Fall Classic. All that mattered now was redemption. Someone asked Walter O'Malley, the owner, which team he wanted to play in the World Series. With his rimless glasses and puffy face and three-piece suit, O'Malley looked like Mr. Potato Head dressed as a small-town accountant. But he had the soul of an assassin and the mind of a ward politician. No one poured champagne on him. The only moisture on his head was the oil that kept his straight dark hair in place. "I want to beat the Yankees," O'Malley said. "We have to beat the Yankees once, sometime or other, and this ought to be the time."

It would be the last time anyone in Brooklyn agreed with Walter O'Malley.

The owner's statement initiated a debate at Jake's counter about the tight American League pennant race. The Yanks, Indians, and White Sox were dancing a little threesome at the top of the standings, switching places almost every day, with no team ever falling more than two games off the pace. I figured a conversation like that would keep my father occupied for some time. I turned to Hubbell to solicit his opinion, but he was oblivious. He was looking out the window at three girls who were approaching Jake's.

Two of the girls were old familiars. Shirley and Roz had been inseparable from the time their mothers had thrown them together in a playpen. Now they had attained that stage of female adolescence in which one affects an air of haughty contempt toward males of the same age and social class. Noses in the air, they sashayed toward the Corner, their mouths, like their butts, in perpetual motion, chewing gum and blabbing. Roz had her platinum hair pulled up in a bun, accentuating an overly long neck. She wore a mint-green tank top, bare at the midriff, her breasts pointing sharply upward like the noses on twin fighter planes. Roz wore falsies, or so I had been informed by the Big Guys.

Shirley did not; the substantial mounds that tested the limits of her tight pink blouse contained no artificial ingredients. Her brown hair was cut in a page boy and tucked behind her ears. Each girl had painted her lips too red and her eyelids too black, and each wore pedal pushers, one lime-green, the other white, which hugged their hips so tightly they seemed to be walking on stilts. The pants revealed the truth of an observation once made by Ignazio Corso: if you could graft Shirley's excess baby fat onto Roz's bones you would have two pinup-quality babes.

Hubbell was watching neither Shirley nor Roz. He was gazing, with rapt appreciation, at the more perfect form of their companion, Grace Kelly. For that was the comparison the stranger invoked. She was tall and slim, and she moved with natural grace and elegance in a powder-blue summer dress, a gazelle flanked by an ostrich and a mule. Her hair, naturally gold as a sunflower, with the texture of silk, was swept up in a buoyant flip at the ends, like a hairdo in a Breck ad. Her face was a soft oval with cheekbones that suggested a smile even though her lips, unadorned but lush as a peach, were in perfect, dignified repose. The cheekbones offset perfectly a pair of eyes the color of a blue jay, or at least the color I imagined a jay would be if one ever got lost and ended up in my neighborhood.

The girls entered Jake's. Hubbell shuddered.

"Who's this, Miss Rheingold?" said Mr. Big.

"Lord, have mercy," Dizzy exclaimed.

"Va va va voom!" said Harry the Horse.

"You're so *couth*, Horse," said Shirley. She maneuvered a wad of gum from one side of her mouth to the other, making a loud clicking sound when she bit down on it. She guided her companion toward a booth as if protecting her from contamination, while Roz fetched three 7-Ups from the ice box and put twenty-seven cents on the counter for Jake. The newcomer was so self-contained she might have been entering an art museum, not filing past a tribe of teens whose hormones were engaged in civil war.

"Hey, Roz," said Marty Klinger, "ain't you gonna introduce me to your friend?" He pronounced it *innaduce.*

"I wouldn't introduce you to my dog," said Roz as she slid into a booth with her friends. "You might give it rabies."

Glass shattered on the tile floor. My brother had dropped his cherry Coke. As his pals made fun of his clumsiness and complained that the soda had splashed their trousers, Hubbell had, uncharacteristically, nothing to say. He picked up the shards of glass and wiped the floor with a rag that Jake tossed over, and never once did he take his eyes off Grace Kelly. All he could see was the back of her hair, and her tanned, athletic arm, and the creamy curve of her neck and shoulder, but that was evidently sufficient. I could practically hear his heart, pounding like Otis Hicks on his drums. Then I remembered a conversation to which I'd been privy, in which Hubbell expressed a certain curiosity about a tall blonde he had seen in the company of Shirley. Benny had promised to make inquiries.

For all his gregarious ways and his affable nature, when it came to girls, my brother was shy. Perhaps it was because he was one year younger than his female classmates, or because he was so cute that herds of dorks had flirted brazenly with him throughout his life, causing him to retreat, or because Ignazio Corso had set unrealistic standards for all the boys in the neighborhood, standards that he flaunted especially to Hubbell. For the envy that Marty Klinger held for Iggy was matched by Iggy's jealousy toward Hubbell. Throughout his childhood, Iggy was compared to Hubbell and he'd always come up short. Hubbell was naturally superior in every activity that mattered to boys and drew accolades from parents, whereas Iggy was the kind of kid whose mother would say, "Why can't you be like Hubbell?" His rival's status as heir to Cyclone Frankie Stone and Dodger of the Future ate away at Iggy's developing ego and served as a catalytic enzyme to his mother's sensuous spaghetti sauce. Iggy's procession of female conquests was, therefore, held up to Hubbell as if to say, "You can have Ebbets Field, chump. I'll take the chicks."

Whatever the reason, in the presence of a pretty girl, my articulate, loquacious brother became as mute as Round Man's pet snake Cecil. Hubbell had overcome his shyness often enough during adolescence to be considered normal if not a ladies' man, but dating took the kind of willpower and perseverance he devoted to baseball.

I was familiar with three of his ex-girlfriends. Sandy, a blonde pixie whose four-foot, ten-inch stature earned her the nickname Toulouse, dropped Hubbell for a six-foot, six-inch basketball player. Elizabeth, a cheerleader with long legs and green eyes and a chestnut-colored ponytail, had been Hubbell's steady girl the previous fall. The relationship had progressed to where Hubbell had given Elizabeth an ankle bracelet with twin hearts on it for Christmas, and on New Year's Eve, in a bedroom of the house where the gang had held its party, something transpired that had the Big Guys needling Hubbell for weeks. Elizabeth was beautiful and smart, but she was something of a nag. She harassed Hubbell so much about goofing off with his schoolwork that they bickered in public. When she graduated a semester early and entered Hunter College, Hubbell chose not to compete with college guys, and Elizabeth drifted away. Then there was Beverly, a brunette with substantive breasts and a sexy overbite, about whom much of a romantic nature had been said when Hubbell escorted her to the senior prom, but whose name had since been uttered in tones of dismay and even contempt.

"Scouting report, Big Ben?" said Hubbell.

In a clandestine whisper, Benny provided the facts. "Shirley's cousin. Name: Diane Brooks. Just moved down from Boston. Lives in Flatbush. Big old house. Father teaches English at Brooklyn College." Hubbell focused on the data as if he were being briefed for a mission by J. Edgar Hoover. He liked what he heard. I myself would have preferred someone from a less eggheadish lineage, and I was not crazy about having a sister-in-law with the name of the hurricane that had, in alliance with The Thing, recently ravaged the East Coast. Sure, her last name was one of the Dodgers' nicknames, but she would lose it one day anyway.

"Dig it, Hub," said Dizzy. "Go meet the chick."

I had always believed that if the bases were loaded and Mickey Mantle was at the plate, my brother would grab the ball and stride to the mound with a smile on his face as if he'd rather be nowhere else on earth. He always seemed that confident. Now he was offered the chance to meet the girl of his dreams, and beads of sweat appeared on his forehead like translucent whiteheads. He wanted to do it, he knew he should, but his legs would not cooperate. He ordered another cherry Coke.

My father, who was at the counter with his contemporaries, signaled that he wanted to leave. Checking the clock, I figured my mother would still need more time, and besides, I wanted to see what Hubbell would do. I held up my egg cream to indicate that I would like to finish it. Dad jerked his head toward the door; we were leaving. Then Irv mentioned Sonny Scott's latest aspersion.

My father said, "So-Called Sonny Scott knows as much about baseball as I know about polo, that putz."

Irv wiped his face of the spit from my father's passionate pronunciation of the letter *p*. "He was a pretty good ballplayer, that Solly."

"Skapinsky *talked* a good game," my father replied.

"He played doity," said Burt. "Tell him, Frankie. Tell him how the sonofabitch ruined your career."

My father acted reluctant to go into it, but he allowed some gentle encouragement to persuade him. He ordered a jelly doughnut and a cup of coffee. Stalling him was turning out to be a breeze.

Dizzy and Benny whispered guy-talk patter in Hubbell's ears, like infielders pepping up a pitcher. Inspired, my brother belted down the cherry Coke, breathed deeply, took one step toward the girls, and froze. Dizzy shoved him. He stumbled, regained his balance, and eased into a self-conscious lope. He was trying desperately to look cool.

Shirley made it easy for him. In her eyes, Hubbell was one of the few boys who deserved a civilized greeting. "What's doin', Hub?" she said. "Didja meet Diane? Diane, this is Hubbell. He's gonna be a Dodger, ain'tcha Hub?"

"Well . . ." said Hubbell. He cleared his throat.

"He's modest," said Roz.

"How exciting," said Diane. "What position do you play?" Her voice was like maple syrup.

"I'm a, uh . . . a pitcher," said Hubbell. His voice was like Cracker Jacks.

"Diane's my cousin," Shirley said. "Her father's a professor. He writes books and stuff."

"Really? What kind of books?" asked Hubbell.

"Well, he just published a biography of James Joyce," Diane replied.

"Oh, right, James Joyce," said Hubbell. "*From Here to Eternity.* Great book."

Gently, and with exquisite tact, Diane said, "You must have thought I said James *Jones*."

"Oh, right, of course," said Hubbell, but his face turned the color of the cardinal on St. Louis uniforms. It struck me as more than coincidental that, in one day, both my brother and I had been found ignorant of this James Joyce fellow. Maybe Hubbell too was thinking about that love scene with the waves and the sand and Deborah Kerr's legs.

"Oh, everyone gets those two mixed up," said Diane. I was beginning to reconsider my opinion of this girl; she clearly had a soul to match her looks.

A blade of sunlight flashed in my eyes. The door had opened to admit the lanky figure of Ignazio Corso. The Cunt Man, as he was respectfully called, advanced toward us in long strides, a Lucky dangling from his lips. The smoke curled into his eyes, causing them to narrow like Bogart's. He wore black chinos with a buckle in the back and a white T-shirt, one sleeve of which served as a pocket for his smokes. His hair was as shiny and black as a Halloween cat, and he combed it as he walked. Then he returned his arms to where they had been before he groomed himself—around the two girls he'd earlier seduced into riding with him.

"The boss with the hot sauce," said Dizzy.

Iggy greeted his admirers; his female companions surveyed the scene. In the booth, Shirley and Roz had acquired expressions of disdain. "I for one do not care to be in the same room as them tramps," said Roz.

"Me neither," said Shirley. "Let's went."

They clambered out of the booth. Diane, clearly confused, stood also. She smiled pleasantly at Hubbell, whose return smile had a distinct Alfred E. Neuman quality about it. "Nice to meet you," she said.

"Me too," said Hubbell. "I mean, you know . . . to meet *you.*"

"Where yez goin'?" said one of Iggy's girls.

"Wouldn't *you* like to know," said Roz. She hoisted high her nose and joined Shirley in a synchronized exit. Diane followed. The rejected girls wrinkled their noses and stuck out their tongues, then commandeered the booth. Hubbell, dazed, stared at Diane as she swayed gracefully out of the luncheonette.

Iggy got the picture. He sidled up to Hubbell with his upper lip curled to one side. "How inconsiderate of me," he said. "Here I am with two chicks and you don't even have one."

Hubbell shot him a dirty look.

"So, uh, who's the new babe?" asked Iggy. "The blonde with the cute behind. I dig chicks like that, don't you, Mr. Stone?"

"She's not your type, Corso," said Hubbell. "I hear she has a brain." He appeared rather pleased by that one.

Iggy grinned. "Oh, uh, I almost forgot," he said. "Beverly sends her regards. She says to tell you she kind of likes not being a virgin no more."

Hubbell was wounded. Iggy waited for a retort, and when none was forthcoming, he laughed. "Hey, fellas," he said to the guys at the counter, "who's the blonde chick with Shoiley and Roz?"

"What the hell do you care, greaseball?" said Klinger. "She's too classy for you any day."

"Mr. Horse," said Iggy to Harry, "please inform Mr. Dingleberry here that he must stop underestimating me."

"You think you're hot shit, don'tcha, Corso," said Klinger.

Now there was an expression I could never figure out. It seemed to me that shit at room temperature was disgusting enough, and that heating it up would only make it worse. Why, then, was hot shit something anyone would aspire to?

"My man Ignazio always gets the girl," said Dizzy.

"Not this one," countered Klinger. Adrenaline gushed into his arteries.

"Would you care to put your money where your mouth is, Mr. Dinger?" asked Iggy.

"You mess with my name once more and—"

"Ten simoleons says I get a date with the chick before the World Series is over." Time was measured by such datemarks in my neighborhood.

All eyes turned to Klinger. Hubbell's were wide with apprehension; they darted back and forth between the two adversaries and the door, as if he was willing Diane to return.

"Ten?" snorted Klinger. "Waddayou, chicken shit?"

"All right, Mr. Dinger, if you insist, I will bet you twenty bucks that I not only go out with the young lady, but I get her to park with me at the Holy Shrine."

Everyone gasped. Hubbell groped his way to a stool. The Holy Shrine was a secluded clearing in a forest of tall reeds in the marshlands near Canarsie. It was named in honor of all the virgins that had been sacrificed there.

Klinger rubbed his palms together. "I don't want your fucking greaseball money. If you lose . . . *when* you lose . . . if you don't park with her for, like, a half an hour, then you gotta be my chauffeur for a whole friggin' day. You gotta drive me anywheres I want to go, *with* the top down. You gotta wear one of them hats and shit and open the door for me and everything."

Clearly proud of his imaginative proposal, Klinger beamed as if he were already stretched out in the backseat of the Buick and Iggy was calling him sir. Hubbell looked like the soldier in a war movie who meets the girl of his dreams at a USO dance only to learn he is being shipped out the next morning.

Iggy nodded thoughtfully. A diabolical smile took shape. What he had in mind evidently pleased him as much as the prospect of parking with the lovely Diane. He let his words drip out

slowly and deliberately. "You got it, Mr. Shitflinger. And if *I* win
. . . you shall appear on the Corner . . . at the exact time designated
by yours truly . . . and you shall get down on your knees . . . and
you shall kiss . . . my . . . naked . . . ass."

"Owooooo!" howled Dizzy. "Too much!" He pounded out
a quick riff on his trumpet case.

Before Klinger could think of a face-saving way to alter the
terms of the bet, Harry the Horse grabbed Marty's right hand and
entwined Klinger's pinky with Iggy's. Mr. Big broke the pinky
lock with the edge of his hand. With judicial solemnity, Benny
pronounced, "The bet is official."

Dizzy closed the proceedings by quoting his favorite deejay,
Jocko: "Solid Ted, 'nuff said, take what you got and go ahead."

Iggy puffed himself up as if he'd already won the bet. "Would
you care to get in on the action, Mr. Stone?"

"I don't bet on girls like they're racehorses," Hubbell replied. And he staggered, pale as chalk, out the door.

"What's his story?" said Harry the Horse. "He eat something that don't agree with him, or what?"

Chapter Six

As I walked behind him up the steps, my father looked weary again, more like old Jack Kass carting home his Sphinx than the stickball king and schoolyard legend. In the small square area that served as a common foyer for the four apartments on our landing, Otis Hicks swept the floor with a broom whose handle, I noted, would make one hell of a stickball bat. From behind, his slow, deliberate movements seemed to be those of a worker bored with his task and indifferent to its completion. But Otis's face belied that interpretation. He hummed a tune and smiled as if he could not be happier, and when he saw my father and me, the smile became a grin.

"Hey, little man, how y'all doing? Hey, Mr. Stone."

"Call me Frank, will you, Otis, I can't stand that mister shit."

"I didn't call you Mr. Shit." Otis let loose a laugh that sounded like Benny Goodman's clarinet running through the chromatic scale, from the deepest bass to the squeal at the top end. "Just kidding, man, just kidding."

"I saw you playing the drums before," I told the super's son. "I watched you, in the cellar."

"You was there? How come I didn't see you?"

I shrugged. If he didn't know, I surely didn't, and I was not about to tell him that he had looked right at me.

"I'moan keep my eye out for you, little man," he said. I thought, *I'moan,* now there's an expression I can use to stump Henny Horowitz.

Entering the apartment ahead of me, my father announced his arrival and strode toward the kitchen with, I imagined, a big smile, anticipating one of the moments he lived for. I heard my mother's voice: "I'll call you later, Cecille." I smelled nothing cooking. By the time I got to the kitchen, my father's long arms were wrapped around his woman, crushing her tiny frame against

90

his bulk. He bent over and puckered; my mother stood on her toes and lifted her chin. They kissed.

And they kissed.

When Hubbell came out of his room and saw them, he announced, "This could be a new world's record, ladies and gentlemen." And when the couple came up for air and returned to their normal height, Hubbell shoved a large wooden mixing spoon in their faces and asked, "How does this compare with your other famous kisses?"

"Terrific," said my father. "She's in top form."

"He had garlic for lunch," said my mother.

Hubbell turned as if to a camera. "How about that, fans. Mr. and Mrs. Smooch, a new world's record."

"What are you, Vin Scully?" said Dad. He looked around the kitchen, perplexed. "What's for supper, babe?"

"Well . . . something came up, sweetheart. I'm running kind of late."

"You're running late? *How* late?"

"Well . . . we can eat in, oh, maybe forty-five minutes."

"Forty-five minutes? I'm starving."

"I'm sorry, honey, really. I just lost track of time."

He tried to control himself, he really did. He took a deep breath and paced in a half circle and clenched his fists. "You lost track of time? Christ, you'd lose track of your head if it wasn't attached to your neck. What are you, too busy bullshitting with your friends? You like to dig up dirt? Go work for Roto-Rooter!"

In all fairness, although I sympathized with my mother's dislike of convention, and had, in fact, been an accomplice in this instance, I understood my father's reaction. I knew what it was like to be hungry and have to wait to be fed. It's not that my mother was inconsiderate, although I suppose it would be hard to spare her that verdict on all occasions. It's just that she frequently slipped into a time zone all her own, and the rest of us would end up with jet lag. She would announce that supper would be served at such and such time, only to storm into the house about five minutes before the appointed hour, throw on an apron over her coat, and start chopping and thawing and boiling and slinging ingredients around. It was as if, in her mind, the alarm had been set to cook, not to eat.

She was no Angie Corso in the kitchen either, but she was a reasonably good cook for someone who did not care much for the job. She owned no cookbooks, filed no recipes in boxes of three-by-five cards. When other housewives exchanged culinary tips, my mother drifted away. She would forget to buy necessary ingredients even when she wrote them down, although the refrigerator always had packages of Swiss cheese, on which she nibbled the way some people snacked on candy, and the cupboard always had pounds of pistachio nuts, because for reasons none of us could comprehend, she purchased these items every time she shopped. She was, however, a competent improviser with a knack for manifesting tasty meals out of meager raw materials. Unfortunately, there seemed to be a chronic disjunction between our stomachs and her personal clock, which is why her sons had developed a talent, rare in males of that era, for whipping together sandwiches and snacks of singular distinction. Hubbell, for example, was the omelette king of Brownsville. I, in addition to a skill with home-made egg creams that rivaled Jake's, was developing an artisan's skill with triple-decker Dagwood sandwiches. Hank specialized in beverages and desserts. My father, on the other hand, couldn't even fry an egg.

"I wasn't gossiping, Frank," Mom said. "You don't want the PTA to be taken over by bigots and fascists, do you?"

"The PTA? The PTA? I gotta starve to death because of the PTA?"

He was about to erupt. His face was rapidly approaching the critical shade of maroon. The volume and ferocity of my father's tantrums had made them the most terrifying events of my early childhood. It had taken years of experience and a lot of counseling by my mother, but I had finally learned not to take the episodes personally, regardless of the context. As Mom explained, Dad, like a pressure cooker, had to make some noise when the pressure inside got too high, as it did when he had to contend with too many traffic jams, lousy tippers, and drivers from New Jersey. Pennant races and close ball games also drove up the pressure. When a Dodger manager made a stupid decision or a player forgot to cover a base or booted an easy ground ball, my father would shout a curse and throw his house slipper at the television. Fortunately, Cyclone Frankie Stone hit better than he threw; he never once broke a picture tube.

The tantrums presented no immediate danger, Mom assured me; the fierce bark would never become a bite. And so, I had learned to watch the fireworks with the detachment of a spectator at a Fourth of July exhibition. How my mother could understand her mate so well and still not have learned to give the man his supper on time was a mystery.

Over the years, my father's outbursts occurred with about the frequency of a full moon. Of late, however, he had erupted more often, due to his growing dissatisfaction with his occupation and the accumulation of losing bets. With the promotion of Sy Kramer to dispatcher, they had begun to manifest approximately once a week.

He raised his head as if addressing the upper deck at Ebbets Field and roared, "You hear this? My wife thinks she's Winston Churchill. I can't eat because she's leading the fight against fascism in the PTA!"

Having heard my father's voice, Round Man rolled into the kitchen. He was wearing an old pilot's helmet of cracked and faded leather, with goggles over his eyes. On his shoulder was a green and red parrot whose squawk sounded like the younger Mrs. Kass. "Dad, look what I did. I taught Gleason to talk."

"Very nice, Hank," said my father. Hank could have been showing off a pterodactyl. It still would not have earned him any attention. Dad then went face-to-face with his wife. "I work my ass off all day. I expect a decent meal when I get home. Is that too much to ask? Do I have to beg like a dog? Huh? Like a dog?"

I estimated that his voice was now carrying at least to the Corsos' apartment. With an arch of an eyebrow, my mother calmly reached into her left ear and plucked out the earphone of her hearing aid.

"Very funny, very funny," said my father. He raised his voice to compensate for the out-of-service hearing aid. "You think it's a picnic driving around in bumper-to-bumper traffic on days like this? You think it's a goddamn pleasure cruise riding home on the subway like a sardine?"

My mother decided it was time to initiate civil defense procedures. She wailed, "WAAaaa, AAAaaa, AAAaaa . . ." in modulating tones, like a siren.

Hubbell took up the cue. "Take cover! Air raid! Proceed to fallout shelter immediately!" He kicked a chair out of the way and crawled under the table. Mom and I followed, then Hank squeezed in, a tight fit indeed.

"You think it's funny?" roared my father. "Huh? You think it's a joke?"

He slammed the table. We covered our heads with our arms, as we had been instructed in air raid drills at school. We tried to hold back our laughter, but with each increase in my father's decibel count, the task became more and more futile.

"A man deserves a little respect when he gets home. I work hard so you clowns can have a roof over your head and food on your—" Gleason buzzed his head like a kamikaze pilot. Dad jerked out of the way in time and took a swing at the parrot; he connected only with the string on the light fixture.

"That's another thing," my father bellowed. "I'm sick and tired of all these beasts around here. I feel like I'm living on Noah's ark half the time."

Gleason made another attempt to dive-bomb my father, who again swung and missed.

"Don't hit him!" said Round Man.

"Don't hit him?" said my father. "Did you hear that, Jeannie? His fine-feathered friend nearly decapitated his father, and he's worried about the bird. Is that how you're raising my kids?"

Under the table the effort to suppress my laughter was causing my rib cage to burn. Hubbell and Mom clenched their teeth so tightly their faces turned crimson. Hank fought it so hard that spittle poured down his series of chins like a stream cascading over embankments of rocks. A guffaw, like a sneeze, burst from his mouth.

"You think it's funny, Hank?" said my father. "Next time there's no supper, we'll eat parrot soup!"

I could hold it back no longer. A laugh exploded from my diaphragm like a cannonball. Hubbell and Mom followed suit. My father pounded the table, sending tremors through our shelter. "I will not be a laughingstock in my own house. Do you hear me? Let me tell you—"

The next sound emerged from a different orifice. He interrupted himself with a fart, a short, sharp blast that sounded off-key although it was a tune unto itself.

"How sweet it is!" squawked Gleason.

"He said it!" yelled Round Man. "I trained him!"

The bird's statement was like a fanfare that signaled the end of all restraint. Seized by currents of laughter, my mother and brothers and I howled and cackled. We spilled out from under the table, twitching and rolling on the floor, colliding with each other and the chrome legs of the chairs.

My father tried to hold it in. He tried to maintain the stern look in his eyes and the snarl on his lips. But he could not. It was contagious. He waved his arm as if throwing in the towel. And he laughed. The sound fluttered out from between his lips like a series of soap bubbles. "All clear!" yelled my mother. "All clear," her sons repeated.

"How sweet it is," said Gleason.

A few minutes later, when all five of us were laughed out, my mother stood up and threw her arms around her husband. My father blushed. "So, sue me, I blew off a little steam."

"It's okay," said Mom. "You're under a lot of pressure. Did you talk to Kramer?"

My father shook his head. "It wasn't the right time. I'll talk to him, don't worry."

"You're not asking for the moon, Frank. You deserve better after all these years."

"Shut up and kiss me."

She did as he asked. Round Man and I competed for who could make the ugliest grimace of disgust.

To atone for his tantrum and to celebrate the pennant-clinching, my father put up only token resistance to our proposed evening at Coney Island. Coney had actually been a peninsula ever since the tidal creek that had kept it apart from the mainland of Brooklyn had been filled in. Though people lived there, it was principally a place of amusement, and had been since the nineteenth century, when its ornate hotels and opulent restaurants were host to high society and its racetracks attracted dandies with a penchant for wagering. When, in the twenties, the expansion of the subway lines made the area accessible to the masses, Coney was democratized. On a hot Sunday as much as fifteen percent of New York's population might squeeze into its few square miles of beach, boardwalk, amusements, and eateries. Even on the cool September night of our visit, the area around Nathan's Famous was shoulder to shoulder with people stuffing their faces and trying to keep mustard and ketchup off their clothing.

Nathan's had opened in 1920, a small stand kitty-cornered from an elevated subway station. Its proprietor, Nathan Handwerker, cut in half the going rate of ten cents per hot dog. The price drew customers away from older emporiums, and the unique taste of Nathan's frankfurters brought them back again and again. By the time Round Man was old enough to knock off eight dogs at a sitting (or standing, since no one sat at Nathan's), the establishment occupied a full block of choice Coney Island real estate and its legend had spread across the nation. It was impossible to bite into one of Nathan's specialties without proclaiming, no matter how redundant, "These are the best damn hot dogs in the world." Exactly what mysterious ingredients Nathan Handwerker had used to elevate his weiners above the commonplace was the source of much conjecture. The secret was never revealed. In later years, when Nathan's cloned itself in Long Island and Times Square and eventually even the San Fernando Valley of Los Angeles, aficionados would swear, in vehement opposition to the restaurant's claims, that the hot dogs in Coney Island were different from those at other locations. Maybe it was the salt in the air.

Nathan's was our first stop. The family consumed, among us, thirteen hot dogs, six heaping orders of fries, four ears of sweet corn, two-dozen clams, three hamburgers, one chow mein sandwich on a bun (a Round Man favorite), and five orange drinks. Afterward, we took turns trying to knock down plastic milk bottles with baseballs—an activity that Hubbell was forbidden to join—flip hoops over dolls and toss Ping-Pong balls into fish bowls. We won only a stuffed Mickey Mouse doll, a popular item that year, Disneyland having opened to much fanfare and *The Mickey Mouse Club* about to debut on afternoon TV. Ersatz animals were offensive to Round Man, however, unless they were realistic models. He gave the doll to a grateful waif.

We visited a haunted house; we rode the Cyclone, the world's most famous roller coaster; we banged each other around in the chaos of a bumper-car course, blue sparks flashing off the electrified ceiling when a collision jarred loose the copper-tipped poles that energized the cars; we rode the Wonder Wheel, selecting one of the brightly colored boxcars rather than a white one. The choice of Wonder Wheel cars was a litmus test, separating the adventurous from the bland; white cars clung securely to the perimeter of the structure, circling in traditional Ferris Wheel fashion, while colored cars broke loose from the humdrum circumnavigation and zoomed into the center, rocked up and back, then zoomed again to the opposite rim on a thrilling upswing. I imagined that Yankee fans rode in the white cars.

When we rode the bobsled, my parents took a car of their own. My mother once told me that my father had kissed her for the first time in the long, dark tunnel that the cars climbed through to start the ride. Frank Stone was nothing if not sentimental. The bobsled mimicked the winter sport of the same name. You sat in low-slung, bullet-shaped cars with your legs outstretched, one rider between the legs of the companion behind him, and you rocketed at breakneck speed up and down hills, hurtling up the sides of embankments so quickly you would instinctively brace yourself for getting flung into the air like a pebble from a slingshot. Round Man sat in front of me, pinning my legs to the sides of the car. I wished he were half his size, a wish that plunged headlong into a fantasy—a premonition, as it turned out—in which my bobsled companion was a supple girl with soft raven hair and a fear of the dark and a little something to hold onto when centrifugal force took control of my hands.

After the bobsled, we waited around for Hubbell, who had wandered off on his own. We stood next to a fun house entrance, near a larger-than-life mechanical woman that rocked back and forth emitting a hysterical, ear-piercing laugh. My father sidled up to the rollicking doll.

"Did you hear the one about the traveling salesman?" he asked. The doll laughed louder. "Oh, you've heard it," said Dad. By now an appreciative crowd had gathered. Again he addressed the mechanical woman. "How about this one? This priest says to a rabbi, 'Come on, Hymie, waddaya say? Try a ham sandwich just once.' And the rabbi says, 'Okay, Murphy, I promise I'll eat a ham sandwich . . . at your wedding.' " The doll, and the crowd, laughed uproariously.

When his performance ended, he walked proudly down the bustling midway with my mother's arm in his. I edged closer and heard him say, "Hubbell's goofing off lately, Jeannie. I can tell. He's not going at it with the old intensity."

"He *needs* to goof off a little, Frank," my mother reasoned. "He's young, and he's worked so hard at it. He just needs to find his own way."

"This is not the time for that," said Dad. "You know that friend of mine who used to work for the Dodgers? Well, his brother-in-law's friend introduced me to a scout, and you know who it turns out to be? Teddy Ryan. Remember Teddy from the old days? He's a scout! A big one. And he's gonna come down and watch Hubbell, only I don't want Hubbell to know because it'll put too much pressure on him."

"That's terrific, Frank."

"You bet it is. We're in like Flynn, only he can't slack off. I want him tuned up like a Rolls-Royce."

I was excited by this news, but I had to keep it to myself. If my father knew that I knew, he'd find it necessary to remind me hourly not to tell Hubbell.

Round Man and I were seatmates again in the tenuous chairs of the Parachute Jump. This landmark, erected next to the boardwalk in 1941, was designed to simulate a paratrooper's descent from a plane. In our open chair with only two leather straps supporting our backs and a pole for each of us to hold, we were lifted by a powerful engine for the slow ascent. We rode in silence. Round Man nibbled at a jelly apple. I marveled at the view, which expanded magnificently with each foot we climbed. The multicolored lights of Coney blended together like the stars of the Milky Way, and the noises—the clickety-clack of the roller coaster, the squeals of children, the raspy cajoling of vendors and hawkers, the organ music of the carousel, the cackles of the mechanical laughing lady—coalesced into a single chorus. The big sign for Steeplechase, the Funny Place, with the familiar logo of a man's face with an almost grotesque, literally ear-to-ear grin, shrunk to the size of a postcard. Before us, the vast blackness of

Jamaica Bay opened out to the Atlantic. A cargo ship crawled slowly toward the narrows that would one day be spanned by the Verrazano Bridge. Against the distant sky, the silhouette of Staten Island's hills was crowned by a line of lights.

It was 250 feet to the peak of the Parachute Jump. The pace lent itself to reflection. With trepidation, I thought about the following week, when school would open. Who would be my teacher? Smart sixth-graders typically ended up with either Miss Gutoff, who was young and pretty and good-natured, or with Mrs. Schaefer, who was a witch. I wondered which kids would be in my class, and who would sit in my vicinity, uncontrollable conditions that could make or break a school year. I contemplated the happy convergence of signs and omens that pointed to the Dodger's first World Championship, and I asked myself if I really wanted to face the Yankees in the Series. Yes, I decided, bring them Bombers on and end the curse. I thought of my older brother. Hubbell had indeed been goofing off; my father didn't know half of his transgressions. What did it portend? What impact would it have on me and my future?

"Do you think, when Hubbell's on the Dodgers, he could get me a job as a bat boy or something?" Round Man asked, his mouth encircled by the red residue of his jelly apple.

"You?" I replied. "I'm older. I get first dibs."

"That's not fair. You'll get to be a player. I won't."

"I thought you want to be a zoologist."

"That's 'cause I stink at baseball." Round Man took another bite of his jelly apple, then opened Pandora's Box. "Maybe Hubbell won't be a Dodger anyway."

"Don't worry," I said. "The scouts were probably waiting till they clinched the pennant. Now they can get down to business and sign up new guys and stuff."

"What if they don't?" said Round Man. "What if they don't sign him up?"

"Dad has a backup plan. Hubbell will spend the winter at Uncle Jack's place in Florida so he can practice outdoors, then he'll go to spring training and—"

"Maybe he won't go. Maybe he changed his mind."

He said that as if he knew something I did not. He denied it, but I sensed that he was lying.

Suddenly, we were jolted; the ride hit the top. We plunged toward earth in a free-fall, letting loose loud shrieks, not out of fear, for we'd been through this dozens of times, but for the sake of custom and the sheer joy of yelling at the top of our lungs. Gravity must have pulled the rest of my body faster than my stomach because my esophagus filled with the remains of hot dogs and orange drink. Then, abruptly, the parachute opened and the dive ended in a jarring jerk. The food dropped back into my belly. The parachute wasn't really necessary, of course; the ride was controlled by machinery. But the sight of the white sail billowing above our heads lent the experience a verisimilitude that was part of its appeal.

We drifted down exhilarated. Slowly, objects on the ground assumed their customary size and shape. Round Man chomped on his jelly apple.

"Tell me, Hank," I commanded.

"Tell you what?"

"Don't give me that. Tell me about Hubbell."

"I can't."

"Tell me," I insisted.

"You can't make me."

I grabbed a chunk of flesh on the outer part of his arm and squeezed. It was a relatively light pinch; I did not like to hurt my brother unless it was absolutely necessary. Not that I was compassionate. It's just that, when pushed, he fought back, and what he lacked in agility and truculence he made up for with raw power. Hank gritted his teeth to ward off the anticipated pain.

"Tell me," I demanded, and when he did not give in, I squeezed harder, twisting his skin. He yelped and lost his grip on the jelly apple. He tried to snatch it out of the air, but he missed, and it rolled down his leg. He jerked his feet upward in hopes of kicking the apple back into his lap, but he succeeded only in shaking our seat so hard I had to grab the pole with both hands to keep from being tossed into the night. The apple plummeted earthward like a bomb.

"Banzai!" I shouted.

The jelly apple landed on a wooden platform about ten feet from the mechanic who operated the ride, splattering red and white shrapnel but injuring no one. I tried to punish Round Man by telling my parents he'd eaten almost the whole apple before it fell, but they bought him a new one anyway. I determined to find a way to break his silence. As it turned out, I didn't have to.

The five of us strolled on the splintery boardwalk. Sailors in white cake-mold caps ran past us with giddy girlfriends on their arms, hurrying to get in as much fun as they could before they had to return to their ship at the Brooklyn Navy Yard. Two old women on their nightly promenade watched Round Man blissfully chomp on his new jelly apple and admired his healthy appetite. A girl in a dress with yellow flowers bawled because her cotton candy had fallen from her hand and rolled around the boardwalk like sagebrush gathering sand.

My mother led her husband to the railing to look out at the empty beach and the black sea. My brothers and I stood beside them, next to a row of parked wicker carriages that, by day, were used to push sightseers up and down the wooden boulevard. Hank and I read aloud a sign with a big NO and a list of all things forbidden on the beach or boardwalk: peddling, advertising, littering, dogs, fires, bicycling, roller skating, vehicles other than baby carriages and wheelchairs for invalids, newspapers other than for reading, sitting on railing or steps, bathing rings, rafts, inflated or buoyant devices, masks, goggles or fins, persons on beach from midnight to dawn, acrobatics, ball playing, throwing of missiles or sand, dressing or undressing, tents or shelters, articles hung on signs, benches, baskets, railings or fences, ropes, umbrellas, boats launched or beached, fishing, flying of kites, flags or pennants, digging of holes, creating hazards or committing nuisances, bathing near jetties.

"You can't do nothing," summed up Round Man.

"Anything," my mother corrected. Double negatives, like misused words and vulgarisms such as *ain't,* seldom got past her.

We could hear the gentle waves slap against the shore and the sizzling sound of the ocean sucking itself back over shells and rocks. Faint giggles and whispers reached us from beneath the boardwalk, where lovers lay together on the cold sand, a mating ritual so common that the dark dominion under the boards was known as Hotel Underwood. The night was moonless and clear, lit by a gaggle of stars. My mother breathed deep of the salty air and hummed the tune to "Stardust."

A shooting star streaked through the sky. We gasped in awe. Such an event was so rare in Brooklyn that it jarred loose a long-forgotten memory trace in my father's brain. He emoted grandly, his accent an odd marriage of Olivier and Damon Runyon: "The rude sea grew civil at her song, and certain stars shot madly from their spheres, to hear the sea-maid's music."

"Holy mackerel," said my mother. She stared at her mate with a mixture of melancholy and shock; for a moment she saw the young romantic with the broad shoulders and thick dark hair who, without damaged pride, let her introduce him to the things she loved. In the last days of their courtship and the early days of their marriage, Jeannie had tried to cultivate the dormant sensitivity she had perceived in Cyclone Frankie Stone. She saw in him an intelligent young man with innate good taste that belied his coarse exterior and his street-corner education. She dragged her beau to concerts and theatres. She sat him down and read him poetry. She played recordings of Chopin and Rachmaninoff. She even got him to act with her in amateur plays. And all of it was fine with Frank as long as he could be with Jeannie with the light brown hair.

When it became obvious that he would never play in the big leagues, my father began to dream of a son who would carry the torch. He himself would study journalism and become a sportswriter. He married his Jeannie toward the end of the Depression, when the couple was lucky to get an affordable apartment in the building where my mother's parents lived. Greenwich Village would have to wait. So would Frank's schooling. He drove a cab, then joined the Army when the war came. Jeannie and her son moved in with her parents to save money. She saw her soldier husband only on short-lived furloughs, including the ones in which Hank and I were conceived. By war's end she had three children, and her dreams got stuffed into the trunks of the cabs that my father drove to support his family. Now she wondered how, with Times Square only forty minutes away by subway, she had let art and culture slip unnoticed from her life.

"That was from *A Midsummer Night's Dream*," she told us. "We were in it together, before you kids were born. Believe it or not, the old boy was a pretty decent actor."

"Yeah?" said Hubbell. "Which role did he play? Putz?"

"That's *Puck,* wise guy," said my father. He gave Hubbell's arm—his nonpitching arm—a playful punch. "No, I was too big to play Puck," he added. "I was Oberon, King of the Fairies."

This went right to the funny bone. Round Man picked up on my lead and we minced along the boardwalk with limp wrists, lisping, "He's king of the fairies. He's king of the fairies." We had learned of such things by observing men who complained about their wives' perverse fondness for Liberace.

"Let's get these comedians home," said my father. "It's getting late."

Now it was my mother's turn to emote. "My fairy lord, this must be done with haste, for night's swift dragons cut the clouds full fast."

We walked in silence, Round Man and I flanking my mother, Hubbell walking up ahead with my father, although not by choice. I could tell by the tone of Dad's voice that he was giving Hubbell one of his Knute Rockne pep talks. Hubbell angled his walk to put some distance between his ear and my father's message, but Dad instinctively closed the gap.

A chill wind blew off the ocean. My father took off his jacket and draped it over Hubbell's pitching arm, which was protected only by a shirtsleeve. Hubbell shrugged the jacket off. My father put it back on. "I don't need it," Hubbell said.

"You don't want to take any chances," said my father. "It's chilly."

"I think I know when I'm cold, Pop. I'm not a baby."

Frank Stone stared at his son; he was not used to intransigence. He might have persisted. He might even have lost his temper. But my mother maneuvered into his line of vision and shot him a look. He draped the jacket over his own arm. "Fine," he said to Hubbell. "Okay, fine, don't wear it, what do I care?"

The front page of that night's *News* declared: DODGERS IN! Beneath that, a smaller headline read: ORDER DEAD HEIRESS' MOTHER ARRESTED IN ABORTION KILLING. My mother extricated the pages that told that sordid tale. I claimed the funnies. The man of the house, as was customary, got first dibs on the sports pages, where the Dodgers' mauling of the Braves and subsequent celebration was detailed. We always read every word of every story on every game, even those whose every pitch we had seen with our very own eyes. The reading never felt redundant; it lent perspective and, in some odd way, validated our experience.

On the way home we had stopped at Meyer's Candystore to pick up a quart of Sealtest cherry-vanilla ice cream, hand-packed. My parents and I ate it while simultaneously reading the paper and watching *Dragnet* on TV, a time-saving art that I would carry with me through life. Round Man had gone to his room with a dish of ice cream and a library book on the care and feeding of cocker spaniels; Hubbell had retired to his room immediately upon arrival, not even pausing to dish out dessert.

At ten o'clock we watched a new half-hour comedy-variety program starring a slim young comic who had previously hosted a quiz show and written monologues for Red Skelton. It was called *The Johnny Carson Show.* During a commercial break, I went to the kitchen for something to drink. I heard sounds coming from Hubbell's room. Ordinarily, this would have been meaningless, but Round Man's secretive behavior on the Parachute Jump had alerted me to trouble, so I tiptoed down the corridor, clinging closely to the wall where the floorboards were less likely to creak. Hubbell's door was slightly ajar, practically inviting me to peek in. What I saw gave me the creeps.

My older brother was seated, legs crossed, one elbow perched on the arm of the chair. Smoke from a cigarette drifted past his face. This was remarkable; to my knowledge, Hubbell did not smoke and never had. His eyes half squinted and his brow was wrinkled in a look of serious regard. When he spoke, his voice was not his own. It was deeper and somehow older, and it contained only a faint trace of Brooklyn. It reminded me of someone I could not, for the moment, place.

"Mr. Stone," he said, "thank you for inviting us to your room. It's charming. Did you decorate it yourself?"

As if it wasn't weird enough that Hubbell was talking to himself as someone else, now he put the cigarette down, uncrossed his legs, maneuvered to the other side of the chair, and spoke in his own voice. "Just a few things I threw together. Oh, sorry, how embarrassing." He tossed a pair of sweat socks toward the closet. "I don't know how those got there. By the way, Mr.

Murrow, that's a new automatic record player over there. You can play a whole stack of forty-fives on it."

He angled into his original position, crossed his legs, puffed on the cigarette and assumed the other voice, which I now understood to be Edward R. Murrow's. My brother was acting out the *Person to Person* show, in which Murrow visited, via remote camera, the homes of celebrities. "Mr. Stone, if I may, I'd like to get right to something that everyone in America is talking about: those persistent rumors that you are thinking about retiring from baseball. Is it true?"

He shifted back to himself. "Well, Ed . . . is it all right if I call you Ed? It's a tough decision. I certainly appreciate all the cards and letters from my fans begging me not to quit, but I have to weigh all the factors and do what's right for me and my family."

This was the spookiest thing I'd seen since Spencer Tracy in *Dr. Jekyll and Mr. Hyde.* Hubbell turned into Edward R. Murrow again: "But you're a darn good ballplayer."

He responded as himself from the other side of the chair: "Yes, but good is not good enough. I mean, you have to be a lot better than good to make the majors. Of course, my father says I'm plenty good enough. My whole life I've believed everything he told me, but he's wrong. I mean, it's not like they're beating down the door to sign me up."

"But you *love* baseball."

"Yeah, I love it. I love to watch it. I love to play it when it's just for fun, but when I play in front of a crowd, like when there's pressure and my father's there watching and everything, it's like . . . well, I never told anyone this before, Mr. Murrow, but . . . well, I throw up before every game."

He shifted seats and cleared his throat; Edward R. Murrow did not approve of such crude talk on nationwide television. "I see," he said. "Well, if you do retire, what do you suppose you'll do? Your whole life has been geared to one thing."

"Well, Ed, that's the sixty-four-thousand-dollar question. I can't believe I let my father talk me out of applying to college. He said it would be a jinx. Do you believe that? My friend Dizzy's going to Juilliard. Benny's going to City College. Other guys are starting jobs or whatever. And they're all jealous of *me*. That's a laugh, isn't it? Say, how did you get where you are, Mr. Murrow?

You and Red Barber and those guys. How'd you get there?"

No answer was forthcoming. Hubbell sighed. "Would you like to see my forty-five collection? I just got 'When You Dance' by the Turbans."

He switched positions and voices and addressed the viewing audience. "Join us next week when we'll visit Kukla, Fran, and Ollie. Until then, good night, and good luck."

I dashed on my toes up the edge of the hallway, my heart pounding with the thrill and terror of revelation. When I got back to the living room, Johnny Carson was introducing a tall, rugged actor who was built like a linebacker. His name was James Arness. He and Johnny talked about the new TV show in which Arness was about to star. Based on a radio series, *Gunsmoke* was to be unveiled the following Saturday night, with the actor portraying Marshal Matt Dillon of Dodge City, Kansas. Johnny joked with his guest about his feature film debut, a 1951 movie in which Arness had played the title role. The movie was called *The Thing.*

"Remember *The Thing*?" my mother asked, her smile suggesting that she remembered well my reaction to it.

"Sort of," I said.

Did I remember the movie? Could I forget it? Would I *ever* forget it, with that monster following me around like a pin caught in the collar of a new shirt? I couldn't relax for one stinking night! And now, in the very living room where I had watched my grandfather's heart grind to a halt, on the very TV with which The Thing had emblazoned the image of Bobby Thomson's iniquity on my innocent brain cells, I would be reminded of the wretch week after week. The Thing was going prime-time.

Bubbly voices urged us to use Ajax, the foaming cleanser, because it floats the dirt right down the drain. I wished I could float The Thing right down the drain, but he was busy delivering a preview of coming attractions.

"Oh, honey, listen to this," said my mother to my father. She was reading the entertainment pages of the newspaper. "They're going to do a musical version of *Pygmalion.* Rex Harrison's going to star in it. Oh, let's go see it."

"*Pygmalion*?" said my father.

"You know, George Bernard Shaw."

"Oh, yeah, the one about Joan of Arc."

"Oh, for God's sake," Mom said, exasperated. "It's about
. . . oh, never mind. I'm sure it'll be wonderful. Lerner and Loewe
are doing the music and—"

"I don't know, babe," my father squirmed. "Them Broadway shows are pretty expensive."

"Oh, phoo," said my mother, "I've got about fifty dollars put
away."

"Fifty bucks?" My father turned his eyes from his wife to the
Ajax commercial in an attempt to conceal the excitement that her
announcement had sparked. He lit a Pall Mall.

"Nickels and dimes, here and there, it adds up," said Mom.
"I've been saving for an occasion. Come on, what do you say, let's
blow the wad. We'll get orchestra seats, we'll have dinner at
Lindy's . . . We haven't done anything like that in years."

"We'll see," said my father. "Jeez, it's getting late. I better
wash up." He stood up, stretched, and, avoiding my mother's
gaze, walked toward the bathroom.

The love of his life scrutinized him carefully. She suspected
something. I *knew* something. My father intended to use that fifty
dollars to pay off Mike the Barber. To The Thing it was all in a
day's work.

Chapter Seven

Wind blew swirls of dust around the angular corridor of the alley. Illuminated by the light from a kitchen window, garments hanging from clothespins kicked and flapped and fluttered like the flags above the scoreboard at Ebbets Field. The wrought-iron gate creaked as it swung open and closed, as if a procession of invisible souls was marching to the cellar to watch Otis Hicks play the drums. From my window I heard a tender blues from Dizzy's muted trumpet, the raspy sound of Yiddish from two tired throats, and the liver-and-onions rondelet: Barney Klinger hollered at his son Marty, who in turn hollered at his mother, who hollered at Barney. The day had been so eventful I could not sleep, so I sat at the window, keeping a watchful eye on Ruth Finkelstein's room in hopes that her light would go on. My curtains, patterned with white aircraft carriers and red planes against a background somewhere in the range of blue between ocean and sky, feathered my face and shoulders as I tried to make sense of the five-month odyssey that had brought the Bums to the brink of another World Series and my family to the brink of crisis.

Before the season, it was widely believed that the Dodgers had blown their best chances between 1950 and 1953, the years of their greatest glory and most ignominious ruin. After the back-to-back traumas of Dick Sisler and Bobby Thomson, the Bums had raised themselves up from their own ashes to win two consecutive pennants, only to be pillaged in each World Series by the Yankees. Last year, 1954, the injury-plagued team struggled all season behind a rookie manager and finished five games behind the Giants. The only joy in Mudville had been watching the upper-crust, lily-white Yankees win 103 games and still lose the pennant to Cleveland, two of whose key players were a Jew, Al Rosen, and a black, Larry Doby.

When the 1955 training camp opened, the fans' expectations

were the lowest they had been since Jackie Robinson burst into Ebbets Field in his odd, pigeon-toed sprint. Key players were old or of questionable fitness, the pitching was dubious, the competition formidable, the manager, we thought, retarded. Walter "Smokey" Alston was beginning his second year at the helm. A quiet, laconic man from Darrtown, Ohio, he was a sharp contrast to profane predecessors like Charlie Dressen and Leo Durocher. Alston seemed as though he'd be more at home in a silo than a major league dugout. Here was a guy who'd had one—count 'em, one—time at bat in the big leagues, and used it to strike out. He was a minor league manager, a man so anonymous the headline of the *News* when his hiring was announced read: WHO, HE? Why had Alston been chosen to replace Dressen? Because, my father contended, Dressen was his own man and Alston was Walter O'Malley's. The owner of the Dodgers did not like his authority challenged.

My father and Hubbell were among Alston's chief detractors; they held him responsible for the previous year's downfall, and believed he could never earn the respect of a veteran squad. In their opinion, Alston's placid character was ill-suited to the team; he treated umpires like a country lawyer deferring to a judge when the job called for a street fighter. Nor did they think the manager could outthink shrewd opponents like Durocher or Milwaukee's Bobby Bragan, not to mention Casey Stengel, should the Bums manage to face the Ol' Perfessor in another World Series. They called for Alston's head.

Word filtered north from spring training that certain players were feuding openly with the manager. Predictably, the most militant dissident was said to be Jackie Robinson. Having already been shifted from second base to third because of his age, Jackie sizzled while Alston toyed with starting a younger player, Don Hoak, at the hot corner. In the opinion of the Stone family, this was further proof of Alston's mental deficiency. Sure, Robby was thirty-six and had lost a step or two. Yes, ground balls he once would have gobbled up like a kid scooping up jacks might now skip past him, and bases he would have reached safely might now recede from his sliding spikes. But he was still indispensable for his contagious intensity and his matchless ability to find a way to win. Word reached Brooklyn that the obscure manager and the celebrated athlete had squared off in a locker room in Louisville before an exhibition game.

As opening day neared, even steadfast gentlemen like Pee Wee Reese and Roy Campanella were said to be mutinous. In one of many experiments with his lineup, Alston had Campy, a two-time Most Valuable Player, batting eighth. The reason for this indignity was Campy's right hand, an injury to which had turned him into a part-time .207 hitter in 1954. If the hand did not recover from off-season surgery, it would be a crushing blow. Not only did we need Campy's bat, we needed him to throw out impertinent base runners, set defensive strategy, and handle the pitchers, a task for which Roy had a mother's touch. And the Flock staff badly needed nurturing. Virtually every hurler was a question mark, the biggest being Don Newcombe, who the previous season had returned from two years in the service as rusty as the bicycle frame in Rooney's Lot. We feared the team would score runs by the bushel but give them up by the barrel.

It was, in all, an uncertain team that barnstormed north in April. Most writers picked them to come in third. The favorites were the Giants, who had scalped the potent Indians in four straight games to bag the '54 World Series; they had solid veterans, an able pitching staff, and Willie Mays, who pummeled pitchers, stole bases with impunity, and patrolled the vast Polo Grounds outfield like a one-man cavalry. Picked to finish second were the Milwaukee Braves, with Henry Aaron, Eddie Matthews, and Warren Spahn.

In the streets of Brownsville and Bensonhurst, Bay Ridge and Borough Park, the Dodger faithful approached the new season with the obligatory displays of optimism, but their predictions had a hollow ring. They were built more on hope than conviction. Their faith was that of the religious who harbor irritating doubts but sustain their belief because they know no other way and would be lost without it. Even never-say-die Frank Stone had subtly changed his tune. His emphatic "We'll win going away" had been replaced by "We got a pretty good shot at it."

On the morning of April 12, the papers reported that Abba Eban, Israel's United Nations representative, had accused Egypt of opening fire along the Sinai border. Adlai Stevenson had called for a joint declaration by the U.S. and its allies to defend the island of Formosa (later Taiwan) from Red Chinese aggression. In Ann Arbor, Michigan, a team of top scientists prepared to announce the results of experiments on an antipolio vaccine. But the minds of the men who sipped Jake's robust coffee before trudging to work, and of the kids who gulped their Wheaties before dashing off to school, were turned to thoughts of baseball. It was opening day.

Opening day stood for something then. It, not the equinox, not crocuses or rosebuds, signified the true beginning of spring. The seasons of sport still behaved themselves. When the soil got soft and moist, bats and gloves sprouted; pucks were stored away, gyms were shut down, shoulder pads and helmets continued to gather dust. The previous Sunday, the Syracuse Nationals had defeated the Fort Wayne Pistons, 92–91, to win the NBA championship; the Red Wings and Canadiens were about to wrap things up on the ice; the Cleveland Browns' 56–10 clobbering of the Detroit Lions for the NFL title was ancient history. It was time for baseball, only baseball.

But the season jumped off to a false start. On opening day it poured from New England to Washington; all three New York teams were rained out. To me, this had all the earmarks of an omen. But of what? I lay in bed that night, searching for an interpretation as rain sprayed my window and Alan Freed spun silken doo-wop songs like the Penguins' "Earth Angel" and "Crying in the Chapel" by the Orioles, already golden oldies at the dawn of the rock era. Then the news came on: the Salk vaccine worked. We could now be immunized to a disease that had crippled millions and had terrified kids every summer when, we were told, heat and dampness helped it to spread. We'd been afraid to step in a puddle lest the polio virus seep through our pores and into our blood and we'd end up in a wheelchair like Franklin Delano Roosevelt. Now, Mayor Robert F. Wagner promised to inoculate all of New York's public school students within weeks.

An epidemic was about to be conquered, a menacing natural force subdued, a seemingly unbeatable foe vanquished. Human beings, underdogs to a powerful virus, would win. This was a sign. Let the games begin! The underdog Dodgers would vanquish seemingly unbeatable foes, subdue the menacing natural force of the New York Yankees, eradicate the epidemic of appalling last-minute defeat. It seemed to me that if we could beat polio, we could conquer the World Series. Strained reasoning, perhaps, but not if you believed that the Brooklyn Dodgers represented all that was deserving about humanity.

Sure enough, the Bums bolted from the starting gate with the speed of Swaps, a Thoroughbred that would bolster my faith the following month by upsetting the great Nashua in the Kentucky Derby. Only seven thousand fans braved the drizzle and fog to see the opener at Ebbets Field. I was not among them. I was stuck in a hard wooden chair in a fifth-grade classroom, looking out the window at the dark gray sky while Mrs. Rutledge, adjusting her bra strap every few seconds, explained what a vaccine was and drilled the class in the principal products of South American countries. When the three o'clock bell finally rang, I picked up my books, placed my brand-new lucky Dodger cap jauntily on my head, and bolted. By the time I got to Jake's, it was the bottom of the seventh inning and the score was Dodgers one, Pirates one. It was then that I began to realize my importance to the team.

No sooner did I have my egg cream in hand than Junior Gilliam socked a homer over the right field scoreboard to break the tie. After a double, a walk, and a sacrifice fly, Jackie Robinson stepped up to bat with runners on first and third. Robby was in the opening lineup after all; not even Walter Alston was dumb enough to keep him out. He bunted. It was a beauty, set down with delicate precision on the damp grass, too hard for the pitcher to field, too slow for the infielders, too shocking to anticipate. All the Pirates could do was ask themselves why a thirty-six-year-old player would bunt with two out and the baseline as slippery as a trout. To score a run and inspire his teammates, that's why. And Robby did both. Swarthy Carl Furillo then cracked a shot that cleared the fence above the Gem Razor Blade sign, and the score was 6–1. Carl Erskine shut down the Bucs the rest of the way. It was only one win over the lowly Pirates, but it was another sign.

In the next game, against the Giants on their home turf, Newcombe faced off against Sal "the Barber" Maglie, a nemesis whose lifetime record against the Bums was 22–8. Newk pitched courageously, and he helped in a way pitchers rarely do; he clouted two home runs. After the Brooks pounded Maglie into the shower, they pounced on the knuckleballs of his replacement,

Hoyt Wilhelm, and by the time the Giants came up to bat in the seventh, the Bums owned a 10–3 lead. Things looked so secure, I went outside to play punchball.

For punchball, bases were outlined in chalk on the black asphalt; the curbs were the foul lines. There were no pitchers. The batter flipped a spaldeen a foot or so in the air and either slapped it with an open hand or punched it with the palm side of his fist. The best players—and I was proud to be numbered among them—did this with a running start that propelled them toward first base once contact was made; they could make the ball curve or slice once it hit the ground, and place the ball precisely where they wanted it to go. The game was as popular as stickball.

Fortunately, you could not go far in the neighborhood without hearing the Dodger score. In my absence, Newcombe gave up five runs. I rushed back to my station at Jake's as the Giants came to bat in the last inning only two runs behind. Monte Irvin clouted a drive to left-center. Snider flew after it. Near the fence, he leaped high, snatched the ball out of the air, and crashed to the warning track. I had returned just in time. With two out and a man on base, the tying run stepped to the plate in the form of a pinch hitter whose name belonged on the desk of a bank president, not a scorecard. Mr. Foster Castleman lofted a long fly to left. Forks and glasses were suspended in midair. Sandy Amoros, the latest in a long line of journeymen to occupy left field, went back to the fence and caught the ball for the final out. It was a close call; I would not let my guard down the rest of the year.

Victories and positive portents multiplied each day. The versatile Flock, perhaps taking out their preseason frustration on opponents, won their first nine games, tying the all-time record for consecutive victories at the start of a season. Maybe Walter Alston was not retarded after all.

I considered Game Ten to be of singular importance. Tying a record is one thing; *breaking* it would be a major sign. However, to accomplish the task the Brooks would have to beat Robin Roberts, who had, over the course of an illustrious career in Philadelphia, won twice as many games at Ebbets Field as he'd lost. I decided to play hooky from school in order to lend my support from the first pitch to the last.

My accomplices were Louie Corso and Artie Finkelstein.

Louie was lean and dark-eyed with thick lips and cheeks that looked like he was sucking them in and holding them between his teeth. He was slightly goofy-looking then, but in a few years, when his cheeks filled out and his oversized lips and jungle of black hair settled into the right proportions, he would become even more handsome than his brother Iggy. Long before that, however, pubescent girls would dedicate their first, innocent sexual encounters to Louie Corso.

At times, if you ignored his size, Louie seemed more like a grown man than a preadolescent. He discussed sex as if he knew what he was talking about from personal experience. Louie was the first to know what a prophylactic was, how a sanitary napkin was used, how to unhook a brassiere. He could inhale a cigarette without coughing. He was even getting some fuzz under his arms. Rapid maturation was evidently a side effect of Angie Corso's spaghetti sauce.

Unlike his brother, Louie did not give the impression that life was an arena for him to goof around in. He shared with his father, Mike the Barber, the air of a savvy con man; he always looked as if he had some big deal cooking. However, Louie did not direct his energy into the customary channels. He was so bad at school, both in performance and conduct, that his teachers concluded he was impossibly dumb and irredeemably naughty. Louie's mother, Angie, thought she saw indications of her son's true calling in his penchant for singing along with Mike's opera recordings. She did not know he was making fun of them. Hence, Louie was coerced into taking piano lessons. He hated sitting still for the time required to practice, for Louie was cursed with what my grandmother called *shpilkas* and psychologists would one day call hyperactivity. One day, when I asked him why he didn't just quit the piano lessons, he explained that they meant a lot to his mother. Not that Louie was motivated by filial duty. The inducement was the extra fifty cents a week that Mike slipped him under the table to keep Angie happy.

That's when I finally understood my friend. Louie wasn't lazy. He was bored by schoolwork. He did not have a conduct problem; he was restless. His nonstop talking and his irritating habit of repeating himself were not signs of stupidity or bad manners. They were part of an energy package that also included darting eyeballs and fidgety legs and hands that stayed in one place about as often as a bee. Louie was always looking for something to do, and he had bigger fish to fry than the times tables and vocabulary lessons. Louie was destined to wheel and deal himself to a fortune.

Artie Finkelstein was a different breed, an introspective kid who didn't speak much but was uncommonly profound when he did. Artie and I had been in the same class for three consecutive years, in 3–1, 4–1, and 5–1, the number 1 designating the smartest class in the grade. But Artie deserved a class of his own. Artie was a brain, although his intelligence was deceptive to the unprepared; he always seemed on the brink of a yawn. He moved slowly; he spoke slowly; his prominent brow and bushy eyebrows gave him a slightly Neanderthal look, which was accentuated by a nose that was too wide for his face. If, when he grew up, Artie had elected to go into business instead of becoming a physicist, he would have shot to the top like a noiseless rocket. He would have lulled his competitors into complacency while picking their pockets. Artie's mind was as quick on the draw as Roy Rogers, whether calculating numbers or recalling a list of dates, or penetrating to the essence of a problem. My friend had rescued me on many occasions, when baseball had diverted my attention from academic duties.

Whereas his older siblings, Dizzy and Ruth, had their father's dark kinky hair and brown eyes, Artie had acquired his mother's coloring. Like Sylvia, he was so fair and blue-eyed that Hitler might have worshiped him despite his Semitic ancestry. He was, however, always unkempt. His shirttails would climb out of his pants like leaves seeking sunlight. His shoelaces were always untying themselves. Food stains materialized on his shirt even when he tucked a napkin into his collar. His hair was unruly no matter how much tonic he applied. He took to using gobs of Vaseline to keep his pompadour in place, but, by midday, locks of hair would shoot up randomly around his head like the soloists in a band.

As with all brains, no one expected Artie to be any good at sports. Here, too, he was deceptive. Although his coordination and skills were mediocre at best, he made up for it with an uncanny ability to know what was going to happen before anyone else did. In the outfield he always managed to station himself exactly where the next ball would be hit. Still, in the robust, high-status sports, Artie was merely average. But when it came to precision games like hit-the-penny or box ball or flipping baseball cards, Artie Finkelstein was the main man. It was as if he understood intuitively the laws of physics that governed the spin of a ball or the fall of a thin piece of cardboard.

When it came to doing something naughty, like playing hooky, Louie Corso required no persuasion. Artie, on the other hand, was not naturally defiant. He was Sylvia Finkelstein's pride and joy, a good boy, not like her Sheldon, aka Dizzy, the no-good beatnik.

Sylvia would pop up on Play Street waving a big white hanky, like a one-woman posse tracking down heedless sweat. She would make Artie eat, on schedule, a diet that included unconscionable quantities of spinach and broccoli, meat so rare you expected it to say ouch when you cut it, and generous servings of prunes to keep her son's bowels more regular than the Long Island Railroad. As part of her preventive hygiene regimen, Sylvia would examine the product of that regularity daily and plot the results for each of her offspring on a graph of stool consistency ranging from watery to rocklike. That summer, however, Dizzy had finally broken his mother of this routine. He obtained from Sharfin the butcher a pound of bloody chicken entrails and planted them in the toilet bowl for her to discover.

As Artie's rebelliousness was still subservient to his fear, he was usually loath to violate rules. In this case, it was easy because, for all his superior intelligence, Artie, like most males in the neighborhood, was unreasonably superstitious when it came to the Dodgers. On days when the team was playing at home, Artie would not step on a crack in the sidewalk; when the team was on the road, he would step on *every* crack. This made for rather awkward perambulation, and, I imagine, a great sense of liberation in winter, when he could walk any way he wanted to. His superstitious nature made it a cinch for Louie and me to convince Artie to ditch school that day and to volunteer his house as a hideout. Neither my mother nor Angie Corso could be counted on to stay away all afternoon, but Sylvia Finkelstein worked from eleven to four in a Pitkin Avenue haberdashery.

The plan was to leave for school in the morning, as always, and meet in the alley behind Sharfin's butcher shop. Artie and I got there first. We sat on the cold ground, shielded by two garbage cans, trying to keep the stench of rotting flesh away from our noses until Louie arrived. He was late because he had to wait for an opportunity to lift a few Chesterfields from his mother's pack. We wound through the alleys like fugitives to Rooney's Lot, where we had a secret hideout: under a row of slanted boards that had once been used as a ramp to lower barrels of pickle brine form the back door of a grocery to the lot, where they were emptied.

In the cramped, dark space, we killed an hour and a half until Sylvia left for work, keeping amused with supplies provided by Louie. We smoked cigarettes, Artie and I making the hideout sound like a tuberculosis ward and Louie puffing away, proud and nonchalant. Then Louie took out a book and a flashlight and we read aloud by turns. The book was called *The Hoods.* Louie had borrowed it from his brother Iggy's room. It was about young Jewish criminals on the Lower East Side a few decades earlier. In the passage Louie had us read, the main character, Noodles, enters the toilet in his tenement to find it already occupied by a plump, busty bowl of pudding with loose morals named Fanny. Fanny offers to let Noodles play between her legs if he promises to buy her a charlotte russe.

Of the two objects involved in the transaction, Artie and I were familiar with only one: the charlotte russe, a confection consisting of sponge cake topped with whipped cream and a maraschino cherry and encased in a cardboard cylinder. Louie seemed to be on more intimate terms with what Noodles obtained in the bargain. He described the terrain between Fanny's legs in graphic, almost clinical, detail, and the whole time Artie reread the passage Louie kept his hand in his pocket. I stuck my hand in my pocket too, but nothing I felt elicited a smile like the one on Louie's face. I resolved to attend Angie's Sunday-night dinners more frequently.

When the time was right, we made our way in stealth to the Finkelsteins' apartment. Taking care not to walk past uncurtained windows, we raided the cupboards and refrigerator, judiciously, so as not to leave behind any evidence. We played a few games of casino with the cards we found in a drawer; we laughed our way through a scrapbook of Finkelstein family snapshots; we tried on some of Sammy's neckties; and we found one of Sylvia's gargantuan brassieres and strapped it on our chests like armor and over our heads like helmets.

At one point, pretending I was going to the bathroom, I sneaked into Ruth Finkelstein's room. It was the neatest, tidiest room I had ever seen. It had blue wallpaper with a pattern of white flowers, a blue and beige twill rug, and diaphanous white curtains, the very curtains I could see fluttering in the wind from my bedroom. The bedspread, also blue to match the rug, did not have a wrinkle. Atop the desk, three textbooks were stacked in a perfect column next to a green ink blotter and a picture of Ruth with a smiling, crew-cut young man in a blazer with an insignia on the pocket. Then I noticed an object that made my blood surge: a pair of white cotton panties.

They were on the seat of the chair I could see from my window, tickled by the toes of a pair of nylons draped over the back. I dropped to my knees, below the windowsill, and crawled over. Shaking with a combination of fear and anticipation, I picked up the bloomers with my thumb and forefinger and lifted them slowly to my nose. I wanted to see if Louie was right, that the area between a girl's legs smelled like fish. I sniffed deeply. The panties did not smell like any seafood I'd ever been close to. The smell was distinct, but it was not fishy. I sniffed again. It was not sweet, like perfume, nor was it foul. It was a little of both. I knew I would never be able to describe the smell, but I also knew it was one that I wanted to sample again.

I replaced the panties just as I had found them, with the crotch toward the wall and the elastic waistline touching the back of the chair. Then I pushed the chair closer to the window. I did not move it far enough for the change of location to be noticed, but, I hoped, far enough to expose more of Ruth when she laid out her undies at night.

At twelve o'clock we opened the paper bags our mothers had packed for lunch. Both Artie and I traded Louie half of our sandwiches, salami and tuna respectively, for half of Angie Corso's meatball special on Italian bread. Even the son of the best cook in the neighborhood was averse to eating his own mother's food. Rejoicing in the discovery of a jar of Fox's U-Bet chocolate syrup, the only product suitable for preparing homemade egg creams, I whipped up three foaming beauties, adhering strictly to Jake's hallowed recipe, as Louie treated us to a series of poems ("Boidie, boidie, in the sky, why you do dat in my eye? I'm sure glad cows can't fly") and riddles ("Why did the moron throw the clock out the window? To see time fly!").

The egg creams were consumed before the National Anthem ended. My lucky hat was in place. Artie had stepped on no cracks. Louie fondled a silver horseshoe. With all that going against him, Robin Roberts, the Phillies' pitcher, may as well have been Marty Klinger tossing spaldeens. The Bums clobbered him. Robinson, Snider, Amoros, and rookie Don Zimmer all socked homers. By the time Sylvia Finkelstein got home, every trace of anyone having been in the apartment had been erased and the Dodgers were emptying their bench. The final score was 14–4. For the first time in the history of the world, a major league team had won ten games in a row to start a season.

That night, after a supper of veal cutlets, mashed potatoes, and peas, the four Stone men munched Oreos while Dad drank coffee and the rest of us milk, for the calcium. We tried to explain the significance of the Dodgers' record winning streak to the only female in the house.

My mother could not grasp it. Not that she didn't understand baseball; she'd have to have been deaf in *both* ears and blind as well to have that shortcoming in our house. No, she just could not comprehend the magnitude of the accomplishment. "Ten games doesn't seem like a hell of a lot," she said as she cleared the table. "There's a hundred and fifty something in a season, isn't there?"

We looked to our father for enlightenment. "She's a girl," he explained.

But this girl had a sixth sense for mischief. As I was brushing my teeth that night, Mom slipped into the bathroom, leaned against the door and said, "Have a good time today?"

I asked her what she meant. It was just a day like any other day.

She smiled. "Did Artie do a good job with my signature?" I was dumbstruck. Artie had forged absence notes for all three hooky players. "Next time you need a day off, discuss it with me," she said. "Maybe I'll write you a real note."

To the air of springtime in Brooklyn, the scent of elation was added. It was a cautious elation, for it would take more than ten wins in a row to overcome our dark ancestral memories. Hardened fans were heard to say, "Dem Bums'll come down ta oit one a dese days."

Them Bums did come down to earth, of course. They took a 4–0 lead into the eighth inning the next day, but the Giants scored five times to pocket the game. The streak was over, but (and this was a sign of no small dimension), another began immediately. By the time the azaleas had blossomed in Prospect Park, the team had opened up a nine and a half game lead. They were 22–2, and the two losses were by one run each. If they could keep up that pace, their record by season's end would be 141–13.

Only eleven-year-olds would dare contemplate such an achievement, of course; no team in history had ever won more than 116. But throughout Brooklyn wounded veterans of campaigns past, who had not dared let their hopes rise, and doomsayers who believed that the Dodgers were over the hill, were rapidly changing their tunes. As always, the expectation of ruin was never far away, but it had been pushed aside far enough for visions of old to crawl up from the dark recesses of our minds and make their way to our lips in bold assertions. We're going all the way. We're invincible. This is the year of destiny.

If the Dodgers' V-8 acceleration through the early schedule was joyous to other fans, to Frank Stone it was bliss, for it juiced up Hubbell just in time for the final step in the master plan. Shortly after the historic ten-game streak, Hubbell's high school team opened its season and my brother picked up a win. Hubbell himself was dissatisfied with his performance; he'd given up three runs and left under siege in the eighth inning. My father was, as ever, encouraged. However, he did notice a late-inning tendency for Hubbell's shoulder to drop when he threw a curveball, perhaps allowing the batter to anticipate the pitch. This, he concluded, was the result of fatigue, and the remedy was weight lifting. To Hubbell's regimen was added daily exercises with a pair of dumbbells, with extra emphasis on squats to build up the leg muscles. As always, he went along with the program, but I could tell he found it tedious.

Hubbell ended his final scholastic season with respectable, although not spectacular, numbers. He earned an honorable mention on the all-city team. After graduation, while his friends took summer jobs, hunted for career opportunities, or set out to get some kicks before starting college, he plunged into step two of the final phase with customary zeal, undeterred, or so it seemed, by the lack of attention he'd received from the scouts. Each day he would pitch to my father or the box spring, rounding up volunteers—even, when necessary, guys with pint-sized strike zones like me—to bat against him, jog through the streets, do wind sprints in the park and calisthenics in Rooney's Lot, squeeze hand grips and flex dumbbells, and study his big league models in person or on TV. Despite the hard work, his first three American Legion games were undistinguished; twice he got knocked out before the sixth inning, and he won a 5–4 game in which he walked six batters.

Self-doubt started to creep into Hubbell's psyche, but my father buoyed him. Frank Stone was sanguine; to him, half the problem was the mediocre team Hubbell had behind him, and the other half was a matter of adjusting to the new competition level. One day, while listening to a Dodger game on the radio as he shuffled passengers around Manhattan, he realized what was missing. Hubbell needed another pitch in his repertoire, a trick pitch, a clutch pitch, a trademark pitch that people would talk about, a pitch that would curve away from right-handed batters, a pitch like the one his namesake had perfected back in the thirties. Why hadn't he thought of this before? It was so damn obvious!

Frank Stone could not contain himself. He dumped his cab in the garage early, told Sy Kramer, the dispatcher, that he had a stomachache, and dashed home to start teaching his son how to throw a screwball. ("Perfect name for one of my husband's ideas," said my mother.) That night, Hubbell ate with his right hand while gripping a baseball in his left and snapping his wrist clockwise over and over again.

For me, liberated from school and still more than a year shy of the landmark birthday that would—as per Frank Stone's negotiated settlement with his wife—initiate the mature phase of my training, July was splendid. The steaming streets, vacant lots, and fetid alleys were, to my friends and me, as fair as the green lawns and manicured courts of a summer camp in the mountains. We played one game after another, from early morning until long after the orange sun dipped behind the apartment buildings and you could barely tell the difference between a flying spaldeen and a moth. At night we convened again, to shoot hoops in school-yards dimly lit by distant street lamps, or to play hide-and-seek and ringolevio in the spooky shadows of alleyways and cellars, or to roast marshmallows and potatoes—*mickeys,* we called them—over a fire in Rooney's Lot.

Two or three times a week we splashed around in Betsy Head pool, a huge public facility with a ten-cent admission charge and enough chlorine to disinfect India. We would carry our bathing trunks rolled up in a towel, undress on long rows of benches and stuff our street clothes into paper bags, which were stored away by an attendant behind a counter. The attendant would give us elastic bands with round, brass wafers on them, each with a number that enabled us to redeem our belongings at day's end. Betsy Head was an early lesson in gender differences. Evidently, girls could be trusted with lockers of their own, but boys had to check paper bags with attendants because they liked to break into other boys' lockers or steal their keys.

On the hottest days Artie, Louie, and I might subway to the sands of Brighton Beach or Far Rockaway. These were long journeys, but major portions were scenic since the routes were largely above ground. Unless beaten to it by riders who boarded earlier, we would stand at the window of the front car and imagine that we were steering the train ourselves. The trek home from the beach always seemed to take twice as long as the ride there, perhaps because we were transporting sand between our toes and in the crotches of our bathing trunks to deposit on our mothers' carpets. When traveling to the beach seemed too daunting a prospect, we cooled off at matinees packed with cartoons and serials in picture palaces whose advertisements promised air-conditioning, or in geysers created by opening fire hydrants with a monkey wrench, or we might take to sea on the Staten Island Ferry like Clark Gable in *Mutiny on the Bounty,* or glide in paddle boats on the lake in Prospect Park. We might let out our aggres-

sion by playing War—one side Americans, the other Germans—
with rifles jerry-rigged from pieces of plywood. This was more a
macabre exercise in acting than in combat strategy; the accolades
one could receive by dying an inventive death made it more
rewarding to get shot than to kill someone else.

Baseball, of course, was a presence as constant as dust. My
Little League team, the Lincoln Savings Bank Pennies, was as hot
as the Dodgers, and I was playing like the Hall of Famer I was
named for. According to my calculations, the Rajah (for that was
my nom de diamond that summer) was batting .464, although
some of my persnickety teammates believed it inappropriate to
award myself a hit when a pop fly was dropped or a ground ball
caromed off the shins of an infielder.

As often as our parents and allowances would permit, my
friends and I availed ourselves of our constitutional right to freedom of worship: we went to Ebbets Field. Our mothers would
wrap sandwiches in waxed paper, toss in a package of Devil Dogs
or Twinkies and a pint of milk that would get too warm to drink
by the time it was opened, and stuff it all into a paper bag. We
would pay our seventy-five cents and hike up the long chain of
ramps to the center field bleachers. As early birds, we could watch
batting practice, soak up the atmosphere of the ballpark, and
exchange baseball gossip and folklore with our fellow partisans.
We preferred front row seats a bit toward left field. On most
plays, this put us directly in line with the broad back of Number
4, the Duke. We would yell down to our hero, knowing he could
hear every word even if he pretended not to.

From those seats we could also see the entire scoreboard, on
which numbers would mysteriously appear in the appropriate
slots to keep us informed of the data on our own game and the
scores and current pitchers for every game in both leagues. A big,
black monolith rising up from the warning track in right field, the
scoreboard was surrounded by a high screen that compensated for
the short distance from home plate to home run territory. The
park had been shoehorned into a swampy lot in what had once
been known as Pigtown; the right field foul pole was a mere 297
feet away, as compared to 348 in left.

Above the scoreboard was a neon beer sign—Schaefer—
whose *h* and *e* would blink to indicate whether a particular play

was ruled a hit or an error. Under the data-bearing part of the scoreboard was a strip of yellow with the words HIT SIGN, WIN SUIT. The offer, from Abe Stark's clothing store on Pitkin Avenue, was redeemed about as often as a no-hitter was pitched, for Carl Furillo patrolled the area in front of it like a settler protecting his ranch. The Reading Rifle was Louie Corso's favorite player, a *paisan* with a compact body and a compact swing and an arm so strong that he was known to field sure singles and throw out the batter at first base. Skoonj (short for *scungilli,* the Italian word for snails) did not let many balls hit that sign. Nevertheless, aided by the prominent ad, Abe Stark's store became prosperous and the proprietor was elected borough president.

The home of the Dodgers had, by then, ascended to the status of legend. Ebbets Field was a place of pilgrimage for baseball fans across the country, even those who had big league stadiums at home. It was a magnet for dignitaries. The King of Iraq paid it homage on a state visit. Politicians vied to throw out ceremonial first balls. Douglas MacArthur showed up shortly after Harry Truman stripped him of command in Korea, remarking, "I've been told that one has not lived unless one has been to Ebbets Field and has watched the Dodgers play baseball." The general was right. Years later it would be hard to figure out who deserved more pity, those who had known Ebbets Field and lost it, or those who never had the privilege of watching a ball game there. The place offered more laughs than a burlesque house, more catharses than a tragedy at Epidaurus, more genuine communal feeling than a church.

When we could not worship in person, we did it from afar. Whatever we did, wherever we went, the Dodgers were with us, in transistor radios and televisions and newspapers and inexhaustible conversations. To our joy, the team won and won and won, despite a barrage of injuries.

At one point the Dodgers' lead grew to thirteen and a half games over the Braves and even more over the Giants. Chests were puffed up and heads carried high from the Battery to Coney. But did anyone think the lead was safe? Would anyone allow confidence to slip into complacency? Not us. Not me. Thirteen and a half games had been precisely the Dodgers' lead in August of 1951, and we, fans and players alike, had become cocky at incalculable cost. After sweeping a three-game series from the Giants, the '51 Flock let their hatred for their rivals get the best of them. They gloated, they taunted, they shouted insults across the thin partition between the two clubhouses, and manager Charlie Dressen proclaimed, "The Giants is dead." But the Giants wasn't dead. Ignited by their manager, Leo the Lip Durocher, they responded to the affront like warriors. They won sixteen games in a row, thirty-seven of their last forty-four, and snatched the pennant right out of the mitts of the astonished, humiliated Bums, burying Grandpa Abe in the bargain.

We would not, God help us, make the same mistake in '55. Older and wiser, the Flock soared past the thirteen-and-a-half-game standard like Chuck Yeager shattering the sound barrier. Then one steamy day, at a newsstand, I saw Roy Campanella's egg-cream-shaded face on the cover of *Time* magazine, and for a moment The Thing peeked back at me from the cover of *Newsweek.* Everyone knew it was a jinx to have your picture on the *Time* cover; I feared for the catcher and the team. But the next day against the Braves, Campy socked a round-tripper with two on and two out in the ninth inning to cap a stunning comeback, 11–10, and bump the lead to fifteen and a half games. It was more than just another victory; it was a convincing sign that 1955 was not 1951. As Dick Young put it in the next day's *News,* Roy "hammered the hex into the left field bleachers."

This year the world was ready for the Dodgers. This year the Academy Award for best picture would go to *Marty,* a black-and-white film about a simple, ordinary working stiff from the Bronx who finds his heart's desire and claims his dignity. This year the Senate, back in the hands of Democrats, had finally throttled the demagogic ravings of Joe McCarthy. This year, by Supreme Court decree, the nation's public schools were to be integrated "with all deliberate speed." This year, Rosa Parks would refuse to give up her seat on a Montgomery, Alabama, bus. In a year like this, could history deny a populist, Democratic team, a team for simple, ordinary working stiffs, a team of underdogs that might, on any given day, send five descendants of slaves onto the playing field at the same time?

That night, after the win over the Braves, my efforts on the April day I'd played hooky with Artie and Louie finally paid off.

I saw Ruth Finkelstein in just her panties and bra, when she leaned over to pick up a slip that had fallen from her chair—the very chair that I had moved closer to the window. It was only a glimpse, but I snuggled contentedly under the covers, and for a moment I swore I could sniff the pungent scent of her panties. On my wall was the *Time* magazine portrait of Campy, along with a blue Dodger pennant, the official team photo, a 1953 scorecard with the autographs of Hodges, Reese, and Furillo, and the front page of the current yearbook with an illustration of a Bum reaching for a star with 1955 written on it. Campy's pudgy image smiled down at me.

As I drifted into sleep, the voice of destiny whispered in my ear: "This is next year."

The neighborhood was as ebullient as Rio before Lent, and Frank Stone was the King of the Carnival. Even under normal conditions, mine was the most popular household in the neighborhood. The Stones were fun and they ran a loose, boisterous home, with few of the regulations that ruled in other apartments. There were no plastic slipcovers on the furniture; kids could put their feet up on the sofa and drape their legs over the arms of the chairs. The cupboard and refrigerator, while often lacking in the principal food groups, were always well-stocked with munchies, and you didn't have to ask permission to raid them. You could relax around the Stones; if a dirty word slipped off your tongue, there would be no admonishments from Frank or Jeannie, for they were likely to use the word themselves.

Now, with the Dodgers power-steering through the National League schedule like my father through early morning traffic, our apartment turned into *The Colgate Comedy Hour.* My parents, always openly affectionate, held hands and hugged with disgusting frequency, and when they kissed, I could sometimes see their tongues lapping each other like two of Round Man's pets. My father even made a rare good business decision: figuring that the rest of the borough was also basking in the Dodger sunshine, he hacked in Brooklyn more than he normally did, and as a result, his tips soared way above average.

My father's spirits were further boosted by the progress Hubbell was making in mastering the screwball; it snapped and crackled like Rice Krispies and was beginning to find the strike zone with some regularity. Factoring in a sum he could reasonably divert from the bonus the Dodgers would soon bestow on his son, my father revised his timetable for owning his own taxi. That the additional pitch had not substantially improved Hubbell's won-lost record or his earned run average did not trouble my father in the least, for such things took time. It bothered Hubbell, though, and what bothered him more was the fact that he had no indication that any scouts were salivating after him with a contract in hand.

My father explained this discrepancy with two theories: first, success might have bred complacency in the Dodger scouting system, in which case he would personally find a way to bring Hubbell to the attention of the right people; and second, the team was too preoccupied by the pennant race to make offers at this time.

"I guarantee you," countered Hubbell, "when they wanted Koufax, they didn't wait for nothing."

Chapter Eight

On a steamy day in early August I unknowingly set in motion a series of events that would change the lives of both my brothers, and, by extension, the whole family. I was sitting on the top step of a stoop on Sterling Place, sipping a bottle of Yoo-Hoo, a sweet chocolate beverage that was the closest thing to a portable egg cream.

Louie removed a deck of cards from his pocket. "Pick a card, any card," he said.

I selected a card and turned it over. It was the five of diamonds, and one of the diamonds was located in the belly of an otherwise naked woman. Louie grinned. He and I examined the rest of the deck while, below us, Artie demonstrated his transcendent skill at stoopball.

Stoopball was an individual sport. The player who was *up* stood in the gutter next to the curb and threw a spaldeen against the stoop of a brownstone or row house. The ideal stoop was ten to fifteen feet wide with four or five steps and solid sides so that errant balls would bounce back to the players instead of careening down the sidewalk, perhaps never to be seen again. If the thrown ball rebounded off the steps and back to the player on one bounce, it was worth five points, assuming it was caught. If it was dropped, or if it bounced more than once, the player was out and the next one took his turn. If the ball hit the crease between two steps and popped back to the player on a fly, it was worth ten points. If it hit the *point* of a step and was caught on a fly, it was a stoopball jackpot, one hundred points.

Artie Finkelstein was so good at stoopball, it was futile to play with him, but we had to indulge him from time to time or he would not join in the games we wanted to play. *Ping* went the ball when it hit the stoop. *Clop* it went when it returned to Artie's hands. Ping, clop, ping, clop. Five points here, ten points there, a hundred—a lethal monotony. Artie had spotted Louie and me two hundred points each in a game in which a thousand won, and he was already way ahead.

"Five hundred," Artie said. Ping, clop. "Five ten." Ping, clop. "Five fifteen." So casual was his stance, so loose and unaimed were his throws, that he seemed not to be paying attention. Artie had mastered the Zen of stoopball. Ping, clop. "Five twenty-five."

He paused briefly to let someone pass. It was my brother. Round Man would normally be courteous enough to walk around a stoopball player instead of between him and the stoop, but he was not himself at the moment. He was wearing a white shirt and red tie, and he was crying. I made him stop and tell me what was wrong.

"Rocky's dead," he said, sniffing wayward snot back into his nostrils.

"Marciano?" said Louie, horrified at the thought.

"No, stupid, my turtle," explained Round Man. Then, to me, he said, "She stepped on him."

"Who did?"

"Mom! Who do you think? She hates my pets."

"She does not. It must've been an accident."

"She did it on purpose," my brother insisted. He was holding a matchbox, which I assumed to be Rocky's coffin, and a cross made by pasting together two Popsicle sticks. "I'm going to bury him in Rooney's Lot," he said.

"What's with the cross?"

"Rocky was Catholic," said Round Man, and he waddled off to conduct the funeral services.

Meanwhile, Artie was in a magical groove. As the ball pinged and clopped, he called out his accumulating score like a bookkeeper reading numbers off an adding machine. Bored, I began to recount for my friends the glorious night of Pee Wee Reese's thirty-seventh birthday party at Ebbets Field. It had been the emotional high point of our triumphant summer. The only captain the Dodgers ever had, the reliable Little Colonel was perhaps the most beloved player on the team, respected not only for his adroit batsmanship and flawless fielding, but for his dignified leadership. Had Pee Wee, a Southerner, not conspicuously befriended Jackie Robinson in his tumultuous season of revolution, baseball's great experiment might have gone askew like a wild pitch. And what had Pee Wee to show for his service? He was the only player in history to play in five World Series for the same team and lose all five to the same opponent.

As instructed by the Dodgers, everyone in the standing-room-only crowd brought matches and cigarette lighters. When the house lights dimmed, 33,033 flames lit the ancient ballpark and the crowd sang "Happy Birthday" to the captain. I described for my buddies the flickering lights and the chorus of ardent voices, and how Happy Felton, the emcee, presented Pee Wee with a string of gifts. I told them how Round Man's pet frog, Merlin, sprang loose from his master's hand and wrought havoc in the crowd until a guy who had had too many beers booted it like a football into the lower deck. Hubbell reared back to punch the drunk, but my father stopped him; not to keep the peace, but to protect his son's pitching hand.

The only thing I did not tell Artie and Louie was how my father wept when Pee Wee made his thank-you speech. Until then, the only other time I had seen him cry was at Grandpa Abe's funeral. That is, except for every Wednesday night between ten and ten-thirty when he watched *This Is Your Life.* I would never know if those ritual tears were tears of contagion, caught from those whose lives Ralph Edwards honored, or tears of remorse for living a life that would never be celebrated outside the neighborhood, much less on national television.

Ping, clop, ping, clop went Artie's spaldeen.

"Eight twenty," said Artie. Ping, clop. "Eight thirty. You know, *we* ought to have a Day for someone."

It was just a casual remark, but its impact would be enormous. Louie picked right up on it. There was a long tradition of Days and Nights to honor the greats, he pointed out. So if Days were such a great thing, why don't we have one too?

"For who?" I asked skeptically.

We ran down a list of names, from older notables such as Jake to illustrious Big Guys like Harry the Horse, but none of the choices seemed satisfactory.

"Game!" said Artie. He had run off 630 points in a row. He

hopped up the steps of the stoop. "Let's have a Day for Round Man," he said.

Artie, the idea man, suggested holding Round Man Day before the annual softball game between the kids of Sterling Place and the kids of Saratoga Avenue. Louie took over from there, shamelessly coercing every merchant in the neighborhood to contribute. He convinced Pincus the printer to engrave invitations for free, and Herbie the mailman to deliver them unstamped. Sam the Fruit Store Man donated watermelons; Happy and Henny Horowitz contributed loaves of rye bread and a pair of salamis; Meyer's Candystore supplied pretzels and licorice sticks; Marvin the seltzer man threw in a few cases of soda, including Round Man's favorite, Dr. Brown's Cel-Ray Tonic. Jake refused my request to whip up a few gallons of egg cream on the grounds that his reputation would suffer if the brew were to lose its distinctive cachet in transit, but he pitched in with a couple of pies and a box of Danish. From other merchants Louie solicited decorations, an assortment of gifts for the honoree, even a public address system.

The event was held in the aboriginal schoolyard of P.S. 144. The cyclone fence—the very one that had been dubbed Frankie's Fence in my father's honor—sagged in places like the shoulders of old Jack Kass, and it had holes big enough for his wife, the Sphinx, to walk through. The playing field was pocked with potholes and cracks that made every ball that hit the ground a high adventure. Behind each foul line were three rows of wooden bleachers, which Louie had gussied up in bunting, but few of the spectators elected to sit in the seats for fear the structure would collapse. Most of the hundred or so attendees—the largest crowd ever assembled for the annual softball game—remained standing; others squatted on the ground, leaned against the solid sections of the fence or sat on their own folding chairs. Louie provided the Stone family with a private box, decked out in red, white, and blue crepe paper, next to the Sterling Place bench.

I sat with Hubbell and our parents while Louie, the master of ceremonies, sermonized with surprising eloquence about the spirit of sportsmanship and the sunny disposition that had earned Hank Stone his Day. He then turned over the microphone to entertainment. Mike the Barber played "Lady of Spain" on the accordion. In bosom-heaving Wagnerian style, Sylvia Finkelstein sang Round Man's favorite song, "How Much is That Doggie in the Window?" And the Big Guys, with Dizzy singing lead and Harry bass, and Hubbell, Benny, and Mr. Big doing harmony, knocked out the crowd with an a cappella rendering of "Sh-Boom," complete with precision choreography. Their nights spent harmonizing in hallways had paid off nicely for Dizzy and the Deans.

Throughout the festivities, Round Man stood, baseball cap in hand, sometimes blushing, always smiling like a Buddha. When the entertainment concluded, Louie presented the honoree with an array of gifts: a free pass to Loew's Pitkin, a case of Oreo cookies, a rare Van Lingle Mungo baseball card, two tickets to the Bronx Zoo, a water gun, a coonskin cap, a Captain Video ring with a special decoder, a Duncan yo-yo that glowed in the dark, a turtle to replace Rocky, and, the pièce de résistance, a cocker spaniel. Without hesitation Round Man named his new pet after Davy Crockett; it was love at first sight. With tears flowing over his apple cheeks, Hank thanked everyone profusely. When he finished, my mother, swallowing her dismay over having a new dog in her life, led the standing ovation. My father cried. He was seeing his third son—the forgotten one, the mistake, the klutz who would spoil the Stones' chance for a big league family hat trick—as if for the first time.

Round Man's glory had only just begun. And my other brother was about to have an epiphany of his own.

The Sterling-Saratoga game was for boys under twelve. The Sterling squad, depleted by a string of inconvenient birth dates, was able to scrape up only ten players. This gave us a single substitute: Round Man, who was assigned—happily, it seemed—the job of coach. And that wasn't our only disadvantage: the Saratoga team was virtually the same as the one that had whipped us by six runs the year before. But, inspired by the pregame festivities and sparked by my scintillating play at shortstop, our team performed beyond its capacity. Entering the ninth inning, we were ahead, 15–7.

That's when the Big Guys started chanting, "We want Round Man!" "We want Round Man!"

As team captain, I called time out and discussed the situation with my teammates. Carried away by emotion, I offered to take myself out of the game and replace myself with my kid brother.

As Hank raced eagerly onto the field to the accompaniment of applause and demeaning, but well-meant, remarks, Hubbell grabbed the microphone. With amplification, his voice was richer and more mellifluous than ever. "Hold everything, sports fans," he announced, "it looks like the Sterling squad is using its secret weapon. Yes, yes, it's the one, the only, Round Man!"

I shifted some personnel around and stationed Hank behind home plate, figuring that, with an eight-run lead, he could do little harm as catcher. However, this strategy not only created annoying delays when one pitched ball after another escaped his clutches, but it turned the Saratogas into a bunch of Jackie Robinsons. They bunted, and bunted again, taking bases with impunity on passed balls and Hank's wild attempts to throw them out. With the score 15–10, I moved Round Man to right field and instructed our swift center fielder, Johnny Owens, a ringer whom I imported from *over there,* to cover for him.

"Hit to right field," yelled Saratoga supporters, their spirits buoyed by their team's rally.

"That's just what the Sterlings want," said Hubbell to the crowd. "They'll sucker 'em into hitting to right field, and Round Man will gobble up every ball."

"Looks like he gobbled up a hundred already," said Marty Klinger.

Johnny Owens could not cover for Round Man. Not even Willie Mays could have covered for Round Man. The first Saratoga batter hit a fly ball to right. Hubbell called it: "Round Man comes in . . . he goes back . . . he comes in . . . It's over his head! How about that!"

Johnny raced the ball down and fired it back to the infield, but not before two runs had scored. The next batter hit one to approximately the same spot. This time Round Man fell down. Next came a ground ball past the first baseman. Round Man charged it, but the ball skipped between his legs, and he fell on his face when he turned to chase it.

"Our statistician has informed me that Hank Stone has just set a league record for falling down," said Hubbell. The spectators were now as interested in his commentary as they were in the game. "He seems a trifle rusty. He's been on the bench a lot, and that's tough on a fierce competitor like Round Man."

"Must be tough on the *bench* too," said Harry the Horse.

"Fans with low IQs may laugh," countered Hubbell, "but remember this: Round Man makes up in spirit what he lacks in skills. Which is exactly why the team rejected that offer to trade him for Ernie Banks. The man is a winner, and winners get the last laugh."

So far the laughs were going Saratoga's way. I watched from the bench, helpless to do anything more than encourage my mates, as one batter after another took advantage of our right fielder. While Hubbell mixed trenchant observations with wise-cracks, like some combination of Red Barber and Groucho Marx, more Saratogas crossed the plate, and soon the score was tied. With two out and the bases loaded, the Saratoga batter lofted a flyball right at Round Man. Johnny Owens, already exhausted from trying to play two positions, sprinted over but had no chance to get there in time. The ball descended. Round Man braced himself. He squinted into the sun. He raised his glove. The ball hit him smack in the forehead.

"That's using your head!" said Hubbell as the three base runners raced toward home plate.

The ball ricocheted high in the air. Round Man bounced to the ground, flat on his back. The ball came down on the perfect dome of his belly. There it paused for one tantalizing moment, as if getting its bearings. Then it rolled down the hillside of Round Man's topography. All seemed lost.

And the ball fell, kerplunk, right into Round Man's glove, which was lying inertly at his side with his hand still in it. "Yer out!" yelled Mr. Big, the umpire.

"Oh, Doctor, a spectacular catch!" Hubbell roared as the crowd went wild. "How about that, ladies and gentlemen! Willie Mays never caught one on his back!"

The Saratogas argued vehemently, but Mr. Big was un-moved. The ball never touched the ground. It was three out, the score still tied. We, the home team, had to score now, for there was no way we could hold off our fired-up opponents with Round Man on the field.

Our first batter popped up. Louie hit a feeble ground ball to the first baseman. My spot in the batting order was due up, which meant that Round Man would bat. We tried to sneak Johnny Owens to the plate instead, but the Saratogas could not be fooled. Their partisans, smelling victory, hooted with fiendish delight when Hank rolled into the batter's box.

The Sterling supporters shouted encouragement: "Go get 'em, Hank!" "You can do it, Round Man!"

With extreme solemnity, Hubbell intoned, "Ladies and gentlemen, this is a historic occasion. This might be the last at-bat in the legendary career of Hammerin' Hank Stone. Yes, Round Man has announced that after this game he will hang up his spikes and go lion hunting in Africa with Ernest Hemingway. His uniform will be sent directly to the Hall of Fame."

Round Man's batting stance resembled a hippopotamus hanging from a subway strap with two hands, its body twisted by the pressure of the other passengers. He swung at the first pitch and missed it by about two feet. The momentum of the bat spun him around like a top and he plopped onto his behind. "A ferocious swing," said Hubbell. "Man, if Round Man connects, look out."

Hank missed the second pitch just as badly, although he managed to keep his feet.

"He has 'em right where he wants 'em," Hubbell admonished the laughing fans. "Round Man is at his best when his back is to the wall."

"Keep your eye on the ball, Hank!" yelled my father. It was the first baseball advice he'd given his third son since Round Man's waistline passed the thirty-inch mark. Hank nodded toward his father like a man to whom the mystery of existence had just been communicated. On the next pitch he kept his eye on the ball, uncorked a robust swing, and managed to catch a piece of it. The ball bounced on home plate, caromed meekly into the air, landed about eight feet in front of the plate, and died.

"A wicked smash!" Hubbell called it.

Round Man put his head down and took off for first base. His arms and legs churned feverishly, but the overall effect was that of a stationary turbine with pumping pistons. The Saratoga catcher, thinking the pitcher would field the ball, broke into a crowd-pleasing imitation of Round Man's style of locomotion.

But the pitcher was absorbed in watching Round Man plod his way up the baseline. When the players realized that neither was going for the ball, they both did. They arrived at the same time, bent down, and bumped their heads together.

"And Round Man outlegs it to first. What blinding speed!" said Hubbell.

The next batter was our first baseman, Big Bad Bobby Berkowitz, an oversized kid who wore his T-shirt sleeves cut off at the shoulder like Ted Kluszewski. Bobby knew his job. He had to hit one out of the park, or else so far that even Round Man could run from first to home before the fielders caught up with it. He came close. He hit a scorcher to straightaway center field that just missed clearing the fence. By the time the Saratoga outfielders caught up to the carom, Bobby was rounding second base. The problem was, so was Round Man. Bobby did everything but pick him up and carry him, but Hank could move no faster than he was already moving.

Round Man continued his courageous gallop toward third. The Saratoga outfielders relayed the ball crisply to the infield and would have had the out if the ball had not bounced on a crack and skipped past the fielders. Our whole team stood along the third base foul line, waving our arms like Ippish, exhorting Round Man to stop. Perhaps he didn't see us, for his eyes had become nothing more than narrow creases in a wet, crimson moonscape.

"Holy cow, he's rounding third!" yelled Hubbell. "He's headed for the plate!"

When the ball arrived in the catcher's mitt, Round Man was about halfway home. The Saratoga catcher, the biggest player on their team, waved an imaginary cape at the onrushing Hank like a matador, and, with a grand flourish, prepared to apply the tag. Round Man never slowed down.

"He won't be denied!" Hubbell shouted.

Hank lowered his shoulder and rammed into the catcher. The two young leviathans crashed to the hot cement in a heap.

"The ball is loose!"

The catcher tried to snatch the errant ball and, at the same time, prevent Round Man from crawling the remaining few feet to home plate by pinning one of Hank's legs between his own.

But my brother tore himself loose and scratched toward his goal, blood dripping from his nose, his lips, his elbows, his knees. The Saratoga pitcher chased the ball down. He took a running leap at Round Man. But a split second before the tag, Hank plopped onto the chalk-drawn plate like a walrus collapsing on an ice floe.

"Safe!" yelled Mr. Big.

"How about that!" said Hubbell. "What an ending! He was a joke, a laughingstock. Now he's a hero! Ladies and gentlemen, if there's a Hall of Fame for guts, Hank Stone should be the first one inducted."

Sterling supporters swarmed their hero and tried to hoist his bruised and bleeding body onto their shoulders, but he was too much weight in too little space and he had no corners for their hands to grip, so they settled for mobbing him.

"That kid's got the heart of a champeen," said my jubilant father as he and my mother rushed to join the throng. "Let that be an inspiration to you guys."

I suddenly knew how Hank must have felt most of his life: left out as his brothers monopolized the attention of the adult population. His pain must have been masked by congeniality, insulated by layers of fat, smoothed over by the unconditional love he received from his animals. My mother must have realized this as well, because from that day forth she made a point of spending more time with her youngest son, and implored Hubbell and me to include him in our activities. I'm certain Round Man never forgot his Day. If, in the future, he should feel self-conscious about his appearance, if ever some psychic scar should surface, etched in his subconscious by the remarks of unfeeling boys or his own sense of shame, he would always have the pre-game ceremonies and his own heroics to remind him of his exemplary virtues.

My older brother would never be the same either. Hubbell's performance at the microphone earned him almost as many plaudits as Round Man.

"You are something else, my man," said Dizzy, slapping both of Hubbell's palms.

"Where the hell did you learn to talk so good?" asked Harry the Horse.

"When you're done playing ball, you should like announce games on TV and shit," suggested Marty Klinger.

"No jive, man," said Dizzy. "You make that chump Sonny Scott sound like Elmer Fudd."

"Actually, you should think about that, Hubbell," said the always-sensible Benny Mason. "TV's going to be big. Pretty soon there'll be one in every home. In *color*."

"Get outta here. Color?" said Harry the Horse.

I looked at Hubbell's eyes. He was having an epiphany. He heard every word, but his mind was somewhere else, perhaps in the broadcasting booth at Ebbets Field.

Chapter Nine

Two weeks after Round Man Day, with the Dodgers coasting toward the pennant, The Thing's sabbatical ended. He blew into town on the forty-mile-per-hour gusts provided by Hurricane Connie.

On the afternoon of his arrival, I was stuck babysitting my cousin, a four-year-old brat named Judy. Judy's mother, my aunt Libby, had a friend who worked for a clothing manufacturer that had botched a line of trousers, cutting the legs too short for normal men. On the assumption that the pants, whose price had been slashed to match the legs, might fit Round Man, Aunt Libby had taken my mother and younger brother to the company's warehouse in Red Hook. I was entrusted with Judy.

After making me watch her play ventriloquist for a coven of dolls on the living room floor, the minx finally got sleepy. I parked her on Round Man's bed just in time to watch *Amos and Andy* in peace. One of my favorite episodes was on that day, the one in which Kingfish sells Andy a cross-country trailer trip and never leaves Central Park. When the show ended, Kingfish's scam having backfired as usual, the news came on the air. John Cameron Swayze informed me that twenty-seven entertainers had been called before the House Un-American Activities Committee to determine whether Communist propaganda was penetrating the brains of moviegoers. I wondered if my mother had burned *all* of my uncle's pinko literature. Then I learned that the Soviets were constructing an atom smasher twice the size of the one America had just built. As if those items weren't chilling enough, Hurricane Connie had alighted on the New York area sooner than expected, and more torrentially; she was flooding thousands of cellars, washing out roads and railroad tracks, shaking loose the restraints of telephone and power lines, and lashing at the ground with the charged wires.

A flash of lightning illuminated the dull brown bricks of the apartment house opposite ours. A crash of thunder rumbled through the streets like the gang of motorcycle hoods in *The Wild One.* A tingle of cold fear crept up my spine. I closed the window that opened out on the fire escape and checked to make sure the front door was locked, as if the hurricane could enter by turning the doorknob. On the way I heard Judy. She had awakened with both lungs blazing. Wailing and weeping like a Greek widow as played by Little Richard, she threw open the bedroom door and demanded food and her mother in that order. As I rushed to the refrigerator, a gust of wind blew the screen off the kitchen window. The flying screen knocked over a plant. The ceramic pot shattered. Soil spilled onto the floor, turning to mud when it mixed with the puddle of rainwater that had streamed in through the top window. I shoved the window closed and wiped up the mud. Judy screamed even louder. I ordered her to shut up and wait.

She did neither. She jerked open the refrigerator door. A bottle of pickles shattered on the floor; briny liquid spread over the green and beige linoleum. Judy bent down to pick up a pickle and grabbed instead a piece of glass. Blood gushed from her finger. I picked her up and hauled her to the bathroom, trying to press her mouth against my shoulder to muzzle her brain-piercing shrieks. But since that position prevented her breathing, she squirmed loose and slid down the side of my body like an unfastened shawl, smearing blood on my shirt. Pinning the child against my leg to keep her from hitting the ground, I gimped the rest of the way to the bathroom. I opened the door. I yanked the string to turn on the light. Nothing happened.

The wind whipped wet and cold through the tiny room. The window shade flapped and fluttered like the eyelids of a demon. The door slammed shut. It was pitch-black. Judy screamed directly into my ear. Then I saw a pair of white eyes in the dark. I kicked the door open and darted out of the room. The Thing was lounging in the bathtub.

Mercifully, my mother and Aunt Libby soon returned and ministered to the traumatized Judy. I mopped up the kitchen floor, plucked the glass shards from the linoleum, and closed the windows on the rain.

Connie and The Thing hung around for days. The closest I could get to the streets I loved was the living room window. From there I watched rivers of rainwater rush down Howard Avenue and gale winds shake the stop signs and hurl trash-can lids into the air like kites. With most ball games rained out, television seemed overrun by anemic shows like *Liberace* and *Father Knows Best.* The latter bowl of mush had just returned to the air after a flood of angry letters greeted its cancellation. Personally, I could not comprehend what the fuss was about. With families like the Cramdens and the Rileys and the Ricardos around—not to mention Kingfish and Sapphire—why would anyone want to endure an evening with the bloodless Andersons?

It was at that time that Hubbell started to act weird. For one thing, he monopolized the television, having developed an attachment to an odd assortment of programs: newscasts, variety shows, documentaries such as *You Are There* and *Person to Person,* quiz shows like *Masquerade Party* and *What's My Line?* He wasn't just watching, he seemed to be *studying* what he saw, even the commercials. At times he would mumble along with Edward R. Murrow or Dave Garroway, as if they were singing a song whose words Hubbell wanted to learn. If I dared make a peep, my brother hushed me with a terrifying hiss. I was helpless against this onslaught of boring television because my mother supported Hubbell's choices. They were, she said, intellectually stimulating.

What made this more than a quirk was the fact that Hubbell was watching television and listening to the radio when he should have been working out. My brother was goofing off and covering up his goldbricking by lying to my father, either describing workouts that I knew had not occurred or creating an excuse such as a minor injury. The latter gambit backfired, however, because it caused my father to step up the fitness portion of the master plan and to administer personally Hubbell's regular rubdowns with Ben-Gay. He used the massage time to reiterate past lessons and reinforce Hubbell's motivation with pep talks. Inclement weather was not a valid excuse, because my father had arranged, through Jesse Hicks, the janitor, for a maintenance man to open the high school gym on request so that Hubbell could work out day or night regardless of the conditions.

One August night the entire family tuned in along with forty-seven million other viewers to *The $64,000 Question*. Gino Prato, a humble little shoemaker from the Bronx, was to tell the nation whether he would keep his thirty-two grand or go for the sixty-four.

"Don't be a jerk, Gino," advised my mother. "Take the money and run."

"Shoot the wad, Gino baby," countered my father. "Go for the whole lasagna."

"Will you guys keep quiet?" said Hubbell.

He was listening closely to Hal March, a beaming quizmaster with Pepsodent teeth and Vitalis hair. Breathlessly, March asked Gino for his decision. The nation hushed. The cobbler read a cablegram from his old papa back in Italy. "It is enough," the message read. "Stay where you are." And that is what the contestant did.

"God bless you, Gino," said Hal March.

My mother applauded. "Attaboy, Gino."

"Schmuck!" yelled my father.

My parents argued about the merits of Gino's decision, a reflection of fundamental philosophical differences that The Thing would soon seize upon in an attempt to wrench my family apart.

"Will you please shut up!" said Hubbell.

I awakened around midnight, having to pee. The hallway was dark except for a stripe of light under Hubbell's door. As I passed his room, I could hear my brother, like a deejay, introduce "Devil or Angel" by the Clovers. His voice was an octave deeper than normal and had a plaintive quality. "This one goes out to Beverly. Someone out there wants to know, are you devil . . . or angel?"

Thus, I concluded that Hubbell's odd behavior could be attributed to girl trouble. He had lost Beverly, his steady girl, under circumstances I was unable to discern, but which involved Iggy Corso and had clearly disturbed my brother.

Slowly, I nudged the bathroom door until I could reach in and pull the light string. Never again would I be trapped in a small dark room with The Thing—and something told me he was in the vicinity.

The Thing was not in the bathroom. He was in my parents' bedroom. I heard their agitated voices when I detoured to the kitchen for a drink. At first I thought they were still arguing about Gino Prato's decision, but their voices had a different, more serious, tone.

"I don't trust them rich New York doctors," my father said. "Big shots. They rush you in and out so they can beat the traffic to the golf course."

"Dr. Goldsmith says he's the best," said my mother.

"What the hell does Goldsmith know? He's the Walter Alston of medicine. I'll tell you one thing, Jeannie, I'm not gonna let some butcher cut up my wife."

"Frank, they may have to cut it out in order to analyze it."

"There's gotta be another way, for chrissake. It's only a little lump."

"My whole breast is only a lump."

"That ain't funny, Jeannie," said my father. "I'm telling you, it's a cyst, that's all. It's gotta be."

That was all I heard. Their voices became indecipherable. I slept with the light on as rain and wind hammered my window. By the next morning, as if it had been a dream, I had forgotten what I'd overheard.

Like President Eisenhower, who had gone fishing and golfing in Colorado that week, The Thing took a brief vacation. Hurricane Connie, satisfied with nine inches of rain and forty-one deaths, swept up the coast to New England. In Switzerland an international contingent of sane people met to discuss peaceful uses of atomic energy. As a show of good faith after a harmonious summit conference, the Soviets announced that they would reduce their armed forces by 640,000 troops.

It was a false calm. The Thing came roaring back on the savage winds of Connie's sister, Hurricane Diane. New York and three of its neighbors declared a state of emergency. Damage was estimated in the billions of dollars. Nearly two hundred people were killed. Thousands more huddled in Red Cross shelters. By the time Diane finally waved goodbye, she left behind enough moisture to keep the humidity in the nineties, matching the temperature point for point. Steam rose from the puddles and hung in the stagnant air. Water molecules seeped into people's nerve cells, shortening their fuses. It was so hot I slept on the fire escape, as did scores of our neighbors.

Meanwhile, the Dodgers, on a road trip, were losing more games than they won. Not only that, their clubhouse resembled the Mayo Clinic; half the pitchers were in various stages of incapacity, other players were ailing, and the healthy ones were slumping, none more so than Duke Snider, whose batting average had plummeted from .331 to .299.

When he grounded out with the bases loaded in a close game against Cincinnati, the center fielder who had been idolized above all Bums was actually booed by the faithful. The Duke of Flatbush was a good-looking young man, a natural athlete with a smooth grace in the outfield and a swing so pretty it was almost as thrilling to watch him strike out as to see him loft a home run over the screen and into the service station on Bedford Avenue. But Duke was temperamental. He was somewhat insecure, and perhaps too immature to know that boos were a sign of affection. Dodger fans reserved the right to jeer loudest the heroes they admired and depended on most. And much was expected of Number 4, the only prominent left-handed batter on the team.

"They are the worst fans in baseball," Duke told reporters. "They don't deserve the pennant. That's why we're going to Jersey City next year."

Jersey City? *Jersey City!!!* What's this about Jersey City? It seems that while Hurricane Diane was tearing up New York, The Thing had arranged for der Führer, Walter O'Malley, to schedule eight of next year's home games across the Hudson River, down the road from the worthless Palisades Amusement Park. It was the first salvo in the war between the team's owner and the borough of Brooklyn, which would end, two years later, in the shameful exodus to Los Angeles. Ebbets Field had outlived its usefulness, The O'Malley contended. Its 31,902 seats were insufficient. Public transportation was inadequate. Parking was virtually nonexistent, a distinct drawback given the numbers of fans who were shuffling off in Chevys and Mercuries to the green suburban lawns of Long Island.

To O'Malley, Ebbets Field was not a shrine, but a place to sell a product—like a department store. He insisted that he had every intention of keeping the team where it belonged. But if Brooklyn did not find a way to build a modern stadium with convenient rest rooms and comfortable chairs and no obstructed views, in a choice location with acres of parking, well . . .

"Get outta here. He's fullashit. He ain't goin' nowheres." That was the general reaction to the implied threat. To Brooklynites it was inconceivable that the Bums would play anywhere else. It was like asking the Pope to leave Rome and set up shop in Beirut. All right, Ebbets Field was old, but so was the Vatican. So was Jerusalem, and look what a fuss they were making over that joint. So, go ahead, modernize a little, snazz up the old ballpark, build a parking lot. Not that 31,902 seats is chopped liver, mind you. Not when you fill them up. Only the Braves were drawing as many fans as the Dodgers, and they were still a novelty in Milwaukee. One losing season and they'd be lucky to fill up the press box. But, what the hell, go ahead, add some chairs if you have to. Only please, dear God, don't go nowheres!

"O'Malley is bluffing," we said. "The greedy sonofabitch, he's just looking to make a juicy deal for himself. Guys like that, they're always gettin' away wit' moider."

That's what we said. But we were worried. We wuz pertoibed. Guys like O'Malley, guys who know a buck, you don't take guys like that for granted. Just look around: the whole damn country was on wheels already; the suburbs were sprouting split-levels like ragweed; sweltering outposts like Texas and Arizona were becoming air-conditioned. And baseball had become as restless as the populace. Between 1903 and 1952 stability had reigned; the same eight teams represented each league for half a century—no interlopers, no deserters. Then the Braves relocated from Boston to Milwaukee. The next year the St. Louis Browns became the Baltimore Orioles. In 1955 the Athletics moved from Philadelphia to Kansas City. New York and Chicago were the only cities left with more than one team. Where would it stop? When would it stop?

The Bums dropped a doubleheader to Cincinnati. It was time for some in-person support, and fortunately, Louie, Artie, and I had tickets for the next game. We had saved up six Borden's ice cream wrappers apiece (Elsie wrappers, we called them, after the cow on the Borden's logo), and this earned us grandstand seats behind third base.

That morning we were tossing a spaldeen around on the Corner when, to my surprise, I saw my father heading toward us in his good blue slacks and a white shirt. I threw him the ball. He caught it effortlessly, but instead of throwing it back, he held it. His gait was labored, his gaze pinned to the sidewalk.

"Hey, Frank, throw me a curve," said Louie.

There were ways to squeeze a spaldeen with one's knuckles and release the ball so that, when it hit the ground, it would bounce sharply to the left or right in a variety of angles. These were tricks that young boys viewed with awe because their fingers were too small to pull them off with a grownup's panache. My father, who had a thrilling repertoire of spaldeen stunts, flipped the ball underhanded toward Louie. Louie braced himself to thrust either arm to the side when the ball bounced. The ball hit the ground about a foot in front of him . . . and hopped straight back to my father. "That's not fair!" Louie whined. "How'd you do that?"

"Magic fingers," said my father.

But he was not in a playful mood. He took me aside. "Your mother wants to see you," he said.

"Now? I can't, we're going to the game soon."

"There's plenty of time," he said. "Do me a favor. It's important."

"Why? What's wrong?"

"Nothing's wrong. Just do what I'm asking."

"Something's wrong," I insisted. "I can tell. Why aren't you working? Why are you dressed up? Why are you playing with your keys like you're nervous?"

"What are you, Dick Tracy?" said my father. "Shut up and go upstairs."

"That's no way to treat a guy who saved your life."

My father had been in the Army when I was born, stationed at Camp Gordon, Georgia. His commanding officer, a dues-paying member of the Ku Klux Klan, did not feel obliged to give a wiseass New York Jew a furlough to see his wife and newborn child. So, with the help of forged papers, my father went AWOL.

He hopped a freight train to New York and spent a week with my mother and me, an interlude he would recall with sweet affection but which I could not remember no matter how hard I tried. He returned to the Army in the company of the Military Police; soon he was court-martialed and sent to the brig. While he stewed in jail with killers and thieves, his company was shipped overseas. Not one of the soldiers returned alive. I never let him forget that had I not left my mother's womb when I did . . .

"Get upstairs or you're not going to the game."

I sped past the Sphinx and took the steps two at a time. My mother sat at the kitchen table with her usual paraphernalia: a cup of coffee, almost black; an ashtray, almost full; a pack of Camels, almost empty. But something was different. There was no book or magazine, no telephone, no dishes, no vegetables to chop or flour to mix. She just sat there, staring at the sugar bowl. Moreover, she wasn't wearing her usual daytime attire, an old rumpled housecoat; she was wearing a dress with nylon stockings and high heels. At her feet was a small suitcase.

She looked older. Across from her sat The Thing.

My mother explained that she would be spending the night in a hospital and that the next morning she would undergo some sort of test. When I asked why Dr. Goldsmith couldn't do it in his office, she said it was a special test that could be performed only in a hospital by a specialist.

I asked her what kind of test it was. She looked me over, lit a cigarette with the butt of her previous one, and decided to tell me the truth. "I have a lump on my breast," she said. "Tomorrow, they'll cut it out and analyze it. It's probably nothing, and I'll be home in a couple of days."

"What if it's *not* nothing?"

"Well, there's a slight possibility . . ." She got no further because my father entered. He knew immediately that she had revealed more than he considered appropriate.

"What are you telling him?" he asked.

Sensing that my father would censor any further discussion, I pressed for more information. "What happens if it's not nothing?"

"They'll remove my breast."

My father smacked his forehead. "Jesus Christ, Jeannie! Why

don't you draw him a picture while you're at it?" He turned to me. "Don't pay attention to her, champ. Your mother has a wild imagination."

"That's what they did to Esther, isn't it?" I asked.

My mother nodded. Her friend Esther, I knew, had only one breast. The other one had been removed; in its place was a wad of foam rubber. I did not understand why each time this subject came up, everyone became so solemn. My mother had foam rubber breasts also, two of them in fact, little rounded cones called falsies that my brothers and I would sometimes clown around with when we found them in the bathroom. Once we had planned to wear them on our heads as yarmulkes to someone's bar mitzvah but we lost our nerve. Even my parents made jokes about falsies, but not about Esther's. Why hers were so different, and why having a breast removed was not the same as losing an appendix or a set of tonsils or any other superfluous organ, I could not comprehend. It was not like losing an arm or a leg. Even if you gave birth, a baby could suck on only one breast at a time, and besides, there were bottles nowadays. Nevertheless, I was frightened, not by anything that had been said, but by the tension in the room. It was as palpable and noxious as the smoke from my mother's cigarette.

"Look at that, you scared him already," said my father.

"He has a right to know," my mother replied. "He ought to be prepared, just in case."

"Just in case what?" I asked.

"Don't listen to her," said Dad. "Your mother has a little cyst. It's nothing. They'll take it out and that's that, like when Hubbell had those warts removed. No big deal." He managed a cheerful smile. "What do you say we go to the chink's tonight, huh? Just us guys. We'll get some spare ribs, some chop suey. Maybe I'll take yez all to the pool room afterward, huh?"

When it came to life's tragedies, my father, by example, taught us to seek refuge neither in religion nor in reality.

In our grandstand seats, in the cool shadow created by the upper deck, my buddies and I were close enough to see the sweat on Jackie Robinson's neck; to hear the arcane patois of the third base coaches; to catch a foul pop if we got lucky; to hear the raspy voice and clanging cowbells of Hilda Chester, the most famous Dodger fanatic of all; to watch the Dodger Sym-Phony, five guys from Williamsburg who dressed up like tattered bums and played, on battered horns and drums, tunes to harass the opposition and the umpires. They would serenade the umps with "Three Blind Mice," and when an enemy batter trudged back to his dugout after striking out, they would play "The Army Duff"—ta-dum ta-dum, ta-dum ta-dum, ta-dum ta-da-da-da-dum ta-dum . . . holding their last cymbal crash and bass-drum boom for the precise moment when the player's butt hit the bench.

Hilda and the Sym-Phony were celebrities, but there were thousands of other regulars who yelled and cheered and cursed and razzed in glorious anonymity, making life in the stands as memorable as anything that happened on the playing field. With the team on a losing streak and O'Malley issuing threats and heroic Duke throwing out insults instead of enemy base runners, the tension at Ebbets belied the Dodgers' still-lofty place in the standings. We were hurt, and the pain brought out our natural ingenuity. MAYBE JERSEY CITY AIN'T FAR ENOUGH AWAY, postulated one banner. Pleaded another: LEAVE US NOT GO TO THAT JOISEY.

Roughly half the fans in our section booed when Number 4 stepped into the cage to take batting practice. They taunted, "Crybaby, crybaby, nah nah na-na nah." The other half, myself included, gave the Duke an ovation, for he had repented, in a manner of speaking, in the morning papers. "There are some good Brooklyn fans," he'd allowed. "But maybe there are more bad ones." Contrite it wasn't, but for me it was good enough.

Duke smacked three base hits that day, but the Flock lost again. Their lead was down to ten games, the lowest it had been in over two months. Evidently, the presence of me and my cap was not entirely foolproof. As they moped up the concrete steps to the exits, the careworn fans mopped their necks and brows with soiled handkerchiefs. "No sweat. They'll snap out of it. No way they could blow it this time, are you kidding?" That's what we said. What we thought was terrifying, and The Thing made sure we thought it. He was at the gate, dressed in an usher's uniform, saying, "Watch your step. Remember 1951."

"Let's walk home," I suggested to my companions when we reached the street.

"What'd you, spend your carfare or what?" asked Louie.

"I have my carfare," I assured him.

"Oh, I figured you musta spent your carfare or something." He pronounced it *somftin*. "Else why do you wanna walk home?"

There are times when a man needs to think, that's why, and a crowded bus with the climate of a steam bath is not the place to do it. But I did not know how to explain that to a guy with raw nerve endings who was plainly not given to contemplation. Nor did I want to walk alone. "Come on, you guys, let's walk."

" 'Cause if you spent your carfare or somftin, I could lend you," said Louie.

"I have money. I just feel like walking."

"You're cuckoo, you know that? If we take the bus, we could get in a coupla games of punchball or somftin."

I looked to Artie, the voice of reason, hoping he would cast the deciding vote in my favor. He was as neutral as Switzerland, sorting out baseball cards as if he hadn't been listening.

"Hey, Artie, this guy's cuckoo," said Louie, twirling his index finger counterclockwise beside his ear in case Artie did not know what cuckoo meant.

"If we walk," I pointed out, "you can use your carfare to buy a Creamsicle."

"I hate Creamsicles. Fudgsicles I like, but I hate Creamsicles. I like Fudgsicles."

How could one reason with a guy who preferred the chocolate monotony of a Fudgsicle to the Creamsicle's delicate blend of orange ices and vanilla ice cream?

"So buy a goddamn Fudgsicle."

"I could lend you the carfare."

I controlled myself, remembering what my mother always said about Louie: "He means well, dear."

Thankfully, Artie came through. "Let's walk," he said.

We walked north up Franklin Avenue, then east on Eastern Parkway, a broad, tree-lined boulevard that had been built along a terminal moraine formed by the movement of a primordial glacier. Lined with huge, prestigious apartment buildings, some of which housed the highest-priced doctors in the borough, Eastern Parkway was the neighborhood's principal link to downtown Brooklyn and the bold bridges that leaped the East River. Streams of cars hurtled down the elegant artery from Manhattan. Herds of secretaries and businessmen spilled out of subway exits. On benches beneath the shade trees, old men and women whose garments were far too heavy for the weather passed the time with conversation or the Yiddish newspaper, the *Daily Forward*.

I walked slightly behind my companions, preferring silence. The Dodgers have to snap out of it, I thought. If they blow it again, the results would be too unbearable to contemplate: an epidemic of psychosomatic illnesses; enough souls falling off their rockers to fill all the loony bins in New York; a skyrocketing divorce rate; plummeting life spans. Throughout the so-called Borough of Churches, houses of worship would close their doors due to the death of faith. Attendance at Ebbets Field would drop to seven—the Sym-Phony, Hilda Chester, and organist Gladys Gooding, who would play "The Mexican Hat Dance" during the seventh-inning stretch to empty seats with no one to clap along. Millions of fans would defect, filing suit in saloons and street corners for alienation of affection. Millions of subconscious minds would be poisoned forever. Men would spend the rest of their days anticipating betrayal in love, defeat in battle, failure in enterprise. "Wait till next year" would lose whatever shred of uplift it still contained. It would be replaced by another expression, already a fixture in the lingo: "Can't get a break."

I remembered that my mother was, at that moment, in a hospital bed, probably being poked and prodded by strange doctors, or maybe rallying the nurses and orderlies to rise up against their oppressors and demand better working conditions. Taking my father's advice, I had not worried about her during the game. But losing again to Cincinnati did not stimulate positive thinking. Even though my father assured me it was just a routine operation, like the removal of a wart, I remembered that terrible, unexpected things can happen in a hospital. I knew a kid who almost died because some surgeon screwed up his tonsillectomy, and a friend's father who had a bad reaction to medicine and couldn't move the left side of his face. At that very moment The Thing could be on his way uptown to my mother's hospital.

As we waited for a light, a woman walked past us and came to a stop in what seemed to be a predetermined place. She wore a pillbox hat with a veil, under which was a chalk-white face blotched with lipstick and rouge and black, penciled-in eyebrows. She reached into a shopping bag, removed a handful of bread crumbs, and tossed them into the air, like Tinker Bell sprinkling fairy dust. From hiding places in the upper branches of trees and the eaves of buildings, a flock of hysterical pigeons descended in a frenzy of flapping wings. The woman, delighting in the free-for-all, extended both her arms, Christlike, as befits a feeder of multitudes. Several pigeons perched on her arms and fed directly from her hands. One strutted to her shoulder. The woman turned her head, puckered her lips and fed the bird a chunk of Wonder Bread, mouth to beak.

"Get the hell outta here with dem goddamn boids!" The voice, loud and raw, belonged to an old man on a bench who wore a straw hat, a thirty-year-old brown suit, and a green tie with the face of a horse on it. The woman ignored him. Her antagonist waved his hand as if applying a curse, then returned to his previous position, hunched over, staring at the small octagonal blocks of cement with which the sidewalk was paved, as if waiting for one to open up so he could dive into his grave. His wrinkled face was yellow, as were his eyes, discolored by the slow acid drip of regret. He coughed and spat up yellow phlegm, and talked to someone who was not here. Not just talked; he growled rebuke, hissed damnation. This was a man who had done lifelong battle with The Thing.

His was the fate that my mother beseeched me to avoid when she sang the words to "Young at Heart." But if the Dodgers blow the pennant this year, I thought, there I'll be, six or seven decades from now, sitting on a bench on Eastern Parkway, motherless all those years, scowling at the octagonal blocks, whining at old ladies whose only pleasure was feeding pigeons, coughing up phlegm, and cursing. "Goddamn Bums. Farshtunkener Alston. They blew it, them bastards, them doity rotten dawgs. Ptooey! Goddamn O'Malley, that no-good Nazi son of a bitch, may he rot in hell. Aaah, they shoulda walked Thomson in 'fifty-one . . ."

I was back on Eastern Parkway the next day, heading in the opposite direction in my uncle's blue and cream Bel Air. We had no car of our own at the time, my father having sold our '48 Packard to pay off some debts, so Uncle Sid insisted we borrow his. It would not do, he felt, to take the subway to visit his twin sister in the hospital. I sat in the backseat, spending much of the ride with my head out the window so I could see the sights unimpeded and open my mouth to let the hot wind dry my tongue and inner cheeks, a sensation that gave me a peculiar pleasure. Hubbell sat up front next to my father, ambling from one radio station to another like a window shopper. Having been deemed too young for the occasion, Hank remained at home, content with his pets and a macaroni luncheon catered by Angie Corso.

It started out a perversely quiet ride, measurably different from my family's usual high-decibel outings. Hubbell and my father were lost in sober reflection. I began to suspect they were not leveling with me about my mother's condition. The night before, at the Chinese restaurant, my father hardly spoke. When Hank or I mentioned my mother, Hubbell shot us such a look, you would think we'd blown our noses in the chow mein. My father acted as though his wife was luxuriating at a spa. Just a little lump, he would say, then comment on the food or the waiters. When the subject of the Dodgers came up, he was equally sanguine. Just a little slump, he would say. But he did not finish his spare ribs, and he left a five-dollar tip, like a Catholic hoping to purchase a blessing. A little lump, a little slump, I thought. Nothing to worry about. But I slept fitfully, and in the morning, when I told Jesse Hicks where we were going, the janitor said, ominously, "Why do it always happen to the good ones?" I skipped the singing of my usual car song—a spirited rendition of Dinah Shore's "See the U.S.A. in your Chevrolet . . ."

We stopped for a light on Eastern Parkway. Just as it turned green, an old man in a straw hat crossed the street, forcing us to wait, something my father, like all cab drivers, did not do well. With his back bent like a sickle, the old man crept slowly past the hood of the car, then turned and scowled at us, as if he could read our minds and was rebuking us for disrespectful thoughts. To my astonishment, it was the same bilious codger I had seen the day before snapping at the lady feeding the pigeons.

"Old fart thinks he owns the street," said my father. "Reminds me of your grandfather." He was referring to my mother's father, who died when I was five. We resumed the journey. "He never liked me, that hypocritical son of a bitch. Thought I wasn't good enough for his daughter. Wanted her to marry an educated man. Even tried to arrange it once with some Columbia professor. A biologist. Ha! Your mother left that egghead sitting in a restaurant. He's probably still there."

The floodgates had opened. Hubbell and I were treated once again to the story of the courtship of Frank and Jeannie Stone. It began in the early days of the Depression. My father, the oldest male in his family, had been forced to take any job he could get, small jobs, big jobs, anything to bring in a buck. Once, he ran an errand for a classy-looking man in a silk suit who gave him a generous tip and offered him full-time employment. My father accepted. After he'd done odd jobs for a week, his dapper boss showed up at the schoolyard and watched the last few innings of a softball game. Afterward, he complimented Cyclone Frankie Stone on his smooth, powerful swing, and asked if he wouldn't mind swinging a bat at targets other than a ball, like, say, someone's head. If so, he would like him to meet his employer, one Louis Lepke. My father had heard the name. Mr. Lepke's firm was known as Murder Incorporated.

One did not easily walk away from such employment. But thanks to the intervention of a well-placed friend of Grandpa Abe's, Frank Stone was able to turn down the promotion and still walk safely on the streets of Brownsville. While on those streets, he was stopped one afternoon by a nice woman with snow-white hair and gentle blue eyes. She was looking for someone tall, like him, to wash her windows. She offered him fifty cents. He took the job.

He was on a stepladder, scrubbing grime off the high windows, when he saw the woman's daughter. He had seen the girl around the neighborhood, had watched her from a distance, but had never summoned the nerve to speak to her. Nor did he speak to her that day. But he kept going back to wash the nice woman's windows, accepting only a modest lunch as payment.

It took a while, but eventually Frank Stone asked the girl for a date and she consented. My father was in love, terminally, but Skinny Jeannie was not prepared even to date him exclusively. She liked him, but she was young and gay and popular, and she did not wish to be tied down. He courted, one of her many beaus, and one day while washing the windows in the small apartment, he proposed marriage just as her date, Solly Skapinsky, rang the doorbell. Jeannie didn't think she could say yes at that time. Frank said he would wait. He waited four years.

"I never went out with anyone else," he said as we drove past the Brooklyn Museum and the Botanical Gardens.

"You never went out with another girl?" asked Hubbell, incredulous.

"Not on an actual date," my father explained. "We went out in groups. You know, a bunch of guys and gals, to a dance or the beach or whatever. Your mother, she went out with all kinds of guys, even friends of mine, even Skapinsky, that son of a bitch. But me, I never cared to date anyone else."

"Not once?" asked Hubbell.

"I'm a one-woman man," my father declared.

At Grand Army Plaza, by the big public library where my mother would take us to find books, we picked up the Flatbush Avenue Extension, drove north past furniture showrooms and discount stores to downtown Brooklyn, where stately buildings housed the borough's officials, and department stores such as Abraham & Strauss offered bargains not to be found in Manhattan. We drove past the grand theatres, once home to vaudeville shows. At the Fox was a double bill, *Land of the Pharaohs* and *Devil Girl from Mars*. The Paramount featured *The Seven Little Foys* with Bob Hope. Soon, the marquee informed us, Alan Freed's Labor Day stage show would present The Cardinals, The Harptones, The Rhythmettes, The Nutmegs, and Chuck Berry, whose songs had yet to gain widespread attention. Freed was aggressively offering white audiences the sort of rhythm and blues revues that the Apollo and other black theatres had been showing for years. To make it more palatable, he had booked a somewhat incongruous headliner, Tony Bennett.

My eyes were drawn to the Albee Theatre, where *The Seven Year Itch* was playing. Above the marquee was the enormous figure of Marilyn Monroe, her white dress blown up over her thighs by the wind from a subway grating, her lips parted in a secret pleasure that I sensed only a girl could comprehend. As we passed beneath her, I leaned out and craned my neck, hoping I might see further up the dress. Recalling Ruth Finkelstein's bloomers, I wondered how Marilyn's might smell.

"That's where we went on our first date," said my father. "The Albee. We saw *Grand Hotel* with Garbo and Barrymore. I was so goddamn nervous, I nearly peed in my pants."

We drove up the ramp of the Manhattan Bridge, its heavy cables curving gracefully against the oyster-gray sky. The car wiggled slightly as the road beneath it turned from solid asphalt to a steel grid. We were above the waters of the East River. Rainbows swirled with the currents, marking places where oil had been deposited. Ahead of us were the skyscrapers of the great island we called New York, not Manhattan, as if we who lived in the borough of Kings needed to declare our independence from the rest of the city. I could pick out an office building that Grandpa Abe had worked on. A barge the size of Ebbets Field passed beneath us, pulled by a tugboat toward the open sea. To our left was the older, more elegant Brooklyn Bridge, and beyond it the cluster of buildings on Wall Street where, I imagined, Yankee fans sat behind mahogany desks smoking Cuban cigars and barking orders to buy and sell the world.

Beyond those towers I could see the Statue of Liberty and Ellis Island, where my ancestors' journey from the Old World had terminated. Three of my grandparents had passed through that island. The fourth, Grandpa Abe, was born on the Lower East Side, at the foot of the bridge to my right, the Williamsburg. My mother's parents were educated people from the city of Minsk. Her mother, the kind lady with the blue eyes and dirty windows, read Shakespeare to her children in Yiddish and raised a pianist, a painter, a mystic, and a playwright, none of whom could earn a living at his passion. Her husband spent most of his time reading books about science and philosophy, and he scornfully flaunted his learning before the young man who came to wash windows and court his youngest daughter.

"Son of a bitch thought he knew everything," my father told us. "But the bum couldn't even support his own family. He had a bicycle shop. He sold wallpaper and linoleum. He did this, he did that, but nothing worked out because he thought he was above honest labor. All he did was read and putz around with some big secret project that was going to make him famous. At one time he had a laundry and it was doing real good, but the schmuck sold it and sank all his money into this . . . this *thing* he was building. You know what it was? A goddamn perpetual motion machine. He had the whole thing figured out, how you could build it, how it would keep running forever. Turned out, to get the thing started, you needed something like an atom bomb. He was out of his mind. Your grandmother, she was a saint. Told him she'd leave him if he didn't shut up and let me marry his daughter. Bastard drove that poor woman to an early grave."

Late in life my grandfather had found religion. He started wearing a yarmulke and a prayer shawl. For the first time, he observed to the letter every ritual, every injunction, every holy day his ancestors had decreed, and he tried to force the whole package on his children and their families. Unlike other late-life converts, however, my grandfather did not acquire contentment. He became more bitter and cantankerous than ever. This turned my mother from an indifferent agnostic into a radical atheist. She not only refused to cooperate with the old man's religious demands, she blatantly violated them. She allowed Hubbell, her firstborn, to reject a bar mitzvah. She served us ham and bacon— and made sure her father knew about it. At Passover she carried home loaves of forbidden bread—without bags, so everyone would be sure to know about her sin. On Yom Kippur, while other Jews fasted and atoned, we would go to a Chinese restaurant and feast on roast pork, a tradition we maintained even after my grandfather's death. All this made my father—himself an agnostic, albeit less militant—love his wife even more.

My father's forebears on his mother's side were peasants from the Jewish villages, the shtetls, near Kiev. His mother was a short, plump woman with enormous breasts and enough energy to start her in-law's perpetual motion machine. I saw Grandma Rosie without an apron on only a handful of occasions. Long after her four children were grown, she still spent most of her time in the kitchen. The first thing she did when her husband died was whip up a vat of chicken soup, admonishing her family, "Eat, eat! You need strength to worry." She never seemed to learn from all her experience, however. To me, Grandma was The Thing's answer to Betty Crocker. Grandpa Abe's descendants had also come from the shtetls, but he was born in the New World. He tried to get his wife to assimilate. Every year, he would force her to enroll in an English class for immigrants, and every year she would buy a black composition book and start her lessons, and every year she would quit before she could read or write a sentence. Part of Grandma Rosie never wanted to leave the shtetl.

Those two streams of chromosomes from town and village had converged in my cells like the two rivers that flowed into the bay around Ellis Island. I contemplated the consequences of this inheritance as my father wheeled the borrowed car uptown along the Bowery, where real bums squatted in the shadow of discount jewelry stores.

He had been silent since the approach to the bridge, lost in thought. Now he blurted forth the continuation, as if he had been interrupted routinely for station identification. "I kept on proposing. My friends said I was nuts, but I couldn't help it. It made me happy just to be around her. She wasn't gorgeous or anything, not like a movie star, but I loved to look at her. And what a mind she had, smart like a whip, smarter than I'll ever be, I'll tell you that, and a heart of gold. There's no one like her, boys. You ought to have a Day for your mother, like you did for Hank. Jeannie's Day, that's the ticket."

He took out a handkerchief and wiped his eyes. "Wind," he explained.

The walls of the small, square waiting room looked as if they'd been painted with the green and yellow product of a sneeze. Its casement windows had no shades to block the sun, which had angled between two office buildings to beam directly into the room. Every seat was occupied. A young Puerto Rican woman with unshaven legs rocked a baby on her knee. An elderly couple sat close together, holding hands. They said nothing, read nothing, just looked at each other from time to time and sighed. A young black couple looked at their watches anxiously and read magazines. Hubbell sat by the window, peering out at the traffic, shifting his transistor radio from one ear to the other, sometimes silently mouthing the words to whatever he heard. I read *Sport* magazine. My father prowled the room like a caged buffalo.

My father lit one Pall Mall after another, crushing them out aggressively in an ashtray overflowing with butts. "Why the hell don't they empty the damn ashtrays?" he growled. He picked up a magazine, opened it at random, and threw it down on the pile without reading.

"Oh, no, Carmen Miranda died," said the Puerto Rican woman, crossing herself. She had learned this from the Spanish language newspaper she was reading.

"How do you like that," said my father. "No one invited me to the funeral."

"You knew her?" said the lady, very impressed.

"Just kidding."

"Oh, she was wonderful." The woman sang a chorus of "Chiquita Banana" in a slow tempo as a kind of memorial tribute.

The sluggish passage of time wore on my father's nerves; the room could not contain him. "I'm gonna take a leak," he would say, and he would return in five minutes with another cup of coffee. He had more leaks that day than the *Titanic.*

From time to time a nurse would enter the room and my father would pounce on her, eyes wide in anticipation of news. Her name was Miss Gallagher. Her red hair was tucked neatly under her nurse's cap and her green eyes sparkled with compassion above a constellation of freckles. "I'm sorry, Mr. Stone," she would say, "there's still no news about your wife."

"What the hell's taking so long?" Dad would ask. "What are they doing to her?"

"Oh, this is perfectly normal," said Miss Gallagher, placing a calming hand on his arm. "Just sit down and relax, Mr. Stone. Can I get you anything?" If Harry Truman had had a voice like hers, the Japanese would have said, "Sorry," and Hiroshima would still be standing.

"No, thanks, I'm fine," my father would say. "Just find out what's going on. *Please.*"

And Miss Gallagher would address herself to the party she had come to see. First the black couple, then the elderly couple left the room with her, only to be replaced by others. The room was always crowded.

At lunchtime Hubbell brought us sandwiches; my father did

not want to leave the area, in case he was needed. He did not eat his lunch. Hubbell tuned in to the Dodger pregame show, reporting to us what he heard.

"Guess who's pitching today," he said, and when my father and I guessed incorrectly, he told us, "Koufax."

"What are you, kidding me?" said my father. "What the hell is Alston doing, giving the pennant away?"

To him, the idea of trying to stop a losing streak by sending to the mound a nineteen-year-old with one previous start, whose control was as reliable as Walter O'Malley's promises, was evidence of treason. This was especially true if the pitcher in question was a lefty and you were playing in Ebbets Field. The compact park was hell on southpaws; visiting managers would juggle their staffs so only right-handers would pitch there. Alston's decision was proof that he'd been lucky so far, that his rangy bearing and phlegmatic stoicism was emblematic not of a Gary Cooper–like valor, but of a Mrs. Kass–like dementia.

Sandy Koufax had spent the previous year at the University of Cincinnati on a basketball scholarship. As a student at Lafayette High School, he hadn't pitched a single game. But he pitched four times in college after the basketball season, and he tried out for the Dodgers, who saw potential in his jet-powered arm, not to mention a public relations bonanza in having a Brooklyn-born Jew on the mound. The team's previous Jew, Cal Abrams, had been popular until his baserunning cost the Bums the pennant in 1950. To make room for Koufax, the club released a pitcher named Tommy Lasorda. Unfortunately, Koufax's vicious fastballs were as likely to hit the press box as the catcher's mitt. He was wasting space on the roster, most fans believed. But Sandy was a bonus baby, and being a bonus baby meant never having to say minor leagues. In a policy intended to prevent rich clubs like the Yankees from tying up all the talent, baseball had decreed that any team that gave a rookie more than four thousand dollars to sign had to keep him on the roster for at least two years.

"Alston doesn't have much choice," Hubbell said. "Everyone's either tired or injured."

"The man's an idiot," said my father. "He's pissing away the goddamn pennant." He started to kick the radiator, but stopped himself. He sat down on the edge of a chair and leaned forward wearily, resting his elbows on his knees. My father was taking personally the news about today's starter, as if Walter Alston had selected the day of Jeannie Stone's surgery to sacrifice a young Jewish pitcher.

After a long silence Dad mumbled, "It's malignant. Why the hell else would it take so long? It's cancer."

It was the first time the word had been mentioned in my presence. Now I understood what all the fuss was about. To me, the possible removal of an organ whose only purpose other than feeding babies was purely cosmetic, did not seem to warrant a great deal of anxiety, especially if you needed foam rubber help to begin with. But cancer was another story. People died of that. In fact, one of my mother's brothers, the would-be playwright, had died of cancer before he turned fifty. As I understood it, the dreaded disease involved rebellious cells going wild inside vital organs, like the juvenile delinquents in *Blackboard Jungle.* The cells in my own mother's breast might be engaged in gang warfare that could spill out into other areas. The Thing peeked into the waiting room, dressed in a white smock.

My father slumped farther forward, as if his back was not strong enough to hold up his fear. He reached for a cigarette. Finding that his pack was empty, he crushed it and threw it at the wastebasket, cursing. I looked to my big brother, hoping he might say something that would calm our father down. Hubbell looked as helpless as I felt.

"Here you go, mister, have one of mine." The offer came from a man on the other end of the room.

He handed a pack of Lucky Strikes to Hubbell, who started to relay them when he had an idea perhaps intended to cheer up my father. He held up the cigarettes like a TV pitchman and said, in a chipper baritone, "L.S.M.F.T. Lucky Strike means fine tobacco. Light up a Lucky. It's light-up time."

My father stared at his eldest son as if he had suddenly begun to speak Chinese. It was a measure of his gloom that he passed up the opportunity for a wisecrack. He lit up a Lucky and walked across the room to return the pack to his benefactor, wiping the back of his neck with a handkerchief. "Thanks, pal. Jeez, you'd think they could get a fan for this place. They charge you an arm and a leg, and it's like a *schvitz* in here."

"What's a shpitz?" said the Puerto Rican lady, looking to me for enlightenment.

"It's a steam bath," I said. "It's pronounced schvitz."

She found this a delightful discovery. "Shpitz." She laughed, and repeated the word several times to the child bouncing on her knee, as if she wanted him to memorize it.

"Mister, you're tall," said another woman to my father. "Why don't you open the window on the top?"

His eyebrows lifted at the irony. "That's how I met my wife," he said.

"What, you peeked in her window?" said the Puerto Rican lady.

"No, no, I was tall, so . . . never mind."

"And Koufax mows down the Reds one-two-three in the first," announced Hubbell.

"Anyone can pitch one good inning," said my father.

Unable to reach the handle on the top window, he slid over a small table and stood on it. This gave him better leverage but it also exposed his face to the direct beams of the sun. Squinting, his face illuminated as if by a spotlight, he grabbed the handle and pulled. It did not budge. He yanked it several times, then smacked it with the heel of his hand, and with each new failure he cursed still louder, the sweat poured faster, and he turned a deeper shade of red.

"Forget it, mister," said the Puerto Rican lady, "you'll give yourself a hernia like my Pablo."

"You want air or not?" Dad pounded the window and yanked at the handle and cursed, until Hubbell announced, with relish, "It's going, going . . . *gone!* A round-tripper by Furillo with two on. It's three to nothing, Dodgers."

It was the sort of news that would normally cheer my father. But he snarled, "They'll need more than three runs with that rookie on the mound." He smacked the window again. "Move, you son of a bitch!" He frequently swore at inanimate objects that refused to cooperate.

"What seems to be the trouble, Mr. Stone?" It was Nurse Gallagher.

Like a kindergarten child caught pouring fingerpaint in a

classmate's shoe, my father looked down sheepishly from his perch. "Nothing, nothing, I, uh . . . it was hot . . ."

"Yeah, it's a real shpitz!" said the Puerto Rican lady, and she howled with laughter.

In the sultry room Miss Gallagher was like a white Christmas with her red hair and green eyes and her snow-white uniform and sugarplum voice. I wondered if she would go for a scrawny guy with a mop of unmanageable brown hair, ears like wings, and teeth parted down the middle. The nurse informed my father that the window was sealed shut, but she did it in such a way that he emerged redeemed, not embarrassed. She offered him a dainty hand, but he elected to hop off the table unassisted.

"Would you like a sedative, Mr. Stone?" asked the nurse.

"I don't need no sedative, I just need my wife. What the hell are them butchers doing to her?"

"Your wife is in good hands, Mr. Stone," said the nurse. "Just relax. I'll have a fan sent in." As she escorted another person out of the room, she smiled at me and patted my head. I thought of removing my Dodger cap in case she repeated the gesture; I knew her hand would be warm and soft on my scalp. If I had a teacher like Miss Gallagher, I thought, I would never play hooky again. I watched her leave, her hips twitching from side to side against the crisp white uniform, and I wondered what she would say if I offered her a charlotte russe.

"Hey, lover boy, what are you looking at?" said my father.

"Nothing," I said. And I repeated the answer emphatically to counter the three-way smile that passed among Hubbell, my father, and the Puerto Rican lady. It was the first time Frank Stone had smiled all day.

In the fourth inning, according to Hubbell's report, Jackie Robinson did what no one did better: materialize runs from the ether and galvanize his teammates. Robby legged out an infield single. Then, on consecutive pitches, he stole second and third, putting himself in position to score on a ground ball by Sandy Amoros, the swift Cuban left fielder.

"Amoros, he's my boy," said the Puerto Rican lady. She balanced her baby on her lap, held both hands above her left shoulder and flexed her wrists back and forth. She was emulating

Amoros's batting stance; he waved his bat like a metronome above his left shoulder, just as the Sphinx might have done if she'd been a ballplayer, not a minstrel.

Miraculously, Koufax's missiles kept finding their target. This had an even more salubrious effect on my father than Nurse Gallagher. "It's benign," he said as the Reds went down hitless once again. "What the hell are we worried about? It's gotta be benign. She's too damn young to get cancer."

When Nurse Gallagher entered again, there was a doctor at her side. He was taller than my father, but slender, with thick, silver hair and a matching pencil-thin mustache. He referred to his clipboard. I expected a deep, distinguished voice, but his was falsetto. "Mr. Stone?"

My father stood like he'd been shocked by a cattle prod. His face broke out in sweat; a puddle formed in the crevice above his upper lip. He started to reach for the doctor's hand, then remembered he had a cigarette in his. He reached down to crush it but it slid off the side of the ashtray onto the table and a cluster of old butts followed. Miss Gallagher calmly snuffed out the sparks before they burned the table; she returned the butts to the ashtray.

"Mr. Stone . . ." said the doctor.

"Give it to me straight, Doc, I can take it. Just tell me the truth." He winced like a child about to be smacked in the face.

"The tumor was benign," said the doctor. "Your wife is perfectly fine."

My father did not know whom to kiss first. He kissed me, then he kissed Hubbell, then he kissed the Puerto Rican lady, then Miss Gallagher. Blushing from that last, impulsive transaction, he grabbed the doctor's hand and shook it so hard you would think the surgeon himself had made the tumor benign. Throughout this celebration, my father blabbered, "I knew it. Never any doubt. It had to be benign. No question about it." Then he shouted "Benign!" as if it were "Remember the Alamo!" and he fainted flat out on the floor.

As Miss Gallagher administered smelling salts, the Puerto Rican lady looked down at my father and said, "That man, he love his wife something fierce."

———

Sandy Koufax shut out the Reds on two hits and fourteen strike-outs. My mother shut out cancer. She returned home with both breasts intact, her cells at peace, and the men in her life fawning over her like court retainers. She seemed more chipper than ever, and so did the Dodgers. Koufax's performance put an end to the losing streak and set in motion an opposite trend. Defying torn ligaments, pulled muscles, twisted ankles, and pitching arms hanging by threads, the Bums were never again threatened, and on the afternoon of September 8—with me watching at Jake's, significantly—they climaxed the season with their fifth pennant in my lifetime.

As I recalled these events that night, the Klingers hollered themselves out. Ruth Finkelstein's room lit up briefly, but all I could see were shadows. The gusty winds fell silent and a cluster of stars appeared above the rooftops. I crawled into bed. It had been a triumphant day. But, I cautioned myself, don't get complacent; The Thing could snap out of his slump at any time.

Part Two

Chapter Ten

I could not look out the classroom window without finding Eleanor Krinski in my line of vision. A passive profile would have been bad enough, but Eleanor's radar could detect the slightest microturn of my head, and she would face me, flashing a dorky smile, with her pink spongy tongue showing between two rows of braces that were thicker than the chrome streaks on Iggy Corso's convertible. Her eyes, the grayish brown of sparrows that had flown too close to a smokestack, zeroed in on mine. Her eyelids opened and closed as if spelling out *I have a crush on you* in semaphore. Even if I did not turn toward her, I could not ignore Eleanor's presence at the desk next to mine, for no sooner did I tune her out than the gold barrette that kept her black, kinky hair from springing into space like the Bride of Frankenstein's would clang on her desk, or she would pump her bony legs up and down, causing her black-and-white saddle shoes to squeak out a beat against the wooden floor. The Thing had gotten hold of the Class 6–1 seating plan.

That was not all he'd accomplished since the Dodgers clinched the pennant. In front of my classroom he had placed the biggest, meanest hen in captivity: Mrs. Schaefer, with her dancing gullet, her beak of a nose, her beady eyes, and her long, veiny, wrinkled hands. Schaefer had it in for me. I was the son of Jeannie Stone, who had not only defied and insulted her when Hubbell was her pupil, but was currently leading the campaign to make Vivian Mason, Benny's mother, the Jackie Robinson of the PTA. Vivian was the perfect candidate for PTA president; she was a college graduate, a professional bookkeeper, the mother of a bright fourth-grader, not to mention a college freshman, and the wife of a junior high math teacher. Mrs. Schaefer championed the fascist candidate, a woman named Mrs. Hess, whose main qualifi-

cation, according to my mother, was her ability to outshout anyone in a room.

I heard Schaefer's voice: "Mr. Stone. Mr. Stone! Are you
with us? What is the answer, please?"

Hell, no, I'm not with you, lady. And I not only don't know
the answer, I don't know the question. I don't even know the
subject. I was thinking about more important matters, like how
to get my seat changed, and why I was in school in the first place
instead of at Jake's with my lucky hat on my head watching the
first game of the World Series. Today's was the first Series game
ever televised in living color, and I didn't even have a radio.
Other kids, like Louie Corso, were less deprived; their teachers
allowed radios in the classroom on World Series days, and certain
pupils were charged with keeping their ears to the speaker to
report significant developments to their classmates. Why, I wondered, did they not play the Fall Classic at night, or, better yet,
declare a national holiday, so that hardworking men and schoolchildren—the very heart and soul of American fandom—could
exercise this most fundamental freedom? It seemed to me a violation of the Bill of Rights.

And why, of all times, had my mother chosen now to make
a stand for discipline and good attendance? She did not permit
Hank and me to stay home from school because, she said, there
are more important things than the World Series (as if she could
name one convincing example), and we would be among the
privileged to attend in person the games to be played on the
weekend. It did not register on my mother that with me stuck in
a classroom from Wednesday to Friday with my lucky cap in a
briefcase under the desk, the World Series might be all but over
by the weekend. Not that Hank and I were the only ones in this
ignominious condition. Fearing an epidemic of hooky-playing, a
bunch of moms had banded together to form a chain of sentries;
there was no way to walk to P.S. 144 without passing one of them
stationed in a window, looking for missing children like Happy
Horowitz watching for German submarines off the Virginia coast.

"Mr. Stone?" Schaefer repeated, smoke and flames shooting
out of her nostrils in anticipation of a kill.

I heard a whisper: "Twenty-four." It was Eleanor Krinski,

trying to win me over with a rescue attempt. I had no choice but to give her that satisfaction.

"Twenty-four," I said.

"I suggest you pay attention, Mr. Stone," said the hag, "and tell your mother to help you with your homework instead of playing politics. The answer, class, is twenty-eight."

This time I *chose* to look at Eleanor's face. I glared at it. It was red with shame, bowed with contrition. She stared at her desk. And, of all things, I found myself feeling sorry for the little reptile. I fought this disturbing impulse and took advantage of Eleanor's lapse of attention to look out the window and beam my attention northward, in the general direction of the Bronx. Like Brooklyn, the Bronx was a sprawling borough of ethnic enclaves that was treated by Manhattan like the crude cousin you had to invite to family affairs but whom you hoped would not call attention to himself. On a map, Manhattan was a double-pointed dagger with one tip aimed at the ass of the Bronx and the other at the neck of Brooklyn. However, I felt no kinship with the home of Yankee Stadium, where so many World Championship flags had been raised. Toward the Bronx I directed a curse on the Yankees and a stream of mental cheers for my underdog Bums.

The previous night, after watching the season premiere of Milton Berle's show with John Wayne and Esther Williams, I had convened with Artie and Louie in Rooney's Lot to roast up some mickeys and discuss the World Series. Ritual gatherings like ours were taking place throughout the neighborhood; my father and his pals were at Mickey's Saloon, Hubbell and his were at Jake's.

It was cool and damp, with dark clouds shielding a waxing moon, and the fire felt warm on our hands and faces. The weather report said there was a fifty percent chance of rain the next day. A rainout would help the Yankees, experts believed. Having fought for their pennant up to season's end, the Bombers could use an extra day of rest, especially since Mickey Mantle, their best hitter and the American League home run champ, needed more time to heal a pulled thigh muscle. The Mick would not be able to play the next day. The boys and I decided to root for a rainout because we wanted our victory to be untainted by Yankee excuses and we wanted the earliest games to come on the weekend when we would be in attendance. If not a rainout, then at least a rain *delay,* which would push game time back to, say, after the three o'clock school bell.

Most pundits picked the Yankees to once again prevail. The bookies fixed the odds at 13–10. The consensus among sportswriters was about the same; even Dick Young, who covered the Dodgers, picked the Yankees to win in seven games. Predictably, Joe DiMaggio, retired from baseball but not yet Marilyn's husband, forecast another Dodger defeat. ("I guess the only thing that could cure them is a brainwashing," said Jolting Joe.) So did Billy Cox, the ex-Dodger third baseman, who asserted that all the Yankees had to do to win was show up in their pinstripes with the N.Y. emblem on the chest. Billy Cox, I figured, was still bitter at having been traded to Pittsburgh.

Puffing on the Chesterfields that Louie had brought along, we listed all the reasons why the Dodgers should win. They'd had three weeks to rest and prepare, and, with the exception of Carl Erskine's sore arm, their only health problem was Carl Furillo's cold, which should be taken care of with penicillin. With Clem Labine and Ed Roebuck, the Brooks had a better bullpen than the Yankees, an important factor in a match between two hard-hitting teams. Furthermore, the Bums had not only run through the National League schedule like Ex-Lax, to use a simile that Louie had picked up from Mike the Barber, but they were more mature now than when they'd lost Fall Classics to the Yankees in the past. And they might have been more formidable: the '55 Flock led the National League in runs scored, home runs, team batting average, slugging percentage, doubles, stolen bases, earned run average, saves, and strikeouts.

Perhaps more important, the Yankees were not as dominating as they once had been; they'd lost the pennant the year before and barely squeaked it out this year. They no longer had fireballing right-handers Allie Reynolds and Vic Raschi to neutralize the Dodger's righty sluggers. The current Yankee pitching staff had one star, Whitey Ford, and a bunch of mediocrities. Casey Stengel announced he would start lefties—Ford and Tommy Byrne—in the first two games, and the entire season only one southpaw had managed even to complete a game against the Bums, and he'd *lost.*

"We gotta win," said Louie. "If we don't win this year, then there's no God."

"I don't know about God," I said. "All I know is, dreams have to come true sometimes."

"If we don't win, there's no God," said Louie.

"We'll win," Artie asserted. Like his hero, Gil Hodges, Artie was quiet, but he was as emphatic in his convictions as Gil was when swinging at an inside fastball.

"I sure hope so," I said.

Louie sensed the uncertainty in my voice. "You think they won't win?" he asked.

"Damn straight they'll win."

" 'Cause it sounded like you're not sure. What do you think—they won't win or somftin?"

"They'll win. They're ten times better than the Yankees."

" 'Cause you sounded like maybe they won't win."

Although I was not about to spoil the occasion by listing them, I had plenty of reasons for trepidation. What if the long layoff had made the Dodgers rusty, not rested? What if the Yankees had momentum going for them? They were as hot as a roasted mickey at the end of the season, winning nine of ten games to nail down the flag. Watching their stretch run had filled me with a perplexing ambivalence: I rooted for them because I wanted the satisfaction of beating them in the Series, but it went against my natural instincts; every inning was a struggle because I hated them so much I kept forgetting that I wanted them to win. In the second game of a doubleheader against the Red Sox, Ted Williams came to bat with the bases loaded and the Yanks holding a 2–1 lead. Whitey Ford took the mound in relief and coerced Teddy Ballgame into hitting a double play ball, and the Yankees clinched the pennant. I felt like I did when I found myself cheering for the cavalry even though my mother had explained exactly why the Indians were really the good guys.

The Red Sox game convinced me that the Yankees were still the Yankees, the franchise that had won twenty-one pennants in thirty-five years. They were still the luckiest team in the world, and Casey Stengel was the greatest magician since Houdini. Those guys found ways to win when they had to win. They may have slipped in '54, but before that they had won the World

Championship five straight years, sixteen times all together, more than any other franchise and exactly sixteen more times than the Dodgers. For the Yankees, tradition was like a great relief pitcher—an extra edge, something to turn to when the going got tough. A legacy like theirs makes a team bold and the opposition wonder if mysterious forces were conspiring against them. Maybe, when the Dodgers walked into Yankee Stadium, they would freeze like I did when I walked into the 6–1 classroom and saw Mrs. Schaefer. The spirit of Yankees past might rise up and make the Dodgers' knees tremble in awe.

Nor were ghosts the only thing the Yankees had going for them in the Stadium. The alley in left-center field, where the Dodgers' right-handed batters were accustomed to slamming home runs and extra base hits, was cavernous; balls that would sail out of Ebbets Field were routinely caught in the Bronx. And the Yanks had the home field advantage; the first two games and the last two, if needed, would be played in the Stadium.

And what about Carl Erskine's injured shoulder? This was no small thing. If Oisk couldn't play, the Dodgers would lose their pitching advantage. Don Newcombe, great as he was, seemed to hibernate in October; he had never won a World Series game. In addition, Clem Labine wasn't feeling well, and Johnny Podres had just returned from the disabled list. The Flock also had a problem in left field. Alston announced he was starting Jim Gilliam instead of Sandy Amoros to get another right-handed batter in the lineup against Ford. But Gilliam was inexperienced in the outfield; what might happen in the spacious pasture of Yankee Stadium? The decision also meant that Don Zimmer would be playing second base, and I wasn't so sure that the rookie could handle the pressure. To top it off, Duke Snider had not hit a home run since Labor Day, three weeks earlier.

Doubts such as these could be countered convincingly. It was the nonbaseball signs that really troubled me, and these I could not discuss with Louie and Artie because they did not share my sensitivity to omens, nor my intimate acquaintance with The Thing.

For starters, on the same day the Yankees clinched the pennant, an all-white jury in Mississippi acquitted the two men suspected of killing Emmett Till, the black teenager who allegedly wolf-whistled a white woman. It had taken all of two hours for the defense to convince the twelve men that someone out to destroy the Southern way of life had deliberately thrown a corpse in a river so it would be identified as Emmett Till. I knew this to be a bad sign; the fate of Jackie Robinson's team correlated strongly with racial justice. Making the issue even more complicated, the Yankees, sensing a shift in the direction of destiny, were no longer entirely Caucasian. Elston Howard, whom a *News* writer called "the team's Negro," had been a major contributor in his rookie season, catching, playing the outfield, and hitting close to .300. Even someone unfamiliar with the larger dimensions of the racial picture would know that the acquisition of a Negro was a significant advantage; in the previous seven years, blacks had won six National League Rookie of the Year awards and five Most Valuable Player awards.

The day after the Yankees clinched, The Thing struck at the heart of the nation: President Eisenhower had a coronary. He was in a Denver hospital, in an oxygen tent. Analysts postulated that, if he survived, Ike might resign the presidency for health reasons. Surely he would not run for reelection in 1956. Although Paul Dudley White, the nation's preeminent heart specialist, declared the president's chances of a full recovery "reasonably good," the nation pondered a future without its chief executive. On Monday the stock market saw its heaviest trading in eighteen years and the worst single-day dive since the Crash of 1929.

I was, by heritage and inclination, a Democrat. I wore an Adlai Stevenson button in 1952. I voted for Robert F. Wagner in my school's mock mayoral election. Moreover, I was certain that the Dodgers were Democrats; if not in their actual voting habits, then certainly in spirit, for they were the workingman's team. One would, therefore, expect me to interpret as a positive omen a tragedy befalling a prominent Republican. But Eisenhower's heart attack was a bad sign for one reason: Richard M. Nixon was vice-president. This was no war hero. This was not a general who led the Allies to victory against Hitler. This was not a man who could have been a Democrat had the party been smart enough to recruit him. No, this was a bona fide Republican, a shady-looking character who sent chills up the spine when he smiled, a man who had persecuted Alger Hiss and allied himself with Joe McCarthy, a man who, in my mother's view, was surely in the thrall of big business. At least Eisenhower was a stabilizing force and a respected international figure; Nixon, age forty-two, was a nobody. Worse than a nobody. If the slope-nosed phony wasn't a Yankee fan, I'd eat my lucky cap.

That The Thing had managed to infiltrate the White House and sabotage justice in Mississippi was a measure of his strength, for he'd spent most of his time that September in my house. I'd been feeling like an orphan, what with my father obsessed with Hubbell and my mother on two campaigns—one to elect Vivian Mason, and one to make up for the neglect of Round Man. When she wasn't recruiting for Vivian, she was going places with Hank. But that was the least of it. My older brother's mysterious behavior had become even stranger, and his intentions were mutinous.

The day after 300,000 Brooklynites turned out for the team's parade, Hubbell was scheduled to pitch his last sandlot game of the summer. My father prepped him with a full schedule of work-outs and a series of pep talks so intense that if you saw silent footage of him, you'd think it was Jeff Chandler rallying his warriors for a last-ditch battle. I knew that my father had arranged for Teddy Ryan, the Dodger scout, to be at the game; Hubbell did not. I also knew something my father did not: Hubbell wasn't doing half of what he was supposed to do to prepare for the game.

I watched from the sideline behind third base with my father and Teddy Ryan. The scout was a tall, lean man with a thick crop of gray hair and eyes to match. His face was browned and lined from years of squinting in the sun. He said nothing, communicating whatever he had to with a nod, a tilt of the head, an angled lip, a raised eyebrow. He chewed and puffed on a cigar, and spit so much brown juice I was sure the grass in his vicinity would die.

My father smoked one Pall Mall after another and talked incessantly. When he wasn't shouting instruction and encouragement to Hubbell, he provided Ryan with a nervous commentary, not just about his son, but every player on the field, advising the scout on which kids had big league potential and how the organization would have to coach them to bring them up to snuff. He told Ryan that the batter was an opposite-field hitter who couldn't hit an inside pitch, and, on cue, the ball was hit to the opposite field. He knew when someone was about to bunt. He knew who would swing at anything above the chest. He knew who could be had with a curveball out of the strike zone.

"Look how the sucker's leaning," he said of one batter. Then he yelled to Hubbell, "Give him the curve, babe!" Then back to Ryan: "Watch this, Teddy, curve on the outside corner. He's got a great curve, it breaks like this." And he described a sharp, downward arc with this hand.

Ryan spit.

Hubbell pitched decently in the first inning. He walked one batter and got lucky when another hit a scorching line drive right at the third baseman. Two fly balls to the outfield and he was out of the inning. "Way to go, champ!" yelled my father. "He gets better as he warms up," he told Ryan. "But his best weapon is his head. He knows the game. He outsmarts 'em."

As Hubbell reached the sideline, a teammate pointed in our direction and told him something. Hubbell looked surprised. He hurried to the locker room, and when he returned, barely on time to start the second inning, his face was faintly green.

It went downhill from there. Hubbell struggled through five innings, giving up four runs, eight hits, and four walks, and the worse it got, the more desperate and anxious my father became. "Show 'em some heat, champ, low and in!" he'd shout. "Bear down, champ! Come on, these guys can't hit! Let's go, babe, give him your best. Use that screwball." But he couldn't do the pitching. When a batter socked one over the fence, he told Ryan, "I don't believe it. He *never* gives up the long ball. His shoulder must still be bothering him." Then he caught himself. "It's fine, actually. The shoulder's fine. No problem." He couldn't have it both ways.

It was pathetic. Teddy Ryan said nothing, but his spit was eloquent. Occasionally he seemed impressed by my father's comments; at other times it seemed he wanted to shove a resin bag in my father's mouth. When the other team loaded the bases in the sixth, Dad was sweating more than Hubbell. He was desperate. "Even on an off day you can see what great stuff he has, right, Teddy?" he said. "How he moves the ball around, how he knows the game, how he don't get rattled with men on base . . ."

The manager of Hubbell's team walked to the mound.

"No!" yelled my father. "Don't take him out! Let him find the groove."

The manager waved for a new pitcher. Hubbell handed him the ball. "Leave him in there, you moron!" my father roared. "Teddy, say something." Teddy Ryan turned to my father. He squinted long and hard, his gray eyes filled with cold pity. He spit and walked away.

On the pitcher's mound the manager gave Hubbell a pat on the butt. My brother walked off the field, swinging his arms as if he'd been relieved in more ways than one. When he got to the bench, he accepted briefly the comfort of his teammates, then trudged to the locker room. My father chased after Teddy Ryan.

I caught up with them in the parking lot. Ryan had his hand on the door of his Oldsmobile. My father entreated, "Come on, Teddy, everyone has off days, you know that. Jesus, I saw Bob Feller get the shit kicked out of him on more than—"

"Frank!" Ryan interrupted. His voice was surprisingly smooth. The gravel I'd expected to hear had been polished by phlegm and coated by fifths of bourbon consumed in lonesome motels. "Frank, this ain't the first time I've seen the kid. I've seen him pitch four, five times."

My father was stunned. "You think we don't keep an eye on our own backyard?" said Ryan. "I gotta tell you, Frank, you know the game better than half the scouts in the business. You got eyes like an eagle. But you can't see your own kid. He's got talent, sure, but in all honesty, we're talking a big project here. Semipro ball for a few years, then maybe the low minors for who knows how long, then maybe, *maybe*, if he works at it and stays healthy and gets a few breaks, maybe he gets a shot at the bigs. But I wouldn't bet on it. I'm sorry, Frank."

He got behind the wheel and started the motor. My father's voice lost its authority. "Take another look at him, willya Teddy?" he implored. "In Florida maybe, a workout in spring training?"

"Sure, Frank," said Ryan. "Take care." He drove off, the wind from the car's acceleration sweeping a gob of brown spit onto my father's pants. He didn't notice.

When Hubbell finally got home late that night, we were

watching Perry Como on TV. My father, having downed a few belts at Mickey's Saloon, tried to lift his son's spirits. "Hey there, champ," he said. "Don't sweat it. Everyone has off days."

"Why didn't you tell me you had a scout coming down?" Hubbell asked.

"Didn't want you to think about it. Didn't want you to do anything different. No big deal. Some days you just don't have your stuff."

"I had my stuff, Pop. It just wasn't good enough."

"Just a little setback," said my father. "Let me tell you, Teddy Ryan, he could see your potential, even on an off day. He said it won't be easy, but with your talent and some hard work, the sky's the limit."

Had I heard the same conversation my father was referring to? Had I been in the right parking lot?

"You know what else Ryan said?" Dad told Hubbell. "He said I can see things out there he doesn't see himself. He said I have better eyes than most of his scouts. And you know what I saw? I saw a damn good pitcher who needs to work on that screwball because the righties are waiting on your curve. And you know what else? I want you to learn a forkball. The way your fastball rises—"

"Forget it, Pop," said Hubbell. "New pitches are not gonna turn me into Carl Hubbell. It's over. I'm not cut out to be a ballplayer."

"What are you talking about?" my father said. "You *are* a ballplayer. That's what you are. You can't let a little adversity throw you off the path. No, no, I did not raise a quitter. You're tired. You're disappointed. These things happen. You'll get some rest. We'll reconsider a few things, and we'll move on. This winter you'll go to Florida, you'll stay with Uncle Jack."

"I'm not going to Florida."

"What do you mean, you're not going to Florida? It's the plan."

"It's *your* plan. Maybe I have other plans."

"There *is* no other plan!" my father yelled. "Baseball is the plan!"

He had never encountered such impertinence from his children. Confused, he looked to my mother for clarification. Her eyes warned him against losing his temper. He got a grip on himself. "Look, champ," he said, "the thing is, some guys, they're naturals. Mantle, Mays, DiMaggio . . . guys like that, they're blessed. All they have to do is show up. The rest, they have to get there with sweat and blood. They have to push themselves to the limit to make the most of what they've got. I was one of those guys. You are too. It didn't work out for me, but it can for you. Don't lose faith. Now go and rest up. Go ahead, we'll talk another time."

Hubbell had heard it all before. This time, clearly, he didn't buy it, but he was too weary to argue. He shuffled to his room.

"Lay off him, Frank," said my mother.

"You don't understand. You never wanted him to be a ball-player in the first place."

"I understand this. If it doesn't come from inside him, there's nothing you can do about it. You don't make the big leagues because you want to make your father happy."

My father waved his hand in disgust. He never had time for my mother's fancy theories about child-rearing. But this idea was uncomplicated and eminently sensible. He ruminated for a while, then turned to his wife and said, "You're right. I'll leave him alone for a while. No kidding, I promise. Let him take a little vacation till . . . yeah, that's it, till the World Series. That's the ticket. The Series, that'll get the old juices flowing. When the Dodgers win, boy, he'll get right back on the program, full speed ahead. Thanks, babe, you always set me straight."

My mother examined him through a gray haze of cigarette smoke. She wasn't so sure he'd been set straight.

Nevertheless, he stuck to his word. For over a week the only time my father mentioned baseball to Hubbell was in the context of the approaching World Series and the tight American League race to see who would play the Dodgers. As if to avoid temptation, he kept a distance from his older son.

At first this worked out nicely for me. I was restored to the position of prominence to which I had become accustomed. Without Hubbell to work out with, my father spent more time with me in the afternoons and on weekends. We played catch. He hit me fungoes to sharpen my fielding skills. We would recruit Round Man or Artie and Louie to shag the balls, and my father would pitch to me so I could practice my hitting. The afternoons on the dusty diamonds were sweet, but after a while they soured. Unable to get Hubbell off his mind, Dad missed the sense of urgency that had marked their workouts. As a result, he gradually turned our own sessions into toil, driving me the way he drove Hubbell. The irony did not escape me when I began to make up excuses, even stooping to afternoon homework, to get out of doing the one thing I'd loved most about the first eleven years of my life: playing ball with my father.

At the same time, I was plagued by Hubbell's behavior. Was he betraying the family dream? Was it just some rampaging hormone, a condition that would pass, like acne? Was it part of The Thing's overall plan? Was it a sign that had some bearing on the World Series? And what did it portend for me? I'd always seen my future as a train hitched to Hubbell's locomotive. Ever since I'd decided, some years earlier, not to model my life after Hopalong Cassidy, I had not considered an alternative to baseball.

Hubbell just got weirder. When he wasn't on the living room floor a foot away from the television or holding a radio to his ear, he was reading newspapers and magazines out loud to himself, pacing around the house and mumbling in a deep baritone. Prominent, tongue-twisting names emanated from his mouth: Mao Tse Tung. Nikita Khrushchev. Charles de Gaulle. Patrice Lumumba. Jawaharlal Nehru. Gina Lollobrigida. Sometimes he'd pronounce a series of ordinary words: these, those, third, going to, Long Island, give me that, thirty, dirty, oyster. Was my brother turning into one of those maniacs who talked to phantoms in the street? Would they let me visit him in the insane asylum? Do they have baseball fields at those institutions?

One afternoon I was fixing myself a triple-decker sandwich with bologna, mayonnaise, peanut butter, grape jelly, and Swiss cheese, when I realized that I was like the ingredients in a sandwich—a sane sandwich on nut bread. I was the normal one sandwiched between an older brother who broadcast to himself in incomplete sentences and an oversized younger brother who was a cross between Clyde Beatty, the lion tamer, and Marlin Perkins, the host of *Zoo Parade.* Round Man, wearing an infantry helmet, was kneeling in a corner of the kitchen, his butt thrust skyward. Will he never learn? I wondered, as I reached into my pocket for my bobby pin stinger. But when I saw what he was doing, I forgot about stinging him. Hank was holding aloft a safety pin straightened to form a long spear. It was aimed at a huge cockroach, which was trapped in the corner. "What are you, dueling with roaches?" I asked.

"Shhh," said Round Man. "They have to die, but they deserve a fair chance." He angled down with the pin. The roach swiveled to the right. Hank adjusted. Suddenly, he stabbed at his prey. But the roach darted out of the way. Again, Hank thrust downward with his lance, but once more the roach dodged it.

"It's Rommel," Hank concluded. "No one else has moves like that."

"It has a name?"

Just then Hubbell arrived. "Hey, guys, listen to this, willya," he said. I turned in his direction. Hubbell held up a pack of Marlboros and intoned, just like a guy in a TV commercial, "The new filter cigarette from Philip Morris. The filter doesn't get between you and the flavor." Then, in his normal voice, he asked, "How does that sound? Do I have an accent?"

I said he sounded fine. Round Man had no opinion. He was busy with his stakeout. I explained to Hubbell what Hank was doing. He looked at the wall as if there were a camera imbedded in it and spoke like John Cameron Swayze: "Ladies and gentlemen, we're here on the dusty plains of North Africa, where General Round Man Patton is stalking his archenemy, Rommel, the Killer Roach."

Hank shot us a nasty look. Rommel seized the moment. He darted left. My brother stabbed at it. Rommel stopped dead in his tracks. The lance landed just in front of him and lodged in the linoleum. Hank yanked it out, stabbed again, but this time Rommel sped to the right. The spear hit the floor at an angle and bent like a leg broken at the shin. "You made me miss!" Round Man yelled as Rommel escaped into a crack in the wall. He warned his prey, "You got away this time, Rommel, but you're a marked man."

Hubbell faced his imaginary camera again. "Ladies and gentlemen, this demented young man needs your help. Won't you send your check today to the Round Man Memorial Booby Hatch Fund, Post Office Box—"

"Very funny!" said Hank. "*You're* the crazy one, walking around like you're on TV when you should be practicing your screwball."

"I have better things to do," said Hubbell.

That was the first indication that there was some purpose behind Hubbell's odd behavior. The second came the day we woke up before dawn to wait on line outside Ebbets Field for World Series tickets. As the line inched toward the ticket window, Round Man and I stood in front of Hubbell and Benny. My brother read out loud from the newspaper while his friend coached him. "Give it more life," Benny would say, and Hubbell would rev up his delivery. Or Benny would interrupt to correct his pronounciation: "You said *dat dey,*" or, "No, no, you said *fawced* to have a *toid pawty,*" and Hubbell would read the line again, taking pains to say *that they* and *forced* to have a *third party.*

The strange monotony ended only when a guy on line objected, "Hey, what's the story? Your friend can't read? Draw him a friggin' pitcher."

After we secured our tickets, we went to the record store on Pitkin Avenue where Dizzy worked. Hubbell wanted to buy "Story Untold," a ballad of lost love by the Nutmegs that was too maudlin for my taste. Hank was interested in "The Ballad of Davy Crockett" because whenever it came on the radio, his two hamsters would career around their cage like Fred Astaire and Gene Kelly. My choice was "Why Do Fools Fall in Love?" by the Teenagers. I liked the beat, I liked Frankie Lymon's pubescent falsetto, and I hoped that by listening to it repeatedly I might figure out the answer to the question posed by the title.

As Hank and I browsed the bins of 45's, Hubbell and Benny spoke earnestly about career choices. Benny said he was now thinking of majoring in sociology because civil rights was going to be big. My brother said something about *getting in* and *acing the test,* but just as I edged close enough to hear him better, the music on the store's speakers changed to the McGuire Sisters' "Sincerely," and Dizzy, furious, shouted to his boss, an obese man with a black duck's tail haircut, "Hey, dig it, Charlie, turn that shit off, man. That's the Moonglows' song. Those bitches stole it."

"Hey, who woiks for who around here?" said Charlie. His

voice wheezed as if he'd just sprinted a hundred yards to get there on time. "And watch your friggin' language or you're out on your ass."

"Benny, man," said Dizzy, "you ought to major in business and get a job in the record industry and straighten this shit out."

"Hmm, records *are* going to be big," mused Benny.

"See what I mean," said Hubbell. "You guys have alternatives. You can do whatever—"

His jaw fell open so abruptly I thought it would shatter against his chest. Everyone followed his eyes. At the door Grace Kelly was getting her bearings. Benny and Dizzy watched Hubbell stare at her, then sang, in harmony, "Ea-earth angel, earth angel . . . will you be mi-ine?"

"Shut up, you idiots," said Hubbell.

She was wearing a peach-colored dress and silver earrings with a deep blue stone that offset her eyes. Beads of sweat the size of pearls formed on Hubbell's forehead and under his nose. Diane moved closer to where we stood, surveying the record bins for the right category. Then she spotted my brother. "Hubbell?" she said. "Hi, remember me?"

Hubbell tried so hard to be cool his voice cracked like ice. "Oh, sure, uh . . . Shirley's cousin, right? Diane."

She smiled; her teeth were as straight and white as the paper in a brand-new notebook. She looked at the rest of us, waiting to be introduced. But Hubbell was paralyzed.

"Hello," she said to Benny. "I'm Diane."

"Oh, I'm sorry, jeez . . . I thought . . . you know . . ." said Hubbell. "Um, this is Benny. Mason. And this is, uh . . . Sheldon. He works here."

"You may call me Dizzy," said Dizzy, and he bowed.

Diane looked down at Hank and me. Round Man shifted nervously, as if wondering whether he too was supposed to bow.

"Oh, uh, these are my brothers," said Hubbell. "This is Hank and this is Roger."

"Hello, Hank. Hello, Roger," she said. Her cordial smile and the musical way she pronounced my name were so endearing, I thought I might be able to give up Nurse Gallagher for her.

Gesturing with their eyes, Benny and Dizzy urged Hubbell to make conversation. Hubbell strained to think of something to say. Then he saw what Diane was carrying and, for a moment, forgot his fear and became his real, natural self. "Wow, *The Catcher in the Rye*," he said. "I loved that book."

"Really?" said Diane. "You read it?"

"Oh, yeah, my mom gave it to me. She's always giving me books."

"My father does that too," said Diane. "Do you think he's crazy? Holden Caulfield, I mean. My mother says he's neurotic, but I think he's just . . . I don't know . . . sensitive."

"Oh, no, you're right, for sure," Hubbell declared. "He's not crazy, he just sees through all the phonies out there and it gets to him."

"That's what I think too." They stared at each other for a long, nauseating moment, like those scenes in movies when they want to make you believe that two perfect strangers have just found true love. "Don't tell me how it ends," Diane urged. "Maybe we can discuss it when I'm finished."

The exchange was interrupted by the proprietor. "Hey, Dizzy, go take a break with your friends. I got a business to run here."

Outside, Benny put a hand on my shoulder and Dizzy grabbed Hank's; they were slowing us down so that Hubbell could walk alone with Diane. We had to pretend to be window-shopping at Woolworth's while the two of them talked at the bus stop. Hubbell shuffled and fidgeted so much I thought he would drill a hole in the concrete with his sneakers. Finally, Diane's bus arrived. She got on, waving goodbye to us, and Hubbell floated our way.

"How'd it go, babe?" asked Dizzy. "Did you ask her out?"

"Well," said Hubbell, "not exactly."

"What does that mean, *not exactly*?" Benny inquired. "Did you or didn't you?"

"I couldn't. There were too many people around."

Disappointed, Dizzy said, "Shit, man, would that stop Iggy? This was like a golden opportunity. You gotta strike while the bull is hot . . . or the horns, or some such shit."

"The iron," said Benny. "Strike while the iron is hot. Take the bull by the horns."

"Same difference," said Dizzy. He and Benny eyeballed Hubbell, demanding an explanation.

"Don't bug me," said Hubbell. "Some old woman was like two inches away, listening to every word I said. I'll call her, okay? I'll ask Shirley for her number."

His friends were skeptical. Hubbell vowed he would ask her out, and to strengthen his chances he made us stop in a bookstore to buy something that would impress Diane. He marched straight to the fiction section, perused the James Joyce titles, and settled on *Ulysses,* despite its bulk, because he assumed it was the same story as the movie we had seen that summer starring Kirk Douglas.

When we reached Play Street, some of the Big Guys were playing stoopball. Hank excused himself to go home and play "The Ballad of Davy Crockett" for Bruno and Gorgeous George. I hung out in hopes of getting into a punchball game with the Big Guys; nothing gave me more pleasure than to slap a slicing two-hopper past a lunging pair of teenage hands. Hubbell leaned on the stoop and scanned *Ulysses.* "Jesus Christ," he said, "where the hell's the periods in this thing?" Additional scanning elicited another revelation. "What the hell! This can't be the same as that movie. That was Greece. This is like Ireland or someplace."

The big, black Buick of Iggy Corso rolled slowly up the street. "Here he comes, Klinger," said Mr. Big. "You can find out for yourself."

"He's fullashit," said Klinger. "He don't have no date with her."

"Yes, he does," said Harry the Horse. "I asked Shirley."

If the news irritated Klinger, it was poison ivy to Hubbell. He squirmed as though his skin itched in places he couldn't stratch. Iggy pulled up to the curb. "Hello, Mr. Dinger," he said. "Keeping those lips nice and soft for my ass?"

"Just warm up that backseat for me, shithead," said Klinger. "And get a haircut. I don't like no shaggy-ass, greaseball chauffeurs."

"My backseat is always warm," said Iggy. "Say, uh, Mr. Stone, I can't decide which of these to use. Can you help me out?"

He held out his palm. In it were two flat, square packages, one silver, the other red. Each had a circle inscribed in the square, as if it housed a wafer or a fifty-cent coin. "I'm kind of used to Trojans," Iggy said, "but maybe something a little classier for the blonde chick. What do you think?"

Hubbell burned. He wanted to say something devastatingly clever, but before he could think of anything, Iggy said, "Maybe I should ask someone with a little more experience." With a guffaw he sped away. Hubbell put the book down, grabbed the spaldeen out of Mr. Big's hand, and marched to the curb. He fired the ball at the stoop.

We watched, flabbergasted, as Hubbell caught the rebound and threw the spaldeen again. "Hubbell, what are you doing?" said Harry. "You ain't supposed to throw spaldeens!"

"Fuck it, I want to play stoopball." He threw the ball with all his might. It bounced hard off the step, hit the side of the stoop and bounced to Benny. "Gimme the ball," said Hubbell.

Benny hesitated. "Don't mess with me," warned Hubbell. "If I want to play stoopball, or stickball, or punchball, or any goddamn ball, no one's gonna stop me. I'm sick and tired of this bullshit." He twisted Benny's wrist and removed the ball from his grip. Horrified, I watched him throw the ball, catch it, throw it, catch it, throw it harder and harder. The way my father described what throwing spaldeens could do to a pitcher, I expected my brother's arm to drop from its hinges like an old door. Then I saw something even more horrifying: Frank Stone himself was on the Corner, arguing with Mike the Barber. My father said something that appeared to be unequivocal. Mike shrugged and made an entry in his memo pad. My father, impervious to the urgent messages I was beaming his way, turned and saw the left arm that carried the standard of his baseball dreams being used to throw a small, pink rubber ball.

That night, in the kitchen, my father tried to contain his fury as he rubbed Ben-Gay into Hubbell's shoulder. Hubbell said his arm felt fine, but my father insisted on preventive measures. My mother washed the supper dishes. I oiled my glove. We could hear, faintly but discernably, a robust chorus singing "The Ballad of Davy Crockett" over and over, while, I imagined, Round Man choreographed a routine for two rodents with top hats and canes.

"What a day," my father groaned. "Traffic. Sy Kramer. Goddamn bunch of convention drunks. Now this. You gotta *care* for this arm, for chrissake, it's a precision instrument."

"It's no big deal," said Hubbell. "You didn't have to embarrass me in front of my friends."

"No big deal? Do you hear this, Jeannie? No big deal, he says, like he can pitch with his *other* arm if this one's out of commission."

My mother spotted Hubbell's copy of *Ulysses* on the counter and thought it a perfect excuse for changing the subject. "My my, what ambitious reading. What'd you do, meet a girl who reads Joyce?"

Hubbell didn't have to answer. From the look on his face, my mother knew she was right.

"Jeannie, do you mind?" said my father. "We're discussing something important here."

"Books are important," my mother countered.

Hank entered the room, carrying a long, green snake. He stroked its cold, scaly skin as if it was chinchilla.

"First thing in the morning, I want you to do windmills with the arm," Dad told Hubbell. "Slowly, no strain, just to see how it feels."

"Mom, didn't Joyce write anything easier than that?" asked Hubbell.

"Try *Dubliners.* It's a collection of short stories."

"Enough with the literature!" Dad yelled.

Hank tried to maneuver close to my father so he could show him his snake, but my father's position as he kneaded the muscles in Hubbell's back and shoulder made it difficult to achieve the right angle. "Look, Dad," he said.

But Dad was intent on explaining to Hubbell what Hubbell had heard a thousand times. "This arm is the key to your future, champ. You don't want to—"

"How come you always know what I want and what I don't want?" This was not a simple question like, say, "Didn't Joyce write anything easier?" You could hear in my brother's voice years of reflection and a lengthy accumulation of courage. My mother watched her husband, poised to intervene if he erupted. Dad tried hard to control himself.

"How do I know?" he said. "Because I've been there. That's

how I know. Because we've been working for one thing ever since your hands were smaller than a baseball. Because all our hard work can go right down the toilet in one minute. Because you can't break in a forkball with a bad arm."

Hubbell stared at the leftover scraps of pot roast and pasty pebbles of mashed potatoes and peas. In his mind, lined up like bullets, were things he wanted to say but could not bring himself to utter. Nor could he stand any longer the touch of my father's hands on his skin. He reached for the shirt draped over an adjacent chair.

Hank took advantage of the opening. "Look what I got, Dad," he said, thrusting the snake between my father and Hubbell. My father turned toward him.

"Not now, Hank . . . Yaaaaaahhhhh!" Seeing the serpent inches from his nose, he jerked back so hard he almost knocked the chair out from under himself. He turned the same shade of green as the snake. "Jesus Christ, get that reptile out of here!"

"He won't hurt you," Hank assured him.

"Take it away. You'll scare your mother."

My mother found his gallantry amusing.

"Come on, Cecil," said Hank to his pet. "They don't appreciate nothing around here." He sulked toward his room.

"Hubbell, I think that arm can use a hot shower," said Mom.

Hubbell got the message. "Ladies and gentlemen," he said, "the show's over. Good night, and good luck."

"Get back here!" ordered my father. "I ain't through yet."

Hubbell kept walking. My father stood up, the veins bulging on his neck. My mother stepped in front of him. "Let him go," she whispered firmly. "Go talk to Hank. I'm sorry he's not an athlete, but he is your son. You have three, in case you forgot."

My father slammed the Ben-Gay tube onto the table. "Snakes, for cryin' out loud," he said, and he shuffled off to Hank's room.

"Let me tell you, Roger," my mother sighed, "sometimes this is not an easy team to manage."

I did not discover the purpose behind Hubbell's madness until the day before the World Series opened. I was in the bathroom early that morning when I heard my brother's footsteps in the corridor leading to the front door. Then I heard my mother.

"Okay, Hubbell, where are you going all dressed up, and why have you been acting so weird lately?"

I peeked out to see my brother, dressed in a suit and tie, turning back to face Mom. He checked his watch and, evidently calculating that he had time to spare, returned to the kitchen to explain himself. Standing in the bathroom with the door ajar, I couldn't help but overhear.

That summer, Hubbell had realized that he was not cut out to be a baseball player. He had finally come to accept what his father and mentor did not, or could not—that reaching the big leagues was, at best, a long shot, at worst a pipe dream. To make it he would have to dedicate himself entirely to the goal, work his tail off day and night, be prepared to endure years of toil in semipro or minor league ball in hopes of someday having a shot at a major league roster. He did not think he had it in him. He said he did not want to be hanging around the Corner when he was forty, talking about the good old days.

He had a new goal, he said, one that had arisen without bidding from deep inside. He wanted to be a broadcaster. He wanted to be like Mel Allen and Red Barber and Vin Scully, or maybe even a classy news guy like Edward R. Murrow or Douglas Edwards. In a sense, Hubbell said, he'd been in training for that his whole life, every bit as much as he'd prepared for baseball. A few weeks earlier he had discovered through Mr. Putterman, the guidance counselor at his high school, that NBC operated a broadcast school, and that it was considered an excellent way to break into the field, especially for someone with no college plans. He applied, passed the written test, impressed his interviewer, and today, that morning, he was going to take the subway up to Rockefeller Center for the big step: an audition, at which he would be asked to read extemporaneously from news copy. He felt more confident about this challenge than he ever felt when taking the mound to pitch with the aftertaste of vomit in his mouth. "I want this, Mom," he said. "I want it as much as I ever wanted baseball, maybe more because this is *my* dream, nobody else's."

Now I understood the TV watching, the play-by-play commentaries, the reading aloud, the pronunciation drills. I even understood why Hubbell had been so interested in Yankee games—not because of the pennant race, but because he was studying Mel Allen and Red Barber. I understood why, when guys rehashed the old arguments over who was better, Mantle or Mays or Snider, Campanella or Berra, Rizzuto or Reese, Hubbell would start arguments over the relative merits of Allen and Barber, Vin Scully and Russ Hodges.

He apologized to Mom for not telling her sooner. He hadn't told a soul, he explained, except for Benny, who helped him prepare for the audition. Keeping the secret had been difficult because he was so excited he wanted to share it with everyone, but he dared not risk his father finding out. He couldn't bear the thought of telling him, he said, not so much out of fear—he knew that the bark of Cyclone Frankie Stone was far more ferocious than his bite—but because he did not want to hurt him.

My mother was moved. She reached out and held Hubbell's hand. "He'll take it hard. He has an awful lot riding on you. Too much, if you ask me. I've been living with this since before you were born, you know, since the minute he realized he'd never make it himself."

"It's not my fault he got injured, Mom. Why should I have to make up for it?"

"You don't, honey. Just do me a favor and pick your moment carefully. He's going through a rough period, and remember, he always did what he thought was best for you."

Hubbell nodded. "I figured I'd wait till after the Series. When the Dodgers win, he'll be a lot easier to deal with."

This promises to be one hell of a postgame celebration, I thought, with my father depending on the Bums winning to get Hubbell back on the baseball program, and Hubbell waiting for the same moment to tell Dad he was going to *talk* about baseball instead of playing it.

I could not tell if the tears in my mother's eyes were from sorrow or pride. "You know," she said, "I went along with the baseball thing reluctantly, but I have to admit, I really wanted to see you pitch in Ebbets Field."

"Jesus, not you too," said Hubbell. "Hank and Roger want to be batboys. Sal and those guys have bets on how much money I'll make. Dizzy wants to play the National Anthem on his trumpet the first time I pitch. Everyone has a stake in me."

"Don't worry. I'm on your side. I'm very proud of you." She checked her watch. "You'd better go."

They stood up. She hugged him. "Break a leg, kiddo," she said, and shoved him toward the door with a pat on the butt. As my brother, my idol, dashed down the corridor toward a new future, I closed the bathroom door so he wouldn't see me. I braced myself in anticipation of finding The Thing stretched out in the bathtub. But the tub was empty. Maybe The Thing was not responsible for mangling Hubbell's brain. Maybe he was in Denver adjusting the knobs on President Eisenhower's oxygen tent, or in the Bronx making preparations for the World Series. Or maybe what was happening to Hubbell was, somehow, not a bad thing.

Life had always been simple. The important truths were axiomatic. My brother would be a Dodger, and I would follow. My father would be robust and cheerful and funny, and would drive a cab and one day own his own. My mother would always be there when I needed her, ready to stick up for me in matters such as the occasional day off from school. The Dodgers would one day win the World Series, and they would always be in Ebbets Field. Now things were topsy-turvy. I had never encountered uncertainty of this magnitude. I couldn't decide anything. Late that night, after roasting mickeys with Artie and Louie, I lay in bed as rain pelted my window. I couldn't decide if I wanted the opening game to be rained out. I couldn't decide whether I wanted Iggy Corso or Marty Klinger to win their stupid bet. I thought Iggy was the coolest guy in the world, and I hated Klinger, but on the other hand if Iggy won, it would break Hubbell's heart. Then again, what did I care about Hubbell? He was a traitor. He was betraying the family cause. On the other hand, maybe he was doing the right thing. My mother seemed to think so. And if he was, what would it mean to my future? I *wanted* to be a ballplayer, damn it! The only thing I knew for sure was that I would not tell anyone what I knew because if it got back to my father, no fallout shelter would be strong enough to withstand the impact.

It did not take long for Eleanor Krinski to get over the humiliation of feeding me the wrong answer. I was beaming my most powerful hexes toward the Yankees, who, by my estimates, ought to be batting in the third inning, when she leaned back directly into my field of vision. Her eyes cloudy with tears, her pale, quivering lips arched in a pout, she whispered, "I'm sorry, Roger."

They will stop at nothing, these dames. I ignored her. I turned to my notebook and tried hard to fall into step with Schaefer's lesson in long division. Anything to take my mind off the impossible task of divining what was happening in Yankee Stadium.

Soon, a boy entered the room and announced, "Dodgers two, Yankees nothing." For the first time since school had started three weeks earlier, the room witnessed an outpouring of joy. We cheered so loud that the messenger did not hear what the smoldering Mrs. Schaefer was trying to tell him before he left to spread the good news to other classes.

I was relieved, but I remained frustrated. How had they scored? What inning was it? How was Newcombe pitching? One needed to know such things to get a reading of the signs.

A short time later the messenger reappeared. "The score is two to two," he said. The Yankees had tied the score. But how? When? This time there was no cheer, only a low grumble, and even that was too boisterous for the dragon lady.

"Class!" Schaefer bellowed. We shut up. She stopped the bearer of ill tidings as he attempted to continue his rounds. "Just a minute, young man. Who sent you here?"

"Mr. Newman," the boy said, trembling. "I'm going to all the rooms on this floor."

"Well, I do not want to see you again. Tell Mr. Newman that his messages are not welcome in this classroom. Do you understand?"

"Yes, ma'am," said the boy.

About twenty minutes later Louie Corso's head popped briefly into view in the window of the classroom door. In a moment it appeared again. Louie was jumping up and down. Once he knew that I'd spotted him, his hands appeared in the window. On one hand, three fingers were held up; on the other, two. So, that was the score. But who was winning? An okay sign appeared in the window. Clearly, it was 3–2 Dodgers.

Louie never returned. My classroom was blacked out for over an hour. It was agonizing. I could not keep myself from turning toward the window, as if I expected a scoreboard to appear above the rooftops or a plane to trace a message in smoke, and each time I turned that way Eleanor Krinski would take it as evidence that I forgave her and her crush on me was requited. When I couldn't take it any longer, I raised my hand and asked if I might leave the room.

Schaefer knew what I was up to. She wanted to refuse. But she couldn't. Suppose I really did have to go to the bathroom and I ended up peeing in my pants or collapsing on the floor with cramps from holding it in? She'd be in big trouble. Scowling, she handed me a pass. "Make it quick," she said.

The boys' bathroom was down a long corridor. I ran. The idea was to use up as little time as possible in search of a radio or someone who was up on the game. Continuing past the bathroom, I paused briefly at each door in hopes of hearing the sounds of baseball. I heard nothing, so I dashed down a flight of stairs, scurried past another line of rooms, and again heard no radios. Then I turned a corner and heard what I was after: the voice of Vin Scully. I followed it to a supply room. I entered, fearlessly, and found myself in a narrow aisle flanked by shelves of pads, pens, pencils, paste, blackboard erasers, and chalk. Miss Wolf, a stoop-shouldered woman with a dark mustache who worked as a clerk in the Adminstration Office, was stacking the shelves and listening to the game on a transistor radio. She looked glum. With some trepidation, I asked, "What's the score?"

I shocked her, but she recovered quickly and responded, frowning, "Six-three, Yankees."

I was crushed. But I had to know more, and luckily Miss Wolf knew her baseball. It was the eighth inning. The Dodgers had jumped out to a quick lead in the second when Furillo sliced a home run to right field. Robinson followed with a triple that was hit so far it would have been a home run at Ebbets Field. Robby scored on Zimmer's bloop single. But the Yanks came right back, Elston Howard lining a two-run shot into the left field seats.

Howard, the Yankees' only Negro, had hit a home run his very first time at bat in a World Series. This was a bad sign. The Dodgers regained the lead in the third, Miss Wolf told me, when Duke Snider popped one. A good sign—the Duke's quiet bat had awakened when needed. But the Yankees tied it up when Newcombe committed the cardinal sin of walking the pitcher, Whitey Ford, who eventually scored on a ground out. The very next inning Joe Collins, the Yankee first baseman, hit a home run to put the Bronx ahead. And, in the sixth, Collins connected again, this time with a man on base.

We were losing six to three because some stiff who hit .234 in the summer decided to become Babe Ruth in the fall. It was the timing of guys like Joe Collins that had made Casey Stengel a genius.

My companion in the supply room was the most knowledgeable female I had ever met. I wondered why she was a lowly clerk instead of a teacher. She told me that the Dodgers were getting men on base off Ford in the early innings, but were not coming through with clutch hits. She said that Newcombe had been rocky all game and had finally been removed after Collins's second home run. In her opinion he should not have pitched that long.

Even in a cramped room without my hat, my presence made a difference. As we spoke, Furillo cracked a single. Then Robinson smacked what might have been a double play ball but which skidded through the hands of Gil McDougald for a two-base error. Zimmer followed with a sacrifice fly, making it 6–4, Robby moving to third. Frank Kellert pinch-hit. Ford's first serve was a ball. On the second pitch Robinson broke for the plate and slid under the tag of Yogi Berra. Robby, his hair gray and his waistline inflated, had stolen home for the nineteenth time in his career. Quite a rhubarb ensued, according to Scully. Yogi jumped up and down and screamed in the umpire's face, certain he had applied the tag before Robinson's foot touched the plate. Like all arguments, this one did not change the score: it was now 6–5.

I was aware that I'd been away from class long enough to have peed in Coney Island, but I didn't care. I was alive again. Jackie Robinson had once again done the miraculous, and I just knew it would be the turning point. And sure enough, no sooner had the dust settled than Kellert looped a base hit. Don Hoak ran for him. The tying run was on base and Gilliam, a switch hitter, was at bat.

Then a shadow passed along the shelves between me and my new friend, and a deep voice echoed around the room like an iron door closing on a dungeon: "What have we here?"

It was Dr. Gross, the principal. Gross was The Thing's chief agent in P.S. 144. Mrs. Schaefer's ally and superior, he had a few years earlier embraced the McCarthy cause and fired three teachers for alleged subversion. Like Schaefer, he had it in for the Stone family and backed the fascist candidate for PTA president. He was as happy to see me as I had been to see Miss Wolf, only his pleasure was so perverse, I expected him to drool. "Miss Wolf, this will not do," he said. "I will see you in my office." She left, trembling. Then Gross looked down at me, placed a hairy hand on the muscle that ran from my shoulder to my neck and squeezed. "Come with me, young man."

In the corridor Dr. Gross informed me that I was to report to his office at three o'clock to spend an hour in detention. This was intolerable. The game was too close. If I made good time getting to Jake's when the bell rang, I might still make a difference. "I can't," I told him.

"Really? Well, I'm afraid I insist."

"I have to be somewhere."

"What a pity. You'll have to tell your friends you were unavoidably detained."

"I have a dentist's appointment," I said. "I had a bad toothache all night." Sometimes my ability to come up with quick, effective lies scared me.

As with Schaefer, I had Gross in a tight spot. Suppose I was telling the truth? Would he want to face an irate dentist, not to mention my mother, who would then have cause to accuse him of picking on her children for political gain? He thought it over. "Make plans to stay after school tomorrow," he said. "Now get back to your room. I think Mrs. Schaefer might have some ideas of her own for you."

As I ambled down the corridor, Miss Wolf, who was walking up ahead with the radio to her ear, turned and shook her head. It was a gesture of neither sympathy nor camaraderie. It was a baseball message; the Dodgers had failed to tie the score.

Schaefer greeted my return by announcing publicly that I must have a kidney disorder to need so much time in the bathroom. She said she would discuss it with me after class. I started to tell her about my dental appointment, but she snapped, "Not a word! Take your seat!"

When the three o'clock bell rang, I bolted for the door. Schaefer shouted my name, but I kept going. On the way down the steps I passed other boys whose intentions were the same as mine. One of them was Round Man, who bounced along in a fury. I burst into the afternoon light and, without pausing to let my eyes get used to it, fought half-blind through the crowd, dodging bodies like Crazy Legs Hirsch. Without breaking stride, I fixed my cap extra firmly on my head and raced recklessly through the streets, heedless of traffic. I did not stop for lights. At one point I nearly collided with Barney Klinger's enormous Lincoln. He screeched to a stop, yelled at me to watch where the fuck I was going, and went back to what he was doing: growling at a shrinking, cowering man in the passenger seat who was begging for mercy. Barney was worse than a Yankee fan. He was indifferent; he did not even have the radio on. But everyone else did, and as I ran past windows and shops, I heard fragments of commentary: "Strike . . . Snider . . . base . . . ninth . . . foul . . . six-five . . ."

I burst through Jake's door. No one budged. All eyes—Hubbell's, Dizzy's, Benny's, Harry's, Mister Big's, Sal's, Jake's, Burt's—remained fixed on the TV screen. Hitler could have stormed in with a dozen SS troops and no one would have noticed. I stood next to Hubbell and surveyed the scene. Snider was on first base. Furillo was at the plate. Bob Grim, not Whitey Ford, was on the mound. The faces around me matched the pitcher's name. "Come on, Skoonj!" whispered Hubbell. But Furillo swung and missed.

Hank barreled into the luncheonette.

"Too late, Round Man," I said. On screen, Duke walked dejectedly off the field. Yogi Berra jogged to the mound and shook the pitcher's hand. In the Yankee dugout, looking natty in pinstripes, The Thing patted Casey Stengel on the butt.

Chapter Eleven

My father arrived home looking as old as the national pastime itself. That morning, as if to get the World Series off on the right foot, Sy Kramer, the dispatcher, had taken his time assigning a cab to my father, causing him to miss an hour of peak driving time. At day's end Kramer greeted Dad's return to the garage with the verbal equivalent of grinding horseradish into an open sore, gloating over the Yankees' victory as if he had personally whispered in Whitey Ford's ear the requisite wisdom to stifle Dodger bats.

My mother's mood had nothing to do with the game, except insofar as it was easier in Brooklyn to escape the effects of humidity than the collective gloom of a Dodger defeat. Mom was aggravated by the failure of the forces of good to rally the PTA membership behind Vivian Mason. Several key supporters had, that afternoon, switched allegiances. Hence, Mom was not amenable to rational arguments about why Hank and I should be permitted to stay home from school the next day. For an open-minded person, my mother was remarkably hidebound when it came to matters such as my lucky cap or the metaphysical link between her cause and my own. And she was shockingly unsympathetic about my difficulties with Eleanor Krinski and the Schaefer-Gross axis.

She was also late with supper, a lapse that did not sit well with her husband, whose lunch had consisted of two gobbled-down Sabrett hot dogs, with sauerkraut, purchased at a red light from a street vendor. I anticipated a tantrum and a Take Cover drill, but Mom cut that off deftly by telling my father, "If you want pot roast, shut up and wait. If you want canned soup, go ahead and blow your stack." He opted for the pot roast, and let his stack simmer in silence.

Even Round Man was ornery. He chose the worst possible

time to try to convince my mother to let him add a new frog to his menagerie. "But it'll help me capture Rommel," he whined.

"I don't care if it turns into Prince Charming," Mom replied. "There will be no amphibians hopping around my house."

For reasons that were not yet clear to me, Hank was particularly nasty to Hubbell. My older brother joined our brooding foursome halfway through supper, blowing in with a jaunty strut and a big smile, as if he'd just returned from another dimension where the good guys won World Series openers. "Chin up, Hank," he said, patting the sack of flesh between Round Man's mouth and chest. "It's just one game. Don't let it get you down."

Hank slapped his hand away. "Get outta here, drop dead, you don't know nothin'."

"Jeez, don't take it out on me," said Hubbell. He offered the mourners a more upbeat view of current events: "Look at it this way. We lost by one run to their best pitcher. Who do they start tomorrow? Tommy Byrne! A stiff. Thirty-five years old, for God's sake. *Lefty*. We'll kill him. Then we're home for three straight games."

I figured something good must have happened between him and the blonde he had a crush on. Later that night I would find out the real reason for his incongruous gaiety. Once again I caught him talking to himself, only this time he wasn't Edward R. Murrow. He was Red Barber and Mel Allen. He shifted from one sportscaster's voice to the other:

"Well, Mel, Hubbell Stone is in the catbird seat. That telegram from NBC just about clinched it for him."

"How about that, Red. It doesn't surprise me in the least. He was at the top of his game for that audition, and he belted a real Ballantine Blast."

"Oh, Doctor, did he ever! And it couldn't happen to a more deserving young man. Of course, they'll be tearing up the pea patch when he breaks the news to his father."

"I'm afraid so, Red. And there is that small matter of how he's going to pay the tuition."

This told me two things: my brother had been accepted to broadcast school—and he had lost his mind. I hoped the Dodgers, or any team for that matter, would sign him up before it was too late and he either went ahead with this stupid plan or ended up broadcasting to a padded wall. I thought about squealing to my father, but changed my mind on the theory that he would find out soon enough and I would not have to subject myself to Hubbell's revenge; it would be, I calculated, at least five or six years before I was big enough to fight him even up. I wished he would lose his voice. I wished his tongue would fall out. I wished he would fall asleep in the sun so his lips would swell up like balloons and he'd never be able to talk again. I wished he'd lose the girl. I had been ambivalent about the Klinger-Corso bet, wanting to see Diane's honor upheld, but also looking forward to seeing Marty bend down and kiss Iggy's ass. Now I would root for Iggy on the theory that Hubbell would be so crushed and humiliated he would come to his senses.

"He's got a point," said my father about Hubbell's argument. I could practically see the opposing factions in his brain waging a tug-of-war. One side wanted to take Hubbell's opening and run with it, turn that optimism into a good old Cyclone Frankie Stone pep talk about sacrifice, destiny, and faith in dreams of baseball glory. The other side, the one that remembered his promise to leave Hubbell alone, prevailed, aided by a muscular glance from my mother.

Dad expanded on Hubbell's views, listing several additional reasons why Tommy Byrne could not beat the Dodgers in a million years. Overlooked in this analysis was the fact that, owing to the injury to reliable Carl Erskine, the Flock's starting pitcher for Game Two would be Billy Loes, a twenty-five-year-old nut from Queens whose surname was an anagram for both *sole,* as in the bottom of a foot, and *lose.* Loes had already blown one World Series. In 1952 the Dodgers had a three-games-to-two advantage when the flake took the mound for Game Six with a chance to bring home the marbles. Instead, he lost his. The Bums were leading 2–1 in the seventh inning when, with a Yankee on first, Loes went into a stretch . . . and let the ball slip out of his hand. The balk put the tying run in scoring position. The opposing pitcher, weak-hitting Vic Raschi, then hit a grounder back to the mound. The ball ricocheted off Loes's leg and into right field. The score was tied. Next inning, Loes tossed up a gopher ball to Mickey Mantle. The Bums never recovered. After the game Loes said he'd lost the ground ball in the sun.

My father chose instead to remember that Loes had won a game in the 1953 Series; he had a feeling the pitcher was due for a big performance. After supper, compelled by his renewed faith, he made a clandestine phone call to Mike the Barber. "What's the price on the whole Series?" he asked. Whatever Mike replied, it made my father's eyes light up. "Do it," he said.

As bedtime approached, I pondered ways to use my knowledge of the phone call to blackmail my father into helping me ditch school the next day. Dad should have been a natural ally in that cause, but he had long ago agreed to defer to my mother in educational matters. We were watching the Arthur Godfrey show. When Julius LaRosa sang "And This Is My Beloved," my mother, visibly choked up, rose from her chair and announced, "That does it. I'm going to get tickets for *My Fair Lady*."

"Wait a minute," said my father. "Where are you going?"

"To get that money I put away. The show opens in a few months, and I want the best damn seats I can get."

"No!" said Dad. "Wait. Hold on. I, uh . . . I don't know if that's a good idea."

"It's a great idea," said Mom. "If you won't join me, I'll go with someone else." And she disappeared into the kitchen.

My father followed. So did I, my heart pounding with the knowledge that the fabric of my whole existence could be ripped apart like an old undershirt being converted into rags if my mother found out that her money had been used to pay off a bet. Only two days after he learned about the secret fund, I had seen my father hand fifty bucks in ones, fives, and coins to Mike the Barber.

My mother opened the broom closet. She reached toward the back of a shelf on which were stacked light bulbs, an iron, an extension cord, boxes of thumbtacks and nails, a roll of masking tape, and some loose balls of string and twine that had tangled around each other like ivy and bougainvillea competing for sunlight. She was groping for a red and black tin box that had once contained Chinese tea.

"Wait a minute, babe," said my father. "It's not that I don't want to go. It's just . . . well, you know, I'm trying to save for that medallion and—"

"Fifty bucks won't make a whole lot of difference."

"Every nickel counts, sweetheart. The sooner I can get my own cab—"

"Oh, Frank, wake up!" She now had the box in hand. "Fine, so you won't have Sy Kramer to deal with, but you'll still be doing the same thing every day, hustling fares, fighting traffic, all the things you complain about. And for what? A few more bucks a week? Drop it, Frank. Do something else with your life while you still have your health and your sanity. Be honest. You *hate* your job. It eats away at you. You're a smart man. You can do *more.* Quit, Frank! Find something worthy of you."

"Quit?" said my father. "Just like that, huh? Sure, I'll quit. And do what? I got mouths to feed. I got rent to pay. You don't just walk away from your livelihood, for chrissake."

"Oh, piddle! We'll manage. We always have. I'll get a job. The kids are old enough to—"

"If you get a job, I'll *never* eat!"

"The point is, owning your own cab is not the answer," Mom argued. "You used to have passion, Frank. You used to care about things. Lately, all you care about are those damn Dodgers and Hubbell's career, and I'll tell you something, sweetheart, you can't control either one, and that's not healthy. Don't get old on me, Frank. It's not too late. Find something else before you end up like Willy Loman."

"Willy Loman? Who's—"

"Oh, for God's sake! I give up. Do what you want, Frank, but I'm ready to make some changes."

As if going to see *My Fair Lady* would somehow enable her to be her own Pygmalion, she placed the tea box on the counter and started to open it.

I knew that The Thing would pop out of that box like a genie and curse the entire family. I yelled, "Mom!"

She turned toward me, astonished to find me there in the first place and wondering why in the world I had screamed. She stared at me, her fingers poised to pry open the lid.

What could I say? "Don't open the box"? I said, "Can I stay up to watch *I've Got a Secret?*"

"Go to bed," said Mom. She opened the box. I winced, ready to cover my ears with my hands and run to my room. But The Thing did not pop out. Nor was the box empty. My mother reached in and pulled out a stack of bills and two handfuls of coins. "I'm buying two tickets tomorrow," she told my father. "I hope you come with me." She stuffed the money into the pocket of her housecoat and lit a cigarette. On her way out of the kitchen, she said, without bothering to turn around, "Willy Loman's the guy in *Death of a Salesman*."

Artie Finkelstein, bless his calculating mind, figured out a way to outsmart Mrs. Schaefer. He obtained a transistor radio and an earplug with a long cord, placed the radio in his briefcase and the briefcase between his legs, and ran the wire through his fly and up his shirt to his ear. In this manner, Artie was able to listen to Game Two, and, because he was a brain, he was able to answer any questions the Mad Hen threw his way even though he was preoccupied. Through a system of prearranged signals, he kept me abreast inning by inning from his location one row over and four seats down. The system provided some measure of satisfaction, but in many ways it served only to frustrate me more.

I approached Game Two somewhat buoyed by the signs. First, doctors had declared that President Eisenhower was making satisfactory progress and had allowed him to do some business from his hospital bed. Second, Mickey Mantle would once again watch the game from the bench. And third, gentle Roy Campanella was still steamed over the incident in the first game in which he tagged out Billy Martin on an attempted steal of home and the two collided and got all tangled up like my father and Solly Skapinsky. When they struggled to their feet, Martin threw an elbow at Campy's face. The *News* quoted the catcher as saying, "He didn't come close with that (delete) arm of his. Just let him take two steps toward me and I'll take care of that little (delete). He's been too damned smart for too long. Anytime that (delete) thinks he's gonna run over me, little as he is, I'll break every (delete) bone in his (delete) body." Maybe, I thought, Campy would be so fired up he'd knock in a run for each delete.

After three scoreless innings the Dodgers added substance to my hope. Artie raised his thumb, followed by one finger. The Bums had scored a run. However, within ten minutes, as Schaefer drilled the class on United States geography, Artie's leg started motoring up and down and he rapped the eraser end of his pencil rhythmically on his desk like Otis Hicks playing drums. He chewed on a knuckle. He shook his head. He dropped his head abruptly onto his desk, as if he'd been shot from behind. He turned, quickly and surreptitiously, to show me his pain. He pointed his thumb downward toward the floor, then flashed four fingers. The Yankees had scored four runs.

Suddenly I heard that most despised voice. "Mr. Stone, what is the capital of Vermont?"

"Montpelier!" I barked. Schaefer was startled, not because I knew the answer but because I delivered it like a gob of spit. Pow! Right in her kisser. She scowled. Her eyebrows, tweezed and penciled-in, joined together in the shape of a V, and her lips pressed so hard against her teeth that they drained of color. Then she raised one corner of those thin lips in what vaguely resembled a smile, as if thinking ahead to how she might torment me.

Down 4–1 with me and my lucky hat stuck in that torture chamber with Mrs. Thing, I felt as helpless as I had the day in the hospital waiting room as they carved the tumor out of my mother's breast.

Signs of hope appeared: Artie punched the air with a clenched fist. Then he leaned forward as if to see more clearly. Something was happening. Artie was rooting.

Schaefer saw an opening. "Arthur, what is the capital of Rhode Island?"

"Robinson! I mean, Providence."

Schaefer eyed him suspiciously, but Artie recovered nicely. He repeated the correct answer and added, for good measure, the population of our smallest state.

Soon Artie displayed a thumbs-up and a single digit. The Bums had scored a run, but I knew from the way my friend shook his head that they should have scored more.

The score remained 4–2 through the sixth inning as Schaefer segued into her favorite topic: the Soviet Union. The weasel probably lit candles before a picture of Senator Joe McCarthy, during whose days of infamy she exhorted her students to report any signs of pinko activity in their homes, such as publications with the word workers in their titles and phrases like one world or means of production. It was even said that her husband had divorced her because she spied on him. Now, after explaining precisely how Khrushchev's lackeys were taking over the United Nations and how we should not be surprised if one day soon a flotilla of Red Chinese gunboats appeared off the coast of Coney Island, she drew a line down the blackboard to form two columns. On one side she wrote COMMUNISM, on the other DEMOCRACY. My mother had explained to me exactly why such a dichotomy was illogical and the terms not necessarily incompatable. One was a way to organize an economy and the other was a system of government. I wanted very much to make this distinction, but, prudently, I kept my mouth shut while Schaefer solicited entries for her lists. Meanwhile, Artie's signals indicated that the Bums had gone down scoreless in the seventh inning.

Then, with well-honed timing designed to subtract years from our innocent lives, the Lizard Lady yelled, "Take cover!" To the sound of seats clattering against back rests and flesh and bones colliding with wood and metal, we dove as one under our desks. The routine was familiar, the drill well-rehearsed—posters headed WHEN YOU SEE THE FLASH, DUCK AND COVER were on every wall—but it never failed to terrify. Normally, the clamor lasted only seconds and was followed by a frightful hush. Absolute silence was mandatory, the better to hear the buzz of Russian planes, the shrill whistle of descending missiles, and, of course, the deafening detonation of atomic bombs. This time, however, the noise gave way to the voice of Vin Scully. As he dove under his seat, Artie had yanked loose his earplug. Scully's words burst forth into the silence like bazooka shells: "Hodges is going . . . Strike three! The throw to second . . . double play!" The Dodgers' eighth inning rally had been snuffed.

Throttling the giggles of girls and the curses of boys with a sharp, "Silence!" Schaefer stormed over to Artie's desk, yanked him up by the shirt collar, turned off the radio, and declared that she was shocked that a boy of his character would exhibit such disgraceful conduct. She added that certain friends of his—exactly who was unmistakable—had evidently become a bad influence. She confiscated the radio and ordered Artie to resume Take Cover position with the rest of us.

On my knees and elbows, with my arms covering my head to protect it from falling bricks and shattered glass, I found comfort in knowing that, because we had to face away from the windows so as not to be blinded by the flash of a nuclear blast, my ass was aimed directly at Eleanor Krinski's face.

From the sound of the metal taps on her high heels and the yardstick she slapped against her palm, I tried to gauge the exact location of Fräu Hitler as she strolled the aisles inspecting our bunker. Judging that she was too far away to see me, I risked raising my head to see if I could catch Artie's eye. I couldn't, but I did catch a more intriguing sight. The skirt of Donna Ackerman, whose seat was to the left of mine, had gotten snagged around her hips. Facing me, within arm's reach, was a blue moon of bloomers with a hole the size of a quarter revealing a patch of pink, plump tushie.

I tried to talk myself out of it, I really did, but reason lost out to instinct. At the risk of dislocating my elbow, I maneuvered my hand into my pocket and found, among marbles, handkerchief, and keys, my bobby pin stinger. I twisted the hammer into firing position, angled my eyes above my folded arm, and slowly reached across the aisle toward the hole in Donna's bloomers. The instant I felt the firm resistance of flesh, I pressed. Snap! Sting! Bull's-eye!

Donna yelled "Ow!" Her head jerked up and crashed against the underside of her desk. "Ow!" she repeated, this time louder.

As I pulled my arm back, Schaefer's yardstick crashed down on the back of my hand. Her bony claw encircled my wrist. She pried loose my stinger. "Up!" she commanded. Too enraged to wait for me to comply on my own volition, she yanked my arm, forcing me to rise so awkwardly I bumped my knee against the iron leg of the desk.

Then Empress Fang noticed I was not wearing my dog tag. Every student had been issued one of these tin wafers; we were to wear them on a chain around our necks for purpose of identification in the event of an enemy attack. Imprinted in raised figures on the tags were the bearer's name, address, date of birth, sex, eye and hair color, race, religion, and, most ominiously, blood type. At first I kind of liked my dog tag. I liked the clicking sound it made when I ran it up and down the beaded links of the chain. I liked sticking it in my mouth at moments of contemplation in lieu of a pen or Popsicle stick. When my mother instigated a militant, and futile, protest to the school board on the grounds that warmongers had no right to force schoolchildren to wear military gear, I lodged a dissenting vote. But each time Generalissimo Schaefer explained why it was necessary to wear the tin necklace, I grew to hate it more and more. The feel of it against my chest evoked images of me lying in a gutter, bleeding profusely from multiple wounds as the swirling red light of an ambulance made eerie reflections on the rain-soaked asphalt. I would hear voices:

"His dog tag says type A, Doctor, and I'm afraid we're all out of that."

"Well, then, pack up those arms and legs, nurse, and ship them to the address on the dog tag."

During the second week of school I shoved the tag into my underwear drawer, and there it had remained.

Schaefer grabbed me by the hair and wheeled me around to face the class, only there were no faces to face because no one dared look up from Take Cover position.

It was small satisfaction, but at least I forced the shrew to cut short the drill. "All clear!" she yelled. "Get up, class. Look at your classmate. He is not wearing a dog tag! It is people like him, who do not take our nation's defense seriously and do not follow instructions, who will be responsible for all of us losing our lives during an attack."

I resisted the urge to bow.

The Bums had been beaten by a thirty-five-year-old pitcher who, two years before, couldn't even make the St. Louis Browns or the Washington Senators, and who spent the previous season in the bush leagues. Tommy Byrne was the first lefty in over a year to earn a complete game victory over the Dodgers. He not only shut down the offense on five hits, he also lined a two-run single with the bases loaded and two out to top off the Yankees' four-run fourth inning. The Bums had several opportunities to score more runs, but they failed to capitalize, hitting into three double plays. Final score: The Thing 4, Good Guys 2.

All this I learned later, of course. I heard nothing of the game firsthand. I had to spend the hour from three o'clock to four outside the principal's office, sitting on the opposite end of a long bench from Artie. Dr. Gross was a bearish man with hair everywhere on his body—ears, cheekbones, knuckles, climbing out of the front and back of his shirt—except on top of his head. He had foul breath too. I caught a whiff of it when he grabbed my comrade and me by our collars after Schaefer handed us over. The look that passed between teacher and principal was the same as that exchanged by commandants in World War II movies when they got their hands on prisoners of war. Gross kept opening his door—breathing heavily, his belly challenging the buttons of his stained blue suit—to make sure we were writing, until told to stop, "I will never again disrupt my classroom."

No team had ever won a World Series after losing the first two games. None. Ever. On his postgame show, So-Called Sonny Scott made sure to emphasize this fact. In his opinion, Brooklyn fans would be moaning "Wait till next year" two days hence. "Only this time there won't *be* a next year," he added. "I say the Bums will relocate. Let's face it, the ballpark's an ancient ruin. In fact, the whole borough's going down the toilet, just like the team."

As Artie and I trudged home, I did, in fact, feel rather like a used wad of toilet paper being sucked inexorably down the vortex of a bowl, to be washed with the rest of the borough's wretched debris into the polluted waters of Jamaica Bay. The weather was perfect for baseball, fair and sunny with temperatures around seventy degrees, but it felt as if a dark cloud hovered over the entire neighborhood, like the one that rained perpetually on the character Joe Btfsplk in "Li'l Abner." That's what I felt like: sad old gloomy Joe Btfsplk.

To make matters worse, it was the day I had agreed to get my hair cut. After Mike butchered my pompadour and made my ears stick out like wings, I watched him commit a similar atrocity on my father's scalp. With my cap squooshing around on my head every time I moved because the barber had been overly generous with a green, gooey hair tonic called Dan-Dee, I studied magazines that featured more flesh than words, and listened to the two men discuss baseball and family. Mike compared the Dodgers to girls who sent you home with a disease he referred to as blue balls. I inferred that this had something to do with being either cold or wet, since, in my experience, the only body parts that turned blue were lips if you stayed in the water too long.

My father once again expressed his disdain for So-Called Sonny Scott. "The man's a moron," said Dad. "Tonight he predicted a sweep. Can you believe that? He also said the Dodgers will leave Brooklyn. Leave Brooklyn! Jeez, I'd love to see that putz eat his words. What's the price now, Mike? On the Series."

"Jeez, it must be four to one, at least," said Mike. "Maybe five." My father winked. "Frankie, lay off willya?" Mike added. "You shouldn't bet on—"

"I'm affirming my faith."

I was building up an arsenal for future extortion. As Mike shaved an arc around my father's ear, Dad talked about Hubbell. "I don't know what to do, Mikey. He's breaking my heart."

"Ah, these kids," said Mike, wiggling his stogie from one side of his mouth to the other. "They wanna be rebels. It's that friggin' jungle music they listen to. You listen to *good* music—Vic Damone, Jerry Vale, Sinatra—you don't act like an animal. You respect your parents."

"It's a fad," said my father. "It'll rock and roll right into the sewer, I guarantee it."

"Take my Ignazio, that bum. I says to him, finish school, loin a trade, *do* something with your life, for chrissake. All he thinks about is broads, broads, broads. He even makes bets now, whether he'll get laid or not."

"No kidding," said my father. He started to shake his head in dismay, but Mike reminded him that he had a razor in his hand.

"Don't you worry about Hubbell," said Mike. "He'll come around. After the Series, like you said. He's still the son of Cyclone Frankie Stone."

"That's why the Bums have to fight back, Mikey. There's a lot riding on it. If they come back, he'll snap right out of it, guaranteed."

He was right. A lot was riding on the Dodgers indeed. I decided then and there, for my father's sake, for Hubbell's sake, for the sake of the entire borough, that tomorrow I would be at Jake's, egg cream in hand, for Game Three.

Through repeated illustrations, my mother had taught me that there was good and bad in everyone. This usually meant trying to find something good to say about someone who acted like a jerk. However, where my older brother was concerned, my mother's principle was operating in reverse. I had idolized Hubbell all my life. To me, he could do no wrong. Now, with time and repeated observation, I was discovering he could also be a jerk.

It was the night of Iggy Corso's big date. The Big Guys were going to follow the couple in Harry the Horse's borrowed car to determine whether Iggy did or did not fulfill the terms of the bet: to park with Diane at the Holy Shrine for at least thirty minutes. Because I felt a desperate need to get my mind off the World Series, and because I wanted to witness my brother's humiliation firsthand, I begged Hubbell to take me with him. He refused, and he did it nastily, without a shred of sympathy, regret, or humor. He was not in the same chipper mood he'd been in the night before. He might have been accepted to broadcast school, he might have been accepted to the Supreme Court for that matter, but being down two games to none while the girl of your dreams goes out with the league leader in making out does not make for sunny dispositions.

Hubbell told Benny and Dizzy, who had come to pick him up, "This is gonna be rich. Wait'll she gets a load of the real Corso. This'll be the shortest date of his career. Are you kidding? A classy girl like that with a Neanderthal like him? Forget about it." But he was nervous. He couldn't stop fiddling with his clothes and fixing his hair in the mirror, as if he, not Iggy, was going on a date.

Because Hubbell would not let me tag along, I sat home and watched television while Round Man commiserated with his animals and my father joined his cronies for communal wailing and rending of garments at Mickey's Saloon. My mother spent the evening gabbing on the telephone with the Vivian Mason delegation to the PTA. When she joined me in the living room, it was only to say, "Roger, I'm going over to Mickey's to get your father. I'm afraid he'll drink himself to oblivion over those damn Dodgers."

"I wish I could drink," I said. "Then I'd get a hangover and I'd *have* to stay home from school."

She must have felt guilty about her continuing refusal to let me stay home because she agreed to take me to Mickey's with her even though it meant I would return well past my bedtime. I expected the bar to be smoky and crowded and to smell of beer, and I expected the denizens to be morose. I was right about all but one. The denizens were not morose, although they no doubt had been before my father decided to whip them into shape with a rip-roaring, never-say-die pep talk. His legs were unsteady and his speech veered into occasional woozy slurs, but he was magnetic. He seemed to occupy the whole room, moving from one clique to another, slapping backs and shaking hands and downing swigs of beer from other people's mugs.

"Are we going to give up?" he bellowed. "Are we just going to roll over and die? Do we think it's all over? That the Yankees are invincible? Hell, no! So what if no one's ever come back from two down! There's a first time for everything, right? They say it's four to one against us. I say, put your money on the table. We *can* come back. We *will* come back! This is not just a ball game. This is not just a World Series. This is a crusade. A crusade for redemption. Vindication! We will be vindicated! This is for every honest bum who ever got a bad break. It's for every underdog who ever had to fight against the odds. It's for the guys in the trenches. The ordinary Joes hustling for a paycheck. The housewives trying to make ends meet. The construction workers. The truck drivers. The shopkeepers. It's for the dreamers! It's for the Regular Guys. It's for *us*! The Brooklyn Dodgers are *us*! And we will prevail. It is our destiny!"

A roar went up and glasses were hoisted, and someone led a "Hip, hip, hooray!" My father downed the rest of his beer and opened his arms to accept perfunctory hugs and hearty slaps on his back. With his lifelong friends surrounding him and "Roll Out the Barrel" being sung, Cyclone Frankie Stone was in his glory, and his glory was increased by the arrival of half of his family. One arm high, the other low, he embraced my mother and me simultaneously.

"When you're ready to stop driving a cab," Mom told her man, "you can write speeches for Winston Churchill." She turned to the others. "Hi boys. Your friend here stood me up tonight. What do you think of that?"

"Hey, Frankie, watsammatter wichyou?" said Sal.

"Some guys, they don't know how lucky they are," said Jake.

For a man with living memories of applause, there could be no more perfect exit than to walk slightly tipsy through a grinning, singing crowd of admirers with the best girl in town on one side and a proud son with a Dodger cap on the other. Grandly, my father bid good night to his pals and aimed us toward the door. I could detect a slight stagger in his step. Then a burst of light sprayed the dimly lit bar. It emanated from a sequined dress and a bouquet of oversized jewels. Behind the two bodies in the door frame, lit by a street lamp, I glimpsed the front end of a shiny pink Cadillac.

The door closed. The new arrivals came into focus. It was Solly So-Called Sonny Scott Skapinsky in a black suit that might have cost as much as the taxi medallion my father coveted. His cigar was the size of a bat. On his arm was a platinum blonde in a sparkling, skin-hugging red dress. She had an hourglass body like Jayne Mansfield's, only she had a bulge or two where hourglasses don't bulge. I knew she was not Elsie Rubin, the neighborhood girl who had married Solly Skapinsky.

"Well, well," said Mike the Barber, "if it ain't old Mighty Mouth himself."

Every eye in the place was directed at Skapinsky and his doll. He raised his chin and rotated it while wiggling the Windsor knot on his tie, although the tie needed no straightening. This was a gesture he repeated every time he spoke. "Hello, fellas," he said. "Long time no see."

"Not long enough, Solly," said Burt.

Skapinsky eyed my parents. "Frank and Jeannie, what do you know. So, you're still together."

My father looked like a drunk who understands his condition and suspects that what he sees is an alcohol delusion. He squinted at the couple before him as if they were pink elephants he hoped would disappear.

"Life's full of surprises, eh, Solly?" said my mother.

"What's wit' the Solly bit?" asked the girlfriend. She had the nasal whine of Judy Holliday. Skapinsky ignored her question.

"So, what's a big star like you doing around here?" asked Jake. "Slumming or what?"

"Jeez," said Skapinsky, "can't a guy visit the old neighborhood?"

"Don't bullshit us, you bum," said Sal. "You ain't been around here in years. What's the story?"

"Actually, the station wants me to do a story on the Brooklyn fans," Skapinsky admitted. "So, I figured, hey, why not shoot around here, put my old friends on television?"

By now my father was convinced that what he saw was real. His primal hatred for Solly Skapinsky was as sobering as a cup of black coffee. "What do you think we are, stupid?" he said. "You wouldn't be here if it was your Yankees who were down two games. You just want to show us up on television."

"You come around here to make us look bad?" said Burt. "I say fuck you and the bus you rode in on."

Solly's girlfriend gasped as if she'd never heard such language in her life. "Well, I never!" she exclaimed. "You gonna stand for that, Sonny?"

Skapinsky did the maneuver with his chin and the tie. "Actually, I rode in on a new Eldorado."

"Yeah, well ride it the hell outta here," said Burt.

I saw the door open and Hubbell enter the bar. He must have been curious about the Cadillac parked out front, or else he figured Mickey would give him a shot of whiskey even though he was underage, because he looked like he needed a drink. I knew instantly that things had not worked out to his liking. Iggy Corso had won the bet and was probably still at the Holy Shrine having his way with Grace Kelly. It was precisely the result I had rooted for, but now I found myself consumed by shame. I felt sorry for my brother. All these topsy-turvy emotions were getting to me. Maybe, I thought, it was just one of those *phases* that grown-ups talked about.

Hubbell was stunned to see what was going on. He found a place along a wall where he would not be seen by any of the principals who now commanded the attention of the whole saloon.

Skapinsky straightened his tie again, making sure his adversaries noticed the diamonds on his cuff links. "Well, you know what they say, a prophet in his own land. . . ."

"This is not your land, Skapinsky," said my father. "You don't belong here."

"Who the hell's Skapinsky?" said the blonde. "Say, what's going on here anyways?"

"Quiet, doll," said Skapinsky. He turned to my father. "Gee, Frank, you're not being very friendly."

"What do you want, Solly, the red carpet?" asked my mother.

"Yeah," said Sal. "You wanna give out autographs? Go to the friggin' Bronx! Around here, we don't forget. You try to break a guy's leg with a dirty slide—"

"That was a clean slide," Skapinsky asserted.

"Bullshit," said Jake. "You were gunning for him, you son of a bitch. You ruin a guy's whole career and you come around here acting like a—"

"Holy shit!" said Solly. "I don't believe this. You morons think that cockamamie injury's what kept this bum out of the bigs? It was nothing. He was dropped because he didn't have a snowball's chance in hell of making it. He would've been dropped anyway." With contempt he elongated every vowel in my father's name. "Cyclone Frankie Stone. Ha! Around here, he was a big fish in a scummy little pond. But out there he was garbage. He was a piece of shit. Ptooey!"

"You lying son of a bitch," said my father. "You jealous bastard."

"What kind of stories you been telling all these years, Frank?"

"You change your name and your whole fucking biography, and *you* ask *me* about stories? You dirty dog, I oughta—"

"You oughta what?" said Skapinsky. "You gonna make something of this, you fucking weasel?"

"Solly, why don't you take off before it gets ugly," suggested my mother. Everyone in the bar had moved a few steps closer to Skapinsky. The babe in the sequins was already clutching her necklace and tugging on her boyfriend's arm. Only Hubbell stayed where he was. He was too stunned to move.

Skapinsky smiled crookedly at my mother. He straightened his tie. "Still a humanitarian, eh, Jeannie? That was always your problem. Too big a heart. I could've given you a life. Instead, you picked a loser, and you're stuck in this decrepit neighborhood."

I had, of course, seen my father blow his stack innumerable times. I had seen him take out his anger and frustration on tables, chairs, fenders, television sets, decks of cards, newspapers, telephones, and dishware. But I had never seen him strike another person. That night, like a racehorse sprinting down the stretch, his bite took the lead from his bark. He lunged at Skapinsky and grabbed him around the throat. Solly tried to pry his fingers loose, but he couldn't. My father was about to push that Windsor knot through the broadcaster's Adam's apple and into his esophagus. But the other men intervened. They pulled my father off his rival and held him by the arms. Mike grabbed Skapinsky and tried to usher him toward the door, but Solly took offense at this. He gave the barber a hard shove, and Mike went crashing into a bar stool.

Seeing his friend abused, my father shook loose and lurched toward Skapinsky again, but Jake grabbed one of his sleeves and he veered off target like a fighter plane that lost a wing. Solly took advantage of the situation and landed the first blow, a right cross that grazed my father's head. My father went wild. His friends could not hold him back. He scored a solid left to his enemy's jaw. Skapinsky kept his feet only because other men caught him and tried to haul him toward the door. But he was a big, burly guy, and he shook them off. He tried to retaliate. He and my father stood toe to toe in the middle of the room, swinging their arms like windmills, so wild and furious that no one could get close enough to grab them. Neither was able to land a punch anywhere except to the other guy's elbow or the top of his head, the kind of blows that hurt the puncher more than the victim. Meanwhile, Skapinsky's bimbo was shrieking at the top of her lungs. "Stop, you animals! What the hell are yez doing?"

My father got a headlock on his opponent. Skapinsky tried to wrench his way loose. When he succeeded, I thought he'd been decapitated, but the object that flew into the air was not his entire head but his toupee. Beads of sweat glistened on the skull of So-Called Sonny Scott like the sequins on his girlfriend's dress.

The combatants were finally subdued. They tried to break free, but they could not; they settled for spitting curses at each other. It looked to be all over.

"Better get your boyfriend out of here, Bubbles," my mother advised the blonde.

"Who you calling Bubbles, you skinny malink?" said Bubbles.

When the grip on his arms was relaxed, Skapinsky took two steps toward his girlfriend as if to escort her away. Then he lashed out. Catching my father looking away, he landed a sneak punch to the side of the head. My father crashed into a table and tumbled over it, defenseless. Skapinsky pounced on him. Mom jumped on Skapinsky. She rode his back, pinning his arms to his sides. Bubbles grabbed my mother by the blouse and tried to pull her off. It looked like a conga line of spastics.

Now was my chance. I had been looking for an opportunity to contribute—something suitable for my size, like a shin to kick, a toe to stomp on, a finger to bite. I grabbed the bimbo's belt. It was made of something slippery, like snakeskin, and it served no purpose other than to carve an isthmus between the two curvaceous land masses on the continent of Bubbles. I pulled. I tried to yank her loose from my mother, but it wasn't easy to get enough leverage with Mom's momentum pulling her in the other direction and my feet sliding on the sawdust that Mickey sprinkled over the wooden floor.

I lost my balance and fell. At the same time, my mother let go of Skapinsky, wheeled around, and gave Bubbles a mighty shove. Never, in all the times Louie Corso and I had pulled this trick on Artie and other unsuspecting victims, had it worked as perfectly as it did, unplanned, for my mother and me. Bubbles went toppling over my back, landing on her head. Her legs shot into the air like two shapely flagpoles. For my valiant effort I was rewarded with a close-up view, albeit brief, of the pink underside of thighs, striped by the clasps of a garter belt, and a V-shaped splash of red satin panties.

By jumping on Skapinsky's back, my mother had given Dad enough time to recover. He shoved Solly, sending him crashing into the bar. But just when it looked like my father would finish him off, Skapinsky grabbed a beer bottle. He cocked his arm and took aim at my father's head. Screams filled the bar. And suddenly Hubbell appeared, like Errol Flynn to the rescue. He intercepted Skapinsky's arm as it started to strike. The bottle flew into the air and shattered on a wall. Hubbell reared back like he was on a pitcher's mound and popped a high, hard one on the outside corner of So-Called Sonny Scott's meal ticket. Blood spurting from his lip, Skapinsky tried to retaliate, but Hubbell adroitly sidestepped the blows and landed a one-two combination: a right to the gut, a left to the chin. Scott hit the deck.

Bubbles flew to his aid, yelling, "Yez are all a bunch of friggin' animals!" My father, always aware of his priorities, ran straight to his son and examined his left hand. "How's the hand? You didn't hurt the hand, did you, champ? Is the hand okay?"

Solly So-Called Sonny Scott Skapinsky—Yankee fan, Republican, bogus Ivy Leaguer, Cadillac-driving celebrity, wrecker of dreams—struggled to his feet with sawdust clinging to his custom-made suit and his girlfriend's hankie helping his blood to coagulate. He straightened his tie. He glared at Hubbell. "You'll be sorry, kid," he said.

"Touch my son and you're dead," said my father.

"Better get out of here while you can, Solly," said the girl whose hand he tried to win twenty years before. Looking at the sea of hostile faces, he saw the wisdom in my mother's advice. He grabbed Bubbles by the arm and led her away. "Oh, Solly," my mother called. "Better get this dry-cleaned." And she tossed him his wig.

Skapinsky grabbed his head, shocked to find it naked. To raucous, mocking laughter, he hastened toward the streets of his youth, dragging his girlfriend by the wrist. "Hold your friggin' horses," said Bubbles, teetering on her spiked heels. Only a few minutes earlier I had felt nothing but contempt for that birdbrain. Now, for reasons I could not explain, I did not want her to leave. I felt sorry for her. I couldn't wait for this phase to end.

Round Man leaned against the sink, trying to blink the sleep from his eyes while petting a fluffy white rabbit named Harriet. His pajamas looked as though they had been created by pasting together the pages of an illustrated version of "Old MacDonald Had a Farm."

"Hank, you should've seen her," said my father, kissing my mother on the cheek. He worked the kitchen like he worked Mickey's Saloon, shrinking the room by waving his arms with grand enthusiasm. "She jumped on his back just like in the movies, and man, she belted that floozy a good one. Right in the kisser. And Roger! Oh, boy, he jumped right in there, put himself right on the line to help us out. Then Hubbell came to the rescue. Unbelievable. He floored that pompous bastard with a combination, just like Sugar Ray. Wham, bam, boom, you're out! Like lightning."

He turned to Hubbell. "How's the hand, champ? The hand all right? Jeez, I'm proud of you. You were great. Just great. That's the fighting spirit I always knew you had. Man, you direct that energy into your pitching and there's no stopping you. Beeline to Ebbets Field. No doubt about it."

Hubbell knew there was no putting off his declaration. "Pop, I'm not going to be a ballplayer." He said it gently.

I could practically hear the air escape from the hole in my father's chest where Hubbell's words had penetrated. He laughed nervously. "What are you talking? Of course you're gonna be—"

"It's over, Pop."

"What's over? How can it be over? We're just getting started."

Hubbell searched his mind for the right words. But Round Man beat him to it, blurting out precisely the wrong ones. "He's gonna be an announcer, like So-Called Sonny Scott!"

"Oh boy," said my mother.

"What's this?" said Dad. He looked from Hubbell to my mother to Hubbell again. "It's a joke, right? Tell me it's a joke."

"I'm going to broadcast school," Hubbell said. "I've been accepted to the best—"

"Broadcast school? You're going to *broadcast school*? What the hell are you talking about?"

"It's what I want to do."

"Broadcast school? What does this mean? You want to sit in a booth in a suit and tie and talk into a stupid microphone? You want to sell beer? Jeannie, did you know about this? Did you keep this from me?" He did not wait for an answer. He banged his fist on the table and yelled, "What the hell is going on around here? My own family is keeping secrets from me? They operate behind my back? They betray me? I will not stand for this!"

"Take cover!" yelled Round Man.

"Not now, Hank." Mom put her arm around her youngest son, who in turn soothed his rabbit with a gentle touch.

My father addressed Hubbell directly, punctuating his words by stabbing his finger within inches of my brother's nose. Hubbell folded his arms and stood his ground. "I will not let you piss away all our work. One little setback and you're folding up your tent? You can stand up to a bully with a bottle in his hand, but you don't have the guts to fight back from adversity? Jesus Christ, that bunny rabbit's got more balls than you."

"It's a girl," said Round Man.

"Try to understand, Pop," said Hubbell. "I'm not cut out for it. I'm not good enough. I don't want it bad enough."

"You stopped believing in yourself. You can't ever stop believing in yourself."

"I'm just facing facts, Pop. I found something I really want to do, and I believe in myself enough to know I'll make it."

"You're a quitter! How did this happen? Jeannie, how did we raise a quitter?"

Hubbell proposed an answer. "Maybe I learned it from you, Pop. Are you a quitter? Huh? Did you give up? Was your injury really that bad? Maybe you just weren't good enough. Maybe you gave up."

These were questions I had never considered. When Skapinsky threw out his accusation in the bar, I figured he was lying, just like he lied about everything else. So did everyone in the saloon. No one would entertain for a second the notion that Cyclone Frankie Stone's march to glory had been curtailed by anything other than the injury inflicted by Solly Skapinsky. What Hubbell was doing was like reading *The Communist Manifesto* into the *Congressional Record,* like screaming "God is dead!" in St. Peter's Basilica. I was too scared to be appalled.

My father's eyes opened wide. His nostrils flared. "You're questioning me? *You're* questioning *me?* You let that son of a bitch Skapinsky poison your mind? I don't believe it. Jeannie, I'm being stabbed in the back by my own flesh and blood."

"Frank, forget about Solly," said Mom. "This is about Hubbell's future."

"You're on his side. I see it all now. You never wanted him to be a ballplayer. You subverted me behind my back."

"She had nothing to do with it," said Hubbell. "It's me. It's my life."

"Oh, it's your life?" said my father. "Okay, it's your life. You want to betray everything we've worked for? You want to *talk* for a living? Fine. Okay. It's your life. Well, *go live it*! Pack your bags. Get outta here. I will not have traitors in my house!"

"Whatever you say, Pop." Hubbell turned on his heel and headed for his room.

"Quitter!" my father yelled at his back. "Coward! Traitor!"

"Shut up, Frank," said Mom. "I have something to say about this too. I will not have you evicting my children."

"It's all your fault," said my father. "You didn't cooperate with the plan. You held me back."

"Oh, Frank, wake up! Don't you see what's going on? You're forty-two years old, you're stuck in a dead-end job and you're living vicariously through your son."

"Don't give me that Freudian crap, willya Jeannie?"

"All right, I'll give it to you straight. Keep it up and you won't just lose a ballplayer, you'll lose a *son*. Maybe two or three sons. Let go, Frank. Give it up. He's got to live his own way."

"He doesn't know what he wants," my father argued. "He's confused."

"At least Hubbell has the guts to face reality and change his life," Mom countered. "But look at you. You're like an ostrich. You're too blind to see what's happening and too scared to do anything about it. *That's* quitting, Frank. That's really quitting."

"What am I supposed to do, let him walk away from—"

"Frank!" She splashed his name in his face like ice water. "Frank! This is about *you*!"

"Aaahhh," said my father. He waved his hand and stalked out of the kitchen, fumbling with a pack of Pall Malls.

I felt like shouting, "Wait, Dad! To hell with Hubbell. Let him be a broadcaster if he wants. Who cares? You still have me. *I'll* do it. *I'll* get to the big leagues. *I'll* wear your glove in Ebbets Field. Come on, Dad, get the balls. Get the gloves. Let's go practice. Hit me some fungoes . . ."

In the corridor, Hubbell emerged from his room. He was carrying a duffel bag and wearing a jacket. "Where are you going?" asked my mother.

"I'm sleeping at Benny's."

"Oh no, you're not. You're my son too, and this is your home."

"I don't want to stay here if he's going to drive me crazy."

"It's just one of his tantrums," Mom explained. "You know how he is. He's just trying to do what he thinks is best for you. He'll get over it."

"Call me when he's ready to listen to me," said Hubbell. "You can reach me at the Masons'."

He kissed my mother on the cheek and marched to the front door. "See you, guys," he called to Hank and me. And he left.

My mother leaned wearily against the wall. "I sure hope those Dodgers win. I can't take this anymore."

That night I had a dream. I was a contestant on *The $64,000 Question*. I was in an isolation booth. The quizmaster was The Thing, complete with a slick pompadour and sparkling smile, only his included fangs. Next to him was his lovely and talented side-kick, Mrs. Schaefer. She was in a sequined gown like the one Bubbles wore in Mickey's Saloon, only she was built like an ironing board, not an hourglass.

"And now, for sixty-four thousand dollars," said The Thing, "what is the real reason Cyclone Frankie Stone did not make the major leagues?"

The theme music played. The clock ticked off the seconds. In the isolation booth I felt trapped and claustrophobic. I did not know the answer, and I was not sure I wanted to know. "Stop the music," I demanded. "Let me out of here."

"What's the answer?" insisted The Thing. "Was your old man screwed by an injury, or was he a bum who couldn't make it anyway?"

"I don't know. Let me out!" I reached for the doorknob, but there was none. I pushed on the door. Nothing happened. I pounded. I shook the booth. Outside, The Thing laughed maniacally, and Mrs. Schaefer gestured to the audience to join in the fun.

Chapter Twelve

I had fallen asleep to the brittle sound of bickering, and I awakened to the same sound, only more clamorous; my parents were going at it by the front door, not their bedroom. "It was a small bet, for cryin' out loud," said my father. His voice had a pleading quality. "Why are you making such a big deal out of it?"

"I don't care if it was a nickel," my mother rejoined. "I don't care if you won, I don't care if you lost. You made me a promise and you broke it."

"Look, I gotta go to work. We'll talk later. You'll feel better. You're upset about Hubbell."

"Go on, get out of here. Stop at Mike's and bet on whether I'll be here when you get back."

"Jeannie, for God's sake . . ."

There was a pause. I imagined them flying into each other's arms, hearts throbbing with contrition and forgiveness. I was wrong. Momentarily, I heard my mother's light but determined footsteps pad down the corridor toward the kitchen. "Jeannie," called my father, the final vowel elongating with desperation like the twisting twang of an electric guitar. I heard the front door open, then, after a hopeful pause, it closed, and my father's heavy footsteps reverberated in the stairwell.

There were boxes of Sugar Frosted Flakes, Wheaties, and Rice Krispies on the kitchen table, with milk, bowls, spoons, and sugar. Round Man was already seated when I arrived. He seemed as disturbed as I was. "Make yourselves cereal," Mom called from the living room. "There's bananas if you want them." Hank and I ate quickly, speaking cursorily, and only of the World Series, because we did not know how to speak about what was on our minds.

When it was time to leave for school, we went to the living room, where my mother lay on the sofa in her nightgown and robe. She drew on a Camel, exhaled, and watched the smoke rise to the ceiling and spread like bad news. "I'll see you at lunchtime," I said. It was more a question than a statement. She nodded.

"You'll be here, right?" I asked.

She looked at Hank and me for the first time, and nodded again. I thought I spotted an opportunity. "Are you okay?" I asked. "I mean, I could stay home if you need me."

"Me too," offered Round Man.

"I'm fine," said Mom. "Go to school."

As if the strength of my thoughts the day before had made it materialize, a dark, gloomy, Joe Btfsplk cloud enshrouded the neighborhood. I eschewed the customary companionship of Artie and Louie and walked to school alone. I needed time to think. The Thing was attacking on a new front: psychological warfare. He was trying to confuse me by mixing up my feelings about everyone in my family. I hated Round Man for blurting out the truth about Hubbell the night before, but I also understood why he did it; the poor kid was just as hurt by Hubbell's betrayal as I was, and he felt left out again. He didn't even get to see the encounter with Skapinsky and Bubbles, let alone contribute to the triumph. I hated Hubbell for spitting in the eye of the family dream, but I also felt bad that he was forced to live in exile, and I admired his guts in springing to my father's aid in the bar and then standing up to him at home. I hated my mother for assenting to Hubbell's mutiny, for playing into The Thing's hands by making me miss the first two games of the Series, and for condemning my father's bets to the point where she just might be forced to walk out on us. But I loved her for defending her son's right to make up his own mind, for leaping into the fray with Skapinsky, and for forcing my father to account for his actions. I loved my father for doggedly defending the family honor, against both Skapinsky and his eldest son. But I hated him for gambling again, and losing his temper, and throwing Hubbell out of the house, and I was plagued by the questions raised in my quiz show dream: was Cyclone Frankie Stone a one-time sure thing whose glory was cut off at the knees by a jealous tyrant, or just another wanabee who couldn't make the grade?

One thing remained as clear and unambiguous as a ball game,

where knowing which team you rooted for made everything else fall neatly into place: the tag team of Schaefer and Gross were in league with The Thing. As I crossed the street to school, I saw my teacher land her broomstick, enter the schoolyard, and line up the class for forced entry into the building. I started working out ways to get out of returning after lunch, and became so absorbed in these machinations that I walked right past the schoolyard entrance. Before long I was at the next corner and everyone else was walking past me in the opposite direction toward school. The feeling of being the only salmon in a parade of downstream-swimming fish was so exhilarating, I kept right on going. The crossing guard paid me no notice despite the fact that I was dressed for school and was carrying a briefcase. I kept walking, and walking, and walking, my heart pounding harder with each step. No one stopped me. Before long the counterstream of school kids ended. The scenery changed. The houses and store-fronts were more dilapidated, the smell more acrid, the people darker. They looked at me with great curiosity and shrugged at each other when I passed. The thought crossed my mind that I ought to turn around before it got so late I would not be able to walk into class without being reprimanded, and possibly punished, for tardiness. And still I kept walking.

Soon I was on a street where half the windows were broken and the doors looked as though they hadn't been painted since World War I. The voices that escaped through the windows were more lilting, the music thumped more insistently. I was *over there.* Suddenly, my path was blocked by three sets of muscular arms folded against tall, lean torsos. I looked up to see a trio of black teenagers in identical jackets—red with the words CORSAIR LORDS stenciled in white on the left breast above two crossed swords. They seemed to find my presence both exotic and amusing. "Wachu doin' here, boy?" said the one who did the talking. They were like a doo-wop group with a lead singer and two guys harmonizing background sounds: "Mmmm," "Yeah," "Ooooh," "That's right."

My inquisitor did not wait for an answer, which was fine with me because I had none. "Wachu got in there?" he asked, gesturing at my briefcase.

"Books," I said. "For school. And some pencils. And a pen."

"Books, huh," he said. "You got some money?"

"No," I said. I had forgotten the first lesson of urban survival: give them what they ask for.

The lead singer did not believe me. "Wachu got in your pockets?" he asked.

"My pockets? A marble, and my keys, and a bobby pin stinger and—"

"If I find me some money, I 'moan whup yo' ass."

"Oh, that's right," I said, as if I'd just remembered something, silly me. "I have some money. Sure. Here." I dug into my pocket and held out the contents: thirty-seven cents. "Take it. It's yours. Here."

"That's all you got?"

"I swear, that's it. Take the marble if you want. And my Captain Video ring. And the books. You want the books?"

"Don't need no books, boy. But I likes yo' hat."

He plucked the cap off my head. "That's my Dodger cap," I protested.

"I know what it is, boy," said the leader. "I could use me one o' these." He put it on his head.

"It's way too small," I pointed out. "You could keep the thirty-seven cents and get sixty-three more and buy one that fits. I'll bring you the sixty-three cents, I swear."

My offer amused them. "But I likes this one," the lead singer said. "I might have to give it to my baby brother."

"But it's my lucky hat!"

"Yo' lucky hat, huh? Sheeeit, I could use me some luck."

"Yeah," said the bass singer.

"It's only lucky if I wear it," I explained. "If I don't wear it, the Dodgers lose."

They laughed in three-part harmony. "How you know I ain't no Yankee fan?" asked the leader.

Because you couldn't be, I thought. You couldn't root against Jackie Robinson's team. Even blacks who lived a block from Yankee Stadium didn't root for the Bronx Bigots.

"Keep the money," I offered. "Take my briefcase. It's worth a lot more than the hat. Take my shirt." I was holding back the baseball cards as the final bargaining chip.

"Jus' might take everything you got, boy, and whup yo' white ass too, you don't mind your manners." He gripped my nose between two of his fingers and twisted. "Now say, 'Please keep my hat, Mr. Cook.' "

The pain radiated out from my nose and covered my face. I was prepared to spend the rest of my life with my nostrils facing up like an elephant holding its trunk out for peanuts. I was prepared to walk home naked. I was prepared to deliver the hats of Mr. Cook's choice to his whole family. But I could not say, "Please keep my hat."

"Say it, boy," he insisted. "Tell me you be honored if I keep dis here hat."

I could not say it. I could not say anything. He twisted harder. Sounds of pain leaped from my throat. I heard the backup singers laughing, and the pounding of drums from a nearby radio, and suddenly I remembered Otis Hicks: "Any of them bad-ass nigger boys bother you, little man, you tell 'em you's a friend of Otis Hicks."

I said it. "I'm a friend of Otis Hicks." But my voice was so distorted by the hand that was trying to rearrange my nose that it came out, "Ibafrenaotahik."

"Say what?"

"Ibafrenaotahik." They howled. I tried to angle my head to get some air into my nostrils. This increased the pain, but enabled me to blurt out, decipherably, "Otis Hicks!"

They stopped laughing. The leader let go of my nose. "What about Otis Hicks, boy? You know Otis Hicks?"

"He's my friend," I said, touching my nose to see if it was still there.

He folded his arms and narrowed his eyes. His chest muscles bulged against his red jacket, elongating the crossed swords and the letters of CORSAIR LORDS. His hands tightened into two massive fists, the brown skin around his knuckles fading to off-white. "You in trouble, boy," he said. "You know what I do to friends of Otis Hicks?"

I had thought of death on three previous occasions: when an explosion jolted Ebbets Field and I took cover under my bleacher seat; when I got caught in an undertow at Coney Island; and in the rumble seat of Grandpa Abe's old Studebaker when he mistook a tree for a garage entrance. The explosion turned out not to be a Russian attack but a mishap at the Brooklyn Navy Yard, and I survived the other two occasions with a mouthful of salt water and a bump on the forehead. Now I would be left to die in an alley *over there,* and if my body was ever found it would not be identifiable because my nose would be upside down and I was not wearing my dog tag.

Then I heard a new, deeper voice: "I hear someone say Otis Hicks?"

Three new black teenagers stood among the original three, staring them down menacingly. They wore yellow satin jackets with the word CRUSADERS on the back. It was the same jacket I'd seen Otis Hicks wear. They must belong to the same band, I inferred. This was the battle of the bands. "Otis Hicks my main man," said the new guy. He looked at me. "You know Otis, kid?"

"He's my main man," I said.

"These chumps botherin' you?"

"He took my hat."

My new friend turned to my nemesis. "You took this boy's hat, nigger?"

"You don't like it?" said the Corsair Lord. "Wachu gon' do about it?"

"You don't give it back, I 'moan bust you upside yo' haid."

I loved this *I moan* thing. If I should make it out of there alive, I vowed, I would use it on Henny Horowitz at first opportunity: "Give me a sentence with *I moan* in it."

The Corsair Lords and the Crusaders lined up face to face. My hat, however, was still on the lead singer's head. "Go on, mu-thafuckah," he said to his counterpart. "Try and take it."

The Crusader's left hand shot out from his side and knocked the hat off his rival's head. The Corsair Lord missed with a round-house right. The groups squared off, one on one, three fights in one ring. They sparred, jabbed, danced around looking for an opening. Then one of the Corsairs flashed a switchblade. The Crusaders reached for their own. I grabbed my hat, jammed it tightly onto my head and ran. I ran and ran and ran, without looking back, crossing streets without slowing down, until my chest was on fire and every breath I took fanned the flames. By then I was on familiar turf. I turned around: not a Corsair Lord in sight. Able to breathe again, I got my bearings and made my way to Rooney's Lot and then to the familiar alleys that led to my building.

I ran straight to the cellar in search of Otis Hicks. I wanted to tell him he had saved my life, and I hoped that he would let me hide out with him until twelve o'clock. I thought I could go home for lunch as expected and pretend I was afflicted with debilitating symptoms that would force my mother to let me stay home for the afternoon. That had been my mistake all along, I realized. I had chosen the honest route, figuring that if I faked an illness I would have to watch the games at home, not at Jake's, and I would not be nearly as effective. The strategy had backfired, and now I was willing to settle for whatever I could get.

I opened the cellar door noiselessly, so as not to disturb Otis or Jesse. It was dark except for a wide shaft of dusty sunlight that entered through a window and slanted into a storage area like a spotlight. I heard voices. One belonged to Otis. The other required a few seconds to identify. It was Barney Klinger. Something in their furtive tones told me to remain out of sight. I crept along a wall until I could see them. Otis rolled one sleeve above his elbow. Barney handed him what looked like a piece of a bicycle inner tube. Otis wrapped it around his bicep and knotted it with his teeth and his free hand.

"That's right," said Barney. "Very good." He held a hypodermic needle up to the light and eyed its contents. Then he injected it, not in Otis's upper arm or behind, but in the joint between the bicep and the forearm.

Otis closed his eyes and tilted his head back like he did when I saw him play the drums. He sucked a stream of air through his teeth. Hsssssss.

"There you go, my friend," said Barney Klinger. "Next time I'll show you how to do it by yourself."

"Yeah," said Otis.

"Don't forget to tell your friends. But no names, understand?"

"Yeah."

In one fell swoop I had solved two mysteries: why Otis had been acting so weird, and how Barney Klinger had fixed himself up with star sapphire rings, sharkskin suits, and a Lincoln Continental. Otis had diabetes, and Barney was moonlighting as a doctor.

My mother was at the kitchen table, a cigarette and a coffee cup in one hand and in the other the telephone receiver pressed against her hearing aid. She was as surprised to see me as I was to see the suitcase at her feet. "I'll call you back, Cecille," she said, and hung up the phone.

"Where are you going?" I asked.

"What are you doing home?" she replied.

"I asked you first."

"I'm your mother."

The argument was not convincing, but it was effective. I told her the truth, as I had determined to do when I decided to go home after leaving the cellar. In a crisis, I reasoned, Mom would surely stand up for me, just as she had stood up for Hubbell last night. I told her I had been held up by three bullies, and after barely escaping with my life and lucky cap, I was just too upset to go to school. Okay, so I changed the order of things slightly, but it was, essentially, the truth.

Mom was horrified. She reached out and pulled me close to her. She rubbed my back. I assured her that I was all right, that they hadn't hurt me. "Boy, oh boy," she said. "Is this what you guys call a losing streak?"

Now it was my turn to ask questions. Her answers were candid. She said that she and Dad had had a disagreement and they both needed some time to think about it. She said she was going to stay with Uncle Sid, her twin brother, and do some things she'd been wanting to do—see some shows, attend some concerts. She told me not to worry, that it was just a little vacation, that we would talk on the phone and she would stop by to make sure there was plenty of food in the house, that she would leave me money to get anything I needed, and that I should take advantage of the situation and get my father to take Hank and me to all our favorite restaurants.

"Why can't you stay here and think?" I asked.

"Sometimes you think better if you get away."

"When will you be back?" I pointed out that her suitcase was pretty big.

"When I come back depends on your father," she said. "This is like a little trick I'm playing. I want to see what he does."

I was all in favor of tricks, but somehow this one did not seem like Halloween. In an attempt to change her mind, I suggested that I might have a delayed reaction to my mugging. She pointed out that Uncle Sid's apartment was only five bus stops and fifteen walking minutes from home and that I knew his phone number by heart. Oh, well, I told myself, if I could survive the tension, the boredom, and the bad food of her stay in the hospital, I could survive this too.

I told Mom about Otis's illness and Barney Klinger's moonlighting. She found the story gripping. "I bet he's not a real doctor," I concluded. "I bet he doesn't have a license or anything. He even put the needle in the wrong place."

I could tell she was proud of my observations. "I want you to tell your father everything you saw. But tell him privately. Don't say a word to anyone else. Promise?"

I promised. "Because we don't want anyone tipping off Barney, right?"

She concurred. "We'll take care of this ourselves."

"Gotcha," I said.

I ate lunch early and headed for Play Street to see if there was anything going on. I had plenty of time to have some fun and still secure my seat and an egg cream well before the National Anthem. On the way, I heard my name called. It was Hubbell, on his way to the Corner with Benny. He asked how come I wasn't in school. "I didn't feel like going," I said. For some reason, that was all I wanted to say, and I said it with a belligerence that surprised me.

"Is everything okay?" Hubbell asked.

"Yeah, why not?" Again my voice was nastier than intended. I had trouble even looking at him, and I squirmed away when he tried to touch my shoulder.

"Wait a second, kiddo," he said. He held my arm to keep me still and bent over to look me in the eye. Benny discreetly kept on walking. "Let me tell you something," said Hubbell. "You know, when you reach a certain age, you have to make decisions about your life. You have to look at things, and ask yourself some tough questions, and when you get the answers, you have to make sure you're not fooling yourself. You have to do what's right for you, even if it means disappointing the people you love. You understand what I'm saying?"

I nodded. I still could not look at him directly.

"Sometimes, people set a course for themselves and it turns out to be the wrong one. If they're lucky, they wake up in time and find a different course, and they hope that one's right. That's what I'm doing. There's no way I was going to be Rookie of the Year. I was never going to pitch with Newk and Erskine, and make the All-Star team, and all that other stuff we dreamed about. It was a pipe dream. You know what that is? It means it wasn't going to happen. Period. You can still be a ballplayer. You don't need me to pave the way. Understand?"

He looked me square in the eye and would not let me look away until I answered. "Yeah," I said. And I did understand, I just did not want to believe it.

"Hey, how's this?" Hubbell went on. "I'll be in the broadcasting booth on opening day, 1964." He slipped into an announcer's voice. "Up steps Roger Stone, the fine young rookie making his major league debut at shortstop for the Dodgers. Here's the pitch . . . It's a long drive. It's way out there! It's going, going . . . it's *gone*! How about that, ladies and gentlemen, Roger Stone hits a home run his first at-bat in the majors!"

"Will you let me sit in the booth with you?" I asked.

"Sure," said Hubbell. "Maybe I'll even let you do play-by-play." He put his arm around my shoulder. "Come on, I'll buy you an egg cream."

When we got to the Corner, Harry the Horse, Dizzy, and Mr. Big were trying to haul Klinger to Iggy Corso, who waited, triumphant and arrogant. "Pucker up, Mr. Dinger," he said.

"Fuck you, guinea!" yelled Klinger. He tried to jerk his arms free. He dug in his heels to resist the push and pull of the other guys.

"Come on, Marty, he won fair and square," reasoned Mr. Big.

"Fuck you too, midget!"

The boys dragged Klinger within reach of his adversary. Iggy undid his belt and ceremoniously dropped his black chinos to his knees. He lowered his jockey shorts. His ass was pale and hairy. "Oh, Dinger, give me those hot lips."

"Kiss the bootie, baby," said Dizzy.

"Go on. It won't bite," urged Big.

Harry tried to push Klinger's head down toward Iggy's ass, but Klinger struggled mightily, his neck muscles quivering from the strain. "Don't make me hurt you, Marty," said Horse. Then, with his lips less than a foot from the target, Klinger summoned up all the liver-and-onion energy he could muster and burst free. He cursed Iggy and took off running down the street.

"Fuck him, let him go," said Iggy. "He'll pay up one of these days." He hitched up his pants and combed his hair.

"So, Ig, you gonna tell us what happened, or what?" asked Harry.

"Lay it on us, man," Dizzy implored.

"Hey, fellas," said Iggy, lighting up a Lucky, "whatsamatter wich you? You know I don't like to spoil a girl's reputation."

The boys practically begged him to tell his story. Finally Iggy agreed. They headed for a stoop. Everyone but Hubbell. He could not bear to listen. He started to leave, but Iggy wanted him in attendance. "I think you'll find this inneresting, Mr. Stone."

Hubbell said he had better things to do. Iggy informed the others that he would not tell his tale unless Hubbell remained. They looked at Hubbell in such a way that he knew the rest of his life would be miserable if he left. He joined the others on the stoop. I sat on the lowest step and pretended to be absorbed in organizing a stack of baseball cards. I feared that if I appeared to pay attention, my companions might be overcome by a fit of Big Guy rectitude and chase me away to protect the morals of a minor.

As with Jake's account of the invention of the egg cream, no one knew if Iggy's sagas of sexual conquest were true, but, with some exceptions, no one cared. The telling was the important thing, and Iggy told hot stories better than Harold Robbins. He said he had softened up Diane by taking her to see *To Catch a Thief.* He wanted her to see the scene where Grace Kelly and Cary Grant are having a picnic in a sports car, and Grace says, suggestively, "Do you want a breast or a leg?" Cary replies, "I'll leave the choice up to you."

Having thus set the table, Iggy drove Diane to the Holy Shrine. When they got there, he talked. He did not want her to panic, or to think he was interested only in getting into her drawers, he said. This was very important with certain kinds of chicks, and Diane figured to be one of them. "Man, did I have her pegged wrong," he said. "There I am, talking about this and that, and asking her shit about herself, like where she grew up and shit like that, 'cause certain chicks, man, they like can't stand it when guys only talk about themselves, you know? But after a while, she like slides across the seat, and she says, 'You didn't bring me here just to talk, did you?' I like couldn't believe my ears. I said, 'Well, you know, I figured we'd get to know each other.' And she says, 'I know a better way to do that.' And she kisses me. I mean *kisses* me. This chick had lips like vacuum cleaners. Her tongue was like a snake, slipping and sliding all around my mouth and shit, and nearly choking me, and it was like she had eighty-seven hands, like a fucking centipede or something. They were all over me, man."

Iggy's imagery may not have been Byronesque, but he knew how to grab his audience. The guys were working up a sweat. Dizzy padded a beat with his fingers on his trumpet case and punctuated Iggy's solo with throaty exclamations like *yes* and *owwww*. Hubbell looked as though he would rather be getting root-canal, but he could not tear himself away. I felt sorry for him. In yet another flip-flop of feelings, his speech earlier had won me over, and now I was rooting against Iggy.

Iggy stepped up the pace. The girl he described sounded nothing like the sweetheart I'd met in the record store. She was a vamp, a tramp, a trollop, a tootsie, a harlot, a nympho, a red-hot mama, a whore, which, in my neighborhood, was pronounced to rhyme with *sewer*. If Iggy was telling the truth, she did everything his brother Louie told me that whores did, only she did them for free, without even being asked, and she did them with amazing dexterity. This was better than reading *The Hoods.* Soon the couple moved to the backseat, at Diane's suggestion, and when they got there, said Iggy, her blouse was already unbuttoned and she was wearing no brassiere.

This fact alone nearly burst the blood vessels of every guy on the stoop. "Too much!" howled Dizzy.

Iggy described his date's breasts as firm but soft, with round brown nipples, just the way he likes them. "Like they were custom-made for me," he said, just the right size, not too small, but not too big either, which was important because "more than a mouthful is wasted." I sensed that this might be a philosophy worth noting for future reference.

Iggy described Diane's moist, silky thighs and her white lace panties, and how she wanted it—and I knew what *it* was—so badly she practically begged for it. "Give it to me, give it to me now." And she ripped off his belt and yanked his pants down and moaned, "Now. I want you inside me, now, now, now."

He stopped and lit a Lucky. He took a deep drag and blew out the longest, slowest stream of smoke I had ever seen. He gazed up at the dark, threatening sky and smiled as if he could look directly into his own head and see the juiciest memory ever recorded on his neurons. Then he looked over the pale, sweaty faces with the slung-open jaws and dry mouths. They fixed him with their eyes, as if fearing that if they blinked or looked to the side they would miss the rest of his tale. Hubbell was the only one who turned away; he looked as if every sentence Iggy uttered was another stroke of a saw that was cutting off his legs.

"Get on with it, for chrissake," Harry exploded.

Iggy took another drag and continued. "There I was, about to enter the pearly gates. I thought, Take your time, man, 'cause this is it. This is the pinochle." He meant, we knew, *pinnacle.* "After this, you might as well jerk off the rest of your life. I opened her legs and I leaned into the task, and suddenly . . . a light flashes in my face."

"Holy shit!" the gang exclaimed in unison.

"It was a flashlight," Iggy continued. "It shined right in my eyes, then it shined on her, and I could see who it was. It was a cop."

"Holy shit."

"He was a mean, ugly motherfucker," said Iggy. "The chick, she went nuts. She screamed. She grabbed anything she could and

covered herself with it. She was scared shit, man, and I gotta tell
you I was too, only she was crying like a baby. And this fucking
cop, man, he was getting his rocks off just watching. I could hear
him breathing hard. I only seen the one hand with the flashlight.
It wouldn't surprise me if he was beating his meat with the other
one. And he says, 'Well, well, what have we here? I sure hope
the young lady's eighteen, lover boy, or you're in big trouble.' "

"Holy shit."

Iggy smiled his pre-Elvis smirk. "I said, 'Look, officer, do
whatever you want with me, but let her go, all right? What do you
say? She's from a good family. Her old man's like a perfessor and
shit. You don't want to ruin a girl's reputation, do you?'

"And she's still crying and trying to cover every inch of her
body, like her ankles and her fingers and everything, and the
fucking cop is digging every minute of it. He's chewing on this
toothpick like it's a tit, and making faces like he's thinking the
whole thing over very carefully. And finally he says to me, 'I'll
tell you what, big shot. I'll let the both of yez go, on one condition . . .'" Iggy inhaled deeply, then added: " 'I'm next.' "

"Holy shit!"

"We should report him," said Benny. "Did you get his badge
number?"

"Fuck the badge number," said Harry the Horse.

"What happened, man? What'd you do?" urged Dizzy.

Iggy got deadly serious, like older men when they recalled
missions behind enemy lines from which their best buddies never
returned. "I didn't know *what* the fuck to do. I was thinking real
hard, and all the while the cop is looking us over and grinning
like a fucking cat who got a mouse in the corner. Then he's tired
of waiting. He says, 'Come on, Romeo, I ain't got all night. Am
I next, or what?'

"And I says, 'Well . . . I don't know, officer . . . I never fucked
a cop before!' "

Iggy's mouth spread open like the grinning face on the Steeplechase sign. He had just delivered the punch line to a long,
carefully choreographed joke and he expected everyone to laugh.
But no one uttered a sound. They were in shock. They sat there,
frozen, staring at the storyteller and trying to get their bearings.

"Whatsamatter, you don't get it?" said Iggy. Slowly, his audi-

ence eased out of its collective trance. They made eye contact, one
with the other. Iggy stopped smiling. Warily, he stood up and
smoothed out the legs of his chinos.

My brother was the first to act. He yelled, "You son of a
bitch!" and lunged at Iggy. Iggy dodged him. The others leaped
to their feet. Dizzy almost grabbed his arm, but Iggy shook loose
and ran. They chased him down Play Street, sidestepping kids on
their way home for lunch and women wheeling shopping carts,
but they never quite got close enough until they reached the
Corner, when Hubbell, the fastest of the lot and the most motivated, grabbed hold of his rival's shirt. Iggy struggled to break
free. His shirt ripped all the way down the back. But Hubbell
held on. Then Ippish, the retarded traffic cop, left his post and
stepped between them. "Break it up, break it up," he said, and
he wedged his burly body between the combatants.

"Get the fuck out of here, Ippish," commanded my brother,
desperately clutching Iggy's shirt.

"Break it up, no fighting," said Ippish, and he pushed them
apart just enough for Iggy to break loose, leaving Hubbell with
a swatch of white cotton big enough to wash a car with. As the
others closed in, Iggy darted into Howard Avenue. He made it
across just as a series of oncoming cars, released a moment earlier
from a red light a block away, sped past the guys, blocking their
pursuit. The delay gave Iggy enough time to build an insurmount-
able lead and disappear into an alley on Sterling Place.

Gratefully, I sipped the frisky foam of one of Jake's better egg
creams. I was perched on my customary stool with my blue talisman on my head. Nearby sat my older brother, homeless and
broken hearted, trying to make sense of what had just occurred.
"He's full of shit," he said to his friends. "Nothing he said is true
except he parked with her. This we know because we followed
him. After that, it's all bullshit, not just the cop part, the whole
thing. It has to be."

"I'm sure you're right, Hubbell," said Benny.

"I don't know, man," said Dizzy, "I don't put nothin' past the
Ig."

Benny shot him a look. "Don't listen to him," he advised
Hubbell. "Look at it this way, if Iggy made it all up, there's

nothing stopping you from going out with her. And if any part of it is true, well, you have to tell yourself, 'Hey, she's not the girl I thought she was, and I'm glad I didn't get mixed up with her.' See what I mean? That's positive thinking."

"You're right, Benny," said Hubbell. "Either way, it works out." He nodded his head once, sharply, as if putting a period on the episode. But a moment later he barked, "Shit!" and pounded his fist on an empty stool, making it ring like a church bell as it vibrated on its stand.

I loved my brother once again. I hoped everything Iggy said was false and that what he described would happen to me someday. But I had more important things on my mind. It was nearly game time. Jake's was filling up with men who were starting their weekend a half day early and kids who had found a way to ditch their Friday afternoon classes at Jefferson High.

The signs were not all good. Carl Erskine would not be pitching as expected; his sore arm was still not ready. On top of that, it was announced that Don Newcombe was also injured and might not pitch again for the rest of the Series. As if it wasn't hard enough to make a comeback that no other team in history had achieved, the Bums would have to do it without their two best hurlers. The starter in today's must-win game would be Johnny Podres, a southpaw from Witherbee, New York, with a well-known hankering for girls and racetracks. It was Johnny's twenty-third birthday. When he first joined the team in 1953, Podres had been a fireballer, but under the tutelage of Campanella and the coaching staff, he had learned to change speeds and to think on the mound. His first two seasons had been decent; he posted records of 9–4 and 11–7, although his one World Series appearance had been a disaster.

This year had started out splendidly for Johnny, as it had for the team. At one point in the summer he was 7–3. Then, like just about every other pitcher on the staff, he hurt his arm and found himself on the disabled list for a month. He worked himself back into shape, but never quite returned to his previous form, and in September he injured himself again in a freak accident when, before a game, the grounds crew accidentally ran him over when wheeling the batting cage onto the field. With his rib cage bruised so badly he could hardly breathe, Podres was almost scratched from the roster, which would have made him ineligible for the World Series. Alston and the front office decided to keep him on, however, and on such inconspicuous choices does the wheel of history turn.

At the time, I could not devine the destiny of Johnny Podres. All I knew was, after his 7–3 start, he had finished the season 9–10 and had not pitched a complete game since June 14. Furthermore, he was a southpaw pitching in Ebbets Field with its close left field porch, and today a strong breeze was blowing out in that direction, as if Mickey Mantle, who was back in the Yankee lineup, needed help from nature. To top it off, some egghead sportswriter had discovered that the last time the first three games of a Fall Classic had all been won by lefties was 1919, the year the White Sox threw the Series. Personally, I would not have started a young lefty in a game this crucial. I'd have taken Clem Labine out of the bullpen and given the assignment to him. It was not time for birthday presents.

On the other hand, the Bums were back in the friendly confines of Ebbets Field; Eisenhower's progress was excellent and he was expected to sleep that night outside the oxygen tent; the Yanks were starting Bullet Bob Turley, a hard-throwing righty with a 17–13 record, lots of strikeouts, and a tendency toward wildness that I just knew would get away from him in Brooklyn; and, of course, I was in place with all my rituals in order.

It did not take long to get things back on track. In the first inning Campanella stepped up to bat with Pee Wee on base on a walk. Campy had been hitless in eight trips to the plate thus far in the Series, but this time he drove a Turley fastball into the left field seats.

The quick 2–0 lead, mixed with the anger and libidinous energy stirred up by Iggy Corso's performance, made the Big Guys a little frisky. With the exception of Hubbell, they started clowning around between innings, and at one point Harry the Horse bumped into me and my hat fell off. Harry picked it up, offered it to me, then pulled it away just as I touched the brim. He did it again. Then he said, "Here, take it, just kidding," and when I reached for it, he tossed it to Klinger, who had returned when he learned that Iggy was not likely to demand payment of his debt that afternoon.

"Gimme my hat," I demanded. Klinger held it out to me. I snapped at it, but he yanked it away, and when I charged, he tossed it to Mr. Big. I leapt at Big, but once again I was too late. Big threw it to Harry. I felt like I was guarding three Harlem Globetrotters. "You don't understand," I said. "It's a lucky hat. If I don't wear it, the Dodgers lose." For the second time that day this argument was greeted with derisive laughter.

"Yeah, sure, you're a voodoo witch," said Harry. He held the hat just high enough for me to reach it, then, when I leaped for it, jerked it upward. I grabbed his sleeve and tried to pull it down, but he switched the hat to his other hand and flipped it to Klinger.

"Gimme my hat!" I screamed. This was no time to play *salugi* with a good luck charm.

"Give him the hat, Klinger," my brother insisted.

"You gonna make me, Stone?" said Klinger. I lunged, hoping to catch Klinger off guard, but I was a split second too late. He threw the hat to Horse.

"He's not kidding," said Hubbell. "It's a lucky hat."

"Yeah, right," said Harry.

We heard the crack of a bat connecting with a ball. Vin Scully's voice got louder. On screen, Duke Snider stared up at the bleachers, watching Mickey Mantle's home run land about four hundred feet from home plate. "I told you!" I yelled. "You better give it back before it's too late."

For a moment it seemed as though Harry the Horse had seen the light. But Klinger yelped, "Bullshit!" and coaxed Harry into throwing him the hat. Now I was mad. I practically tackled Klinger, but he shoved me aside and kept the hat just out of reach.

"Grow up, willya, Klinger," said Hubbell. "Give him the hat and watch the goddamn game."

"Up yours," said Klinger.

Moose Skowron rocked a double. "Look at that," I yelled. "The tying run's in scoring position." Klinger threw the hat to Horse. Realizing I was undersized and outnumbered, I decided to switch tactics. "All right, don't give it to me," I said. "You'll be sorry."

With Phil Rizzuto at the plate and the pitcher up next with two out, we expected an intentional walk. But, astonishingly,

Alston elected to pitch to the Yankee shortstop. Sure enough, Skooter lined a single. Sandy Amoros, back in left field to add a lefty batter to the lineup, fielded the ball on one hop and fired to the plate. The throw had Skowron beat, but Campanella, understandably eager to avoid a collision with a guy named Moose, tried to sidestep the runner as he applied the tag. The ball flew out of his hand. As Rizzuto raced around the bases, the ball rolled all the way to the dugout. Podres, backing up the play at the plate, couldn't find it. The hat was off my head and the Dodgers were losing theirs. Rizzuto crossed the plate.

There was confusion on the field as the umpires convened and the managers and players tried to influence them. "I told you," I said. "You wouldn't listen." The Big Guys looked at me, then at my hat, which was still in Harry's hands, then at the screen, then at each other. They knew they were in the presence of an awesome mystery. "Let's don't take no chances," said Harry. Contritely, he handed me the hat.

Fate turned instantly. Because the ball had rolled into a nook under the bat rack, the umpires ruled that Rizzuto would have to return to third. Podres got the next batter, Turley, to chop a grounder for the third out. The Dodgers' lead was erased, but we escaped with a tie score. And no one would ever again mess with my hat.

In the Dodger half of the second justice was restored. Robinson singled. Then, as if the home field was a tonic, the juice returned to Jackie's aging legs. He danced off first base, threatening to steal, daring the pitcher to try and pick him off. Turley got so agitated he lost control and hit Amoros with a pitch. Podres bunted. Turley was so anxious to get someone out he got flustered and ended up empty-handed. The bases were loaded. As the pitcher went into his windup, Robby danced off third. With the pitch, he took off down the line as if intending to steal home, then stopped abruptly and walked calmly back toward the base. Turley could not help but look at him; he could not stop himself from thinking about him. He walked Gilliam. Robby jogged pigeon-toed down the line and crossed the plate with the lead run as everyone at Jake's and all 34,209 at Ebbets Field cheered the master of psychological warfare.

Another walk from the shaken Turley gave the Bums a two-run lead again. In the fourth they added another pair. Meanwhile, Podres settled down; he kept the Yankees off balance with an artful mix of heaters and change-ups. We had a slight scare in the sixth when Mantle came up with two men on base. But Podres fed the Mick a double play pill to end the inning. In the Dodgers' seventh Robinson did it again. He lined a double down the left field line, then rounded second base so far that Elston Howard, retrieving the ball in the corner, was suckered into throwing behind Robby to second—and Robby dashed to third, sliding into the bag just ahead of the relay. He scored on an Amoros single, and once again the crowd let him know that everything he stood for was appreciated.

The final score was 8–3. The birthday boy pitched all the way, yielding only seven hits; Campy was back on track, hitting safely three times; and Robinson had located the fountain of youth.

"Don't let that hat out of your sight," Hubbell advised me as we watched the postgame show.

The victory seemed to have soothed the torment in my brother's heart. But his tranquility was short-lived.

Sylvia Finkelstein entered the luncheonette. "That's him," she said. She pointed out Hubbell to a young man in a Western Union uniform.

"Hubbell Stone?" he inquired. "Telegram." He stood with his hand out until Jake tossed him a quarter. Hubbell opened the telegram. I read it over his shoulder:

REGRET TO INFORM YOU THAT YOU ARE NOT AC-CEPTED TO NBC BROADCAST SCHOOL STOP DISREGARD PREVIOUS NOTICE STOP

Hubbell started to hyperventilate.

Benny tried to calm him down. "It must be a mistake," he said. "Call them up. Go down there. If you leave right now, you can get there before five o'clock."

"You're right, it must be a mistake," said Hubbell. He ran to the subway station.

Later that night, I saw him on the corner with Benny and Dizzy. He looked like a different person, troubled, sad, confused, angry—like a grown-up. At NBC he had learned that the decision to admit him to broadcast school had been reversed. It was not a mistake. No explanation was forthcoming. But Hubbell uncovered one illuminating fact: So-Called Sonny Scott was a senior member of the committee that screened the candidates.

Chapter Thirteen

If Ebbets Field was a house of worship, on the weekend of October 1 and 2, 1955, it was host to a feet-pounding, tambourine-clashing, Hallelujah-shouting gospel revival. As Saturday's game opened, a tentative ripple of confidence ran through the gathering like the early bubbles in a pot of water heating to a boil. We were encouraged by Friday's victory, but we were wary, for we knew we had to win both remaining games in Brooklyn or face the prospect of winning two straight in Yankee Stadium.

While my personal won-lost record at Ebbets Field was even better than it was at Jake's—an amazing eighteen victories in the twenty-two games I had attended that season—it was not perfect, and in a game where the best of hitters reached base only three of ten times and the best of teams lost every third game, even an .818 winning percentage could not, I knew, guarantee victory on any given day. Yesterday's win had restored a measure of faith, but in truth all it had done was ensure that the Yankees would not sweep the Series, small satisfaction for someone who knew the ways of The Thing. The Thing would not find a sweep fulfilling; far more satisfying to make it close, to let his victims sniff the sweet smell of victory and taste its nectar on their tongues, only to yank it away and leave them with nothing to swallow.

The delegation from the neighborhood occupied two rows in the upper deck along the left field foul line. We were so high up that we could not see all of foul territory, but we felt close to the action nonetheless, not only because of the park's intimate dimensions, but because of the sense one had of being at home among family. My own family, however, was divided. In a fit of wishful thinking, Dad had purchased a ticket for my mother, but her seat was occupied instead by Henny Horowitz, while the intended occupant, having spent the night at Uncle Sid's apartment, was reportedly on Broadway attending a matinee of *Cat on a Hot Tin*

Roof. My father sat on one end of our section with his friends, while Hubbell sat with his at the other end and one row down, as far from the patriarch as he could get. I was stationed midway between them, with Artie and Louie on one side, and on the other, Round Man, who, when he was not eating hot dogs and peanuts, fondled his own lucky charms—four rabbit's feet, which had been removed earlier in the season by a taxidermist from the stiff, furry corpse of Ozzie, the mate of the widowed Harriet. Ozzie had died of natural causes before the couple could populate Round Man's bedroom with litters of little Davids and Rickys. According to Hank, it was Ozzie's feet, not my hat alone, that had propelled the Dodgers' pennant drive.

The game started off not like a gospel chorus but a dirge; the Yankees scored a run in each of the first two innings. They seemed always on the brink of exploding, but, pitching more with courage than his injured arm, Erskine managed to keep the enemy from opening up a big lead. Meanwhile, the Bums mounted little offense against Yankee starter Don Larsen. They scratched out a run in the third when Amoros walked and scored all the way from first on Gilliam's hit-and-run double. In the Yankee fourth, Berra led off with a single and Joe Collins, the villain of Game One, drew a pass. Much as we loved Oisk, who owned the World Series record for strikeouts in a game, we respectfully called for his removal. Alston complied, bringing in rookie Don Bessent, who comported himself well, but yielded a bloop single to make the score 3–1.

We knew the Dodgers had to unleash some power before it was too late. Isolated entreaties rose from the long-suffering throats of congregants and mixed with the steady rhythm of restless limbs and anxious conversations until it swelled and echoed through the temple like the plaintive hymn of the long-oppressed. The response was swift and decisive. Campanella opened the fourth frame with a drive that buzzed through the sunlit air and into the left field seats like a drill going through cardboard. Furillo looped a broken-bat single over the pitcher's head. Then Hodges lofted a high fly toward right-center. At first it looked as though it would come down into the waiting hands of Mickey Mantle. But the collective body English of the partisans kept it afloat like a feather in a stream of air. As I watched the flight of the horsehide, willing it to carry, I saw in neon script atop the scoreboard the word: Schaefer. To the other 36,241 fans, it spelled the name of the beer company that sponsored Dodger broadcasts; to me, it was the hated name of The Thing's consort, and it radiated a force field that acted like a gale in opposition to our will. The forces of good prevailed; the ball cleared the scoreboard. We had taken the lead, 4–3.

The Yankees fought right back, loading the bases off Bessent. We called for the man we wished had been on the mound four years earlier when Bobby Thomson stepped to the plate in the Polo Grounds. A lean righthander from Providence, Rhode Island, with a wicked, sinking fastball, Clem Labine was the man to summon from the bullpen when the chips were down. He was our late-inning closer, and while it was only the fifth inning, conditions demanded a fireman. Clem came through, inducing Joe Collins to bounce out meekly to end the threat.

The Bums immediately cushioned their lead. Gilliam walked, Pee Wee legged out a hit, and Duke scorched one so hard, the evil rays of the Schaefer sign could barely slow down its progress to Bedford Avenue. The three-run homer gave us a comfortable four-run cushion, to which we added one more in the seventh inning. With Labine pitching superbly, the only suspense the rest of the way came in the eighth when a foul pop floated into our area. As the crowd closed in on the coveted souvenir, my cap got knocked off my head and tumbled down into the lower rows. Horrified, Harry the Horse and Mr. Big clambered over chairs and the backs of spectators to retrieve the talisman before it got crushed underfoot, or pocketed, or flew over the barrier into the lower deck. The Big Guys had learned their lesson.

On Sunday, 36,796 fans—the most ever to attend a World Series game in Brooklyn—showed up for the tiebreaker, filling every conceivable space like water seeping into the interstices of a reef. That day, President Eisenhower, whose recovery was progressing to the satisfaction of his doctors, rested comfortably in Colorado. Juan Perón, recently ousted after twelve years of dictatorial rule, fled from Argentina into exile in Paraguay. Raising hackles in the U.S. and Europe, Egyptian President Gamal Abdel Nasser announced he would purchase arms from the Soviet Bloc. The *Daily News* editorialized about the "grim, humorless, Kremlin slavemasters," claiming that Russian scientists were planning to build a dam across the Bering Strait in order to pump warm water into their territory and freeze or flood the United States. And the Yankees and Dodgers each started their fifth different pitcher in five games, only the second time in World Series history that such egalitarian mound assignments had been made.

With both sides saving their lefties for the return trip to the Bronx, the Yanks called on Bob Grim, who was normally their number-one relief pitcher. The Dodgers countered with Roger Craig, one of several players that season whose surprising contribution had made Walter Alston look more like a big league manager than a rube. In July, with the pitching staff depleted by injury, Alston brought up Craig and Don Bessent from the minors and had the newcomers start each game of a doubleheader. They won both, bolstering the sense that destiny was in our favor. The rookies finished the year with a combined record of 13–4, and ERAs under three runs per game.

Now, in his first World Series game, my namesake demonstrated major league poise. Roger held the Bombers to two runs before being replaced in the seventh, to a standing ovation, by Labine. Casey Stengel, too, turned to his bullpen for relief, but the man he normally looked for, Bob Grim, was the one on the mound waiting to be replaced.

The Dodgers were powered by the long ball: one homer by Amoros and two by the Duke, which rocketed unimpeded over the Schaefer sign and caromed like pinballs among the cars parked in the lot across the street. Snider's round-trippers gave him four for the Series—making him the first player to accomplish that feat twice—and a career total of nine, more than any other National Leaguer in history. The congregation emphatically informed the Duke of Flatbush that they appreciated the magnitude of his achievement and had forgiven his trespasses of the dog days of August, when he growled that Dodger fans did not deserve a pennant.

Labine, making his fourth appearance in five games, conducted his relief efforts with the efficiency of the Red Cross; the Yankees managed a total of six hits. With the 5–3 win, the Dodgers became the first team ever to win three straight Series games after losing the opening pair. We had only to win one of two in

Yankee Stadium to bring to Mudville the singular joy that could mend its collective heart.

We knew, of course, that winning two straight at home was a task the Yankees had historically dispatched as adroitly as a cook in a greasy spoon whipped up ham and eggs. Only three years earlier, behind the same 3–2 in games, they won the final pair *in Brooklyn.* While history served as an awning, nonetheless a slender beam of elation penetrated our hearts. None were more elated than my father and older brother.

Throughout both games they had cautiously glanced at each other. I could see the pain in their eyes, a mixture of betrayal, guilt, and disillusionment, but each Dodger run was like a stone under their feet, leading them from the swamp of despair to dry land, where broadcast school and a chaste Diane Brooks awaited my brother, and Frank Stone would come home to a forgiving wife and a ballplaying son. On someone's radio, Vin Scully recapped the game and the Dodgers' weekend comeback.

"That'll be your voice someday, Hubbell," Benny told my brother. "You'll bounce back too."

Hubbell had a familiar look in his eye, one of determination and anticipated triumph that he used to get when toeing a pitcher's mound with his spikes. He slapped the palms of Benny and Dizzy. "I'll catch you back home," he said. "I'm gonna see a certain young lady." He pushed his way through the crowd toward the exit.

My father, too, was inspired. When the last out was recorded, he sprang to his feet, let loose an inchoate roar from the depths of his being, and kissed Burt and Sal on the cheek.

"Jeez, Frankie," said Sal, "save it for Jeannie, willya."

"Jeannie," mused Dad. "My Jeannie." His eyes misted. "I'll bring her home tonight. I know what to do now." Then he saw Hubbell, and the spark in his son's eyes lit up his own. Looking like an agnostic who had spoken to a burning bush, he kept shifting his gaze from Hubbell to the scoreboard, which, to his astonishment, did not change its mind. The score remained Dodgers 5, Yankees 3. "Hubbell's snapping out of it," Dad told his friends. "Look at him. I told you—it's contagious. Soon as we wrap this thing up he'll be his old self again."

Unfortunately, try as I might, I could not figure out a way for each to have everything he wanted. Either my father was right and Hubbell would come around and embrace his true calling, or he would have to wait seven or eight years for me to wear his ragged glove in a big league game. I considered telling Dad that Hubbell's new dream had been sabotaged by So-Called Sonny Scott, on the theory that his hatred of Scott would swing him to Hubbell's side. But Hubbell had sworn me to secrecy. He was determined to work things out for himself.

Like my role models, I too had an agenda, and my hopes too were raised by the Dodgers' comeback. I decided that under no circumstances would I fail to be at Jake's for Monday's game. Further, I vowed to find a way to go permanently AWOL from class 6–1 and rid myself in one stroke of my twin nemeses, SS Officer Schaefer and Eleanor Krinski, who, I learned from Artie, had started a rumor that she and I were engaged.

While life at the ballpark was a carnival, home that weekend reminded me of the time my mother took Round Man and me to see a production of *Hamlet* on the theory that it is never too early to expose a child to the classics. Despite the consuming distraction of a World Series, my father had become the Melancholy Jew, moping around the house in boxer shorts and a sleeveless undershirt in lieu of tights and tunic. Muttering incoherently, he sat before the television with knit eyebrows and clenched jaw, paying no attention to the screen, smoking one Pall Mall after another, expelling an occasional "Goddamn it!" with the smoke, and pounding his fist into the arm of his easy chair where the blue upholstery had faded into a dull gray.

When my mother was in the hospital in August, I had come to realize how much her personality influenced the everyday texture of our lives, and how, despite her frequent lapses, she managed, like an unseen command post, to keep her troops fed, clothed, cleaned, on schedule, and functioning as a unit. During the current, strictly voluntary sabbatical, not only did I miss Mom and her cheering, comforting presence, but I also had to do without Hubbell. In certain ways I missed him more. At some point in the previous few years, I had taken to observing my brother closely, examining what he said and how he said it, what he wore, how he gestured, walked, and stood. It was as if I understood on some level that Hubbell was, by virtue of his greater proximity in age and character, a more appropriate role model than my father. While he had always spent too little time at home for my taste, each of Hubbell's arrivals would fill me with a certain excitement. Now he was gone, perhaps never to return. Half my reference points were missing in action. I found myself disoriented, like a stroke victim who had lost the use of one side of his body.

During the hospital siege, the four of us guys had been drawn together by a common threat, and we responded like a team, pitching in, cooperating, providing comfort and humor for each other and for Mom. If the present situation was analogous to a battle, we were not only handicapped by the loss of one comrade, but the nature of the opponent was nebulous. I did not know whom to blame for the crisis. Furthermore, the first time around, my father had been a worried, anxious soul, but he was also determined to keep his chin up in the presence of his kids. He tried to entertain, to distract, to cast the situation in a positive light, and while his efforts were as transparent as the cellophane wrapper on a box of Necco wafers, they sometimes succeeded and were always appreciated. Although, by virtue of his genes, my father was inclined to seize any opportunity to feel guilty, he could not blame himself for the lump on his wife's breast, and while the threat was deadly, it was out of his control. He was forced, at one point, to surrender to biology.

This time, when not at Ebbets Field or talking about the Series, he was as self-absorbed as the mop with which Jesse Hicks scrubbed the hallway floors. In his ruminations, he was his own chief suspect; he brooded over his complicity, darkly charting his errors. His face was marked not only with grief and fear, as before, but with doubt, regret, and self-recrimination. When he wasn't doleful, he was irritable, snapping at Round Man and me at the slightest pretext, only to hate himself a moment later and offer appeasement, usually in the form of something sweet to eat.

On Friday, he arrived home with a bouquet of flowers, which looked as incongruous in his mitts as a wrench in the hands of Marilyn Monroe. When he found a note in place of his wife, he stuffed the flowers into the trash and slipped into a daze, where he spent the rest of the evening. Supper consisted of corned beef sandwiches from the delicatessen, eaten off the wax paper wrapping instead of plates, and potato salad, wolfed down straight from the container. My father said nothing. As Mom had explained, he needed time to think.

His brooding silence was fine with me; it made it easier to avoid him. Certain thoughts had become too unpleasant to think, and I was learning how, with no more effort than switching channels on a TV set, I could get rid of them. But at the sight of my father, those unwelcome thoughts rushed back into my brain: Hubbell would be banished forever; I would see Mom only on visiting days, like a prisoner; Cyclone Frankie Stone, the legend, would turn out to be the Great Pretender. I spent my time on the phone with Artie, gloating over the adventure I had that day while he was interned by Mrs. Hun.

However, a man with covert responsibilities could not avoid his father all night; I had to disclose my classified information about Barney Klinger. I approached him in the living room. He stared blankly at the television, his eyes sopping wet even though he was watching *The Life of Riley* with William Bendix, not *This Is Your Life.* He was thinking about the members of his family who would not, because of him, be sleeping home that night.

Like my mother, Dad was proud of my intelligence work. We took a vow of secrecy, then he called his buddies to arrange a clandestine meeting with Jesse Hicks. To my surprise, he said nothing about medicine, unless the word *pusher* was the colloquial term for someone who practiced without a license.

On Saturday night, despite the fact that afternoon services had ended with a deadlocked World Series, Dad was silent through most of our supper at Bo Ling. He did not even offer his ritual joke when we entered under the neon sign: "This place used to be a bowling alley, but the *w* went off, so they made it a Chinese restaurant." At the table, he kept turning to the right, as if he expected his Jeannie to be in the seat beside him, as always, adding half a bottle of soy sauce to her moo goo gai pan and gnawing each microscopic morsel of meat from her spare ribs. "Where the hell do you put it all?" he would customarily say. I tried to use the line on Round Man instead, but it clanked like an offkey chord because it was obvious where Round Man put it all.

Back home, Dad planted himself in front of the television with his cigarettes, an ashtray, a bottle of beer, and the evening edition of the Sunday papers. The headline, DODGER HOMERS EVEN IT UP, did not cheer him, nor did the photo of Yankee owner Del Webb getting conked on the head by a foul ball. *Beat the Clock* couldn't do it. *Two for the Money* couldn't do it. *The Honeymooners* couldn't do it. Not even Jimmy Durante could do it. At the end of his show, when the schnozzola said, "Good night, Mrs. Calabash, wherever you are," and walked offstage, pausing in each of a series of spotlights, my father's lips moved as if he were saying good night to Jeannie with the light brown hair, wherever she was.

As Durante departed, my father sprinted to the kitchen, grabbed the telephone, and twirled the dial so emphatically I thought it might start spinning like a propeller and fly off the receiver. "Sid?" he said, when my uncle answered. "Frank. Is she there? . . . Waddaya mean, *who*? Jeannie, for chrissake, who do you think? Eleanor Roosevelt?"

He was informed that my mother was not there. Uncle Sid thought she might have stayed in the city after her matinee, perhaps to catch an evening performance of *Witness for the Prosecution*. Dad hung up. He crushed his Pall Mall and promptly lit another.

Then he saw Round Man, kneeling on the kitchen floor, reaching into the narrow space between a cabinet and the stove. He was trying to capture Rommel the roach in a jar, but his arm was not quite long enough. "What the hell are you doing?" asked my father.

With his voice rising an octave under the strain of wedging his shoulder into the crevice between porcelain and wood, Hank explained his mission.

"What are you, nuts?" Dad responded. "When it comes to cockroaches, you don't take prisoners."

He whipped off his slipper, gripped it by the toe, and wielded it like a club. "Get outta the way," he commanded.

"No!" said Round Man. "I have to do it my way."

My father, while mystified, did not have the patience to ask for an explanation. He wanted Hank out of the way so he could pound the vermin into insect hell and achieve some small measure of control over events in his own home. Round Man refused to budge. He sat, cross-legged, blockading access to Rommel. In his coonskin cap, with his arms folded defiantly atop his bulging tummy, he looked like Sitting Bull gone over to the other side. "Hank, get outta the way or you'll be sorry," said the king of the castle. Round Man puffed up his cheeks and shook his head. Even to his sworn enemy, he was a man of his word.

The stalemate was broken by the fortuitous ring of the telephone. My father pounced on it. But the caller was not my mother, only Mike the Barber. As the two men arranged a morning conclave to discuss the matter of Barney Klinger, Hank tried to take advantage of the distraction. But Rommel was gone, having retreated to some impenetrable fortress behind the stove. Round Man had blown another opportunity, but he had preserved his honor.

We returned to the living room. My father turned to Channel 2, where *Gunsmoke* had just begun. I asked him to switch to George Gobel. He said he couldn't stomach George Gobel. I suggested a show called *Tomorrow's Career* on Channel 7. My father looked at me as if I'd demanded Ibsen. "What's wrong with *Gunsmoke*?" he asked. How could I tell him that what was wrong with *Gunsmoke* was that the main character was really The Thing?

I could have left, of course, but something, perhaps a powerful disinclination to being alone in my room, compelled me to stay. I tried to distract myself by reading the funny papers, but neither "Li'l Abner," nor "Gasoline Alley," nor "Dick Tracy," nor "Brenda Starr" could keep me from masochistically peering over the pages of primary colors to the black and white shadows on the TV screen. The picture I saw was like a psychic negative in which the good guys wore black and the bad guys wore white, and Miss Kitty was Mrs. Schaefer, and, under the big-brimmed hat of Matt Dillon, the alleged lawman, sneered the foul, fanged mouth of The Thing. When he reached for his gun, the hand that slapped the holster was a foot long and clawed.

Another fortuitous phone call saved me from a sleepless night. When he heard the ring, my father sprang from his chair and dashed to the kitchen. He returned with a capricious smile on his lips and one raised eyebrow. It was the nearest thing to mirth he had managed since he opened the door to the apartment after the ball game and found that his wife was still truant. "It's for you," he told me. "It's a girl."

"A gi-i-i-rl," Round Man crooned.

A girl was calling me at ten-thirty on a Saturday night? This was a mystery I was eager to solve, but which I nonetheless approached with trepidation. My voice cracked when I said hello.

"Hell-o-o-o, Roger," answered the high, lilting voice of a flirt. "Do you know who this is?"

My first thought was Nurse Gallagher, but it couldn't be her. Nor Ruth Finkelstein. It was a young girl's voice. I said I did not know who it was.

"It's your secret admirer," sang the honeyed voice. "Can you guess who it is?"

I spoke the first name that came to mind and immediately regretted it because I knew it could be misconstrued as evidence that I, in turn, was *her* secret admirer. "Eleanor Krinski?"

"Ooooh, how did you guess?" she said. I wanted to die. But as soon as she spoke again, I knew something was wrong. Why was she still disguising her voice even after I had identified her? And her next question made me even more suspicious: "Where did you eat tonight, Roger? Did you go out?"

I answered the question and waited for more.

"Are you keeping the bathroom clean? Are you taking the garbage down?"

"What the hell do you care?" I demanded. The laugh that followed gave it away. "Is that you, Mom?"

"Shhhhh." In her normal voice, she said, "Hi, kiddo. I didn't want your father to know it was me." She explained that she had been at Uncle Sid's all evening, but did not want to talk to Dad when he called. It was kind of a test, she said, part of her little scheme to teach him a lesson. She asked how he was doing, and was delighted when I described my father's funk. She asked after all matters concerning the comfort and hygiene of her two youngest sons and told me that if things kept going the way they were, she might be home as early as the next night. She instructed me to fill in Hank on everything she had told me, to tell him she loved us both very much, and to give him a kiss for her. I drew the line at that, as she knew I would. Before we hung up, she added, "Send my regards to Eleanor Krinski."

"I *hate* Eleanor Krinski," I hastened to inform her.

One of the reasons I had decided never to get married was the thought of having to share a bed with another person. There had been times, when visiting relatives, that I had to share one with Round Man, and while I knew I was unlikely to marry someone who occupied as much space as he, I still found repugnant the thought of anyone pulling the covers off me, or jabbing me with an elbow or a knee, or snoring, or exhaling foul breath in my face. I liked being alone in bed. I liked being able to turn on the light to read when I couldn't sleep. I liked listening to the radio whenever I wanted to. I liked being able to sing in bed, and to bounce a bit to get a little rhythm going with the box spring. I liked being able to touch any part of my body I wanted to. I liked not having to hold in my farts all night.

It therefore came as a surprise, both when Mom was in the hospital and on the present weekend, that my father appeared each morning, after sleeping alone, looking like a raccoon with dark rings around his eyes, dragging himself around as if his feet had turned to steel overnight. He looked that way on Sunday morning, although he put up a chipper front when Hank and I emerged for breakfast. On the kitchen table were two paper bags. A small one filled with bialys was propped against the sugar bowl, and a large one, on its side, spilled out its contents of sesame, poppy, and egg bagels. Also displayed was a large silver brick of Philadelphia Cream Cheese, a package of sliced Swiss and another of muenster, and a platter of lox, smoked sturgeon, and whitefish. Dad had learned the low-risk way to provide a hearty Sunday breakfast. During our previous all-male stint, his assault on blueberry pancakes had been enough to turn lily-white the smiling visage of Aunt Jemima. We not only ended up eating toast on that occasion, but we spent half the day scraping crisp black stains from the griddle and removing gobs of pasty batter from every cleft in the stove.

"Sit down, boys," said my father like a proud host. "Look at that spread. Is that beautiful, or what?" He poured three steaming cups of the thickest, blackest coffee I had ever seen. "Yes sir. Who says we can't take care of ourselves? Go ahead, dig in. What are you waiting for?"

He stopped pouring the coffee and stared quizzically at the percolator suspended at an angle in midair. "You guys drink coffee yet?" he asked. We confessed that we did not. "What do you drink? Milk? Juice? Do we have any juice? I'll get some glasses."

"Get some plates while you're at it," said Round Man.

After breakfast we accomplished the cleanup with only one casualty—a broken dish. "What a team," said my father. "Stone, Stone, and Stone. Yes sir, us guys stick together. Right, boys? All for one and one for all. That's what a family is, right?"

"When's Mom coming home?" answered Round Man.

Soon Sal arrived, and Mike the Barber, and Jake, and Burt, and finally, somehow managing to be both dignified and deferential at the same time, Jesse Hicks. In my estimation, their solemnity was inconsistent with the fact that three hours hence they would be in Ebbets Field for the most important game of their lives. Adding to my consternation was my father's nonnegotiable demand that Hank and I exit the room. I could see asking a young kid like Round Man to leave, but why me, the guy who solved the Barney Klinger mystery in the first place?

Their voices were so muted that my snooping from the living room yielded few details. They decided to take care of the Klinger situation themselves because bringing in the police would get Otis into trouble as well. Otis, they concluded, needed a special kind of hospital right away. They promised Jesse they would help him find a way to pay for it. The janitor said he was much obliged. When I returned to the kitchen, on the pretext of needing a glass of water, the meeting was breaking up. Jesse's weary black eyes were filled with tears. As the others rose from their chairs, suggesting with words and gestures that he keep his chin up and have courage, he remained seated, as though grief had rendered his legs unusable. Sal offered him a cigarette. Jake followed with a light. Mike invited him to join us at the game, offering his own wife's ticket. Jesse thanked him kindly, but thought he would be better off sticking close to his son that day.

I was forced to conclude that I had been wrong: Otis did not have diabetes. Jackie Robinson had diabetes and he not only did not need hospitalization, he was still intimidating pitchers and stealing bases. Otis must have a more serious illness, all the more reason to have a real doctor look after him, not an amateur like Barney Klinger. I swelled with pride knowing that I might have saved a life, and a sense of cosmic justice washed over me when I reflected on the fact that I would not have made my discovery had I not been brave enough to ditch school on behalf of the Dodgers. It annoyed me that none of the grownups in that room so much as shook my hand.

The smell of Angie Corso's kitchen, I imagined, was the same that had greeted the liberating GIs when they landed in Sicily, a smell worth fighting for. Fittingly, it was the smell that greeted Round Man, my father, and me after the Dodgers had liberated the Series advantage on Sunday. Angie had accomplished something I thought was impossible: she improved on her cooking. Each bite released ambrosia of unsurpassed savor and a texture so satisfying I could have chewed each molecule forever. From a bottomless pot, Angie kept ladling onto our plates piles of ziti macaroni, adding succulent sausages and meatballs as big as spaldeens, and topping it off with a ripe red sauce as thick and life-giving as Mediterranean soil.

Afterward, with Round Man fast asleep on the sofa and my father and Mike unable to lift themselves from their chairs, Louie and I retired to the living room. We unfastened our belts and compared the sizes of our swollen bellies. Louie then produced three magazines. One, the smallest, contained a collection of black and white photographs that looked like the stills displayed outside movie houses, only in these scenes the actors wore no clothing and were engaged in activities much like those that had allegedly taken place at the Holy Shrine between Iggy and Diane Brooks—only no policeman had stopped the action. Judging from Louie's narration and the location of the women's mouths, I surmised that the word blow had more than one meaning.

As Louie and I analyzed the literature, Mike and my father suddenly appeared. "Waddaya got there?" asked Mike. He was not pleased at Louie's choice of reading material. "Gimme that. Yez are too young for this." He confiscated the small magazine, but not the other, larger and shinier ones that featured color photos of unaccompanied girls. Mike licked his thumb and turned the pages of one periodical until he found the picture he was looking for. "Look at that," he said, whistling. "What a pair of bazooms. How'd you like to sink your teeth into—"

A loaf of Italian bread crashed against his slick, black head. It was Angie. "What are you showing them that filth for?" she said, tomahawking her husband's head with the bread like a squaw out to nab a white man's scalp to hang outside her teepee. "You're disgusting. No wonder Ignazio can't graduate high school. All he can think about is girls."

"Waddaya want him to think about, algebra?" asked Mike, raising his arms to fend off further blows.

Angie jabbed the bread, like a lance, into Mike's crotch. When he instinctively lowered his hands, she whacked him over the head so hard the bread exploded and crumbs sprayed the room like shrapnel. "No good, rotten poivoit!"

A chunk of the loaf bounced off Round Man's face. He awakened, picked the bread off his chest, ate it, and went back to sleep.

Iggy appeared. He had not been at either ball game, nor had he eaten with us, although he was home at the time. I had seen him twice—once when he arrived and went straight to his room, and once when he went to the bathroom. On neither occasion did he speak or acknowledge anyone's presence. He looked sullen and downcast. Both times, Angie and Mike watched their son, shrugged at each other, and shook their heads.

"Take it easy, willya, Ma," said Iggy, puffing on a Lucky. He was wearing a black leather jacket arrayed with silver studs. He turned up the collar.

"Look at him," said Angie. "He looks like a hood, for God's sake. He makes bets on girls! I was never so humiliated—"

"Mind your business Ma," snapped Iggy. "I won the bet, didn't I?"

Angie burst into tears. "Don't talk to your mother like that," said Mike. He smacked Iggy on the back of the head, just hard enough to demonstrate to his wife that his authority was still intact. Angie left the room, wiping her eyes with her apron. Mike held his hands palms up with the fingers and thumbs of each joined at the tips, and he bounced them up and down as if comparing their respective weights. "Women," he said. "What are you gonna do?"

"Lend me fiedollars, all right, Pop?" said Iggy.

Mike peeled off a five-dollar bill from a wad the size of a McIntosh apple. "Come home early," he ordered. "I don't need no more aggravation from your mother."

"I'll be home when I'm home," Iggy sneered.

Again Mike smacked his son's head.

"Lay off," warned Iggy. "I ain't in the mood."

"What the hell's wichyou lately?"

"Don't bug me, all right? Just gimme the fiedollars."

I thought I knew what was wrong with Iggy. He could not appear in public because he did not want to be seen by Hubbell and the other Big Guys; they were still burning over the way he had suckered them into his story, and had been debating the veracity of the tale all weekend. Furthermore, Iggy was in a rotten mood because of what happened at the Holy Shrine. Louie had enlightened me regarding Mike's earlier reference to the condition known as blue balls. He said that when a girl does not let a guy go all the way, the stuff that makes babies builds up like water in a hose, but since it has no place to go, it backs up into the testicles, where it was manufactured, only there's no room left. As a result, Louie said, the guy feels like he has to go to the bathroom all the time but has to hold it in. He postulated that this condition somehow turns the guy's balls blue. Why blue and not red or green, Louie could not say. He promised to look into it, just as he was investigating why, after seven years of marriage, a man's dick starts to itch, as indicated by the Marilyn Monroe movie, *The Seven Year Itch.*

This, then, explained Iggy's irascible mood. Whether or not the story he told was entirely true, he surely did not go all the way with Diane. Hence, he must have a whopping case of blue balls. I, too, would be irritable if I had to walk around like I was holding it in all the time.

I was eager to report my finding to Hubbell, thinking it would be of some consolation to him in case his mission with Diane that night—for I assumed that was where he went when he hustled out of Ebbets Field—was unsuccessful. Only I was wrong.

The cause of Iggy's ill temper was not blue balls, it was a dead movie star.

"I swear, if I didn't know better, I'd think you was a queer," said Mike to his son. "Walking around like a pussy 'cause some actor died. He was in two friggin' pictures, for chrissake."

"Three!" corrected Iggy. "And James Dean, man, he was not just a movie star. He was . . . he was . . . the greatest!" He zipped up his leather jacket as if creating an exclamation point, and strode proudly out of the room.

James Dean, age twenty-four, had broken his neck when his speeding Porsche Spyder collided head-on with another car as he drove from Hollywood to Salinas for a road race. This was clearly a sign, but I did not know whether it was a good sign or a bad sign. On the one hand, a rebellious outsider who sneered at convention was just the sort who would line up cosmically with the Bums. By that reasoning, his demise would be a bad omen. But James Dean was also the idol of juvenile delinquents and, more to the point, of Iggy Corso, and Iggy, having squared off against my brother, had aligned himself with the wrong side whether he liked it or not. By that reasoning, James Dean's death was a positive portent.

That the signs were so impenetrable was an indication of how closely matched the forces of good and evil had become as the World Series entered its final stage.

Uncle Sid and his family lived in the top-floor apartment of a converted brownstone. The narrow street of identical houses was lined with chestnut and maple trees. Their leaves that night were illuminated by the yellow-white glow of the moon, which hovered, nearly full, above the asphalt, as if listening to the sounds of Chopin that sprayed like a drizzle over the street. The simple, elegant melody was familiar—it was one that my uncle played frequently—but the timbre was richer because two sets of hands were at work on the keyboard, Sid's on the bass end and my mother's on the treble. Since childhood the two siblings loved nothing more than to sit side by side on a piano bench and play in unison, sister always two octaves above brother and racing slightly ahead of the tempo, as befits the impatient twin who left the womb first and would drag her timid brother away from the piano and into the streets to experience life.

My father stood between Round Man and me with his hands on our shoulders, waiting respectfully for the nocturne to end. "Look up at the living room window," he instructed us when the air settled into silence. Then he sang, loud and resonant and slightly off-key: "I dream of Jeannie with the light brown hair, borne like a vapor on the summer air. . . ."

Faces appeared at the windows beneath Uncle Sid's apartment and in some in the adjacent buildings. There were probably faces in *all* the buildings, I thought, behind us and up and down the block, and soon a wagon would pull up and guys in white suits would jump out and throw butterfly nets over the three of us. But my mother's face did not appear. "Keep looking up, boys," urged Dad as he took a breath. He resumed crooning, louder than before:

"Oh, I long for Jeannie with the day dawn smile."

"Shaddup down there!" cried a voice from our right.

"Hey, Bing Crosby! It's ten o'clock!" yelled another from the left.

And still there was no sign of life in Uncle Sid's window. My father squeezed us closer to his side and sang louder still.

"Shut up or I'll call the cops!" shouted a voice from behind us. A can landed five feet away and clanged loudly as it bounced along the street.

"Oh, I long for Jeannie and my heart bows low . . ."

"Quiet!"

"Never more to find her where the bright waters flow . . ."

"You asked for it. I'm calling the cops!"

Oblivious to the threats, my father started to sing the next line, but he stopped abruptly because, two stories above us, her brown hair glowing like a halo in the soft light behind her, was his Jeannie. She stared down at us with a scrutinizing, noncommittal smile.

"Come home, sweetheart," pleaded my father.

She narrowed her eyes and said nothing.

"Please come home. We miss you. Your children miss you. You belong with us."

She slid her jaw to the left, then to the right. It was something she did when she was thinking hard, as if the motion lubricated her brain.

"Come home. Everything will be different," my father promised.

"Go home, willya, lady?" roared a voice. "I can't take this no more!"

"Yeah, go home so we can get some peace around here," another voice agreed.

My mother tossed into the moonlit night a white carnation. It landed at my father's feet. He grinned, stooped to pick it up, and gazed again at his wife in hopes of receiving further encouragement. Mom gestured with her hand as if to say, "Come on up," and turned from the window. Dad stuck the flower behind his ear and led the way up the steps of the brownstone.

While my mother and father held a summit meeting alone in the kitchen, Uncle Sid entertained Round Man and me the only way he knew how: he played the piano. But, whereas a normal person charged with keeping two kids occupied might play a singalong ditty like "Row, Row, Row, Your Boat" or a familiar bouncy tune like "Alexander's Ragtime Band," my uncle performed "Rhapsody in Blue." It was the closest thing to a popular song he could think of. On the sofa Aunt Libby mended a pair of black Banlon socks, while, on her lap, my cousin Judy slept with her thumb in her mouth and saliva oozing down her jaw. Round Man stared at a barren bowl of guppies and goldfish, as transfixed as if he were observing dolphins in the wild. I stood beside the piano and watched Uncle Sid.

As he worked his way through Gershwin's composition, sweat built up on his face. The veins in his neck bulged thick and blue. His lips pulled back from his clenched teeth and pressed against his gums as if he were in pain. His head jabbed sharply down and his thick, gray hair fell over his face; then he jerked up as if his head had been yanked by a string, and his hair fell back into place. As the tempo and volume picked up, this meek, soft-voiced man hammered the keys like a convict breaking rocks on a chain gang. His hands moved so rapidly they blurred together like streaks of ribbon. The music seemed no longer to come from the piano but from Uncle Sid himself, not from his fingers but from somewhere deep in his chest. My whole body shivered, like it did when I stood on a subway grate and a train rumbled by below. Then it stopped. The room became as silent as under water. Uncle Sid, his eyes closed and his mouth open, let his head fall slowly forward until his chin came to rest on his chest. I wondered if he suffered from the same disease as Otis Hicks.

When he opened his soft, gray eyes, tears spilled over the lower lids, like a solvent that he hoped would wash clean the stain of his past. Uncle Sid's position at a prestigious music school and his promising concert career had been curtailed in 1951, exactly one week after Dat Day and the death of Grandpa Abe, when an influential impresario learned that he belonged to the Communist Party. It was an affiliation my uncle did not even remember. He had signed on in the thirties so his older brother, the radical, would stop calling him a sissy. Rather than confront his accusers, as my mother urged, Uncle Sid retreated more deeply into his music, as if by playing from his soul he could make everything right. This, along with his refusal to sign a loyalty oath—a stand based on conviction and supported by my mother—was taken as an admission of guilt. Now, as he waited for the tides of history to shift, he eked out a living teaching private students. I felt sorry for this frail, pale man who looked like he still needed his twin sister to fight off bullies for him. I tried to think of a way to tell him what I knew in my heart—that if the Dodgers won either of the next two games, he would be in Carnegie Hall in no time.

Uncle Sid saw me gaping at him. "I get carried away," he said, chuckling self-consciously. Then he looked behind me and smiled, pleased at what he saw: my father, beaming like a bridegroom, holding my mother's hand as if he was afraid she would once again disappear.

"Let's go, boys," said Dad. "We're going home."

Evidently, a lot of negotiating had taken place while Uncle Sid played "Rhapsody in Blue." It was after eleven o'clock as I, dressed in pajamas, watched my father fulfill one of the terms of the deal.

Mom handed him the phone. He dialed and waited, looking as though he hoped no one would answer. When the other party picked up, Dad took a deep breath and summoned up his bravado: "Hello, Sy? Frank . . . Yeah, yeah, I know what time it is

. . . I know you hate getting calls at home . . . No, it *can't* wait . . . Shut up and let me talk, damn it. I just wanted to say, kiss my ass, Sy . . . I said, kiss my fat Jewish ass. I don't need you or your stinking job. I quit! What's more, I'm letting the Hack Bureau know about the graft you've been hustling . . . There's nothing to think over . . . I don't *want* to talk. So long, Sy . . . Oh, and your Yankees are dead meat. It's over, pal. Kiss the Series goodbye."

He slammed the receiver. My mother bounced up and down in her chair, applauding and grinning, like a little girl watching a circus. She hopped to my father's lap and threw her arms around his neck. "Way to go!" she said, kissing him repeatedly. "My hero!"

"Why can't you be a normal wife?" asked Dad. "Most wives would kill if their husbands quit a steady job."

"You'd be bored," my mother explained.

She got up and poured more coffee. As if on cue, each of them lit another cigarette. My father reflected on what he had done. Gradually the smile faded from his face. His mind seemed to shift into reverse. "What am I, nuts? What the hell am I going to do now? How are we gonna live?"

"Don't you worry, kid," said Mom. "It's you and me. We'll work it out. This is the smartest thing you've done since you married me."

Smart was not the word my father would have used to describe quitting his job. He was simply fulfilling the terms of their settlement. But he nodded in agreement with my mother's declaration of faith, as if by doing so her conviction might rub off on him.

"I love you," he said. "Have I told you that lately?"

"You can never say it enough."

My father stood, encircled his wife's lean body with his arms and pulled her close to him. He had won back his Jeannie, but she was the real victor. She had been waging a struggle against Regular Guys Disease for twenty years, and now she had, like the Dodgers, finally taken the lead. She took her husband's face in her hands and planted her lips on his.

I had seen enough. I knew the kiss would last a long time, and it did not surprise me when, a few minutes later, I heard my parents scurry to their bedroom and lock the door behind them.

I took the opportunity to scrutinize my older brother's room. I made a quick survey of Hubbell's closet in search of future hand-me-downs before moving on to the drawers, which I expected to yield more interesting treasures. I did not know exactly what I was looking for, perhaps a clue as to whether Hubbell was making the mistake of his life by abandoning baseball or staking a claim to his true self. I would not have been disappointed to find a diary, or at least a dirty book or two, but I found in his dresser only socks and shirts and underwear, and in his desk only school supplies that he hadn't bothered to throw out after graduation. The only mildly interesting item was his yearbook, but I had already seen the pictures of him in uniform and the entry under his portrait, which predicted that he would be the first alumnus to make it to the big leagues.

I was opening another drawer when I heard the familiar voice behind me. "Find anything interesting?" It was Hubbell.

Hastily, I explained that I couldn't sleep and, since he wasn't home, I thought I might avail myself of his record player. I said I was looking for his records.

He smiled knowingly and pointed to a pair of foot-high stacks of 45's on top of his dresser. He did not seem to believe that I hadn't noticed them. But he was in too good a mood to get Big Guyish on me. His luminous smile did not diminish by a photon. He listened to my feeble attempts to justify my snooping while leaning against the door doing something strange even by teenager standards: he kept sniffing a book as if it were a flower.

Whispering so as not to be heard by our parents, Hubbell explained that he needed some clothes and had waited across the street until he saw the lamp go on in the master bedroom. "You were with that blonde girl, huh?" I said.

"That's for me to know and you to find out," he teased.

He had been with Diane all right, and the evening had been as successful as the ball game that afternoon. I knew this not only because of his charitable mood and the way he floated lightly around the room, but by the book he was sniffing. Titled *Immortal Poems,* it had portraits of wise-looking, old-fashioned men on the cover and it smelled of perfume. When he put it down, I opened the cover and saw *Diane Brooks* inscribed in a soft, blue script that swirled and looped across the page like a ballerina. As if that was not evidence enough, there was the record Hubbell sang along with as he shoved underwear and shirts into a paper bag: "Oh, What a Night," by the Dells.

I did not question him further about Diane, nor did I ask any of the questions that I had been accumulating—about broadcasting school, and So-Called Sonny Scott, and Iggy's story, and whether he would ever move back in or speak to my father again. I was content just having him near, watching him sing, however indirectly, about his night of love, and chatting with him about the World Championship that was now within reach. The spirit of my questions, however, was answered. I could tell by the way he looked at me that I would not lose Hubbell even if my father did.

It was nearly midnight when he returned to his temporary lodgings at Benny's house. I lay on his bed, singing along with the smooth, simple harmonies of "Earth Angel" and "Crying in the Chapel," and the rhythmic falsetto of "When You Dance." I was in no hurry to get to sleep. I could stay in bed as late as I wanted to on Monday morning. For I, too, had done some negotiating that evening. In return for playing the motherless waifs as my father sang his plaintive serenade outside Uncle Sid's house, Round Man and I had been relieved of all academic obligations for the duration of the World Series.

Chapter Fourteen

Game Six was played on October 3, the fourth anniversary of Dat Day; it was over before it began.

Karl Spooner, the rookie who blazed into Brooklyn at the end of the previous season and struck out half the batters he faced, took the mound in Yankee Stadium because Don Newcombe was still not ready for action. The young southpaw with the tenuous shoulder had shut down the Bombers for three innings in Game Two, striking out five and allowing only a bloop single. This time, he was up against the devilish Whitey Ford, who stymied the Bums in the opener and whose .735 winning percentage was the best in the majors.

The Yankees, with their backs to the wall after three straight setbacks in Brooklyn, lashed out at the opening bell. They wrapped two walks around a Spooner strikeout, then Yogi singled in a run, and Hank Bauer did the same, and Bill Skowron hacked a high outside pitch into the right field seats, where Babe Ruth had parked so many of his 714 homers.

Reflecting on the five-run outburst, I had the irritating feeling that it could have been avoided. Spooner had gotten two strikes each on Yogi, Bauer, and Skowron, but could not reel them in before they did their damage. Worse, one runner should have been thrown out trying to steal, but something went wrong—either Campanella got the ball stuck in his webbing or Gilliam was late covering second. And Berra's single should have been a double play ball, but the grounder skipped when it should have hopped, and skidded under Gilliam's glove. Skowron should never have come to bat that inning.

Nothing much happened the rest of the game. Dodger relievers Russ Meyer and Ed Roebuck held the Yankees scoreless, but the Bums could manage only four hits and one run themselves. Whitey tickled them to death with sinking curveballs that they either missed entirely or chopped into the dirt for ground outs. Adding injury to insult, Snider pulled up lame when he stepped into a divot while chasing a fly ball; he had to leave the game after three innings. Based on the Duke's endorsement of Arthur Murray's Dance Studio ("The Mrs. used to bench me every time we went dancing"), I figured he should have been able to pirouette around the hole.

The neighborhood was as quiet as night. It was as if everyone was waiting, hoping that time would collapse like a cardboard box until tomorrow at game time, so they could get it over with one way or the other, let loose the long-awaited celebration or begin once again the requiem, "Wait till next year." Ippish stood with his arms folded on his sweat-soaked chest; the few cars on the road proceeded so politely he had nothing even to wave at, and the ennui induced by the Dodgers' loss had reduced the street games over which he was guardian to some cheerless rounds of boxball and stoopball. The only car that called attention to itself was Barney Klinger's Lincoln Continental, which crossed the intersection with its horn blaring as it swerved around a slower car. Klinger did not, I observed, have an MD license plate.

Women rocked their babies with minimalist art; the springs of the carriages, which on sunny days squeaked like a gathering of cicadas, were as soundless as ants. On her perch atop the stoop, the Sphinx looked more sour and disparaging than ever. The stores were empty of commerce. Sharfin the butcher mopped the blood and sawdust from his floor. Sam the fruit store man rearranged a bin of apples, placing the reddest of the reds and the greenest of the greens in front. Happy Horowitz read a magazine.

In an effort to salvage some pleasure from the afternoon, I stopped by to challenge Henny, who was dusting off shelves of canned goods behind the counter. "Give me a sentence with *I moan* in it," I said.

"I moan close up early and go home," Henny replied. To ease my disappointment, she inserted a thick piece of orange marmalade directly into my mouth. It was no substitute for stumping her, or even for halvah. Was there to be no satisfaction that day beyond my sanctioned sabbatical from school?

In preparation for the shorter, colder days to come, a green coal truck was making a delivery to our building. Black nuggets poured down a long wooden chute, one end of which was inserted into a slot on the side of the truck and the other through a window and into the coal bin in the cellar, where Jesse Hicks angled the chute like a sailor at a rudder. Though he was busy, the janitor was glad to see me. "How's Otis?" I asked.

"Well, Otis isn't feeling too good, Roger," said Jesse, shoveling errant chunks of coal into the bin. "Matter of fact, Otis in the hospital."

"What's wrong with him? Is it diabetes?"

"No, it ain't that. Otis, he got . . . well, he got some rare disease, which I don't even know what to call it. He'll be fine though, just fine. He in good hands."

I was relieved, and not a little proud that my intervention had come in time for Otis to get proper medical care. "What are you guys gonna do to Barney Klinger?" I asked.

The avalanche of coal stopped suddenly. The cellar became as quiet as it was dark. Jesse's eyes darted around as if to make sure spies hadn't infiltrated the bin. He put down the shovel and wiped his brow. "You shouldn't talk about that, son."

I swore that I hadn't said a word to anyone and understood fully the need for secrecy. But I still wanted to know what they were going to do to Barney, since my own father wouldn't even talk about it.

"We'll see about ol' Klinger," said Jesse. We said goodbye in the fetid subterranean corridor that connected the alley to the cellar. Jesse removed his glove and placed his warm, callused hand on my head. "Thanks for letting us know about Otis, son. You done good."

Thanks to the result of the game and the great unresolved issue of Hubbell, which hovered over the family like the cloud of Joe Btfsplk, the atmosphere at supper was as boring as the lamb chops and mashed potatoes on my plate. Mom tried to make conversation, telling us about the shows she had seen and the restaurants she had eaten in during her weekend furlough, but it did not take her long to discern our disinterest. She spent the rest of the meal watching us with an amused, superior air, no doubt wondering how a game played in knickers could elicit from men emotions that the melancholy sorrows of everyday existence could not. She also knew that my father was troubled by more than the Series. The elation of his cathartic phone call to Sy Kramer had been washed away like the chalk marks on Play Street after rain; now he whipped himself with self-reproach because he was unemployed for the first time since the war. He was convinced that Sy Kramer could fix things at the Hack Bureau so he'd never drive again, not even if he raised the money for his own cab. And, though he would never say so, he no doubt also wondered if, thanks to Solly Skapinsky, Cyclone Frankie Stone would now be remembered as a puff of hot air.

I lay in bed staring at the pictures of Dodger players on my wall, wondering whether they could take the field tomorrow with sufficient faith to fuel a victory. I tried to figure out what had gone wrong with my rituals, which I had performed scrupulously. There was only one conclusion: Yankee Stadium was outside my range, just as the USA had, mercifully, been outside the range of German bombers during the war. With Manhattan between my hat and the Bronx, and The Thing's defenses at full strength, I was powerless. I had to take countermeasures. But what?

The answer came to me with the explosiveness of Jackie Robinson stealing home. I dashed out of my room to look for my father; I would need his assistance. The kitchen was empty. I ran to the living room. Only Round Man was there, watching *Ramar of the Jungle* and picking granules of lint from the fur of his rabbit's feet. He too was concerned about his loss of power. Then I saw Mom in the doorway to her bedroom; she looked as if Martians were eating bonbons in her bed.

My father was on his knees with his hands clasped together. From movie screens, picture books, and greeting cards, I recognized it as the posture of prayer. "Uh, Frank," said my mother. "The last time we discussed the matter, you said you were an agnostic, leaning toward atheism."

"Can't take no chances," said my father. "The team needs all the help it can get."

Although my mother was astonished by Dad's sudden piety, I was not. I remembered what happened during the '52 Series, when he was in a three-car pileup. He lay in the gutter, barely clinging to consciousness as the police cleared a path for an ambulance. A priest kneeled over him. "I will pray for you, son. Is there anything you would like to tell God?"

"Yeah, Padre," said Dad, his voice barely audible. "Tell him
to give the Dodgers a break, willya?" And he blacked out.

"The president's in the hospital," Mom pointed out. "The
country's being run by that creep, Nixon. Jews and Arabs are
aiming guns at each other. Negroes are being lynched. And
you're using your first prayer on a baseball game?"

"It's not just a game," said Dad, rising to his feet. "Everything depends on this. If we lose again, Brooklyn will die. Lives
will go down the drain, and one of them will be your son's."

"I know what we can do," I interjected.

"Frank, leave Hubbell alone," said Mom. "If you love
him—"

"I love him more than myself. That's why this is so important.
He's gonna piss his life away."

"I know what we can do," I repeated.

"Look, Frank, I know you love the team, but this is ridicu-
lous."

"You want proof?" said Dad. "I'll give you proof. What
happened with Vivian Mason? When you started that cockamamie campaign, you had lots of support, right? Then what?"

"What does Vivian have to do with—"

"People changed their minds, didn't they? When? I'll tell you
when: Thursday, after the Dodgers lost the first two games. Then
what happened? Three days later, every woman in the PTA was
on your side. Why? We won three straight, that's why. And what
happened this afternoon? What were all those phone calls
about?"

My mother replayed in her mind the roller coaster candidacy
of Vivian Mason. She added it all up, then she thrust her clenched
right fist in the air and said, "Let's go Bums!"

"I *said* I know what we can do!"

The house was of cedar and gray stone, set on a hill as far back
from Cascade Road as the right field fence at Ebbets Field was
from home plate. My father braked Uncle Sid's car to a halt at the
apex of a circular drive carved through a cloister of tall trees. My
mother turned to Hank and me in the backseat and gestured with
her eyes and a nod of her head for us to go fulfill our mission.

Disembarking from either side of the car, my brother and I tried to close our doors quietly so as not to jar the silence, which was thick and opaque despite the clamor of a thousand crickets. The evening air chilled the back of my neck. I sniffed deeply the scent of burning pine and the perfume of something unfamiliar that I knew must be green and moist. Above us the shimmering stars seemed as big as silver dollars on a ceiling.

Only once before had I been so electrified by bucolic sensations: the summer we rented a bungalow in the Catskill Mountains. But the colony was a dense clutch of frail wooden cabins, and the inhabitants brought the sounds of the city with them. This night, in Stamford, Connecticut, I stood for the first time outside a house from which could be seen no other houses, and I felt, if only for seconds, the indelible embrace of nature, heightened by a nerve-exposing sense of anticipation. Hank and I tiptoed to a heavy door of carved wood with a diamond-shaped inset of bullet glass that rendered indiscernible the shapes of objects on the other side. I turned around, looking for reassurance. My parents were outside the car now, leaning on the fender. They signaled, "Go ahead."

I pressed the doorbell. Two round gongs broke the silence. I took a deep breath and removed my Dodger cap. I was trying to prop up my pompadour when the door opened and a woman appeared in the warm glow of light. She was more regal than the pictures of her in the newspapers. Tall, with high cheekbones and intelligent eyes, she wore beige slacks and a dark brown sweater, which offset skin the color of dark coffee. "Can I help you?" she said.

"Yes, ma'am," I said. It was the first time I had ever used the word *ma'am*. "Is Jackie . . . I mean, Mr. Robinson . . . is he home, ma'am?"

"Jackie is resting," said Rachel Robinson. "Tomorrow is a very important game, you know."

"I know, but . . . see, that's why we're here. We drove all the way from Brooklyn. It's real important."

She eyed my parents and concluded that we were relatively harmless. "Well, I don't know . . ."

She had to let us see him. Jackie was the only man for the job. We could have driven to Gil Hodges's house in fifteen minutes, or to Duke's or Erskine's in thirty, and my mother could have been home in time for the season premiere of *I Love Lucy*. But I had lobbied for the ninety-minute drive to Connecticut because Jackie Robinson was not just a ballplayer, he was a liberator; because in his soul burned the desire to prove something more durable than that his team could win a championship; because he had endured trials more exacting than hitting Whitey Ford's curveball and had suffered greater indignities than losing five World Series to the Yankees; because a man of whom it was said "He always finds a way to win" would apprehend immediately the spirit in which I had come.

"Please, Mrs. Robinson." I was prepared to press my case and swear that I would take less than a minute of her husband's time, but the great man himself appeared in the doorway. I had never seen him in person without the baggy flannels with number 42 on the back, and then from only as close as the grandstand. He wore gray slacks and a pale blue shirt, and his well-worn slippers seemed incongruous on feet that flew on spikes. His hair was grayer than I had expected, and he was thicker around the middle, but his black eyes, squinting to size us up in the glare of an overhead porch light, were as intense in the hushed rural night as they were in the roar of the ballpark when he crept in from third base in anticipation of a bunt.

"What is it, boys?" His voice was incongruously high and nasal, but less so in person than through the tinny speaker of a radio or television. I found myself wondering if, when Hubbell became a broadcaster, his voice too would sound higher and more nasal. It was not the only irrelevant thought that intruded on my concentration as I struggled to locate the right words. "Can I do something for you?" Jackie asked.

"Yes," I asserted, my voice crackling like cellophane. "See, this hat, it's a lucky hat and . . . well, I just know if you have it with you tomorrow . . . you know, in the Stadium, at the game . . . well, see, Brooklyn's too far away and . . . if it's with you . . ."

"Sure, son," said Jackie. "I'd be mighty proud to have that hat."

My heart somersaulted. I brushed off the hat on the side of

my leg, and, taking care to hold it straight with the peak facing front, handed it to my hero like a supplicant offering to a priest a lamb for the altar of sacrifice.

"Thank you," I said. When I turned to leave, I remembered that I had not come alone. Round Man had not made a sound, nor had he moved or turned his gaze from Jackie's face the entire time. Now he extended his right arm and opened his fist, revealing a single, impeccably groomed rabbit's foot. Jackie lifted it from his palm and thanked him. Then, to Round Man's surprise, he grabbed the hand, which had remained suspended in air, and gave it a single, vigorous shake. Round Man grinned like a snowman. Jackie smiled too, and the familiar flame in his eyes softened into an ember. Not to be outdone, I reached out my own hand. Jackie gripped it. His hand was tough and soft. I shook it, and kept on shaking, until Jackie yanked it away. He laughed. "I have to throw with that."

Mrs. Robinson gently tugged her husband's arm. As they stepped back into their home, they lifted their gazes to where my parents stood watching. I turned to see my father issue a snappy salute and my mother throw Jackie Robinson a kiss with both hands.

It was sunny and nearly seventy degrees, perfect weather for baseball. The signs on the field favored the Yankees: their southpaws had already won three home games, and today, in the Bronx, the veteran Tommy Byrne would seem to have an edge on young, inconsistent Johnny Podres, who sought to become the first Dodger pitcher ever to win two games in a World Series. Off the field the signs were favorable. The morning papers reported that President Eisenhower had rallied after yesterday's "minor setback," and my older brother achieved a pregame triumph that I hoped would set the tone for the day.

When I arrived at the Corner, feeling naked but oddly exhilarated without my hat, the Big Guys were attempting once again to make Marty Klinger pay off his debt. They dragged him to within inches of Iggy, who started to unbuckle his belt when suddenly Hubbell grabbed him from behind and wrenched his arm into a hammerlock. "Tell them the truth," he demanded.

"What the fuck are you doing, Stone?" Iggy's voice was partially choked by the pressure of my brother's forearm on his Adam's apple.

"Tell them what really happened." Hubbell yanked upward on Iggy's arm, which was pinned to his back with the hand angled upward toward the opposite shoulder.

"Fuck you, I ain't—ow! That hurts, man. Are you crazy or—ow!"

"Tell them!"

"All right, all right. I exaggerated."

"You didn't touch her, did you? You didn't lay a hand on her the whole night, did you? I said, *did* you?"

"Shit, man, let go of my arm."

"Tell them. Tell them all you did was sit in the car and talk."

"We talked, all right? Get off my—"

"Swear to God you never touched her."

"Fuck you, I ain't—ow! All right, all right, I swear, I didn't lay a fucking hand on the bitch."

Hubbell jerked the arm so hard I could hear it snap. "Take it back."

"Take what back?"

"What you just called her."

"What? Bitch? What the fuck's wrong with—*aargh!* All right, I take it back. Jeez!"

Hubbell let him go. "Ladies and gentlemen," he announced, "justice has once again been served." Iggy, rubbing his shoulder, sneered at him with the requisite hint of retribution to come, but it was a feeble gesture, for his eyes betrayed a grudging respect for my brother. The other guys glared at him, contemplating retribution of their own.

"I win!" declared Klinger. "I win the friggin' bet!"

"No, you don't," argued Iggy. "I parked with her for a half an hour. That's what the bet said. It didn't say nothin' about nothin' else."

"Bullshit," said Harry the Horse, "we all know what parking means, and it don't mean sitting in a fucking parked car."

"I won fair and square. Dingleberry owes me a smooch on the ass."

"I'm gonna *kick* your fucking guinea ass, you lying son of a bitch!" Klinger lunged for his adversary's throat, but Harry grabbed him from behind and the others stepped between them.

"We'll figure out what to do later," said Mr. Big, ever the umpire. "Meantime, there's the matter of a World Series, in case you morons forgot."

I was on my stool, egg cream in hand, for the pregame show, which brought to light a mixed bag of news: Mickey Mantle would not start for the Yankees, but Duke Snider *would* be in center field for the Bums, his injured knee having responded to whirlpool treatments; Jackie Robinson, on the other hand, would be on the bench, hobbled by a strained Achilles tendon. In the netherworld where imagination mixes with memory, I saw Robby in the doorway of his home as he and his wife turned away from their unexpected guests. I thought I saw him grimace slightly as his weight shifted to his right foot. What did his absence portend? On the surface, replacing Robby with Don Hoak, a second-year man with a .240 batting average, was a devastating disadvantage. On the other hand, it might be a sign: Jackie would be on the bench with my hat. And I knew the hat would be with him, for Jackie Robinson was a man of honor.

If the overflow crowd at Jake's was typical, attendance at every school in the borough must have hit an all-time low, and supper tables that night would serve a record number of leftovers, for all ages and both sexes were in attendance, standing, leaning, sitting two to a stool and eight to a booth, kneeling and squatting on the tile floor, perched on the counter, the ice box and the jukebox. Hank sat cross-legged like a Buddha on the floor next to my stool, working his three remaining rabbit's feet like worry beads. Hubbell was in a booth with his arm draped casually but proudly around Diane, who looked radiant and relaxed in tan slacks and a light wool sweater, her reputation having been redeemed by the noble young man beside her. Hubbell pretended to ignore my father, who stood at the counter with his cronies, pretending to ignore Hubbell. This charade was easy to play half the time because the older men, adhering to a vision that had come to Sal in a dream, spent the odd innings at Jake's and the even innings at Mickey's Saloon.

Dizzy jazzed up the National Anthem by blowing Satchmo-like trumpet riffs as, on screen, the color guard stood at attention near the center field monuments to Yankee immortals whose ghosts intimidated visiting squads. The home club took the field, incited by the larger portion of 62,465 fans. We countered with exhortations to our Bums, underdogs at seven-to-five. And Cyclone Frankie Stone stood tall against the counter, raised high his cherry Coke, and declaimed:

"Once more unto the breach, dear friends, once more; Or close the wall up with our Brooklyn dead. In peace there's nothing so becomes a man, as modest stillness and humility: But when the blast of war blows in our ears, then imitate the action of the tiger: Stiffen the sinews, summon up the blood—"

He was interrupted by groans and shouts of "Shaddup" and "Sit down."

"That was Shakespeare, you philistines," he replied.

"Shakespeare was from Brooklyn?" queried Marty Klinger.

With two power-hitting teams that had already clouted a record seventeen home runs between them, the last thing anyone expected was a slow, tense pitcher's duel, but that's what we got. It was scoreless in the third when, with two out, Podres encountered a streak of wildness that set the nerves of the faithful on edge. He walked Phil Rizzuto and Billy Martin. Then I received the omen I'd been waiting for—in fact, two of them, back to back. Gil McDougald chopped one down the third base line, too slow for Hoak to get anyone out. But as Rizzuto slid into third, the bouncing ball glanced off his body. Automatic out, inning over, threat extinguished, thank you very much. As the Dodgers jogged to their dugout, the camera found Robinson clapping his hands and shouting encouragement to his teammates. Next to him was a small-sized cap with the Dodger B on the front and the peak curved in a perfectly proportioned arc.

"It's my hat!" I yelled. "Look! It's my hat!"

That I was bareheaded had not, of course, escaped the notice of my compatriots. Everyone had been informed of the family's trek to distant Connecticut and the intended destination of the lucky cap. But until that moment, no one but I had believed that it would actually end up on the Dodgers' bench. Immediately it started to pay higher dividends.

Campanella, who had not had a hit in Yankee Stadium all Series and was batting .070 lifetime in the cavernous park, cracked a double to left. He advanced to third on Furillo's slow grounder. This brought up Gil Hodges. A quiet giant with massive hands who was strong enough to strangle a bear, Gil was among the most respected Dodgers, not only because he lived year-round in Brooklyn, but because he was a charitable man who always had time for autograph hounds. But although he had over twenty homers and a hundred RBIs in each of the last seven seasons, and while he patrolled first base with impeccable grace, the converted catcher had a rap for slumping at the most inopportune times. The reputation was largely a remnant of the 1952 World Series, in which Gil amassed zero hits in twenty-one times at bat, prompting prayers for his redemption throughout the Borough of Churches. It was, therefore, fitting that the key at-bats in this most crucial of games would fall to Number 14. With two out and two strikes on him, Gil nudged an inside curve safely into left field and Campy crossed the plate with the first run of the game.

In the Yankee fourth Podres survived another scare. Yogi lofted a lazy fly to left center. Duke loped in and to his right for the easy catch. But Junior Gilliam—starting in left field in place of Amoros to stack the lineup with righties—also called for the ball. The two outfielders played I-got-it, you-take-it, and then, at the last second, Gilliam backed off and Duke stabbed at the ball with his glove, too late. Yogi ended up with a double, and the mavens at Jake's expressed their displeasure at Alston for sacrificing defense in favor of righty-lefty percentages. With the Stadium fascists screaming for blood, Podres faced three straight power hitters: Hank Bauer, Moose Skowron, and Bob Cerv. He bamboozled them with an audacious assortment of change-ups and curves, preserving the slim lead.

Before the game, Jake had announced that he did not care to miss even a pitch in order to mix drinks and serve snacks; we were on the honor system and could help ourselves. Dry mouths, nerve-induced cravings, and the prospect of easy credit combined to create chaos behind the counter. Between innings, long lines formed outside Jake's one toilet, and the regulars, unaccustomed to women hogging the latrine, struggled to retain their civility. The tension nearly erupted on several occasions. When Marty Klinger failed to apologize adequately for spilling his lime rickey on Burt Sugarman's wife, Burt countered by listing the social inadequacies of the entire Klinger clan. The fight was broken up by peacemakers just as the Dodgers opened the pivotal sixth inning.

Pee Wee led off with a line-drive single to left. Duke, who rarely bunted, pushed a beauty along the third base line and reached first safely when Skowron lost the handle trying to make a tag play. Campanella sacrificed the runners to second and third. Casey Stengel then ordered Furillo walked intentionally, and called for his relief ace, Bob Grim, to pitch to Hodges with the bases loaded. Just in case his RBI single in the fourth had not atoned for the sins of 1952, Gil stroked a fly ball to center, deep enough to score a run.

The next managerial move was perhaps the most salutary decision of Walter Alston's career, although its significance could not have been divined at the time. Hoping to bust open the game, the skipper ordered lefty-swinging George "Shotgun" Shuba to pinch-hit for Don Zimmer. Shuba grounded out to end the inning. But the move made necessary a defensive switch that tied the ribbon on the Dodgers' fate: Alston moved Gilliam from left field to second base to replace Zimmer, and filled Gilliam's spot in the outfield with Sandy Amoros.

Billy Martin, always a hornet in important games, led off the bottom of the sixth by walking on four straight pitches. As Martin jogged to first, the tying run stepped to the plate in the person of Gil McDougald, and the jinx stepped through the door of Jake's Luncheonette in the person of my mother. Everyone was tickled to see her but me. She surveyed the room, called "Hi boys" to Round Man and me, and, when she spotted Hubbell with his arm around Grace Kelly, flashed her older son the okay sign.

"What are you doing here?" I asked.

"Came to see how my Bums are doing."

"It's two to nothing. Satisfied? You can go now." It was not the most diplomatic means of persuasion, but I had no time to waste on niceties. The first pitch to McDougald was a ball.

"That's how you talk to your mother?" said Jake.

"Dad's at Mickey's this inning," I told Mom. "Why don't you walk over there?" She would probably be just as bad a jinx at Mickey's but the Dodgers might get out of the inning before she arrived.

"No, I'll stay here," she said. Ball two on McDougald.

"You can't."

"What do you mean, I can't? What's wrong with you?"

"You're a jinx!" Everyone within earshot turned to me. I felt compelled to reinforce my statement. "She's a jinx. She really is. Whenever she watches, bad things happen."

As if on cue, McDougald laid down a perfect bunt and reached first safely while Martin advanced to second. "See? You didn't believe me about my hat either." The crowd was divided roughly into thirds: those who found my argument nettlesome; those who got a kick out of it; and those who seriously considered throwing my mother out on her ear.

"Roger," said Mom, "some day we'll have to talk to a good shrink about why you think your mother's a jinx."

"You *are*, that's why!" I was getting desperate. The tying run was on base and a squat, pinstriped troll with the number 8 on his back was entering the left-hand hitter's batting box. It was an ominous sight. When a game was on the line, Yogi Berra had an uncanny knack for hitting the ball where no one was.

"Can't you go listen on the radio?" I said.

Mom answered by sticking her tongue out at me.

Yogi connected. The crowd sprang to its feet, like soldiers called to attention. From the trajectory of the ball, it looked at first like a routine fly to left field. But when the camera panned the outfield, it became apparent why the noise at Yankee Stadium was rising in a manner incongruous with an easy out. Sandy Amoros was sprinting across the spacious lawn. He had been stationed nearly in center field because Berra figured to pull the ball. But Yogi being Yogi, he went with Podres's outside pitch and poked it to the opposite field, where no one was. Amoros ran like the wind, but the ball kept slicing away from him, toward the foul line. If it stayed fair, the score would be tied with no out and Yogi at second, maybe third. In my mind flashed visions of Bobby Thomson crossing home plate and Grandpa Abe crossing into the afterlife.

Amoros ran still harder, and the ball sliced farther, but it also remained aloft for what seemed as long as the time it took to get a tooth filled. And at the last possible moment, as he streaked into the corner where the box seats met the foul line, the swift little Cuban thrust out his right hand and the ball plopped into his glove like a potato into a pot of soup. He was still in fair territory. A roar of relief erupted around me, but the fateful play was not yet over. Sandy braked to a stop inches from the restraining wall, wheeled gracefully, and pegged the ball to Pee Wee, who had stationed himself in short left field. The throw hit Reese at chest level, and the savvy captain, who knew where everyone was at all times, relayed the ball across the infield to the outstretched Hodges. It arrived just ahead of McDougald, who had been so sure the ball would land safely that he was on his way to third when it was caught. It was the Dodgers' twelfth double play of the Series, a new record.

The well-informed marveled at the exquisite ironies that make baseball the most literary of sports. If Alston had not pinch-hit for Zimmer, Amoros would not have been in left field, and there was no way Junior Gilliam would have made that catch; he was as fast as Amoros, but not as experienced in the outfield, and, as a righty with his glove on his left hand, he would have had to reach across his body for the ball. Now I knew that the current of history had reversed direction. I turned to my mother with a look of contrition.

"Some jinx," she said.

As the autumn sun slanted behind the storied porticos of the House that Ruth Built, shadows lengthened on the playing field and Roy Campanella, in his wisdom, called for a change in pitching strategy. Podres had been keeping the Yanks off balance with change-ups and slow curves. Now he went to his fast stuff. Destiny picked up steam as well. In the seventh, with a man on base and two out, Mickey Mantle hobbled to the plate to pinch-hit. With his broad shoulders and the lightning-bolt shape of the number 7 on his back, the Mick was a menacing sight squaring off against the little baggy-pants pitcher. With one swing he could tie it up. But Podres would not be intimidated. Mantle popped up to Pee Wee in short left field.

Phil Rizzuto, playing in his last World Series game—his fifty-second, breaking Joe DiMaggio's record—led off the eighth with a single. After Billy Martin flied to right, McDougald slashed a hard grounder to third. It took a bad hop and caromed off the arm of Don Hoak. Again Yogi stepped to the plate with two on base. This time Amoros was positioned more conservatively, and Yogi pulled the ball. Furillo bagged the fly in short right field and unleashed a rocket to the plate, freezing Rizzuto at third. The tension became unbearable as Podres worked on Hank Bauer, a twenty-homer man with an appetite for southpaws. They dueled to a 2–2 count before Johnny reared back and fired a fastball at the shoulders. Bauer swung and missed. We were three outs from paradise.

Now it grew strangely quiet at Jake's, as if no one wanted to say anything that could jinx the outcome. The dominant sounds were of feet shuffling, matches scratching against grainy surfaces, coughs and nervous exhalations, seltzer flowing into glasses, and bottle caps popping off with a fizz.

The Dodgers batted uneventfully in the ninth. As the teams switched places for the Yankees' last stand, the noise level picked up briefly. The bathroom door opened and closed and the toilet flushed, and people requested cigarettes or a light and allowed themselves a remark about how nervous they were. Some issued humble pleas for Johnny Podres not to fall apart now. Darting through our minds, of course, were all the fatal ninth innings of years past, and gnawing thoughts like, "It was all a setup" and "Here comes the heartbreak" and "They'll find a way to blow it."

At the Stadium, Yankee fans, facing the unfamiliar prospect of losing a Fall Classic, tried to shake the aristocratic Bombers out of their doldrums. The first batter, Moose Skowron, smacked a hot hopper back to the mound. Podres snared it, but the ball got stuck in the web of his glove and he ran toward first trying to pull it out. For a moment I thought that disaster might strike in slapstick form, like a Laurel and Hardy movie. Finally the pitcher pried loose the ball and tossed it underhand to Hodges for the first out. He then induced Bob Cerv to fly to Amoros in left.

Now everyone in Jake's was on his feet, packed tightly together in the TV corner, as if the room had tilted. They stood on tiptoe and bobbed their heads from left to right to earn unobstructed views. "Please, God, one more out," whispered Sal, and an incoherent rumble, like the call of an amen corner, answered him. The batter was Elston Howard. Podres challenged him with heaters and hard curves. Howard ran the count to 2–2, then fouled off one pitch after another. "I can't take it no more," shouted Jake. Bursts of nervous laughter, like rifle fire, erupted then died.

Podres delivered a change-up. Howard connected. The ball rolled along the infield grass toward shortstop. What could be more fitting? I thought. It was as if the first and only Negro on the reactionary Yankees decided to put righteousness above corporate loyalty and said to the longest-suffering Dodger, the team captain who escorted Jackie Robinson into history, "Here, Pee Wee, this last out is for you."

The Colonel gobbled up the grounder and, taking a bit too much care, threw low to first. Hodges scooped the ball into his trusty mitt before it hit the dirt.

In the frozen silence before the heavens opened, Vin Scully intoned with quiet dignity, "Ladies and gentlemen, the Brooklyn Dodgers are the champions of the world."

It was the last swatch of quiet, and the last dignified moment, the Borough of Kings would see until the sun came up on another day.

Chapter Fifteen

The roar erupted at once from every corner of Brooklyn, from New Lots to Red Hook, from Sheepshead Bay to Greenpoint. It was heard by the vanquished fans of the Bronx, and in Jersey City, where the Bums would play eight home games the next season, and down South in sharecropper shacks where they rooted for Robinson's team, and in Philadelphia and Chicago and Pittsburgh, where every fall the Dodgers replaced failed home teams in the hearts of baseball lovers, and in California, where they hungered for a major league team, and in Army bases in Korea and Germany, and, I hoped, wherever the spirit of Grandpa Abe had been waiting restlessly for peace.

With the brief exception of Sal, who dropped to one knee and crossed himself, the gang turned Jake's into Coney Island, July the Fourth, and V.E. Day all wrapped into one. Dizzy belted out random bars of John Philip Sousa on his horn. Benny dropped a quarter into the jukebox and pushed the buttons for "Rock Around the Clock" six times. Harry the Horse hoisted Mr. Big into the air and whirled him around like a pompom. People let loose shrieks whose meaning derived not from dictionaries but the vocabulary of euphoria. They hugged whoever was next to them. They kissed anyone of the opposite gender, and many dispensed with even that distinction. They danced, giving their feet permission to make maladroit moves without shame.

Hubbell lifted Diane off the ground and whirled her around and around until there was no more room to spin and they stopped and kissed dizzily in the middle of the room.

Round Man, grinning, jumped up and down, pumping his arms like a penguin trying to take off.

Artie and Louie did him one better; they stood on the counter, flapped their wings, and sang "I'm Flying" like Peter Pan and Wendy.

My father hugged and kissed indiscriminately, shouting "We did it! We did it! We did it!" and when he reached his Jeannie, he wrapped his arms around her and wept like a baby with joy.

Celebrants poured into the luncheonette, colliding with those who spilled into the streets. I kept going back and forth so as not to miss anything. Outside, a thousand drivers leaned on their horns and a thousand church bells pealed. Firecrackers punctuated the other sounds with staccato bursts. A long Pontiac rolled up Howard Avenue with bellowing teenagers draped on the hood, the trunk, and the roof. On a third-floor fire escape someone unfurled a sheet that might have been rotting in a closet since 1941, waiting to display its hand-painted message: WE DOOD IT! Bushels of confetti torn from phone books and newspapers floated in the air like enormous snowflakes. A patrolman danced a jig, then joined a company of spirit-seekers who heard that Mickey the saloonkeeper had offered "Drinks to every bum in the house!"

At the intersection, passengers in one car leaped out to hug the passengers in another. The traffic snarled, but no one cared except Ippish. Aghast and confused, the self-made traffic cop blew desperately on his whistle in an effort to restore order to the sudden chaos around him.

"Ippish," I said. "Ippish, it's okay. The Dodgers won the World Series!"

He looked at me blankly as the words meandered slowly through the matzo ball soup of his brain. I repeated the message. Ippish smiled. "World Series?" he said.

I nodded vigorously.

"I could take the day off," he declared.

Happy and Henny Horowitz handed out slices of marmalade and halvah. Sam the fruit store man tossed grapes and plums to passersby. Gen H. Lee handed lechee nuts to people he could barely see. Even Meyer Weiss, the stingiest merchant in the free world, doled out penny candies to kids, drawing the line, however, at seconds. Sharfin the butcher, with nothing savory to give away, turned to entertainment instead; he whirled along the sidewalk dancing with one old lady after another, like a hoofer at the Follies. From her window Angie Corso banged out bedlam on her pots and pans. Above her someone tossed into the afternoon sky a pair of pillows, which burst open like Roman candles, sending forth a flurry of feathers.

The feathers floated in all directions, and enough of them fell straight down to form a small drift on the hat of Jesse Hicks, who was climbing the cellar steps with tears in his eyes. I ran to Jesse and hugged him.

"We did it, son," he said. "I'm going to call Otis and tell him."

And on my stoop the Sphinx shook like a washing machine with too big a load—not just her hands, but her entire body, from her ponderous shoes to her thin white hair.

Radio reporters conveyed stories of frenzied exhilaration from around the city. Ticker tape rained from Wall Street skyscrapers and the office buildings of downtown Brooklyn. Phone lines to the borough were so jammed that callers could not get through. Motorcades rolled up and down the principal thoroughfares, trumpeting the triumph on their horns. On the Brooklyn Bridge cars stopped and passengers spilled out to dance above the river. Steelworkers shouted and waved from the skeletons of skyscrapers. Construction crews turned jackhammers into party noisemakers. From the waterfront came reports of foghorns blaring and whistles tooting and longshoremen openly weeping. Effigies of the Yankees, complete with top hats, hung from lampposts. And from Borough Hall came a propitious proclamation from Borough President John Cashman: "They must never leave Brooklyn."

In the Dodger locker room, the madness was unrestrained. Players kissed each other. Beer suds wafted across the TV screen, and brew and champagne was poured on the heads of anyone who walked near a bottle. Charley DiGiovanna, the longtime Dodger batboy, walked through the room with a dizzy grin on his face, shouting, "Billy Cox! Billy Cox!"

As if anyone had to be reminded that the ex-Dodger had predicted that his former teammates would cave in to the Yankees, Carl Furillo exhorted the press to "Tell Billy Cox we didn't choke up. Tell him we won it without him."

Johnny Podres, winner of a sports car as Most Valuable Player, tried to hold back the tears as he babbled deliriously, "My fastball really had it . . . I was never worried . . . I can beat those guys seven days a week . . . Don't write that, it sounds too much like I'm popping off . . .''

Laconic Walter Alston of Darrtown, Ohio, beleaguered and ridiculed for two seasons and now the man who brought a championship to Brooklyn at last, allowed himself a wide grin and paid tribute to his players. Sandy Amoros tried to accommodate reporters, but his English did not meet network standards, so we heard about his catch from Duke and Pee Wee. And while the players and the viewers at Jake's recounted the golden moments of the game, all my brother wanted to talk about was the art of broadcasting.

"Did you hear Scully at the end?" Hubbell said to whoever would listen. "Did you hear him? 'Ladies and gentlemen, the Brooklyn Dodgers are the champions of the world.' Is that cool, or what? Is that incredible?"

Then I saw, back to back, the two most satisfying images I would ever see on a TV screen. First, in a corner of the Dodger locker room, his face obscured by other bodies, Number 42 was showing off my hat to a clutch of teammates, whose mouths, it seemed to me, hung open in awe.

Then the screen filled with a panorama of the empty playing field. The camera panned the stands where a few stunned spectators ambled slowly to the exits, then held for a moment on a poignant tableau: in the Yankee dugout, a tall, solitary figure in pinstripes, wearing the number zero, sat bewildered and shaken from fang to claw. I would never see The Thing again.

The demented frenzy continued unabated for everyone but Cyclone Frankie Stone. On the Corner, he found himself face to face with Hubbell. "See that, Champ? Just like I told you. Miracles happen. Nothing's impossible if you believe. Do *you* believe? Are you ready for a miracle? Are you ready to fight for your dream?"

Hubbell looked him squarely in the eye: "Yeah, Pop, I'm ready."

"Attaboy! I knew you'd come around. We'll get to work on that forkball first thing in the—"

"Pop! Baseball is *your* dream. It's not mine anymore. I want to be a broadcaster."

My father's joy plummeted through his body and shattered

in his feet, sending tremors through his legs. "No," he said, "no, you can't do this."

"I'm doing it, Pop. One way or another, I'm doing it."

"No, this can't be happening."

"Pop, listen to me. I love you. I really do. I appreciate everything you tried to do for me, and I'm really sorry if I'm letting you down. But my mind's made up."

My father reeled from shock and the sum of even-numbered innings at Mickey's Saloon. He stared at Hubbell and blinked his eyes in an effort to bring his life into focus.

"I want your blessing, Pop," said Hubbell.

But before my father could refuse—for that was what he was about to do—his jubilant buddies swarmed him and delivered the news that So-Called Sonny Scott would be shooting his show live outside Ebbets Field. After a quick round of fortification at Mickey's, they were heading over to razz the scum-sucking sonofabitch bastard. They grabbed hold of my father and hauled him off, backward. He glared at Hubbell until his friends turned him around and made him walk on his own.

Hubbell stared back. He was sad. He wanted peace. He wanted his family back. And then something clicked in his head. His eyes opened so wide I thought they would overlap. With a sense of urgency he panned the maniacs dancing in the street, and when he located Diane, he ran to her and whispered at length in her ear. She bounced up and down on her toes and clapped her hands like a cheerleader. Then the two of them darted from one Big Guy to another, whispering secrets, and the bunch of them disappeared up the street.

Outside Ebbets Field, about two thousand nuts danced in a conga line around and around the sacred edifice. Lines of cars with crepe-paper streamers and stacks of boozed-up riders circled slowly. Two men with the ticket stubs of every Dodger game they had ever attended stapled to their clothing marched with a long banner held aloft on broomsticks. It read: WOILD CHAMPEENS!

On the streetcorner behind the home plate entrance, at the foot of a curved facade of bricks and archways, two bulky cameras stood ready to capture the image of So-Called Sonny Scott. A small crew hustled about and attempted, with the help of a cadre of cops, to keep the rowdy crowd behind a row of sawhorses and their feet from tangling in the cables and wires. I worked my way through the crush of bigger bodies to a closer viewpoint. A man in a Vandyke beard, whom I assumed was the director, shouted orders and clapped his hands to speed up the progress of his minions. As his face and wig were touched up by a makeup girl, the star of the show was pelted by hecklers: "Go back to da Bronx, where ya belong, ya bum!" "Who's da loser now, big shot?" "Hey Scott! Ya don't know yer ass from yer elbow!"

Skapinsky called to the director, "If any of those idiots gets on the air, your ass is cooked." Then, finding the makeup girl's handiwork wanting, he shoved her aside. "Get outta here, I'll do it myself."

Peering between the jostling figures around me, I saw Hubbell, clutching Diane protectively. He signaled to the Big Guys, who were stationed in pairs, maneuvering like Indians on a raid. I saw Burt, Sal, Mike, and Jake hurling jibes at Skapinsky, gleeful as children launching soap bubbles in the air. And I saw my father, his head hanging from the weight of whiskey and his son's final betrayal, walk away from the celebration he'd been pining for all his life and mope across the street in the direction of a bar.

The director shouted to his crew: it was close to airtime. So-Called Sonny Scott checked himself once more in a mirror, raised his chin and straightened his tie, and walked toward his spot before the cameras.

Suddenly there was commotion. Bodies hurtled in all directions. Shouts of alarm and confusion mixed with whoops of delight. When I elbowed my way to a clearing, I saw something astonishing: standing in front of the cameras with a microphone in his hand, wearing a black blazer and a light blue tie, was my brother. Solly Skapinsky was wrapped in the muscular arms of Harry and Klinger, his mouth sealed tightly by Horse's hand, and, in a moment, a wide swatch of adhesive tape. Benny secured his wrists with a belt; Shirley and Diane tied his ankles together with hair ribbons. One of the crew, a young man with a shiny pompadour and a black turtleneck sweater, didn't know whether to applaud or attack Hubbell with his slate. He decided simply to do his job. "Ten seconds!" he called, and he turned to the director for instruction.

"What the hell's going on here?" yelled the director. Then Mr. Big and Dizzy grabbed his arms, barked an order, and jabbed water guns into his ribs—that is, *I* knew they were water guns, but the director, apparently, did not. "Don't shoot!" he shouted. "I mean . . . Ready to shoot! Five, four, three, two . . ."

A red light blinked on atop a camera. Hubbell, smiling engagingly, performed as if he'd been speaking into microphones all his life; and in a sense, he had been. "Welcome to *Talking Sports.* I'm Hubbell Stone, live from Ebbets Field, where at long last the World Championship flag will soon be raised. Solly Skapinsky, also known as Sonny Scott, couldn't be here today. He has an upset stomach from eating too much crow. Who needs Yankee fans anyway, right gang?" His statement was loudly endorsed by the crowd, who shouted and waved their hats and jostled for position in hopes of being seen on television. "Let me tell you, it's absolutely cuckoo all over Brooklyn. No one's going home, no one's going to work, no one's going to sleep tonight, because next year has finally arrived."

Hubbell looked like he was born to do what he was doing. Any resentment or ambivalence I may have held toward him was erased at that moment. I thought of my father, spilling his sorrowful guts to some bartender and missing the moment of his son's deliverance. He had to see this. If he did, he would forgive Hubbell and endorse his new life, and my family would once again be whole.

I fought my way through the crowd and raced across the street to the tavern. My father was on a bar stool, the lone melancholy figure in a roomful of revelers. "Dad!" I yelled through the din. I ran to him and tugged at his sleeve. "Dad!"

"What the hell are you—"

"Change the channel!" I ordered the bartender. "Quick! Turn on Channel 4!"

The bartender looked as if he had never seen anyone under drinking age. "He wichyou?" he asked my father.

I had no time for introductions. "Hurry up!" I barked.

The bartender reached up to the twenty-one-inch Philco mounted above the racks of whiskey and changed the channel. "What the hell's going on?" my father asked.

"Just watch."

He hoisted a shot glass of shimmering amber, and when he recognized the face on the screen his hand froze and the booze spilled onto his shirt and his mouth formed a long oval of astonishment.

"That's my son!" he yelled. "Shut the hell up!" He looked down at me, and up at the TV, and down at me again, as if trying to figure out if I, too, was a flat reproduction or the living thing.

Seeing Hubbell's face in shades of gray on a small illuminated box, I understood my father's befuddlement. I had to shake my head to rid myself of the thought that everything, even the World Series, was just a dream.

"Let's talk to the fans," said Hubbell, his smile illuminating the screen in sharp contrast to the detested Skapinsky scowl. "This day belongs to them. Come on, cameras, follow me!" He approached the barriers, whipping the cord of his microphone to gain some slack.

"That really your kid, Mac?" asked the bartender.

"Bet your ass it is," said Dad.

"Sure beats that asshole Scott."

"Bet your ass," said Cyclone Frankie Stone.

Jake, Sal, Burt, and Mike burst into the dark saloon like a posse. "Frankie! Frankie! Are you watching?"

"Shut up!" yelled my father.

On screen, Hubbell gestured at a fluttering assemblage of arm-waving, tongue-wagging men. "Look at these maniacs," he said. "Did you ever see such goofy faces in your life?" He aimed the microphone at a middle-aged man with a derby hat and a long cigar. "How happy are you?" he asked.

"Me?" said the man. "I'm astatic. I'm trilled."

"How about you?" said Hubble to another man. "Can you describe how you feel?"

"Are you kiddin'? Dere ain't no woids. Dis is da greatest day of my life."

"Better than your wedding day?"

"My wedding day? Fuhgetaboutit!"

Hubbell pointed the mike at a black man who was blowing kisses at the camera. "Gonna be celebrating awhile?"

"Till the cows come home, Jack. And dey ain't many cows in Brooklyn, I'll tell you that."

Hubbell fixed on the pale, angular face of a man in his seventies. The man's eyes, which were probably blue, twinkled with the special pleasure that comes to those who receive something they deeply desire but had resigned themselves to dying without. "Here's a happy guy," said Hubbell. "How long have you been waiting for this?"

"All my life," said the old man. "I was at the first game they ever played in this joint."

"Get outta here! Are you serious?"

"April fifth, 1913. They were called the Superbas then, not the Dodgers. Beat the Yanks in an exhibition game. And you know what? Casey Stengel hit a home run—for our side."

"Unbelievable!" exclaimed Hubbell. "How about that, fans! Let's hear it for a living legacy!" He led the crowd in an ovation that made the old man giddy with joy. Then, spotting an off-camera signal from the crew, he asked the spectators to quiet down. Amazingly, they did as he asked, so taken were they by Hubbell's one-of-us charm.

My brother turned to the camera, looking now like a mature commentator, humble yet filled with conviction, as poised as a man for whom sharing his thoughts with a few million people was something he did every day. "We're just about out of time, ladies and gentlemen. But before we go, let me say this. My father, who is a very smart man, taught me that this World Series was special. It was fought not just for a baseball team, not just for the borough of Brooklyn, but for all the underdogs and all the dreamers and all the Joe Blows who have to fight for what they want. This victory should serve as a reminder: no matter how bad it gets, you can always fight your way back. On with the celebration!"

The fans engulfed my brother. Inside the tavern a cheer went up and glasses clicked together to toast the speech. Everyone at the bar turned to my father, who looked as tall as he did the day they named a fence after him. The men clapped him on the back and told him his son had a helluva poisonality.

"How the hell did this happen?" asked Jake. "How'd he pull this off?"

Said the proud progenitor, "When my kid wants something, he knows how to get it. I taught him to be resourceful."

"Who knew the kid had such talent?" marveled Burt.

"What are you, kidding?" said my father. "He's a natural. From the time he was this big he had the gift of gab. He could speak whole sentences when he was still in a crib. He could read when he was four. He does play-by-play better than Red Barber . . ."

Never had the lights of Brooklyn seemed so much like stars—the circles of streetlights, the checkerboard squares of windows, the streaks of red and yellow car lights, and, that night, the chandelier galaxies of fireworks. The festivities had continued, slightly more subdued, on the highest roof in the neighborhood. Fresh supplies of beer and soft drinks appeared as if by magic as soon as the ice-filled tubs were empty. In a dozen places the front page of the evening edition of the *Daily News* had been taped to a wall: THIS IS NEXT YEAR! screamed the headline above a picture of Campy and Podres racing toward each other to embrace. Someone had run an extension cord from an apartment to power a record player, and couples danced along the tar to Teresa Brewer's "Ricochet Romance."

I weaved through the crowd, picking at bowls of potato chips and pretzels, and suddenly I saw a sight I had seen only in my imagination, where it had been installed by legend: Skinny Jeannie was tap dancing on the ledge of the roof. My father, chalk-white with terror, stood close by with his arms extended toward his wife, unwilling to try pulling her down for fear of pushing by mistake. He begged her to stop, softly, as if a louder voice might topple her.

My mother capped her performance by leaping into my father's arms. The color slowly returned to his face as he held her close and judiciously moved away from the ledge. He made her promise never to do it again.

Mike the Barber drew from his pocket a roll of bills and peeled some off. "Never been so happy to pay off a bet," he said. "This gets you closer to that medallion, eh, Frankie?" The bills numbered only a few, but the portraits on them were not of Washington or Lincoln or Jackson, but of Benjamin Franklin. Before my father could pocket his winnings, the cash was snatched from his hands.

My mother flipped quickly through the bills and whistled. "Wow. This could help pay for Hubbell's education." She stuffed the wad in her bosom.

She had called NBC to name the skilled interloper on the afternoon broadcast and reveal the ignominious deed that made the intrusion necessary: So-Called Sonny Scott's sabotage. Network officials, who grudgingly admired Hubbell's performance, assured her that justice would be served.

"Go ahead, take it. Give it to Hubbell," said my father of the money. "You were right, babe. You're always right. I got bigger things to do than drive a cab. I've been thinking, maybe I'll put in a call to Teddy Ryan. He said I see things on the field he can't see himself. Remember? He said I know the game like no one else he knows. Maybe he'll open a few doors for me."

"That's the spirit!" said my mother. She stood on her toes and hugged her husband around the neck. With the help of Hubbell and the Brooklyn Dodgers, she had made it permissible for Frank Stone to once again dream for himself.

"Where the hell's Hubbell anyway?" asked Dad. "I'm dying to talk to him."

"He's with that blonde," said Round Man. His tone was so disapproving, you'd think Hubbell and Diane were out torturing bunnies instead of mating like them out at the Holy Shrine. For that, I figured, was what they were doing.

When Hubbell ended his broadcast that afternoon, he was mobbed by admirers. As he made his way through the crowd, escorted by Diane and his buddies, he found himself face to face with Ignazio Corso. For a moment, it looked like Iggy was out to save face by making trouble. "So, uh, Stone. You going out with this chick or what?"

"Yeah," said Hubbell. "What about it?"

"I uh, just figgered, maybe these here would come in handy." Winking, he dangled the keys to his Buick. Hubbell accepted the offer and shook the hand of his lifelong friend and rival.

"Wait till *your* hormones start percolating, young man," my mother told Hank.

"Boys don't have hormones!" he insisted.

Sal and Burt waltzed by singing "Side by Side." As they

passed, they hooked their arms into Mike's and my father's and turned themselves into a quartet. "Oh, we ain't got a barrel of money. Maybe we're ragged and funny . . ." They pranced around the rooftop like a demented chorus line, adding Jake and Happy and others as they went along, and when they finished the song, they collapsed into each other's arms and fell to the ground. They lay in a heap, laughing hysterically, until they looked up and saw Jesse Hicks waiting for the frivolity to end. Slowly, the revelers rose, took leave of their wives, and filed, grim as soldiers, into the stairwell to their appointed task.

Louie dragged Artie and me to a corner of the roof. He had us squat out of sight behind a chimney, then reached into his shirt and pulled out a can of Rheingold beer. He opened it adroitly, sipped the foam that gushed from the triangular hole, then, as Artie and I watched in awe, slugged down the brew as if it were breakfast juice. He offered it to us.

"Him first," said Artie.

It was more bitter than I expected, and decidedly wet for a product that called itself the dry beer, so wet in fact that as much dripped down my chin as into my mouth.

Artie and I were able to help Louie finish off the brew with only one regurgitant episode each. I liked beer, I concluded. It was, as the ads proclaimed, refreshing. I liked it so much, in fact, that I started laughing, although I was mystified by Artie's question: "What's so funny?" When we stood, I felt as if I were walking up a sharply sloping shoreline as the tide receded rapidly by my legs. The lights of Brooklyn swirled in circles and loops. I staggered, clutching Louie's right arm, as Artie did his left.

Soon I found myself dancing—at her invitation or mine, I can't be sure—with Ruth Finkelstein, to the tune of "Cherry Pink and Apple Blossom White." Her left hand held my shoulder, and two of her fingers extended past the border of my T-shirt to rest, intentionally I believed, gently on the nape of my neck. My eyes were at the level of her chest, which afforded me a glimpse, between the buttons of her blouse, of a small patch of the white brassiere that she sometimes draped over the chair by her window. My right hand rested on her hip. I could feel the waistline of her bloomers, the very bloomers, perhaps, whose olfactory tang I recalled as if I'd inhaled it that morning. I believed for a moment that Ruth Finkelstein loved me. I felt a tingle in my groin and I shuddered, recalling the two definitions of the word boner, one of which was *mistake.*

Then a husky galoot in a crew cut tapped me on the back. "Mind if I cut in?" he asked. He did not wait for an answer. He lifted Ruth's hand from mine. She smiled and curtsied. I bowed, and when she rose, I remained bowed for some time because my head felt like a bowling ball.

By the time everything came back into focus, Ruth was gone and in her place was Eleanor Krinski. Before I could prevent it, she was holding me in dancing position. I had no choice but to put my arm around her waist and wobble back and forth in a mimicry of dance.

"You dance nicely, Roger," she said, angling her face so I was forced to look at her. To my surprise, I did not find the sight revolting. It was rather pleasant, actually. She said she missed me in class the previous two days and hoped I was feeling well. Somehow, the way she said it, I felt like apologizing. I assured Eleanor that I never felt better in my life.

To my surprise, I noticed that, despite her braces, Eleanor had an endearing smile, and her eyes, at close-up range, were less the color of ashes than the silvery gray of the ocean on an overcast day. Her freckles, far from the globs of horse manure I remembered, were more like stepping-stones on a wooded path that led to a nose that was somehow cuter and smaller than the one whose profile blocked my view out the window of the 6–1 classroom. Eleanor smelled good. The skin of her hand was velvety soft. Her hair felt like silk, not Brillo, on my face. The flutter of her skirt and the brush of her leg against my thigh sent pleasant sensations through my body. I liked the fact that her size required that my whole arm press against her, whereas with Ruth only my hand could touch. When the song ended, Patti Page's "Tennessee Waltz" began. Eleanor suggested we dance again. I consented and this time, the song being slow, her body pressed closely to mine. In fact, I would have said yes to her all night, whirling merrily with my right arm glued to the curve of her lower back and my cheek against the tickle of her hair, had Artie and Louie not dragged me away to fulfill our pact.

———

We marched, quiet as Indians, over the rough terrain of Rooney's Lot and kneeled in the dark against the cold brick wall of the apartment building. Louie removed the equipment from his pockets and placed it on a dry patch of dirt. Without speaking—for we had reviewed our plan meticulously—Louie and I boosted Artie, the lightest of the Musketeers, up to each of three curtain-shrouded windows. When his reconnaissance was complete, Artie reported that the living room windows were locked, but the kitchen window was open just wide enough for our purposes. Judging from the faint sounds and the dim light reflected on the kitchen wall, he said, Mrs. Schaefer was probably in her bedroom, which faced the front of the building.

We divided the box of matches into three piles. One by one we broke off the heads and discarded the wooden stems. We spread a square of tinfoil on the ground, piled the match heads into the center, sprinkled on shredded rubber from an inner tube, and folded the tinfoil around the mixture until we had squeezed the package into a tight round sphere. Then Louie rolled a piece of cheesecloth into a slim cylinder and inserted it into the tinfoil ball to form a fuse.

Artie and I created a step by grasping each other at the wrists, and boosted Louie up to the kitchen window. When he felt secure, he removed the tinfoil ball from his pocket, lit the fuse, and tossed it into the apartment. The match heads burst into flames, the rubber shreds smoldered, the tinfoil crust sizzled. Smoke billowed and spread, and with it the smell of a thousand farts in an acrid, sulfurous swamp. For good measure, Louie slammed the window shut before he jumped down.

We dashed into the back door of the building for the sole purpose of hiding behind the steps to see Mrs. Schaefer when, as predicted, she ran into the hallway to escape the fumes of the stink bomb. We got a bigger victory than we had bargained for. The door burst open. Out flew the witch, barefoot, clutching the folds of a flannel robe to her bony chest. One leg, ivory-colored with a network of blue veins, poked out of the robe, suggesting that she had been naked when the bomb hit. She coughed. She retched. She tried to wave the smoke out of the apartment like she waved pupils into their places for a fire drill. And with the smoke emerged my deliverance from class 6–1.

Dr. Gross, his bare chest carpeted with thick black hair, stumbled through the door trying to keep his glasses on his nose and button his trousers at the same time. It looked like Papa Bear had decided to raid a closet instead of eating Goldilocks' porridge. Mama Bear, we knew, was not Mrs. Schaefer, but a petite redhead who was probably home caring for the Gross children.

We couldn't hold it in. And we didn't care. We laughed as loud as we pleased and revealed ourselves, for we had enough evidence to blackmail the adulterous swine.

On the front page of Wednesday morning's *News* was a portrait of the Dodgers' symbol: a scruffy, stubble-cheeked bum with a bulbous nose and one lone tooth. His open-mouthed smile was so big it covered nearly half the page. Above it was the headline, WHO'S A BUM!

On the surface it was like any other early morning in October: cars sped down the hill of Howard Avenue toward Eastern Parkway; men in suits raced to the subway or to Jake's for their morning coffee; women in search of the freshest produce wheeled shopping carts toward the markets. But this day was different.

There was a spring to the step of the pedestrians; they looked proud and a little flabbergasted, as if feeling like winners would take some getting used to. Banners proclaiming the Dodgers' redemption still hung from fire escapes; strips of crepe paper and flakes of confetti fluttered in the morning wind; beer cans, soda bottles, potato chip bags, and firecracker cartridges lay beside overflowing garbage cans; alleys reeked of regurgitated alcohol. Scrawled in foot-high letters on at least three walls was Dizzy's victory statement: BIRD LIVES! The neighborhood felt exorcised, like an Old West town the morning after the bad guys had been carted off to Boot Hill. Everything was of a piece. Even the two startling phenomena I observed as I rushed home with the paper fit perfectly the new, liberated fabric of our lives.

First there was the Barney Klinger tableau. His face was discolored and swollen like an oversized biscuit that was burnt in places to the color of indigo. One eye was so battered it would take a crowbar to open the lids. His nose was covered with gauze. His lower lip was so swollen it blended into his chin, making it look as though he had only one lip. Barney limped as he circled his Lincoln Continental to assess the damage. The windshield was shattered in a million pieces. The other windows had holes big enough for pigeons to fly through. The headlights lay in shards on the gutter. The grillwork, fenders, and doors had been used for batting practice. Every tire had been slashed. Through his disfigured lips Barney spit a wretched curse. He had paid a high price for his ambition, and the price would be higher still when he was made to fork over his profits to cover Otis's rehabilitation.

I was halfway to the first landing on the stairwell before I noticed the second incongruity: the Sphinx was not on the stoop. I dashed back to see if I was mistaken. She was not there. Upstairs, the door to the Kasses' apartment was slightly ajar. I heard hushed voices and the sound of someone crying. I peeked in. People milled about the kitchen, drinking coffee and eating bagels. Between them I could see Jack Kass slowly rocking his grandson in his lap as he retreated in his mind to happier times. Relief as well as sorrow was in his eyes. I recognized the Kass children, and Dr. Goldsmith, and some of the women who used to gossip with the Sphinx on the stoop.

For reasons I could not comprehend, I felt compelled to creep into the apartment and look into the bedroom, from which people continued to emerge, tearfully. Before Dr. Goldsmith gestured sternly for me to leave, I was able to see Mrs. Kass on her bed. For her, there would be no more strumming on the old banjo; her hands were folded peacefully above her bosom. Her lips were set in a smile more serene than any she had worn in life; her eyes were closed. I had figured the Sphinx all wrong. The old gal had willed herself to stay alive long past her time, those bursts of shimmering motion acting like battery chargers, so she might see the Dodgers win a World Series.

I entered our apartment holding up the *News* for display, eager to relate what I had seen. But I had no audience. My parents had still not emerged from their bedroom, and Round Man was engrossed in the final moments of his campaign against Rommel the roach. He was standing on a chair by the stove, wearing the white cap of a naval officer. In a pot of slowly boiling water floated a sponge, in the center of which, attached to a toothpick, was a tiny American flag. Skirting warily along the edge of the sponge raft was the captive Rommel. With deft turns of his wrist, Round Man angled a magnifying glass between the window and the pot, until he was able to beam a hot shaft of sunlight onto the sponge. Rommel darted away from the heat, but he had little room to maneuver.

"What the hell are you doing?" I asked.

Without taking his eye off his prisoner, Round Man replied, "It's an execution with honor. He has a choice. He can be burned by solar rays or take his own life by jumping into boiling water."

I was about to inform my younger brother that he was destined to spend his adult years in a straitjacket, drooling spittle in the dungeon of an asylum, when the door opened and Hubbell walked in. From the shade of red in his eyes, his wobbly walk and goofy grin, I inferred that he hadn't slept a wink and would not mind if he never slept again, if only he could spend each night the way he had the last. To my great pleasure, he was carrying his duffel bag, which indicated that he was prepared to move back home.

I told him how great he had been on TV and how I'd run to make sure Dad would see him. I told him how much he had missed at the party on the roof, but he seemed not to mind having been absent. He just looked at me with a blissy grin and took a deep whiff of *Immortal Poems*.

He snapped abruptly into present time when he noticed that Hank was not preparing oatmeal. As if to a camera, he said, "Ladies and gentlemen, we're here at Café Round Man, where the world-renowned chef, Henri le Stone, is preparing his famous dish, poached roach avec sponge."

"He's doing it," Round Man said. We looked into the pot. Rommel the roach, exhausted from evading Hank's sunbeams, marched to the edge of the sponge, where he paused as if delivering his final words or preparing to meet his maker. Then he crawled over the edge to a bubbling grave.

"He chose a hero's death," said Round Man with reverence. Removing his cap, he solemnly scooped up his former adversary with a serving spoon and placed the scalded body into a matchbox.

"There he is!" It was my father, with Mom at his side, still in her nightgown, beaming at the prospect of peace and a reconstituted family. Hubbell's expression was conciliatory but non-committal; he would let the other party make the first move. "Hey there, champ," said Dad. "What can I say? You were great. Terrific. Unbelievable. I mean, seeing you on TV there . . . wow! Who knew?"

"I tried to tell you, Pop," said Hubbell.

"Yeah, well . . . maybe sometimes I don't hear so good. I'm proud of you, kid. You showed real guts. Whatever it's worth, I'm behind you all the way. Whatever it takes."

Hubbell was touched. "Thanks, Pop," he said, but he folded his arms to indicate that what had been said so far was not enough.

"I, uh, I owe you an apology, champ," said my father. "I lost my head. I just . . . I saw it all slipping away. I'd put all my chips on you and . . . well, the thing is, it wasn't fair. You're right. It's your life."

Hubbell's posture softened. "It's okay, Pop. We had some good times, didn't we? And we still can, right? I mean, now it can be fun again."

"You bet," said my father. He took a step toward Hubbell and started to raise his arms as if to hug him. But my brother was not finished.

"There's something I have to know, Pop. Could you have made it? I mean, if you didn't get hurt, would you have made the bigs?"

"Are you kidding? I'd've—" But he caught a look from my mother and dropped the pose. "Ah, the truth is . . . who knows? Maybe I would have made it. Maybe not. There's no way of knowing these things. The fact is . . . lemme put it this way: I was a long shot. Around here, everyone believed I was a sure thing. They turned me into some kind of tragic hero. At first, I figured, fine, who am I to argue? Then one thing led to another, and before I knew it this whole legend got built up, and I got sucked into it myself."

What he didn't have to say was, "For the last twenty years, I'd be driving my cab, or hanging at Mickey's or Jake's, or getting my hair cut, or shooting pool, and guys would talk about Hodges and Furillo and Snider, and I'd think *Why not me? They could've been talking about me.* What was I to do? Tell the world I might never have been good enough, or let them make me a martyr? I chose the way of the Regular Guy."

"How bad was it, Pop? The injury—was it really bad?"

"It was pretty bad. I was never the same after that."

"But how come you didn't keep trying? I mean, you never played organized ball again. How come you didn't give it another shot?" This was a question I had asked myself, but might never have asked anyone else.

My father fidgeted. "Well, I didn't think there was much of a chance. See, the gifted ones, the naturals, those guys can make up for injuries like that, but guys like me . . ."

"That's not the whole story. It doesn't add up. You were the kind of guy who'd try until they made you stop."

"Tell him, Frank," said my mother.

"Jeannie, please."

"Frank, times have changed. You can tell them. If you don't, I will."

"Don't, Jeannie," said Dad. But one look at his wife and he knew she would speak her mind. My father was trapped. What remained was to find the best way to tell the truth. "The thing is . . . I mean . . . well, there were extenuating circumstances. See, it was the Depression. Jobs were hard to come by. I had a chance to drive a cab, and . . . well . . . the thing is—"

"I was pregnant," said my mother.

"Jeannie!"

"With me?" asked Hubbell. My mother nodded. Hubbell, a step ahead of me, did some quick calculations. "I was a love child!"

"Things were different then," said my father. His voice was apologetic, as if he was asking for forgiveness. He was about to tell my brother that it didn't matter, that he was always wanted, that it had no bearing on how he was raised or who he was or anything. But Hubbell required no such explanations. He was in awe.

"Born out of wedlock. That's so cool!"

"You're proud of it?" said my father.

"It's fantastic! It's so romantic! Was it, like, a night of wild, passionate love, or what?"

"It was memorable," said Mom.

"Did you do it in a motel? Or a car? Or under the boardwalk? Was it, like, the first time?"

My father was as embarrassed as he was incredulous. "Look, about this broadcasting business. I think you need to work on a few things—"

"Frank, work on your own life," said my mother.

"Was I a love child too?" asked Round Man. And when the rest of us reacted, he became indignant. "What's so funny? Why can't I be a love child?" My mother hugged him and promised to explain another time.

My father stared at Hubbell. The rejuvenated heart of Cyclone Frankie Stone swelled up and overflowed. "I love you, champ," he sobbed, and he crushed his renegade son to his chest as tears rolled unchecked over his cheeks.

Ordinarily, I might have been jealous, watching my brothers get hugged with no one left to hug me. But on this morning, I felt too good about myself to indulge in such childish emotions. I was, after all, the guy who uncovered the malfeasance of Barney Klinger and the iniquity of Gross and Schaefer, who ensured that my father would be converted by Hubbell's TV debut, and whose hat was responsible for setting straight the history of an entire borough. Besides, I had no time for hugs, nor to try and make sense of everything I'd seen and heard the last twenty-four hours. It was already eight-thirty and I wanted to be in the schoolyard, wearing the silliest grin I could conjure, and perhaps sporting a wicked wink as well, to greet Mrs. Schaefer. For this was to be my last day in class 6-1; my mother was planning to visit Dr. Gross, to negotiate the transfer of me and Artie Finkelstein, and to obtain the principal's unqualified endorsement of Vivian Mason for PTA president.

I also had to stop at Meyer's candystore. I wanted to purchase a charlotte russe for Eleanor Krinski.

About the Author

Like the Dodgers, Philip Goldberg was born and raised in Brooklyn and now lives in Los Angeles. He is the author of 10 nonfiction books and several screenplays. THIS IS NEXT YEAR, currently in development as a feature film, is Mr. Goldberg's first novel and Part One of a projected trilogy.

*Available in a Ballantine Mass Market Edition.